ABOUT THE AUTHOR

Jane Corry is a former magazine journalist who spent three years as the writer-in-residence at a high-security prison. This often hair-raising experience helped inspire her *Sunday Times*-bestselling psychological dramas, which have been translated into sixteen languages and sold over a million copies world-wide. *Coming to Find You* is her eighth novel.

COMING TO FIND YOU

JANE CORRY

PENGUIN BOOKS

PENGUIN BOOKS

UK | USA | Canada | Ireland | Australia
India | New Zealand | South Africa

Penguin Books is part of the Penguin Random House group of companies
whose addresses can be found at global.penguinrandomhouse.com.

First published 2023
001

Set in 12.5/14.75pt Garamond MT Std
Typeset by Jouve (UK), Milton Keynes
Printed and bound in Great Britain by Clays Ltd, Elcograf S.p.A.

The authorized representative in the EEA is Penguin Random House Ireland,
Morrison Chambers, 32 Nassau Street, Dublin D02 YH68

A CIP catalogue record for this book is available from the British Library

ISBN: 978-0-241-99610-2

www.greenpenguin.co.uk

*This book is dedicated to courage, love,
human strength and human frailty.
Also, as always, to my family.*

The Night of the Murder

The knife rack is on the side. I've always thought it was a dangerous thing to have in the house. An armoury of lethal weapons, hiding under the guise of domesticity.

But isn't that exactly what a family is like?

At least, it is with mine. Sharp tongues, bedded next to each other, simmering with resentment.

'It's all your fault!' someone screams.

Everything happens so fast.

I snatch the phone. Dial 999.

But even before I speak, I know it's too late.

Nancy

I

'Have you got somewhere safe to go?' asks the barrister after the verdict. His dark brows knit together with anxiety. Over the last few weeks of the case, I've noticed that this is not uncommon. But right now, the worry lines seem even deeper.

Outside the Old Bailey, the crowds are baying for blood. We're in a small room inside the building. The place is like a rabbit warren, with so many stairs and levels that there's no way I could find my way out alone.

Somewhere safe to go to? It occurs to me that I should have thought of this before.

'Yes,' I say. 'Tall Chimneys.'

Whether it's safe is another matter. Hadn't I always told myself I'd never go back there?

'Where?' he asks.

'It's a sort of family bolt-hole in Devon.'

I think of the beautiful three-storey white Regency 'boarding house', as they used to call it before the term B&B became commonplace. My grandmother's home. The one my mother left me.

He interrupts my thoughts. 'But the locals would know you there.'

'Not necessarily. I was fifteen when I left.' The memories swarm back as I speak. I can't help it. That voice from the past is as clear as if he is standing right next to me now. Stroking the side of my face. Then slowly and deliberately, tracing an invisible line down the side of my throat. Tilting my chin very gently, so I am forced to look straight at him.

'*You've got such beautiful eyes, Nancy.*'

'We could give you a new identity,' chips in the detective inspector, breaking into my thoughts. 'Is this place empty?'

Place? It's not a place, I want to say. *It's more like a person.* At least that's how I had felt when Mum, Dad and I had packed the car every summer and headed south from London for the five-hour drive with the dog, our cases and my father's paints in the back. Before Duncan had wrecked our lives.

'Yes,' I say, numbly. 'My mother rents . . .'

I stop. It still seems impossible that she has gone. Then I force myself to continue.

'My mother *had* been renting it out for years, but the tenants left recently.'

'Convenient,' says the DI.

He speaks as though I have engineered it. As if it was I who had been imprisoned for life instead of Martin.

Not for the first time, I wish my defence barrister had been a woman. The same goes for the DI. I can't help it. I'm naturally distrustful of men.

'I'm afraid that, through no fault of your own, you've been given what is known as a "silent sentence",' says the barrister grimly.

'What do you mean?' I ask.

He shakes his head. 'Crime – like fame – tends to rub off on anyone connected with the accused and the convicted. You're the nearest they can get to Martin.'

My mouth goes dry. 'What might they do to me?'

The DI chips in again. 'Send you nasty emails. Put excrement through your letterbox. You name it. They can do it.'

I wince. The barrister notices.

'These pressures that they put on you, Nancy,' he says in a kind voice, 'might make it hard for you to live a normal life. That's why some families of prisoners say they feel as if they are serving a silent sentence – even if they're innocent.'

Even if they're innocent. Does the Crown Prosecutor still believe that I had something to do with the murder of my own mother and stepfather?

I feel sick inside. 'Who are *they*? And why might they persecute me?'

The DI gives a hoarse laugh. 'Joe Public. Anyone reading the case in the paper or online or hearing someone else talk about it. Someone you might have known years ago, perhaps, and who recognizes your name. A busybody. A fantasist. You'd be amazed at the folk who are glued to murders like this – especially when it's a high-profile victim, as in this case.'

There's a pause for breath. Isn't that enough? But the list continues. 'The press. The man or woman next door. A total stranger. A nutter. Someone who feels that your brother hasn't been punished enough – or that the whole truth hasn't come out.'

'Stepbrother,' I remind him quickly.

'Yes. Of course. Sorry.'

The shouts are getting louder now. '*Get the bastard!*' '*Kill him!*'

'*And the rich bitch too. I don't believe her.*'

'*She's hiding something.*'

Fear tightens my chest. If Mum hadn't been loaded, would they have been so interested? Maybe they don't know that her wealth was virtually an accident. My father's paintings, which he'd struggled to sell during his lifetime, had been 'discovered' after his death by a well-respected critic, which sent prices escalating to heights we'd never imagined. If only my beloved dad could have lived to see this. Maybe that's why I've never taken an interest in the money. It feels wrong to enjoy a fortune that Dad should have benefited from. He deserved the kudos too.

Of course, I could use my inheritance to buy a private jet and hole up somewhere abroad. But I'm sure the press would find me. Besides, it would make me look even guiltier.

I touch my pearl necklace in the way I often do when I need reassurance. My mother gave it to me when I was twenty-one. Before her, it had belonged to my grandmother Adeline. It's the only thing I have of hers. My grandfather had been shot down during the war. My mother told me that the necklace had originally been a present from Adeline's best friend Elizabeth. '*Take care of it, won't you?*' Mum had said.

'We need to get you out the back way,' says the DI curtly. His sharp tone brings me back to the present. 'And quickly. Let's go.'

2

'You can do this,' I say out loud, my hands gripping the wheel. 'You've got to.'

Steeling myself, I edge down the slip road and on to the M3. My hands are sweating. I'm one of those drivers who's reasonably at ease on ordinary roads within fifty miles of somewhere I know well. But motorways have always scared me.

It's the risk you have to take that I don't like; the split-second decision about joining that never-ending stream of traffic that appears to form a solid rank against you. And even if the motorway is comparatively quiet, as it is now, supposing that red car which seems so far away suddenly zips forward? What if my car stops or stalls as I take the plunge and venture out? The one behind might go headlong into me and then . . .

I shake myself. All my life I've thought the worst. Actually, that's not entirely true. Before Dad died, I'd never felt this kind of anxiety. The shock of his death put me on constant alert in case something awful happened to Mum too. Then she married Duncan. I started to feel guilty because Mum persuaded me to take his surname so we'd be a 'proper' family, and it went on from there. But right now, I'm facing the toughest situation of my life. Joining a motorway is small fry in comparison.

Move across! Be brave!! I've done it! I glance in my

rear-view mirror. The red car is behind me. It's closer than it was before but it's still at a respectable distance. No one has been hurt. No one has died.

Not here, anyway.

Taking a deep breath, I switch on the radio. '*Martin Greenfield, the thirty-eight-year-old man who was convicted of slaughtering his father and stepmother in their remote Sussex farmhouse, is starting a life sentence . . .*'

My knees start to judder. Swiftly, I turn it off. That red car is overtaking me. The driver glances across. Is he following me? No. He can't be. Or he'd have stayed behind, waiting to see where I am going. That's if he's a man. It's hard to tell from this distance. Mind you, women can be just as dangerous. Look at me.

'Don't underestimate journalists,' the DI had told me. 'They're like bulls after a red rag. But when the next big story comes along they'll leave you alone. You just have to lie low until then.'

'But I won't ever be able to go back to my normal life, will I?' I'd said. 'People at work know. Everyone does.'

I thought of the advertising agency where I was a senior copywriter. Remember *Banish the blue – find the new you!* for that multivitamin campaign? That was one of mine. But there's no slogan that can help me right now.

I'd told my director about the trial just before it started. I had to. I needed time off. Besides, the case would be reported. His eyes had widened. 'Shit, Nancy. Are you serious?'

No, I'm not. I don't have a dead mother. There are no sirens screaming. No 999 call. No police banging on the farmhouse door. No blood. Not one tiny red drop. See how I can pretend? I'm a creative. I can make anything happen in my mind. I've always made up stories in my head, ever since I was a child.

But I can't stop the news. It attacks me from all directions. Nor can I stop the messages. On my Twitter account, Instagram, Facebook. Most of them furiously disbelieving: *You must have known what he was like!* As if we really know what anyone is like. Let alone a man like my stepbrother. I get a brief flash of Martin as a gangly youth from that summer in Devon.

The red car has disappeared and I force my memories to do the same. But there's a grey car behind me now. It's keeping a steady speed. I'd like to go into the fast lane but I'm too scared. I feel safer in the slow. It's like swimming as a child. I used to panic if I went out of my depth. 'It's all right,' Dad had said. But it hadn't been, had it? I don't mean the swimming but the bigger stuff. Later. When he hadn't been around to save me.

Twenty miles further on the grey car is still there. Five years ago I had sensed someone behind me when I'd been walking down Mile End Road in the dark. His footsteps were getting faster and faster. I was scared that if I ran, he'd run too. So I'd got my phone out and called Martin. 'I think someone's following me.'

'Cross the road,' he said quickly. 'Knock on a door. Any door. Stay on the line. Talk to me all the time so I know you're OK.'

I'd followed his instructions for the first part but I hadn't needed to knock on a door. The person I'd been scared of had simply walked on, minding his own business.

Why had I rung Martin? Because history had already

bound us together. He was – is – the only other person in the world who knows what it was like to live with Duncan. Apart from Mum, of course, and she's dead.

What would Martin say now if he knew a grey car was following me? *Get off the motorway, Nancy. Take this next exit. If the car stays behind you, ring the police.*

So I do. When I reach the roundabout at the bottom of the slip road, I glance in the mirror. Nothing is behind me. I almost choke on the relief in my throat.

My satnav tells me that this road leads to the South West, even though it's going to be a longer journey than the motorway. I decide to go for it.

I'm passing through a small town now. On the left, I spot a hairdresser's. There's a fancy sign on the window with a pair of scissors. Once, during a holiday in Devon before Martin and Duncan had come into our lives, I'd knelt by accident on a pair of cutting-out scissors that I'd left on the carpet while doing my scrapbook. The blood had spurted everywhere. I'd been so shocked that I couldn't talk until the screams had forced their way out.

'It's all right, Nancy,' my father had soothed, scooping me up and carrying me to the cottage hospital near the seafront. The doctor had stitched me up while Dad had held my hands. My mother had always been terrified of blood. 'You're all right now, love.'

Afterwards, he took me down to my favourite ice-cream parlour on the 'front' as he called it. I was allowed to have a chocolate '99' flake with it as a special treat for being so brave. The memory makes me smile now, despite everything.

I slow down. There's an empty parking space on the

road near the hairdresser's. I was booked with Max to have my blonde highlights done this weekend. I'd forgotten to cancel it. Would my stylist be expecting me still? Or would he be telling another client, right now, that one of his regulars was that woman who'd been on the front page of the paper all week? I can imagine his voice now: *I'd been due to do Nancy Greenfield's hair for her wedding last year as well, but it got called off. Some people have a lot of trouble in their lives, don't they?*

The car stops. I don't actually remember pulling in. I'm right outside the salon and there's even a payment machine next to it. Is this a sign?

'I know it's rather last-minute,' I say to the receptionist, 'but I wondered if you had an appointment for a colour.'

My heart is beating fast at the thought of her recognizing me. The tabloids had really gone to town on us. '*Us?*' repeats Martin in my head. '*Glad to see you still think that way.*'

'I don't,' I tell him sharply. Had I said that out loud? If so, the woman doesn't seem to have heard.

'You're in luck,' she chirps. 'Is it highlights you're after?'

'No,' I say, trying to sound casual. 'I fancy a change. I want to go dark.'

When she's finished, I look in the mirror. My heart pounds. This wasn't what I expected. My mother stares back at me. Her hair had been raven black, whereas mine had been blonde like my dad's and then mousey as I moved into my thirties. '*Please come to my birthday party,*' she had pleaded.

Was she kidding? That date will be tarnished for ever in my mind.

'*Why?*' I challenge.

'*Because I want my daughter to be there.*'

'No,' I say to my reflection.

'You don't like it?' asks the hairdresser, startled.

'Yes. No. Sorry. It's great.'

Mum's mirror image makes me shudder as his voice comes back to me again. '*You've got such beautiful eyes, Nancy.*' I used to like them too. But not any more. Not after the summer I turned fifteen and life changed for ever.

I fish about in my bag for cash. No cards, the DI had advised. Not for a while. Too easy to trace.

'Thanks,' she says, looking surprised at the tenner I leave for a tip. I'm not usually so generous but it's to make up for pretending to be asleep while she'd plastered on the dye. Besides, I can afford it now I'm an 'heiress' (another word the headlines had delighted in using).

When I get back into the car, I take a second look at the mirror. If I sweep it back, I look less like Mum. 'You aren't the same Nancy any more,' I tell my thirty-six-year-old self sternly. 'You aren't your mother either. You might not have an official new identity. But this is still your chance to put it all behind you.'

I turn the key in the ignition and drive on.

3

I switch on the radio again only to find that the news is about to start. So I switch it off before I can hear it. I need to stay calm.

PING. I glance across at my mobile, lying on the passenger seat.

Alex.

I ignore it.

It pings again. I stretch across to put it on silent.

As I drive, I try to remember the breathing routine from the meditation app I've been using. But all I can see in my head is Duncan's body and the knife in my hand. *The blood. So much blood.*

And then I see the sea.

I pull into a lay-by and stare. It's as though there's a huge invisible STOP sign on the beach and then . . . nothing. Just miles and miles of water.

'*Are we there yet?*'

I can hear my childish voice from the back of the car.

'*Nearly!*' my father sings back. Sometimes I felt he was more excited than my mother about going to Devon, even though she'd been the one who had grown up there. 'The sea gives me inspiration,' he would say.

I drive on. A road sign announces I have left Dorset and am now in Devon. My satnav tells me there's another forty minutes to go until I reach my destination. I begin to shake. What if reporters are waiting for me? Suppose someone who works at the court has tipped them off? Or the police? Can I trust anyone after what has happened?

I think about my so-called 'silent sentence'. Until now, I'd never considered the implications for the families of criminals. Who does?

Not that I've got a family any more.

Would I have been better hiding in London instead of coming down here with all the memories swarming round my mind? Already I've thought about the past more than I've allowed myself to do in years. I could always turn round and go . . . where? I'd ruled out going abroad, but even a hotel in the UK would be too obvious. Someone could easily recognize me there. The same if I rented a place. No. I have no choice.

The road is feeling vaguely familiar now as it drops down through fields. The hills on either side appear to form strokes going upwards, the sea in the middle of the V.

'*We're there!*' my mother says in my head. '*You'll love it, Duncan!*'

Mum had married him when I was nine. Martin was still living with his mother in France. He was going to join us later for the summer holidays. His school reports that year made my stepfather really cross, though he'd won a prize in history. This stuck in my memory because even then Duncan hadn't been satisfied. 'Why can't the boy be good at something useful like maths?'

Why am I doing this? Why am I coming back to the very house where it all started to go wrong? I have a flash of Martin leaning towards me and begin to shake.

'Tall Chimneys also has happy memories, darling,' I can hear my mother saying now. 'You learned to walk there. And your father taught you to swim, remember?'

Yes. Of course I do. I'd been trying for months in the public baths in Watford, near our main home. But the buoyancy of the sea made it so much easier.

'You clever girl!' said my father, lifting me up into the air and giving me a cuddle when we came out of the water, before wrapping me up in a big towel. Then we'd saunter back, arm in arm, to Tall Chimneys and have a hot chocolate. Later, I'd go to bed in a room that had 'Nancy' on a china plaque on the door, and dream of the waves carrying me safely back to shore.

My grandmother Adeline had inherited the boarding house from her best friend Elizabeth in the 1950s. She'd continued to take in guests, and on her death she'd passed it to my mother, Violet, who'd used it as a holiday home.

Duncan, who was a friend of Dad's, had married Mum shortly after this unexpected wealth appeared. I sensed he both enjoyed the money yet also resented it because my mother 'held the purse strings' – a phrase I often heard during the arguments that took place behind their bedroom door.

'Please don't be so horrid,' I would hear Mum say. I'd often wished she would leave him but Mum was the kind of woman who needed a husband by her side. I always knew I was never going to be like that. That's why I worked my socks off; made things happen for myself. I still want to, even though Mother has left everything to me. Including Tall Chimneys.

'The house is very old, you know,' Mum would say. 'It

goes back to 1812. Just think of everything it's lived through!'

I do a double-take at the WELCOME TO SIDMOUTH sign. I'd been so lost in my memories that I hadn't realized how close I was.

Wow! There's the cinema! I remember going there with my parents and munching Maltesers in the plush maroon seats. We saw *Jungle Book*, and for ages after that, Dad and I would sing the songs together. There's the garage on the corner where they fixed a flat tyre after Mum had reversed into a kerb too hard. Past the row of cottages standing slightly back from the road. And then a tall white house with very high chimneys, surveying it all, like a queen.

Tall Chimneys.

My chest caves in. The magnolia tree has gone.

I'd forgotten it had been there at all until I am reminded by its stark absence. Instead, there's a gravel drive with plenty of parking space. No cars are there. But what do I expect?

I fumble in my bag for the key. The police had given it to me after forensics had finished with the contents of the farmhouse. The fob has TALL CHIMNEYS clearly written on it in my mother's handwriting.

Tears mist my eyes, making it difficult to turn the key in the lock.

'You can do this,' I say to myself. 'Just pretend it's all right.'

I'm in.

Childish memories usually make things much bigger than they really are. But not now. The hall is just as spacious and bright and airy as I remember. The stairs rise through three levels in a gracious Regency spiral above me.

Some of my father's pictures have gone from the walls, leaving only hooks and a dusty outline. Had Duncan persuaded my mother to move them, or even sell them? He was always jealous of our past.

There's a faint whiff of damp and a stale smell – the type you get when a house hasn't been lived in for a while. I open the windows for fresh air and throw the curtains wide (some are closed as though it is night).

Then something amazing happens as the light streams in from the neighbouring house, bathing the side of my face with warmth.

I feel at peace.

All I have to do is lie low. Keep quiet.

Just as Martin had told me to.

4

I wander from room to room.

There are lines of dust on the picture rails and the panels in the doors. The beds are stripped bare. In one of the bathrooms there's a half-empty bottle of green liquid with a label that promises to soothe aching limbs.

There's an Aga in the kitchen but, of course, it's cold to the touch. I've no idea how to light it. I can only vaguely remember how to cook on it. When I open one of the cupboards, I find a not-very-clean-looking sandwich toastie maker. Without a plug. The panel below the cupboard falls out onto the floor. I push it back again, hoping it will stay in place. DIY is the last thing on my mind right now.

My mother had let the house to tenants over recent years, and the previous ones – a family who had come down here to escape the height of the pandemic in London – had left without paying the final lot of rent.

'I might spend some time there myself now,' Mum had said, only a few months before her death. 'Why don't you join me for a weekend?'

'After what happened there? I don't think so.'

She'd looked at me wide-eyed, as if in genuine astonishment. 'What do you mean?'

'You know,' I'd muttered.

'Don't bring that up again,' she'd snapped.

It was the last proper conversation I'd had with her, apart from that final night in the farmhouse. Of course, now I wish it had been different. How I miss her. How impossible it is to think she is gone. But the truth is that I lost my mother years ago, when she got together with Duncan.

What was it they'd said in his obituary in *The Times*? *An upright man with a distinguished military career.*

Upright? Hah!

I make my way past the door to the cellar, trying not to look at it. My heart beats and I feel sick. I can smell the apples my mother would store down there. Or is that my imagination? I've no intention of finding out.

Then I open the patio doors in the sitting room, which I remember my father putting in before he'd died. They're a bit stiff but the effect is instant. A lovely blast of spring air hits me.

That's better. It will clear the stuffiness. I shake out the dust from the cushions on a faded blue-and-pink sofa and take a seat. I don't remember it from before. Maybe Duncan had bought it with my mother. I get off it. I'd rather lie on the floor than touch anything that man had had anything to do with.

As soon as possible, I'll buy a new one. It still seems weird to think I am seriously rich. I could have more if I were to accept the financial offers I've received from several newspapers to tell my side of the story. But I don't need it. And even if I did, there's no way I'd risk it. At some point I'll have to think of ways to use this money to do some good. But it still won't take the guilt away. Or the fear.

I notice that the fridge is completely bare. My stomach is rumbling although I feel sick at the same time. Maybe I should force myself to eat something. There was a small supermarket that I'd seen on my way in. That definitely hadn't been there in my childhood. But I can't help hanging around for a bit, exploring more rooms. When I finally go out – it's almost evening now and dusk is beginning to fall – I notice that the door of the garage is open. It contains a rusty old bike with a wicker basket that has a silver flute-like whistle inside it. I test it out. It works. Then I wonder if I should have put it to my lips before cleaning it. The tyres are flat. Maybe I could get them fixed. I like the idea of cycling around town. Besides, it would be less obvious than my car.

As I go back into the driveway, I jump out of my skin. A woman is advancing towards me with a stick in her hand. 'Who are you?' says a sharp voice. 'And before you answer, don't try to pull any funny tricks. I've dealt with one burglar in the past and I can deal with another.'

'I'm not a burglar,' I bleat. 'I own this house.'

The stick drops to the ground. I take in this tall wiry woman in a yellow jacket, her eyes wide. 'Violet?'

I wince at the sound of my mother's name. 'I'm her daughter,' I stutter. 'Nancy.'

She comes towards me, crunching over the gravel.

'Of course you are. I'm so sorry. It's just that you look so much like her. I read about your poor mother in the paper.'

Hadn't everyone?

'I'm Vera, by the way. I live next door. I didn't mean to give you a fright but you can't be too careful. Those tenants your mother had in, they weren't very responsible. Often left the front door open and had rubbish piling up at the back. You've never seen so many empty bottles. I'm Vera, by the way, did I say that? Vera Robertson. Devonian born and bred, I am. And proud of it. Are you moving in or are you just using the place for holidays?'

All this is said in such a rush that it feels like one long sentence.

'Probably the latter.'

I need to change the subject before she asks any more questions. 'I found an old bike in the garage.'

She chuckles. 'That belonged to your grandmother. I can still remember her tearing around on it.'

That must put Vera at about eighty then, maybe more. She doesn't look that old. I want to find out more about my grandmother Adeline. My mother never seemed to want to talk about her. All I know is she lost her husband in the war, and brought up Mum on her own. But now is not the time. I've got too many practical things to sort out.

'It's very rusty and the tyres are flat,' I say. 'Do you know of anyone who could fix it?'

'You want the bike-shop man in Temple Street. He'll sort you out. Tell him that Vera sent you.'

Temple Street. The name rings a bell, but I can't place it.

'Turn right at the cinema and then straight up for about ten minutes. You'll find it on the left-hand side. Or you can choose the scenic route and go through the Byes. It's a kind of community park that goes on for miles. Take a left at the second bridge, keep going and then turn left.'

'Thanks.'

'It's what neighbours are for, love, isn't it? 'Sides, it's nice to see the house occupied again.'

'I won't be here that long,' I say quickly.

She sniffs. 'Pity. Well, let me know if you need anything else.'

'Thank you. There is one thing. I don't want anyone to know I'm here.'

'That might be difficult. People here notice things. But I'm not going to the papers, if that's what you're asking. I'm not like that.'

Oh dear. Have I offended her?

'If you're staying for a while, you'll need to get that garden sorted out, sooner or later,' she adds in a brisk voice. 'The apple tree by the kitchen window needs pruning back. In fact, there's quite a lot I could tell you about your house when you have time.'

I watch Vera go back into her house, mulling over her words. '*Quite a lot I could tell you*'? Was she talking about the practical side or something else? Once more I feel that sense of unease.

I check that all the doors are locked – Vera's warning has reminded me that I need to be vigilant – and begin to walk towards the town. As I do so, my phone rings. Alex again.

I have a flash of his kind smile. The warmth of his arms around me.

But it's no good. I don't deserve him.

I press Decline.

As I do so, I have a sudden yearning to see the sea, even though I'm hungry.

'Can you hear it?' my father would say whenever we got close.

'Hear what?' my mother would ask teasingly.

'The waves!' I'd call out from the back.

It was part of our holiday ritual. The exchange we always had. I'd buried it for all these years but now the longing is overtaking me. I change direction and run back towards the hump-back bridge that Martin and I used to lean over, playing pooh sticks even when we were teenagers. Right and over the ford – still the same too, thank goodness – and on through a playground that hadn't been there before.

Up to the promenade by the lifeboat station. The doors are shut. There's an emergency number on the front. And there it is. The sea. The waves are choppy. The sun has not quite set but the moon is coming up. I love it when they share the sky like that. A few evening dog-walkers pass one another on the shingle. But the music is the same. Sea music. That's what Dad had called the sound of the waves. Once more I feel that sense of peace I'd felt earlier in the house.

After a while, I walk back through the town. There's the department store that I remember from my childhood. (The clothes in the window look stylish and very chic.) The old bookshop is still there, and a new one too.

And look! The museum! My father often used to take me there when I was a little girl. 'See this?' he would say. 'That's a mammoth tooth from thousands of years ago! Over there is an old gramophone player from the 1920s. History is a wonderful thing, Nancy. Never forget it. It can help us make sense of the present.'

'Evening,' says someone.

I jump. Have I been recognized? A man with a walking

stick nods as he limps past. Then I remember that everyone says 'hello' to strangers here.

At the supermarket, I buy a loaf of bread and a tin of tomato soup. Easy comfort food. I choose the self-service checkout. Keep my head down. Back to the house. It seems even colder than when I'd come in. A sharp shot of fear passes through me as I see why. The patio doors are open. But I'd shut them, hadn't I?

Yet what if I hadn't? My memory is usually good. But since the murder, I keep forgetting the simplest things. Still, it's possible they might have blown open since there's no lock and the doors are rotten.

Even though I know I'm probably being silly, I go round the house, searching for an intruder. Under the beds. Behind the curtains. In some of the wardrobes.

'Let's play hide and seek,' Martin used to say when we were younger. And I agreed, as I'd agreed to so much else he suggested, because he was older. So I 'had to do' as he said. (His words.) Once he freaked us all out by hiding at the bottom of the garden instead of in the house. We formed a search party for him. He was totally unrepentant.

No one is here. No photographer lurking, ready to leap out and demand 'your account of the events'. It must have been me who left the doors open. I have to be more careful. And not just with locking up.

I have two things left to do now. First, get the duvet out from the car – at least I'd had the presence of mind to bring that. In the morning, I'd sort out linen from somewhere.

And the second.

I open my overnight bag and take out the knife. Its steel flashes in the moonlight streaming in through the bedroom window.

My mind shoots back to a different blade I'd been holding, seconds before the police had kicked in the door.

I put it under the bed.

Tomorrow I'll find a safer hiding place.

5

I wake with a start at 4.12 a.m. after one of my nightmares.

I'm in a car, hurtling over the ice with tyres skidding, on the way to the farmhouse. Then suddenly I'm in the undertaker's looking down at my mother's face. In my dream, I know it's my mother, although it doesn't look anything like her. Her jaw has dropped, distorting her features as if she is an overblown image in a fairground mirror. Suddenly she sits up and looks at me. 'Don't say anything to upset him,' she whispers. 'Or we'll all die.'

Then I'm back in the farmhouse. My stepfather is swigging out of a giant whisky bottle that towers over him. Martin is standing next to him, dressed as a clown with huge red lips. He opens his mouth and knives come hurting out. They hit the floor and then bounce on the ceiling. One of them flies towards me. I scream with terror.

That's when I open my eyes.

Dimly aware that I am somewhere other than at home in my London flat, I fall back on my pillows. The next thing I know, the sun is streaming in through the window where the curtains don't quite meet. Where am I?

Then I remember. Tall Chimneys. That feeling of peace from yesterday has gone. I'm suddenly scared.

But I'm so exhausted from yesterday that I drift in and out of sleep for a bit. At some point, I wake again, aware it's much later. Getting up, I look through the window at the flat line dividing the sea from the sky. In between are rooftops with grey slate, red tiles, tall chimneys like the ones this house was named after and short squat ones. Above, I can hear seagulls screaming. It's a far cry from London, with its bustling streets full of courier bikes and people shouting at each other.

I wish I was still there. If I close my eyes, I can pretend it's a normal day. I am going to the office. No one has died.

But my trick of pretending isn't working right now. Maybe it's because of this old childhood room of mine where I would lie in bed and listen to my mother and Duncan arguing, and then making sounds that I couldn't interpret at that age.

'You don't have to sleep here,' I remind myself. The house is mine now. I can do what I like. So I gather my things and go up to the second floor where there's a twin-bedded room which had been used for storage when we came here on holiday. From the beautiful window that drops down to just above floor level there's a view over the back garden. I can see a pink rose that is just coming into flower, even though it's only March. It feels safer up here, especially after finding the patio door open last night.

I go to put my things in the built-in wardrobe. I open it to find the 'back' is actually the wall. As I put in my folded clothes I look a bit closer. Someone has written something there.

Maisie was here. SO WAS SHIRLEY! 8 October 1941

I can't believe I've never noticed this before. Who were they? That year, 1941, was not long after the start of the

Second World War, wasn't it? It seems extraordinary to think of other people living in this house at what must have been a terrifying and uncertain time. It puts my own problems into perspective. Well, some of them.

I go back to my old bedroom and retrieve the knife that I'd hidden under the bed last night. Carefully holding it as I go downstairs, I use my other hand to grip the mahogany bannister that goes round and round, down and down. I'd forgotten how high the house is. 'Never lean over the staircase,' my father had warned me when I was young. 'It was built during a time when there weren't the safety regulations of today.'

'Great exercise!' I remember my mother saying. 'You can't put on weight when you're always running up and down three floors!'

My mother had been obsessed with weight. She wasn't fat – just 'rounded'. My grandmother had apparently been fanatical about feeding her up to compensate for the rationing and general deprivation when she had been young. 'I didn't see a banana until I was five!' my mother had told me. 'Imagine that!'

I couldn't. Mum had been middle-aged when I was born. The Second World War was like ancient history to me.

I hide the knife in the kitchen behind the loose panel I'd dislodged earlier. It gives me some comfort to know it's there.

My stomach is rumbling with hunger, even though I feel sick. I fiddle with the controls of the Aga, hoping to make some porridge, but nothing happens. Looks like it's bread again.

I take my breakfast into the garden – still in my pyjamas – and sit at the wooden table on the patio. It's pretty weather-worn. Daffodils are everywhere. So is the ivy and the bindweed wrapping itself round that early rose, climbing up the brick wall.

Good. Gardening will keep me busy, even though I'm no expert. I wander to the bottom, where there are some raised beds with overgrown vegetables. Then I notice that bits of chicken wire are poking up, and some planks of wood. I heave them aside and gasp. There's a space below that could take six or so people. It reminds me of a picture I'd seen in a supplement recently about air-raid shelters.

I ease myself down – still in my pyjamas. The air is damp and makes me sneeze. The walls are lined with metal sheets and planks of wood. There are noughts and crosses games scored into it. Someone has written something too. *There is nothing to fear in life but fear itself.*

It feels like a personal message. But what about the people who had hidden here? How must they have felt, while bombs dropped around them? What courage that must have taken.

I clamber out, dust myself down and head back to the house to check my phone, which I'd left in the kitchen. Nothing. No messages, not even from Alex. No emails apart from the usual ones that don't matter.

Then I comfort myself with the detective inspector's words: 'When the next big story comes along, they'll leave you alone. You just have to lie low until then.'

Right now, that seems impossible. Everyone at work knows. All my friends, though the only one of them who really matters to me is Claire. She had lived on our road and virtually grown up with me. She'd known what it was like when Dad had died. When Mum had married Duncan. When I'd cancelled my wedding after my mother had died.

I ought to text her. I do. *Am OK. Just hiding until it blows over.*

Her reply comes back almost instantly.

Where are you?

'Don't tell anyone,' the DI had advised.

But Claire is different. We tell each other everything. Almost everything.

Remember those bikinis? I type back.

Mum had bought them for us when Claire first came on holiday with us. We were twelve at the time. The summer had been scorching. We shared my bedroom and nudged each other if we walked past a boy in the street. Any boy. It didn't matter. All we wanted was to actually meet one and fall in love. How we envied the teenagers who had barbecues on the beach and seemed to know each other!

Then Mum bought us matching bikinis. They were candy-pink. Striped. We lay on the beach sunbathing and two boys came up to chat. We barely got beyond the exchanging names stage, but it didn't matter. When you went to an all-girls' school, this was a big deal.

You're in Devon? comes back the reply, bringing me back to the present.

Don't tell anyone, I tap back.

Course not. Take care.

How's the bump? I add.

Claire is heavily pregnant. If she wasn't my best friend, I'd feel jealous. She has everything I've always wanted.

'*Great. She can't wait to meet you.*'

If the baby arrives soon, sod the press, I'll drive straight back to London to meet her. I can't miss the most important time in my best friend's life.

Then I realize something so obvious that I can't believe I haven't thought of it before. My car! Someone might have taken a note of the number plate before I left. It might have been recognized on the motorway.

My heart starts to beat furiously. My blue Mini has been sitting on the driveway since I arrived. Anyone looking for me could have seen it.

Swiftly I run outside, still in my pyjamas, and drive it into the old-fashioned garage. There's not a lot of space and I have to wheel out the old bike to make room. Duncan never used it because his cars were too flash and wide. A cobweb brushes against me as I close the door.

I remember Vera's advice about the bike shop. After getting dressed, I push it up the narrow lanes to Temple Street, glancing over my shoulder every now and then.

There's a woman behind me, carrying a shopping bag. 'Morning, love,' she says.

Is she being chummy or has she recognized me? I walk on faster, gasping a silent sigh of relief when I get to the bike shop.

The owner has a quietly reassuring manner. 'This is rather special,' he says, running an eye over the markings on the frame. 'One of the last of its kind made before the war, if I'm not mistaken. Give me a couple of days and I'll make it roadworthy. Oh and don't forget the whistle in the basket.'

Since it all happened, I keep overlooking things. Brain fog or guilt? Who knows.

I walk back into town – this time through the Byes. I'd forgotten how beautiful it was: a series of green glades with huge trees, many of which must have been planted years ago. There's also a line of allotments with quite a few people working away. My mother had grown vege-tables at the farmhouse. It seems like a dream now.

There's water flooding the path ahead. 'Don't slip, love,' says someone walking past. 'One of the pipes is leaking. We're waiting for the council to come.'

People are so caring here!

Making my way down the high street, I spot several TO LET shop signs that I hadn't noticed on my walk last night. I wonder if they're casualties of the last few years.

Then I stop to take in the sea. Today, it looks grey and uninviting – very different from the memories of my youth. Different, too, from the turquoise-blue waters of Greece, where Alex and I had gone on holiday last year. If only I'd known then what was going to happen . . .

Turning back sharply, I go into the department store opposite the fish market. 'Good morning,' says a lovely assistant with a chignon as I weave my way through the cosmetic and fragrance department. The smell is so beau-tiful here that it's like walking into a florist's. The bedding section is on the first floor. It feels wonderfully normal after what I've been through. Safe. Reassuring. I think of the busy shops in London. Part of me feels slightly nos-talgic for the buzz. The other part of me is comforted by the slower pace here – and relieved to be out of sight.

I pick up a white broderie anglaise duvet cover. It reminds me of one that my mother used to have.

Instantly I see her body covered in blood in the farmhouse kitchen.

I put it down quickly and pick up a primrose yellow design instead. I wait for the blood. But it doesn't come. Emboldened, I buy two pillows.

I'm walking down the left-hand side of the street now – *my* street, although it feels weird to say that – past a terrace of elegant Regency houses. I'm about to cross over when a voice calls out.

'Heard you just moved in! Welcome!'

It's a cheery woman of about my age with a wide smile. She's in a wetsuit and her red hair is damp, as if she has just stepped out of the sea. 'I'm Jasmine.'

'I'm Nancy,' I say. Instantly, I wish I hadn't given out my name. Then again, if I'm going to be living here for a bit, it's only practical, isn't it? Unless I pretend to be someone else. And I'm tired of that.

She beams. 'Where've you come from?'

'London.'

'The bright lights, eh? I lived in Tooting once. Was that near you?'

'Not far,' I say. It's a lie but I don't want to go into details. Has she read about my family? One of the earlier headlines comes into my head: *Stepson arrested after art millionairess hacked to death.*

'What do you do?'

If it wasn't for her friendly manner, this might sound nosy. But somehow it doesn't.

'Actually I work as a copywriter at an advertising agency, but I'm having some time off at the moment,' I say.

'Cool. So do you come up with slogans and stuff?'

I feel a bit embarrassed, as I always do when someone asks this. 'I try to.'

'We ought to get together. Are you here on your own?'

'Yes.'

'Well, come round for a glass of wine sometime.'

Actually, I haven't drunk a drop of alcohol since the night it happened. But I don't want to go into that now.

'By the way,' she adds, 'you've just missed someone.'

My skin prickles.

'Sorry?'

'I was weeding my garden out front and this bloke came over to ask if I'd seen you. Couldn't get a reply when he knocked on the door apparently.'

I can feel my heart thudding in my throat.

'Did he leave his name?'

'No. But I saw him put a message through the door. Not bad looking!' She grins. 'Anyway, I'd better get going. I need to get to work.'

I mumble my thanks and fumble for my house keys, dropping all my shopping on the step. Ignoring it, I open the lock.

There's a business card on the mat. My mouth dries. It carries the name of a well-known newspaper that thrives on gossip. On the back is a scrawled note.

What's your side of the story, Nancy? Ring soon. We'll make it worth your while!

They've found me.

6

When I'm stressed, I clean. It helps me pretend that I'm in control of my life.

I'd scrubbed the flat from top to bottom when I'd told Alex that I couldn't marry him. I'd scrubbed every square inch of the farmhouse after forensics had left. It had been hard to see through my tears but still I worked until every surface was clean. When the first viewer came, the place was like something out of a glossy magazine. That's not why it sold so fast, of course.

'You'd be amazed at the number of people who want to buy houses where a murder has been committed,' said the young estate agent jauntily.

And now I'm scrubbing Tall Chimneys from bottom to top, apart from the cellar and one other room that I can't bring myself to go into. It's filthy with neglect but it's the perfect distraction from the fact that the press have found me.

I find an old bucket and a wire brush in a closet off the kitchen and set to work on the floor tiles. There's a soft broom for the wooden floors and a vacuum cleaner, which hasn't been emptied. When I work out how to change the bag and click it back together again, it still doesn't do the job. So I get down on my hands and knees to use the dust-pan and brush instead.

After that, I wash and dust every surface, and only then

do I realize that I should have done it the other way round because the muck has dropped off onto the floor.

So I wash and sweep all over again. As I do so, a memory comes into my head for no obvious reason. Martin and I are going swimming. I must have been about thirteen: 'Let me carry that for you,' he says, taking my beach bag as we walk down from Tall Chimneys towards the sea. His hand brushes mine. Of course it is an accident. But I move away.

I scrub the floor even harder to wipe him out. And then I go outside with the refuse bags (including the torn-up business card offering me untold wealth) to the dustbins. That's when I find three cars parked on the drive outside.

'Nancy!' calls out a woman in a black quilted coat. Her jolly 'How are you?' tone makes me think for a moment that I must know her. Then I spot the notebook in her hand.

'Nancy!' calls a man leaping out from the car next to her. 'We're writing a piece on family massacres and the effect on the survivors. It will help others in the same situation. It must have been awful to witness your mother's throat being cut. Can you give them any advice?'

'Nancy,' says another woman, getting out of the third car. 'I'd like to give you these, along with our condolences.' She thrusts a massive bouquet of lilies into my hand. 'I'm from the women's page of . . .'

She names a daily paper that I don't read.

'We wondered if you'd like to write us a piece about step-relations and . . .'

No. *No*. NO.

'Just go away. Please. All of you.'

A seagull screams overhead, echoing my panic.

'We understand how you feel,' says the woman in the black quilted coat.

I laugh. 'Really?' I push past them, stuffing the bags into the bins and turning back to the house.

'*My* mother and father are dead too,' she says.

'He wasn't my father.' My voice is as sharp as a blade.

'It doesn't sound like you cared for him very much, Nancy.'

How can I have been so stupid? Don't talk to the press. That's what the DI had told me. Wasn't that why I had come running all the way down here?

'I see you've changed the colour of your hair, Nancy,' says the first woman. 'Is that because you wanted to hide?'

Before my stupid mouth can say any more, there's a ferocious barking. The biggest dog I have ever seen comes rushing towards us, growling and baring its teeth.

They shrink back. I do the same.

'Call off your dog, Nancy!' shouts the man. He can't get back into his car fast enough.

Seizing my chance, I rush into the house, slamming the door.

Seconds later, there's a loud knocking.

'Go away,' I shout.

'Nancy! It's me. Jasmine, from over the road. It's all right. They've gone.'

I open the door a crack. My neighbour is there, this time not in her wetsuit but in joggers and black eyeliner. She's got the dog on a lead now, although there seems no need. It's sitting next to her, quite docile and staring up at me sweetly.

'He's yours?' My voice is a whisper, more from shock at

what's happened than the need to stay quiet just in case there are any more journalists lurking.

'*She*, actually.' Jasmine bends down and strokes the dog's ears. 'This is Sheba. She's one of our rescues from the animal centre where I work. You're in luck. I'd just brought her home for a shower when I saw the cars so thought we'd come out and investigate. You soon sorted out those nasty people, didn't you?'

She's addressing the last sentence to the dog although she's looking at me. Waiting – or so it feels – for me to explain. How much had she heard? I could tell a half-truth, but I'm so grateful to this woman for saving me. Besides, I'm tired of lies. Tired of running.

'You'd better come in,' I say. 'They were journalists. My mother and her husband were . . .'

I stop. When I say it out loud, it trivializes it. Makes it seem normal. But I have to learn how to do it.

'They were murdered in their own home.'

Jasmine's face is frozen with shock.

'Shit,' she says. 'I've never known anyone who was murdered before. I know you weren't murdered, but you know what I mean.'

Actually, there are times when I feel as if it was me who was killed. Since Mum died, I've almost been sleepwalking through life: a ghost of myself.

'Who did it?' she asks. 'If you don't mind me asking.'

'My stepbrother. He's in prison now.'

'Were you there when it happened? Sorry. You don't need to answer that.'

But I want to. I feel an urge to tell some kind stranger who isn't a policeman or a lawyer, or else I might go mad.

'Yes. I was there. We were having a dinner party. It was Mum's birthday. Martin was there too. He was my step-father's son. He was always difficult but on that night . . . well, he went crazy for no obvious reason.'

'That's awful.'

'You didn't read about us in the papers?'

She shakes her red curls almost fiercely. 'Can't be bothered with the news any more. Gave it up during the height of the pandemic. Did my head in.'

I could understand that.

'And now they want my side of the story, as you probably heard,' I say.

'I didn't hear anything, honestly. I just saw the arguing and came over. Listen, why don't I put on the kettle and make you a cuppa?'

'I haven't got a kettle.'

'Don't you worry. I have a spare. Wow, this place smells good. Come on, Sheba.'

But before we can move, there's another knock on the door. 'Can't be them,' says Jasmine quickly, 'or Sheba would be growling. Great judge of character, aren't you, love?'

It's Vera from next door. In the light of day, I can see she has a leathered complexion with inquisitive eyes that dart everywhere. 'Glad to see you sent that pack off with a flea in their ears,' she snorts.

I don't know how to respond. The dog starts sniffing my hand and I can't help stepping back. We'd never had one because Duncan said they were 'a tie'.

'Sheba won't hurt,' says Jasmine quickly. 'She knows you're upset and wants to comfort you.'

Tears prick my eyes. 'I suppose I might as well go back to London,' I say. 'Now I've been found, there's no point. More of them will come down.'

'They'll lose interest,' says Jasmine.

'Murder always sells,' says Vera drily. 'Sorry, love, I don't mean to be blunt. But it won't go on for ever. Do you have a job to get back to?'

I think back to what my boss had said: 'Take a couple of weeks off. You're due some holiday anyway. And to be honest, the last thing we need is for the agency to be pestered.'

'Not for a bit,' I say. 'But I don't fancy dealing with knocks on the door and being stalked.'

I almost tell them about the patio door, but since I can't be sure I didn't leave it open, I let the thought go.

'I've just had an idea!' says Nancy. 'Sheba can look after you. She's the most brilliant guard dog and she'd love it here.'

'I'm not sure,' I say quickly. 'I'm not that keen on big dogs, to be honest.'

'But Sheba is as gentle as a lamb! She only barks at people when she can sense they're bad. She's never bitten anyone in her life.'

'How long have you had her at the centre, then?' asks Vera.

'Three years.'

'And you can't re-home her?'

'The size puts people off. I'd have her myself but I can't afford to feed her. I'm skint enough just paying my rent. Give her a chance, Nancy. You'll be able to sleep at night, knowing she'll make a fuss if someone tries to get in.'

She has a point. 'Well, OK. Maybe I'll take her for a couple of days, see how we get on?'

Jasmine nods. 'It's a deal.'

'You can come back to my place for some hotpot if you like,' says Vera.

In London, the only neighbour I knew was the girl in the flat above me, and that was just on nodding terms. I can't believe these two women are already so involved in my life. So willing to trust me, even though they know my story.

'That's really nice of you,' I say. 'But actually, I've got a lot to be getting on with here.'

The truth is that I need time to myself, but I don't want to hurt her feelings.

'Another time, then. I'll put some seedlings over the fence for you anyway. Got some peas that I've potted early. You can transfer them to the allotment.'

Vera assumes I'm a gardener, which I'm not. That was Mum's department.

'There's an allotment?'

'Only rented, but your mother kept it on. I've been weeding for her so the council don't take it away. They're very hot on sending sharp letters if you do something they don't like.'

'I don't know much about plants,' I admit.

'I'll teach you.'

'But I don't plan on being here for that long.'

She sniffs. 'The place needs living in. Houses are like people, you know. They need company.'

'Talking of company, I'll bring Sheba's bed round, then, and her food,' says Jasmine.

Sheba is lying at the foot of the Aga, which is now mysteriously working. My fiddling with the controls must have done something after all.

'That one's made herself at home, hasn't she?' says Vera. 'Well, I'll be seeing you. Let me know if there's anything I can do.'

The two women leave together.

Shortly afterwards, there's the sound of the post coming through the door. It's later than the delivery at home, but maybe things are different here. Sheba leaps up but she doesn't bark. Perhaps she knows the postman or she's had enough of growling for one day. She brings a letter back in her mouth and drops it at my feet.

It's stamped with a formal mark: HMP. The date is four days ago.

My fingers tremble as I open it.

Martin's round writing – more suited to a child than a man – jumps out at me.

His letter is short, but to the point.

I'm posting this before the verdict, in case it doesn't go the way we hope. If I go down, I WILL get out again, and when I do, I will come and find you. We are bound together for life because of what happened in the farmhouse. I will never forget that, Nancy. I will love you until the day we die. M x

The Night of the Murder

5.30 p.m.

I rifle through my wardrobe. Not that dress. The cleavage is too low. Nor that top. It shows my curves. I don't want him looking at me. Not that way.

A white high-neck blouse and black trousers. That's better.

It looks a bit severe for a birthday dinner party, but Mum's lucky I'm going at all. I'd turned her down flat until Alex had made me change my mind. 'We should go,' he'd said. 'It will be fun.'

But he doesn't know what happened all those summers ago. And I'm too ashamed to tell him.

Then my mobile rings.

'Can't you get back on another flight?' I ask incredulously.

Alex's voice sounds genuinely sorry. 'I've tried, Nancy. There's nothing.'

'Then I'm not going either.'

'You must. You'll upset her if you don't.'

I want to tell him that I don't care. But then I think of Dad. He'd want me to make Mum happy. Besides, my new life with Alex is giving me a clean start. Perhaps I ought to try and put the past behind me now. And so, against my better judgement, I find myself putting on my coat and driving to the farmhouse.

If I hadn't, none of this would have happened.

Elizabeth

7

Autumn 1941

Elizabeth's eyes darted around Victoria station, scanning the crowds. Her goodbye to Robert had been so brief that her heart physically hurt. There had seemed no time at all between her son returning from the conscription office and then leaving on the train to join his new unit in London. 'I'll be fine, Mum,' he'd reassured her, hanging out of the carriage window in Sidmouth station. Then he'd hugged her, his adolescent stubble rubbing against her cheek. She'd clung to him for as long as possible until Henry had broken them up with a 'You'll make him into a right softie. Let the lad go.'

But she needed to say goodbye properly. Needed to tell him so much, like, 'Make sure you keep warm.' Now, with any luck she'd find him before his train departed. Then she could give him the scarf she'd finished knitting, just hours after he'd left Devon.

Everywhere she looked, men in uniform were saying goodbye to loved ones. Women were weeping. Small children stared with bewildered expressions on their faces, wearing satchels round their shoulders and labels bearing their names. Johnnie. Maude. Jean . . .

'Don't worry, love,' she heard one of the adults saying.

'You'll be back in a few weeks. That Hitler's got it coming to him.'

How could the world have changed so much and in such a short time? Men ripped away from their wives, children taken from parents. Added to this was the constant fear that at any minute there might be that piercing scream, warning of an imminent air raid. Stations were prime targets. Everyone knew that.

'Move along there, madam! Move along!'

Elizabeth found herself touching her pearl necklace as a kind of reassurance: a habit when she was nervous. She wanted to shrink into her navy-blue woollen coat, not so much against the autumn cold, but against the brutality of it all.

Because that's what war was, wasn't it? Brutal. A chaotic evil cauldron of terror, with man against man, woman against woman, child against child. Not just here in Victoria station with the hiss of the trains and the dirt getting into your nostrils and that smell of fear because you didn't know what was going to happen or why or how or where.

Not just outside in the London streets, where pillar boxes had been sprayed with a paint that would make them turn yellow as a warning in the event of a gas attack.

Nor just in the houses that had been smashed into smoking rubble, with people furiously digging and calling out, 'Can you hear me?'

But in everyone's hearts. Hearts ripped apart with anguish and fear.

Then her own broken heart quickened. A tall man with auburn hair – a trait from Henry's side of the family – was standing next to a train door, his back to her. It was him! Desperately she tried to squeeze through the crowd to reach him. 'Please,' she begged. '*Please* let me through.'

No one made way. Muscle against muscle. Concrete against concrete. Survival against survival. Fear against fear. Layers of emotions like the pastries that she used to buy from the bakery on the seafront before rationing started.

'Robert!' she shouted out. 'Robert!'

The man was climbing onto the train now. '*Robert!*' she screamed. Her fists began to batter the bodies of anyone in front of her.

'Where's your manners,' someone snapped.

But she ploughed on. Not knowing what she was doing. 'ROBERT!'

Her stockings were laddered. Her face stung where something metallic had scraped it. But nothing else mattered. Nothing in the whole world apart from seeing her boy for one more – possibly last – time. A boy who would not have been going off to war had it not been for her husband.

Almost there now. He was within touching distance! 'ROBERT!'

He turned.

A quizzical expression.

A stranger's face.

Elizabeth's knees buckled. 'I'm sorry,' she said. 'I . . . I thought you were my son.'

Engulfed with embarrassment, she stumbled back through the crowds towards the train home.

'I was crazy to have come here,' she told herself,

attempting to tuck her gas mask under her arm because the strap was hurting her shoulder. *What were you thinking of, Elizabeth, coming all the way to London to give him a scarf to keep him warm in the trenches? You didn't even know what train he was catching, you foolish woman.*

That's what Henry would be saying right now. That's what he *will* say when she gets back. Wasn't that why she'd tiptoed out of the house early that morning without telling him, simply leaving a note on her side of the bed?

She'd left one for Mrs B too. Abandoning your husband for a day at the height of war was one thing. Abandoning guests in a boarding house that was, amazingly, still busy was another. But Beryl (her real name, although Elizabeth had never been invited to call her that even after all these years) would cope. In fact, she'd probably understand more than Henry. She was a mother herself.

The gates onto the platform closed behind her as she neared her train. She'd only just made it. Part of her wished she hadn't. Looking back, Elizabeth saw a crowd of women, their faces pressed against the barriers.

'Make sure you write home, love!' screamed a voice.

'And wash your hands – the countryside's a dirty place with all those cows!' called out another, tears streaming down her face.

Elizabeth had read about the evacuee mothers: the parents who had to decide whether to keep their children at home and risk them being killed by bombs (a whole school had been blasted to smithereens in Coventry recently – what kind of devil could do that?) or send them away for goodness knows how long.

Such a terrible choice to make. Yet if she were given the clock back to make Robert a child again, she would leap at it. Even if *he* had to be evacuated too. It was better than sending him into a foreign country to fight for his life.

She felt the tears threatening again.

'All on board,' yelled the guard, before his whistle pierced the air.

If she didn't obey, it would be too late.

'Make room for the lady,' said a voice. A man reached out an arm and hauled her in. Somehow she managed to find somewhere to place her feet amidst the tangle of legs. Elizabeth tried to say thank you but the words wouldn't come out.

There was a jolt. They were off.

As she attempted to stay upright, her mind went back to when Robert had returned from signing up with a proud expression on his face before going out to 'celebrate' with his friends.

'You can't protect him for ever,' her husband had said sharply. 'He's a man.'

'Seventeen isn't a man,' she'd retorted.

Henry had made that scoffing expression she disliked so much. Sometimes it referred to a meal that she or Mrs B had made if it wasn't to his taste. Or if she'd been out 'too long' on a walk or an errand. 'I was fifteen when I signed up for the Great War.'

'And look what that did to you,' she'd snapped.

'What do you mean?'

'It changed you, Henry. You've told me that yourself. And now you've pushed our son into it. He didn't have to.

He could have waited another year until being officially called.'

'But he wanted to.'

'Only because he hoped to make you proud of him.'

He hadn't answered that.

'Please bring him back,' she whispered out loud now, still half in prayer.

'Are you all right?'

It was the man who had helped her in.

He was sandy-haired and wore glasses, she noticed, and had a group of children around him. Not young but not old either. Maybe eight or nine. Far too young to fight, thank God.

She nodded numbly.

'You can sit on this if you like,' piped up one of the little girls, indicating a battered brown suitcase. 'I was meant to have a satchel so our hands are free but me mam didn't have the pennies for one so the lady next door gave us this instead.'

Such a sweet face! Elizabeth's heart twisted even more. 'One child only,' Henry had stipulated when she'd pleaded for more after Robert was born. 'It's all we can afford.'

But it wasn't about money. He knew that and so did she. How could you have a child if you didn't do what husbands and wives were meant to do? How could you love a man who thrashed around in bed and punched you in his sleep, reliving the Great War in his nightmares? How could you care for a man who called you a whore in his sleep and then denied it in the morning?

Frankly, it was a miracle they'd been able to have Robert.

'Thank you,' Elizabeth said now to the little girl.

'Are you going to the seaside too?' she asked.

'Yes,' she replied. 'I live there.'

'Really?' The sandy-haired man's face took on a keen look. 'Whereabouts?'

A warm feeling swelled Elizabeth's chest as she thought of the place where she had been born and bred; where her parents had lived before her, her grandparents too. 'A town called Sidmouth.'

'We're going to Lyme Regis,' chirped the little girl.

'Really?'

Only part of Elizabeth's brain was taking this in. Her head was still with Robert. Was it possible she had passed him in the station? If so, why hadn't she smelled him? Been drawn to him? Wouldn't she have known that the child she had given birth to was just feet away, maybe inches?

'We're being ee-vac-u-ated,' said the little girl, pronouncing each syllable as a separate word. 'We've got sandwiches to eat. Look! Real fish paste they've got in them. Mam opened the last tin as a special treat.'

Elizabeth's heart felt as if it was being twisted inside her. Was this child's mother one of the desperate women she'd seen at the station, faces pressed against railings for a last glimpse?

'Move along, please.'

It was the guard.

'We can't,' said the man. 'There's no room.'

'Go further down. There's a bit of space in the buffet car.'

Then he glanced at Elizabeth, no doubt taking in her smart hat and coat. What else did he see, she wondered?

A tallish woman with pale blonde hair twisted into a French pleat at the nape of her neck; grey eyes; a smudge of bright red 'going out' lipstick reserved for best because cosmetics were short now; a world-weary expression on her face? Or the young girl inside who could have been so different if she'd made other choices?

'Madam, there's a spare seat going in first class,' offered the guard.

'But I don't have a ticket,' she began.

'Just come with me,' he said.

How embarrassing. But also tempting. The thought of sitting down, closing her eyes and pretending that Robert was sitting next to her was too irresistible.

'Have a safe journey,' she said to the sandy-haired man, hoping he'd understand.

'Thank you. You too.'

She'd need to stay awake, Elizabeth reminded herself. There were no station announcements now, or even station signs. They'd been taken down to confuse the enemy in case of invasion.

But the blackout blinds in the first-class carriage with its soft red-leather upholstery, combined with the emotional exhaustion of the day, proved too much. Holding Robert's scarf against her cheek for comfort, Elizabeth found herself nodding off into a world where none of this existed.

She and Robert were picnicking at the top of Salcombe Hill. They were swimming in the sea, feeling the weightlessness of their bodies in the water . . .

At some point she must have woken up because she was dimly aware of people getting on and off. But then exhaustion took over again. Until suddenly there was a huge noise overhead, followed by a massive jolt. Elizabeth was flung onto the floor of the carriage.

Panic stuck in her throat. Everything was black. People were screaming and shouting.

'We've been hit!'

8

'Blimey,' said a youth next to her. 'Look at that. They could have got us.'

Elizabeth stared in horror at the twisted smouldering metal in front of them. If the Germans had bombed the track just a few moments later, they could all have died.

The train driver had performed a miracle to stop before they hit the wreckage. Then the guard helped them walk along the track for about half an hour to the next station. Some of them had been crying. Most, like Elizabeth, were silently stoical, if shocked; relieved that they were still alive.

'When I smelled that smoke,' said the youth, 'I thought the train was on fire. Bloody lucky. That's what we are.'

Elizabeth nodded numbly. At times, the war seemed like a bad dream that existed only in the newspapers. Of course, there were huge changes like Robert enlisting and shops not having supplies and camouflaged guns on the coast to defend them in case of invasion. But she hadn't actually seen any bombs or damage. Never felt her life was genuinely in danger.

Until now.

'Everyone over here, please,' shouted the guard when they finally reached the next station.

They gathered together, wondering what was going to happen. There was no sign of the children from earlier, or the man escorting them – their teacher, she presumed. *Please don't let them be hurt*, thought Elizabeth worriedly. Eventually, another train arrived from the opposite direction – probably because of the wrecked track – and they were all told to get on.

'I reckon we're going on some kind of detour,' she heard someone say.

Finally, at nearly 3 a.m., they arrived at Sidmouth station.

She walked home in the dark, not even daring to use her precious torch for fear of breaking the blackout rules.

Even though it was late, Henry was waiting up for her.

'Well?' he asked. 'Did you see Robert?'

'No.'

He sniffed. 'Just as well. You'd have embarrassed him.'

'And that's worse than sending your only child to battle, is it?' she retorted.

'You said goodbye to him here when he left. Besides, I've told you. It was his decision.'

She spent what was left of the night sleeping on the other side of the bed, as far away from her husband as she could. There was no point in telling him about the bombing on the train line and their near-escape. She knew what he'd say. 'Well, what else do you expect if you insist on going up to London during a war?'

In the morning, she woke with a start. Where was Robert now? On a boat crossing the Channel? In a truck travelling towards the enemy?

Elizabeth forced herself out of bed. Mrs B was already in the kitchen getting breakfast ready for the paying guests, using the ration books they had brought with them. All three were people with private means who had come here to get away from big cities. There were two spinster sisters – the Patmores – who dressed and looked so alike that it was hard to tell one from the other. And there was a pinched-faced widow, Mrs Norris, whose words were few but generally sharp.

'Got there all right did you?' asked Mrs B.

Some people might take offence at the informal way in which Mrs B addressed her employer, but Elizabeth had known her too long for that.

'Yes,' she said quietly.

'Did you see young Robert in London then?'

'No.'

'I'm sorry.'

Mrs B had sometimes helped with Robert when he'd been a baby. Those were the days when Elizabeth was still trying to work out how to cope with marriage to a war hero who seemed pleasant enough on the outside but hid a multitude of horrors within.

'Mrs Palmer came round half an hour ago but I didn't want to disturb you.'

Adeline Palmer was her best friend although she was younger than her by a few years. Always doing good but stubborn at the same time. She'd come into her element during the war because it had given her, by her own admission, 'a purpose'. She was also Robert's godmother.

'You can do the same for me when it's my turn,' she'd said. But for Adeline, the babies hadn't come and now, like so many other women, she'd have to wait until her husband came home from the front before she could try again.

Mrs B was giving her a hard look. 'Mrs Palmer wants to know if we can have any of these evacuees.'

Henry had already made his position on this quite clear. 'We're not taking in any more mouths to gobble up food,' he'd said. 'It's hard enough feeding everyone in this house.'

'Says she's desperate,' continued Mrs B. 'Wants you to meet her at the Manor Hall. I'd take some lice lotion if I were you.'

Mrs B always spoke like the butter and flour she measured out. Precisely. No more than was necessary. No less.

'Thank you. Did she say when?'

'The sooner the better.'

'I'll help you with breakfast first.'

'No need.'

Elizabeth hesitated. Even though she'd known Mrs B for ever, it wasn't always easy to read her mind. 'How would you feel about the extra work involved if we did take on some evacuees?' she asked.

She shrugged, her fleshy upper arms quivering with the motion. 'Only fair, isn't it? We could have been them if we hadn't been lucky enough to be born here.'

Elizabeth couldn't have put it better herself.

It was a relief to walk along the promenade. To smell the clear air. Hear the screech of the seagulls overhead, ducking and diving in the hope of a spare crumb. Before the war, she and Robert had always swum together, especially in the school holidays, when they liked to go down before breakfast.

Henry couldn't swim because of his shattered leg – not a war injury, as he allowed many to presume, but the result of a pile of wood falling on him in the yard where he worked as the supervisor. The accident had happened shortly after Robert's birth. It had given them both an excuse for the end of any physical intimacy, although the frail hope of more children had also died with it.

But at least she had her son. 'There's nothing like the sea, is there, Mother?' Robert would say, as they dried themselves off on the beach before walking home. 'It makes your mind so calm. So still.'

He often spoke like that. Sometimes, when cleaning his room, she came across little scraps of poems he had written. *Shows great promise*, his English master had remarked in his report.

How would her sensitive son manage with the fighting? Was Henry right when he'd said it 'would make a man of him' and that she'd 'mollycoddled' him for too long. What if he didn't come back? What if he did and he'd changed, just as the war had changed Henry?

'Elizabeth!'

Adeline was waiting for her. Her lovely raven shoulder-length hair was hidden under a scarf knotted at the back – just like a land girl – and she was wearing trousers! Even though more and more women were doing this, Elizabeth didn't dare. Henry would be furious.

'I need two rooms,' said Adeline, getting straight to the point. Her beautiful eyes were steady with intent. 'A teacher and two of his pupils were meant to go to Lyme but there was a mix-up. Let me introduce you. They're by the tea urn.'

Elizabeth found herself face to face with the tall sandy-haired man from the train and the two little girls, who were holding hands with each other. Their faces were streaked with soot and there was a faint whiff of urine from the children's direction.

'You're safe!' she said, her heart flooding with relief.

Adeline looked puzzled. 'Do you know each other?'

'I'll explain later,' said Elizabeth quietly. 'My name is Elizabeth Montague,' she said to the girls, kneeling down so she was on their level. 'What are you called?'

'I'm Maisie,' said the taller of the two, with blue eyes. 'And this is my friend Shirley.' Her companion flicked back her long thick black plaits. What a sweet snub nose, thought Elizabeth, and a mischievous smile. She'd have loved a daughter like that!

'I'm Stephen Smith, their teacher,' said the man. He made to hold out his hand but took it back, as if suddenly remembering it was grimy. 'I apologize for our appearance. The girls kept hanging out of the windows even though I did try to stop them and, well, the facilities were . . . challenging.'

Elizabeth blushed, remembering how she'd been ushered to first class.

'Were you hurt when the train had to stop so suddenly?' she asked.

He put one hand on each of the girls' shoulders in a protective manner. 'Thankfully not.'

'But a lady had her handbag nicked!' piped up Shirley.

Mr Smith shook his head. 'It's very sad that thieves use occasions like this to take advantage of others.'

'Things are nicked all the time where we come from,' said the little girl stoutly.

'Where is that?' asked Elizabeth.

'Elephant and Castle,' said the first child. 'There aren't

really any elephants or castles. But my dad says there's nothing wrong with 'magination.'

Elizabeth noted the dropped 'i', but it felt wrong to correct her. It made her think of Robert's early poems as a child.

'Your father's quite right,' she said.

'Can you take them?' asked Adeline. Her violet eyes were dark with the seriousness of her request. She of all people knew what Henry's thoughts were on this. It wasn't as though this was the first time she'd asked. But it was different now.

Henry owed it to her.

'Yes,' she heard herself say. 'Of course I can.'

'Take us where?' asked Maisie.

Elizabeth knelt down next to her. 'To my home,' she said. 'It's called Tall Chimneys.' Then, crossing her fingers, she added, 'You'll be safe there.'

9

'It smells different from London,' said Maisie as they walked down All Saints Road. Elizabeth's mind was in such turmoil at the thought of what Henry was going to say, that it took her a few moments to answer.

'That will be the sea,' she said. 'You can taste the salt on your tongue.'

'The air is cleaner than at home,' observed Mr Smith. She wasn't sure if he was talking to her or the children. Already she could tell he was one of those teachers who spoke *to* his pupils rather than *at* them. There was also something rather precise about his accent, suggesting a possible private education.

'Where's the sea?' asked Shirley.

'At the bottom of the high street. I'll take you there later if you like. I thought you might want to have a wash down first. We need to tell your parents where you are, too.'

'The school will post details up on the railings,' said Mr Smith.

'But that will take time, won't it? Their parents will be worried. I know I would be. You must use our phone to ring them.'

Mr Smith lowered his voice. 'The girls' parents don't have phones. Very few do.'

She hadn't thought of that.

Meanwhile, Maisie's eyes were darting around as if searching for something. 'Why aren't there any bombed houses and piles of bodies?'

Elizabeth shivered. Was this what the children had been used to?

'The Germans haven't hurt our town,' she said, hoping it wasn't tempting fate. Who knew what Hitler would do next?

'Why not?' asked Maisie.

'Because it's smaller than London,' said the other child. 'That's what me mam said.'

That might be true. But it certainly didn't mean that they were safe, despite her earlier words to the girls. Instead there had been a warning by the government that the town's position on the South-West coast, close to the city of Exeter, made it a prime target for a German landing. The authorities were preparing for that already. Not just with sandbags and blackout curtains but with traps on the beach that were a mixture of old scaffolding and concrete blocks, designed to stop, or at least slow down, any German tanks that might try to cross the beach.

Then there were the guns positioned high up on the hills surrounding the town, camouflaged cleverly by rubble that might look, to enemy aircraft overhead, like bombed houses. And, of course, there were the pillboxes like the one at the top of Jacob's Ladder – concrete lookout posts from which the Home Guard could shoot at any invaders.

It was rumoured, too, that pistols could be bought in a certain pub on the outskirts of town as 'protection for your family'.

Naturally, Elizabeth couldn't tell her new guests any of this. It would scare them. Did Mr Smith realize that his young charges might just have been sent from the frying pan into the fire?

Neither fate was exactly preferable. What a choice – being blown to bits in London or being shot at by German tanks making their way over the beaches and into the streets. Not just shot at, either. There had been terrible reports of women in Poland being . . .

She could hardly think of the word.

'Nearly there now,' she said brightly, forcing the dark thoughts away.

They were turning right by one of the town's two cinemas. It was showing *How Green Was My Valley*, starring Walter Pidgeon and Maureen O'Hara. Maybe she and Adeline could go later this week. Henry always claimed his back hurt too much in the cinema seats, although it didn't stop him playing billiards at the Conservative Club.

They walked down Salcombe Road towards the little hump-back bridge and the ancient toll house that must have seen some sights in its day. A second world war was just one of them. She could only hope there wouldn't ever be a third.

'Here we are. It's called Tall Chimneys.'

'Blimey!' breathed Maisie. 'It's like a picture in a book.'

Mr Smith seemed equally taken aback.

Elizabeth felt both embarrassed and flattered. Her home wasn't as big as some of the enormous houses around here. No. It was more that it was so, well, gracious. Charming. Like an elegant hostess reaching her arms out to the sea beyond and saying 'Welcome'.

For a minute she saw Tall Chimneys through their eyes. Its white Regency fascia with the balcony that ran along the first floor below the second. The imposing black front door with its knocker and bell that she or Mrs B cleaned every day. The large sash windows that they'd 'strengthened' against possible explosions with thick sticky tape and cloaked with blackout curtains every night. There used to be black iron railings outside but they'd been requisitioned for munitions. She was still getting used to their absence.

Even with these recent changes, Elizabeth often had to pinch herself when she saw it. 'I love Tall Chimneys like a person,' she constantly found herself thinking.

Robert had felt the same. 'I'll be back,' he'd promised her during that last goodbye. 'For the house as well as you, Mother. And Dad, of course.'

A chill passed through her. Maybe he was already lying dead in France, riddled with bullets. But she'd know, wouldn't she? That part of her heart that was joined to her son for ever would surely tell her if he had died.

'How long have you lived here for?' asked Mr Smith, breaking into her thoughts.

Partly to hide her distress, Elizabeth found herself coming out with the words that she reserved for those guests who seemed the type who would understand their significance.

'I was born here. The story goes that my grandmother fell in love with Tall Chimneys before she fell in love with my grandfather.'

He was tilting his head to one side in a 'please go on' way.

'Grandfather Joe was apparently drawn to her slim ankles that he glimpsed going up the stairs before him during his dead wife's wake.'

There was a definite glint of interest in his face. Elizabeth allowed herself a wry smile. This story was all part of the hostess act, of course. Then again, hadn't she been acting for years? And if she could keep going, she'd manage to regain some control of her heart, which was still beating furiously at the thought of Robert under fire.

'He had three children, including the baby who had brought about its mother's death during labour. And he had a squat nose and abrupt manner. But he did own Tall Chimneys in a coastal Devonshire town. Initially my grandmother was terrified of the sea – she'd come from a small farming village in the middle of Devon where they rarely travelled to the coast. Eventually, she grew to love it and bathed every day.'

'Do you swim in the sea?' asked Maisie, her eyes shining with interest.

'I do. Every morning before the house is awake.' Robert's excited voice came into her head. *Are you ready, Mum?*

'But what if the fish ate you up!'

Elizabeth tried not to smile for fear of offending the child. But the question made her feel better. It took her back to Robert's childhood, when he was always asking her such funny things.

'The fish are harmless here.'

'And was the marriage a success?' asked Mr Smith.

'Yes and no.' Elizabeth swallowed the lump that came into her throat every time she reached this part of the story. 'They had a child together – my mother – but then my grandfather died unexpectedly from heart trouble, leaving my grandmother with a newborn and three step-children. To her dismay, she discovered there were no savings. The only asset was Tall Chimneys. So his spinster aunt suggested she turned it into a boarding house.'

She took a breath, almost at the end of her potted history now. 'And so began the house's new life. It goes without saying that my mother carried on and that I did the same.'

Elizabeth didn't add that she wondered sometimes if Henry, whom she'd known since Sunday School, had married her because of the financial stability that Tall Chimneys provided. 'Did all right there for yourself,' she'd overheard someone say to him at their wedding. But at the time, she'd only seen a man who had served in the Great War and received a hero's welcome on his return. He'd been such an attentive suitor, so kind with his declarations that he'd 'look after' her. Yet almost as soon as the ring was on her finger and Tall Chimneys had become his as well as hers, he started criticizing everything she did. The accident in the yard had made it worse, with his resentment of the 'unfairness of it all'.

There was a yawn from the little girl with thick black plaits. Shirley.

'I'm sorry,' said Elizabeth quickly. 'There's me chattering on when you must be desperate to freshen up. Come on in and I'll show you to your rooms. I'm afraid you girls will need to share.'

'They're used to that,' said the teacher quietly. 'Shirley's family lives in one room. There are eight of them.'

Eight? To think she'd just spent a good five minutes talking about her own lovely home.

'You're on the top floor,' she said, smiling at Shirley and Maisie. 'Mr Smith, you're on the first. I'll find you some towels and then . . .'

'Good morning.'

Henry stepped out of their bedroom just as they went past, taking her by surprise. Usually he was at the yard by now. His leg must be playing up. Elizabeth's heart sank. She'd hoped to talk to him quietly on their own before they all met.

'I didn't realize we were expecting more guests.'

'Your wife kindly agreed to take us in,' said Mr Smith.

'I see.' Henry's right eyebrow rose; a sign that someone was annoying him. Usually Elizabeth. 'And your name, sir?'

'Stephen Smith. I'm a teacher in charge of evacuee children from London. May I introduce Maisie and Shirley, two of my pupils.'

Henry's mouth was set in a stiff straight line. His upper lip had always been narrower than the lower, but now it was barely visible. 'Elizabeth, a word please.' He glared at her. 'Downstairs in our *private* sitting room.'

He made her feel like a schoolgirl! Usually she would have felt cowed. But it was different now. Her anger about Robert's absence had been growing steadily alongside the gaping hole of loss in her heart.

'I'll be there in five minutes,' she said crisply. 'I need to take our guests to their rooms first.'

Henry glowered. 'I hope you've brought your ration books,' he said. 'We can't feed you for free.'

Elizabeth could barely bring herself to look at the teacher. What must he think of them?

'We have indeed, sir,' he said in a tone that was simultaneously both respectful and cool. 'We are also extremely grateful to you for contributing to the war effort.'

There was little that Henry could say to that. 'Five minutes then,' he retorted, addressing Elizabeth as if the others were not there. Then, holding the bannisters for support, he made his way downstairs.

'I'm afraid we've caused trouble for you,' said Mr Smith in a low voice when they reached the top floor.

'Please don't worry. Now, girls, here's your room.'

'It's so big,' cried out Shirley, her eyes widening.

'It's my son's.' She didn't add that she'd hoped not to give it up to anyone else. Robert's bits and pieces were still there. His shaving brush on the sink. His shoes under the desk. His clothes in the wardrobe. But there wasn't an option. The rest of the house was full with PGs, as they called the paying guests.

Elizabeth felt her throat thickening again. 'I'll find a camp bed to go next to this one.'

'We could top and tail,' said Maisie, yawning. 'Me and my sisters do that at home.'

'There's a bathroom next door but you'll need to share that with some of the other guests who are already here. Here are some towels and . . .'

She stopped. The children were already lying on the bed. One at the top. The other at the bottom. Fast asleep.

'We didn't get much rest on the floor of the hall last night after the train journey,' said Mr Smith quietly.

She should have considered that. 'I'm sorry. Let me

show you your room, unless you'd like something to eat first?'

'I'm not actually hungry, thank you, but bed would be wonderful.' His eyes looked troubled. 'If your husband wishes us to move on, we will try to find alternative accommodation.'

'There will be no need,' she said briskly.

His kindness unsettled her. Very few people in Sidmouth realized what her life was really like. Adeline, of course, was one. Goodness knows what she'd do without her.

'Were you in London to see friends?' he asked.

She was surprised by the question. 'No. I was hoping to see my son before he went off to war. I'd made him a navy-blue scarf that I finished after he'd left. I wanted him to take it with him.'

'That's very touching. He must have been very grateful.'

'I didn't find him,' she said softly.

His eyes were full of sympathy. 'I'm sorry.'

She'd said too much. 'Your room is up here.'

'It can't be easy for you to share your house with total strangers like us,' he said as she showed him the way.

'Actually,' she said, 'I like meeting new people.'

It was true. It meant Henry couldn't be as unkind as he was when it was just the two of them together. Then, in case he took it the wrong way, she added, 'And I want to do my bit for the war.'

He nodded. 'I understand that. Strange how life can suddenly change, isn't it? At times, it's terrifying. Yet at others it feels as though we're being given a chance to do the right thing.'

'I know just what you mean,' she said.

For a second, their eyes met in what felt like understanding.

Then, feeling herself blush with embarrassment, she swiftly turned and went downstairs to help Mrs B in the kitchen. But as the two women chopped up potatoes from the allotment in familial silence, Elizabeth had the strangest feeling that the new arrivals were going to change the lives of all who lived in Tall Chimneys. She just wasn't sure how.

The Night of the Murder

It takes me longer to reach the farmhouse than I'd thought. It's been a while since I visited. The place feels like it's in the middle of nowhere and yet, ironically, it's just fifty-odd miles from London.

Heaven knows why they bought it. Actually, I do. He likes the idea of having a place like this. And she does what he wants.

The long lane is even bumpier than I recall. Then, as I park by the old stables, I see it.

His car.

No one told me Martin was going to be here.

He comes running out like an eager schoolboy. 'Where's the boyfriend?' he asks.

'Fiancé,' I say shortly. 'He couldn't make it.'

'All the more company for me,' he says, making to touch my shoulder. But I'm ready. I walk quickly ahead of him towards the front door.

Just two hours, I tell myself. Then I'll leave.

Nancy

IO

I try to sleep, attempting to put Martin's letter out of my mind. But I toss and turn all night. In the morning, I feel just as exhausted. I need to clear my head. Think. Work out my next move. Pretend I can do this.

So I go downstairs, where Sheba is sleeping on the bed that Jasmine has lent me. I'm a bit nervous about putting on her collar in case she doesn't like it but, on the contrary, Sheba stands very still as if she knows what I'm doing. Then the two of us head for the beach. The early morning sun is streaked across the horizon like a fine palette-knife line of apricot jam. Before us, the sand is as smooth as the marzipan on my wedding cake, which my mother and I made together the week before she died. It's empty apart from a lone dog-walker in the distance.

A seagull screams at me from above as if taunting me. It has every right to jeer. I've landed in this terrible nightmare all by myself. There's no one else to blame. Duncan's glassy stare as he lay on the kitchen floor in the farmhouse looms into my head. If only I'd told the police the truth.

But then what? I might well have been sent to prison myself.

The seagull screams again. Its meaning is almost as clear as if it had spoken. I'm in prison right now. I've never lied before – about important things, anyway. And now I'm paying the price.

Sheba is running ahead of me through the low tide, skirting the frothy fringes without actually going in. I feel for the letter in my pocket. I've reread it so many times in the night that I know the words off by heart.

I'm posting this before the verdict, in case it doesn't go the way we hope. If I go down, I WILL get out again, and when I do, I will come and find you. We are bound together for life because of what happened in the farmhouse. I will never forget that, Nancy. I will love you until the day we die. M x

'*Come and find you.*'
I shiver again.
A wave, faster than the others, bowls up and soaks my trainers. It feels like a warning. I use the silver whistle I found in the bike's basket to call Sheba back – she's obviously been well trained – and put her on the lead so I can text Claire.

I'd like to talk to her in person but I'm scared that the wobble in my voice might give me away. Besides, it's only just after 7 a.m. She might still be asleep. Perhaps I should text later in case the ping wakes her.

But then there's a ping at my end. Claire has texted me first. This often happens. We sometimes joke that we pick up each other's vibes. 'It's because we're best friends,' we tell each other. But what would Claire think now if she knew the truth?

Are you ok? she's written.
Below is a worried emoji.
Claire's texts are usually light-hearted and informal. I tend to spend time editing mine. Rereading. Wondering what to add in. And what to take out.

I've had a letter from Martin in prison, I type back slowly.

WTF? The acronym is accompanied by a startled yellow face. *What did he say???????*

Stuff about never forgetting me, I tap back.

This isn't strictly true, word for word, but I don't want to tell her everything.

I tore it up and put it in the bin, I add.

Good for you. I'm so glad he's behind bars finally.

Claire had never liked Martin from the minute she'd met him. 'There's something creepy about him,' she said. It was during one of the holidays when she'd come down to stay and Duncan and Martin had been there too. We were thirteen and obsessed with boys.

'Do you think so?' He was sullen and quiet with his dad and my mum but OK with me.

'I think he likes you, I can see it in his eyes.' I can almost see her raising an eyebrow now. 'Has he tried to kiss you?'

'NO! He's my stepbrother!'

'It's perfectly legal,' she'd retorted. 'And it's not like you were brought up with him.'

'I don't care. I don't see Martin like that.'

She'd shrugged. 'Have it your way.'

I knew that Claire was desperate to be kissed. More than I was. But she had been right about Martin. He *was* creepy. And I should have listened to her.

My mind goes back to the night of the murder.

If Claire hadn't taken me in after the police had finished questioning me, I don't know what I'd have done. She was the one who had held me. Dried my tears. Steered me into a warm bath, tucked me into bed in the spare room next to hers. Found me a good lawyer – Judith – through one of her old university contacts 'because you're going to need one'. Judith had been there with me through the next police interview. After that, they'd let me go.

Claire was the one who had sat next to me in court during Martin's trial. Who'd reassured me; had held my hand before I gave evidence, telling me that I mustn't worry. The jury would realize I was telling the truth.

She was the one who had burst into tears of relief when Martin had been sentenced to life. 'Thank God! Now we won't have to worry about him ever again.'

We won't have to worry. That's how close we are. Everyone needs a best friend. But sometimes Claire can be a bit pushy. A bit too determined for me to do what she feels is right. I know it's because she's protective towards me after what happened all those years ago. 'Not all men are like him,' she'd told me when I turned down yet another of her invitations to go to a party. But there are some things you can't get out of your head.

I have to go now. Call you later, I text.

Are you sure? Shall I come down to see you?

It's all right, thanks, I tap back. *Just look after yourself.*

Sheba is pawing at a stone as if it's a ball, so I buy her one on the way home from a kiosk on the front. It also sells brightly coloured postcards and buckets and spades. I hear my father's voice. '*Let's make a sandcastle, Nancy!*'

Someone's walking past, speaking urgently into her phone. It sounds like a work call. I get a rush of nostalgia. It feels so strange not being in the office. I miss the routine. The normality. But above all, I miss Dad and Mum. If only she had listened to me, none of this would have happened.

We're climbing a steep slope at Jacob's Ladder where, years ago, donkeys used to carry up crushed limestone to convert into lime. True to its name, there's a very old ladder here as an alternative route, leading to a coffee shop with stunning views over the Jurassic Coast. But I'm not sure if Sheba can manage ladders, which is why we're on the slope instead. When we get to the top, I notice a sign by what looks like a concrete block with a cavity inside: THIS PILLBOX FORMED PART OF THE DEFENCES OF OUR COAST AGAINST INVASION IN 1940 AND WITH THESE CLIFFS AND GARDENS WAS USED IN TRAINING FOR THE D-DAY LANDING ON THE 6 JUNE 1944.

Did someone actually get in there to hide and aim rifles up to the sky? 'It looks so small,' I murmur out loud.

'It's bigger than it looks,' says an old man walking past with a stick. 'There are two rooms inside there, you know.'

'Another world, another life,' I say to myself as I head back to Tall Chimneys. My father used to talk about the war and how his father had been called up. It's only when you see relics like this that you remember other generations had to go through their own bloody battles. Again, my mind shoots back.

'I'm sorry, Nancy,' the paramedic says. 'Your mother is dead.'

Her eyes are staring glassily up at the ceiling. Her face is white. But her hands still feel warm.

'Don't touch,' says the policewoman quickly. 'We need to gather evidence.'

I am shaking now at the memory.

I wipe Sheba's sandy paws and open the front door.

My heart stops. There's an envelope on the mat with a squirly *'By hand'* written in ink.

Not Martin. Please. It doesn't look like his handwriting and there's no HMP stamp, but what if he's got someone else to deliver something?

It's not what I'm expecting.

To the owner of Tall Chimneys

    My name is Jeremy Morton. I am the curator at the Sidmouth Museum and we are currently compiling a history of the town during the Second World War.

    As part of this project, we are gathering documents and photographs from that time.

    We have recently unearthed an old newspaper account that states that someone went missing from your home in 1942. We wondered if you knew anything about this.

    If you are able to help in any way, I would be extremely grateful.

What? Someone went missing? I'd never heard of that before. I rack my brains but I can't remember Dad or Mum mentioning that.

I shiver with unease. I'd only just begun to feel at peace in this place. Was I wrong? Does the house have bad vibes? After all, look what happened to me all those years ago, when I'd been here last.

I walk out into the hall and look up to the top floor through the beautiful spiral staircase. 'It's all right,' the house seems to say.

But what if it's lying? Am I going crazy to think of it as a real person?

Then I recall the writing at the back of the wardrobe.

Maisie was here. SO WAS SHIRLEY! 8 October 1941

Did they have anything to do with this missing person?

My phone starts to ring.

Alex.

I could ignore it like before, but, as Claire says, I have to talk to him at some point.

'Hello,' I say.

'Nancy!'

The relief and the warmth in his voice make me want to cry.

'Please, Alex. Don't call me. It's over.'

Even as I speak, I know I don't mean it. In my head, we're still an 'us'. But I have no choice but to end everything after what happened in the farmhouse.

There's the sound of traffic at his end. I picture him standing in Trafalgar Square, where we often used to spend weekend afternoons browsing round the National Gallery or wandering down to Shaftesbury Avenue in the evening to see if there were any last-minute tickets for a play. I miss him.

'Wait,' he says urgently. 'There's something you need to know. 'You're not safe.'

My throat is dry. 'What?'

He says something, but there's a lot of noise in the background. 'I can't hear you,' I say, unable to keep the desperation from my voice.

'Hang on. I'm going somewhere quieter. I'll call you back.'

I pace up and down, impatient to hear what he has to say. Why am I not safe? Maybe it's busy in the office. Perhaps he has to take another call. Alex is good at getting people to listen to him. I've heard him at work.

'I know it's hard,' he might say to someone whom he wants to interview. 'But your story might help others in the same position.'

His tone is always kind. Caring. Compassionate.

It's partly because Alex truly believes what he is saying. He's a journalist specializing in what he calls 'triumph-over-tragedy stories'. Ordinary people who do extraordinary things, like the mother of the little girl who wanted to be a ballerina even though she was born with only one leg. The mother fought to get the best prosthetic for her daughter and the child performed a solo in the school concert. It brought tears to my eyes to read that article.

And Alex had been right. It did help others. His feature had led to a sackful of letters and emails from moved readers, one of whom wanted to make a substantial donation to charity.

But right now, I can't let him back in my life again. So when he rings again (the line is clear now), I am ready. Or am I? Suddenly I'm scared.

'I don't want to know why I'm not safe,' I sob. 'I just want to live a normal life.'

Sheba begins pawing at me, as if sensing my distress.

'You've got to, Nancy. It's in your interest.'

This was another of his lines. The thing is, he's often right.

I have a flash of our first kiss. He'd waited until our second date partly because I'd told him I needed to go slowly. Of course, I didn't tell him why. But when his lips had touched mine, I didn't feel repulsed. I actually wanted him to kiss me again. We'd only known each other six months before he proposed.

Alex and I set about planning a low-key register office wedding, booked to take place in three months' time. 'I want you to have our babies,' he'd told me.

Maybe I should have come out with the truth right then. But I was too ashamed.

Then Mum invited us to her birthday party dinner at the farmhouse. And everything changed.

Alex's voice is tense. 'I've had a tip-off from a mate at the *Telegraph* that they're running a big piece tomorrow. So are the other dailies. They know where you are, and that means the public soon will too.'

I sink to the floor, my back against the Aga for warmth and my arm around Sheba for comfort.

'Are you still there, Nancy?'

I am. But a horrible thought has occurred to me. Is it possible that the man I still love has sold me out?

'They didn't track me down because of you, did they, Alex? Did you tell them I was here?'

As soon as I say it, I know I'm wrong.

'How could you think that?' he says, clearly hurt. 'For a start, you didn't tell me where you were going. You just disappeared after the trial.'

'I'm sorry, Alex. I just can't do this right now –'

'There's something else,' he butts in. 'Some of the reports are already online.'

'I don't want to talk to you any more.'

'Please, Nancy, listen to me. There are also rumours of an exclusive . . .'

I cut him off. Then I go on to Google, my fingers shaking.

'Farmhouse massacre daughter's dog attacks journalists,' says one headline.

'Where is the grief? Farmhouse murder heiress's million-pound seaside sanctuary,' says another.

Then a third headline, which leaves me cold.

'Blonde bloodbath survivor's brunette disguise. Has she got something to hide?'

There are just two people who know the truth about that night in the farmhouse.

Martin and me.

I can hear his voice as clearly as if he is standing next to me right now. *'No one else must know, Nancy. No one.'*

12

I make sure all the windows and doors at the front of the house are locked, then brew some mint tea and take it into the garden with Sheba. It's chilly, but I need the fresh air to gather my thoughts clearly.

Before the murder, Alex and I would daydream about having a house with a garden. After a lazy Sunday breakfast in bed, we'd pore through the lifestyle sections.

The last time is still fresh in my mind.

'That looks nice,' I'd said, pointing to a rooftop garden with pot plants and cane chairs upholstered in turquoise silk.

'The rent's sky-high,' he pointed out, his arm around me. 'How about escaping to a far-flung Scottish island? We could buy a crofter's cottage and have six children.'

'Six?'

'Maybe five then,' he conceded.

I decided to play along with it. 'Four. It's an even number.'

'You and your superstitions!'

'So long as it's not one,' I added. 'I would have loved a brother or sister.'

'What about your stepbrother?' he asked.

I remember getting out of bed then. 'I've told you before. Martin and I weren't close. He . . . he's always been a bit strange.'

'Is he coming to the wedding?'

'No,' I said brusquely. 'He can't make it.'

The truth was that I hadn't asked him. If it had been up to me, I wouldn't have Duncan or Mum there either. But Alex liked Mum and the feeling was mutual. 'Mind you,' he'd said after their first meeting, 'I sensed a bit of tension between you and your mother.'

'We've had our ups and downs over the years,' I said, 'mainly because of Duncan. It's not easy having a step-parent.'

'I can imagine,' he said.

I don't think so, I almost replied.

Mum thought Alex was 'perfect' for me, but perhaps that was through relief that I was finally settling down. 'Duncan and I could give you some money if you wanted to buy a place of your own.'

'No thanks,' I said. I'd already turned down her offer of help to buy a flat a few years earlier. I wanted to make my own way in life.

'Why not?'

I gave a sarcastic laugh. 'Why do you think?'

Mum had pretended to look confused. 'Honestly, Nancy. I don't know *what* you think half the time. If your father had been here . . .'

'Don't talk to me about Dad. If he'd been here, he'd have listened to me when –'

'I'm not discussing that any more, Nancy.'

'What's going on?' Duncan said as he came in.

'Nothing,' I said. 'I need to go now.'

'Don't be late for your mother's birthday party next week,' Duncan called out just before I slammed the door behind me.

I didn't tell Alex about the conversation or the offer of financial help. Alex was going to be my clean start.

But I did tell Claire.

'You did the right thing, turning down their money,' she said.

'You think so?'

'Definitely. You don't want to be in their debt.'

'Exactly.'

'You're also doing the right thing in marrying Alex,' she said. It was as if she'd picked up on my worries.

'Why are you so sure?'

She didn't answer the question directly. 'Don't tell me you're getting last-minute nerves.'

'There's still enough time to pull out,' I said tightly.

'You can't do that to him.'

'People do.'

'Nancy, I've told you. Alex is a good man. I knew that as soon as I met him.'

Claire might be my best friend but she does like being right. And she takes great delight in telling people that she 'found' Alex for me through an online 'introduction' site, and even contacted him on my behalf because she knew I wouldn't do it.

'You've got to start dating more,' she'd told me. 'I know you're anxious, and that's understandable after what happened . . .'

'Please stop . . .'

'If you really want to stay single, that's fine. But don't do it because of –'

'OK,' I reply quickly. I don't want her to say any more because then it will be real. The only way I can cope is to pretend that it didn't happen. But then the memories and the nightmares come back and I can't get away from it.

'So I'll give him your number then.'

I can't win when Claire is like this. 'If you insist.'

To my amazement, I'd liked Alex immediately we met. He was funny. Kind. Understanding. I didn't feel uncomfortable with him as I usually did with men. He made me laugh and he made me feel safe. He wasn't one of the slick townie types I'd met before – in fact, he'd grown up in the South West. (I briefly told him about our holiday home but didn't go into details.) Claire was jubilant when he proposed. It was almost as if she was getting married herself.

So why haven't I told him about my past? Not just everything about the murder, but also what happened to me during my last summer in Tall Chimneys.

The truth is that there are some things that can't be told to anyone.

I finish my mint tea, which has gone cold. Suddenly Sheba jumps up, barking.

I'm aware that the doorbell is ringing. It's a persistent ring. Urgent.

They're here.

13

I open the door a crack.

It's only Vera, but my heart hasn't caught up with my head and it's still thumping away with fear.

'I'm going for a walk up Salcombe Hill,' she says, her eyes darting from my hair (which I'd shovelled up into an untidy knot) and back into the hall where there's a pile of clothes I'd brought down from my mother's room. A woolly blue jumper that still smells of her. A rainbow-coloured headscarf that I recall my father buying as a surprise present for Mum during the annual folk festival.

'Would you like to join me?'

I'd have thought Sheba would have had enough walks today – I know I have – but she is leaping up with excitement, and it seems rude to turn down the older woman's invitation. And perhaps I can ask her more about my grandmother. My own mother had been quite reticent; now I wonder if this was because she'd missed her as much as I miss Mum.

'You'll need something waterproof,' she says. 'It's going to rain.'

The only thing I can find is one of my mother's old coats in the understairs cupboard. Reluctantly, I put it on. It's bottle-green and the belt is missing. When I put my hands in the pockets to see if it's there, my fingers close round something soft. I bring it out. It's a handkerchief with daisies embroidered round the edge. My mother had inherited a stack of them, along with other linen from my grandmother, and she always carried one. I put it back before the tears come.

'Up here,' Vera instructs me as we set off. For a woman of her age (although it's difficult to ascertain how old she is exactly) she sets a fast pace. 'I love Cliff Road. It gives you a good view down onto the beach. You'll see the new bridge too. Not the same as the old one. Still, the world must move on, I suppose.'

It's the perfect lead-in. 'You said, before, that you remembered my grandmother, Adeline.'

'I do indeed. Very beautiful she was, with those eyes just like yours and your mum's, and always trying to help others. Mind you, she wasn't afraid to speak her mind.'

I rather like the sound of that!

'I used to babysit your mother when she was young,' continues Vera. 'I was only a kid myself then.'

So Vera must be older than I'd thought. Maybe in her nineties.

My eyes prick with tears at the thought of my mother as a baby, not knowing what the future held.

'I'm sorry,' she says, shooting me a sideways look. 'It must have been awful for you.'

'Yes,' I gulp, kneeling down to scoop up Sheba's mess, using the time to compose myself.

'I remember you too, Nancy, from when you were a child. You won't remember me, of course. Always out walking with your dad, you were.'

'Duncan wasn't my . . .'

I hesitate but she ends the sentence for me.

'Your real father? I know that.'

It seems weird to think this woman knew me but I have no recollection of her. Perhaps my mind was on other things.

'The last time I saw you,' she adds, 'you were a teenager. You had a friend staying.'

That must have been Claire.

'I should have written to you after your mother died,' she continues, 'but I didn't have your address. I'm so sorry.'

'It's OK,' I say quietly, thinking of all the letters I'd had to answer, feeling like a fraud.

'Still, I'm glad you came here for refuge. Tall Chimneys is a special house. Your grandmother always used to say that.'

My mind goes back to that letter from the museum. I'd put it to one side after Alex's phone call. 'Actually, there's something I want to ask you,' I say. 'The museum curator wrote to say he'd found a newspaper cutting in the archives about someone going missing from Tall Chimneys in 1942. Do you know anything about that?'

'Missing?' Vera frowns. 'No, I don't. I'd have been about ten then but I can't recall any of the adults talking about it. Still, it wasn't unknown for people to go missing then. Exeter was bombed very heavily during the war and they hit outlying villages and towns too. I do remember a farmer being found dead in a ditch some days later. Then there was a German pilot who was washed up on the beach. Everyone seemed to think that was a good thing.'

I wince. All lives should be precious, shouldn't they?

But if someone has done something wrong, is there an excuse for murder?

'There's lots we don't know about the past,' continues Vera. She stamps her walking stick on the path. 'It's our duty to find out and pass it onto future generations.'

'Do you have children?' I ask.

There's a brief silence. Maybe I shouldn't have asked.

'Too much of a responsibility for me,' she says eventually. 'Besides, it was harder to find a suitable beau when I was growing up. We didn't have these dating sites that you young things have today. What about you? Do you have a boyfriend?'

'I did,' I say slowly. 'We were going to get married. But then . . .'

I stop, not sure why I'm telling her this.

She pats my arm briefly. 'You don't have to say anything. Look!'

Vera points to the horizon. We've just passed a pretty house called Periwinkle Cottage. Below us, the sea has whipped up and there are surfers out there. I marvel at their ballerina-like stance. So tall. So statuesque as they ride the waves. My heart is in my mouth as a white crest rises up and tosses a surfer like a puppet. I watch until I can spot his head surfacing. Then he clambers back on his board.

'You should come down here at sunrise,' says Vera. 'Out of this world, it is.'

I smile, not wanting to steal her thunder by telling her about my morning walk.

Meanwhile, Sheba is having a wonderful time, shooting up the steep field towards the woods.

We're crunching our way over twigs and branches.

'Watch out for this spot,' warns Vera. 'There's a big dip underneath. Rumour has it that they'd leave messages for each other here during the war in what they called "dead-letter boxes".'

'Who's they?' I ask.

'The locals. They trained up, just in case we were invaded.'

'Invaded?'

'There was a real risk of invasion during the war, you know. We're a seaside town, aren't we? The Germans could have landed on the beach. But people forget.' Vera shoots me a kind look. 'Eventually, Nancy, they'll forget what happened to you too, and the press will stop hounding you.'

'But *I* won't forget,' I blurt out.

'No,' she concedes. 'You won't.'

There's a short silence.

'Let's go back down, shall we?' she says. 'We could walk back along the beach. But stay clear of the cliffs. We've had quite a few landslides. Some people are losing part of their back gardens.'

We're walking past tennis courts now. There's a statue of an eagle nearby, which seems rather out of place. 'It's to commemorate the help the Allies gave us during the Second World War,' says Vera, noticing my interest. 'There were quite a lot of Canadians and Americans billeted in Sidmouth.'

I never knew that. It seems almost unreal. 'Were they made to feel welcome?'

'They were here to help us,' she says shortly. 'We wouldn't have won the war without them.'

As she speaks, we reach the seafront. There's a hooting sound that makes me jump. Something that I can only describe as an elegant, elongated, roof-topped carriage with open sides goes past. 'That's the Sidmouth Toastrack,' says Vera. 'It's a restored Austin 20 Charabanc. Very popular for weddings.'

I don't remember it from my childhood, but we can't recall everything. I glance up to my right at the line of beautiful old gracious-looking hotels. On one, high up on a wrought-iron balcony, someone looks as though they are having a cup of tea. It's such a different world from London.

'Sidmouth is a place where you can find peace and come to terms with yourself,' says Vera. 'Now, remember this part? It's called Jacob's Ladder.'

I pause, shocked into stillness by a sudden memory. Transported back in time. How could I have forgotten that day? We're walking past little caves cut into the rock. It's starting to rain now just as it was then. Martin's voice comes back to me. '*We can shelter here, Nancy.*'

'Are you all right?' Vera asks. 'You're looking rather pale.'

'Fine,' I say. 'But I think I'll make my way home now.'

'Well, it was good to have your company.'

She's lonely, I realize. Had I been rude? Too busy thinking about my own problems and not considering hers. Why is it that I always read people wrong?

She walks off. Too late, I realize I should have asked her back for a cup of tea. We're neighbours, after all. But I'm not ready for small-talk. It's too soon for normality. Pretend or otherwise.

As I go in through the front door, my mobile starts to ring in my pocket. When I answer, it goes dead. It's from a 'Caller Unknown'.

I don't like that. But Sheba is wet so I distract myself by towelling her down. A few minutes later, my mobile rings once more. It's Caller Unknown again. I answer. This time I hear breathing.

'Who is that?' I say, trying to sound firm rather than nervous.

There's a shout in the background. 'Greenfield! You're late. Do you want another strike?'

'I've got to be quick before association time ends,' rasps a voice. It's Martin's. But it sounds different. Desperate. Scared. 'Why haven't you visited me, Nancy? I am –'

Then the line goes dead.

How had he got my number? I'd changed it after the trial. And what on earth is 'association time'?

The phone rings again.

'GO AWAY!' I scream into my mobile.

'Nancy?'

It's Judith, my lawyer.

'Are you all right?'

I almost tell her about Martin's phone call but decide it's better she doesn't know.

'Sorry but the press is calling all the time,' I lie.

'I need to ask you something, Nancy. Has Martin written to you from prison?'

I almost deny it. But I can't. 'How do you know?'

'Because a journalist has apparently got hold of his letter and is planning on running an exclusive tomorrow morning. His newspaper's lawyers contacted me and asked if we wanted to comment.'

So Alex's warning was right.

'That's impossible,' I say. 'I tore up the letter and put it in the bin. But I did photograph it first on my phone in case I needed a record.'

'Maybe this journalist took it and pieced it together. I'll speak to the police. Is there anything you want to tell me about the content?'

'No,' I say. 'Martin's a fantasist. He makes things up. You know that from the trial.'

'Very well,' says Judith. 'We'll just have to wait and see what happens. But you should know that if there's anything that . . .' she pauses, clearly choosing her words carefully, 'changes your account of events, the police may want to look at it.'

I put down the phone with a sinking heart.

They're going to come for me. They're going to find out. My legs shaking, I run up the stairs.

I'll go to prison. Just like Martin. And the world will know exactly what I've done.

The Night of the Murder

Martin goes off to hang up my coat. His manners have clearly improved.

Then my mother's husband comes downstairs. I can smell the drink from here. 'Lovely to see you, Nancy. Where's Alex?'

'Stranded in Paris,' I say shortly.

'Oh well. That's what happens when you lead a jet-set life.'

'It's his job,' I snap. 'Where's Mum?'

He rolls his eyes. 'Still getting ready. You women always take an age. But it's worth it.'

I ignore his cheesy comments and the way his eyes are travelling over me.

'May I get you a drink?'

'I'm driving,' I point out.

'Not just one?'

'No thank you.'

He eyes the birthday present in my hands.

'What did you buy her?'

'Something you won't like,' I say.

'That's not very nice.'

I hold his gaze. 'Nor are you.'

And then quickly I go into the sitting room to find the other guests.

'Where is everyone?' I ask.

'They went down with a heavy cold,' says Duncan, behind me. 'Looks like it's just the four of us.'

Elizabeth

14

'Why do you jump when someone knocks on the door or the phone rings?' asked Maisie, helping herself to a slice of toast from the wooden toast rack with the heart-shaped handle that Elizabeth had bought on her honeymoon in Lyme Regis.

'Do I?' asked Elizabeth, blushing.

It was only the second day of the evacuees' arrival but already Elizabeth could tell that Maisie was the kind of child who noticed things. Robert had been like that. Still was, she corrected herself.

The truth was that Elizabeth was constantly listening for that dreaded telegram or a call from Robert's unit.

Mrs Woods at number 7 had received such a telegram last week to say her husband had been shot down over France. They had heard her wails, gradually decreasing into loud incessant sobs, which were even more painful to hear, all down the street. Elizabeth had left a little bunch of late roses on her doorstep with a *Please let me know if I can do anything* note, but Mrs W's curtains had remained resolutely closed.

'In my day,' said Mrs Norris crisply, 'children didn't ask such impertinent questions.'

Oh dear. Elizabeth had wondered how the PGs would

react to having children in the house. They'd adored Robert, of course, who had charmed them all by carrying their bags and asking how Mrs Norris's rheumatism was. For years she had come down for her week's holiday at the end of August. Now retired, she had given up her rented flat in Herne Hill 'to sit out the war by the sea'. She was constantly training her binoculars on the coastline in case 'that devil, Mr Hitler, has the nerve to send his ships'.

Meanwhile, Mrs Norris was helping herself to the last piece of toast and Elizabeth could see the children's faces falling.

'I'll toast a few more slices of bread,' she announced brightly, getting up from the table. 'Any takers?'

'Yes please,' said one of the Patmore sisters brightly. 'But I'll eat it plain. I've decided to give up jam for the rest of the war – my bit for our brave boys who are away fighting – so I'll give my share to the girls.'

Maisie's eyes widened. 'Jam AND butter?'

'You need building up, dear,' said the other sister.

'We're going to school this morning!' piped up Shirley.

'How are they going to find space for you all?' asked Henry without looking up from his newspaper. 'It's crowded enough with our own children.'

'Not now that some of them have been sent off to war,' she muttered.

'Don't, Elizabeth,' he said sharply.

Her old self might have accepted this rebuke. But not now! 'Our son had his sights set on Oxford University,' she announced to the table. 'He was going to read History.'

'And now he's taking part in it himself,' Henry declared.

'I'm sure you're very proud of him,' said Mr Smith.

'Are you now?'

Oh dear. Henry had his bullish voice on. That meant trouble. He'd been furious when the evacuees had arrived but she'd managed to persuade him to allow them to stay by pointing out that the poor children were destitute and that it wouldn't reflect well on him in town if it was known he had turned them away.

On the other hand, it wasn't easy for her husband, Elizabeth reminded herself. Henry had become particularly irritable since men of his age had been called up. With his 'disability' he didn't qualify. Still, at least he had the Home Guard.

'In answer to your question about how they are going to squeeze us all in, I believe we're staggering classes,' continued Mr Smith. 'Some will learn in the morning and others in the afternoon.'

'So our children will suffer by only having half a day of schooling,' said Henry quickly.

Elizabeth couldn't help it. 'As you're always saying, dear, we all have to make sacrifices at the moment.'

Henry stood up. 'I'm off to the yard. I will see you for dinner.'

Then he hobbled out.

Once he'd left, Elizabeth felt a heaviness lifting from her chest. She found her husband's sarcastic comments and continual criticism even harder to bear without the comfort of Robert's presence. When their son had been a child, she had tried to hide arguments from him, but as he'd grown older, it had been impossible. In recent years he had become her crutch. 'Don't worry about Dad,' he would say if Henry stomped out in a mood. 'He's upset because he feels useless now he can't fight.' And then what had happened? Somehow, Henry had encouraged their son to do what he had wanted himself.

'I'll have some lunch ready for you when you come back from school,' she said now to the little girls. 'Then I can take you for a walk to show you where everything is in the town if you like.'

'Thank you,' said Mr Smith. 'That would be very helpful.'

'Can we see the sea?' asked Maisie, her eyes brightening.

Shirley's eyes widened. 'What if there are sharks?'

'There aren't any here,' said Elizabeth gently.

'You have to be careful on the beach,' said Mrs Norris. 'There's barbed wire and mines to stop the enemy from landing.'

'Can the Jerries get us?' Maisie's voice began to tremble.

'No,' said Elizabeth firmly, eyeing Mrs Norris. 'We're well protected.'

It wasn't true, of course. The whole town was terrified that the Germans might land here.

'Mrs Norris is right about the barbed wire and mines. But there are some spots where you are still allowed to go onto the beach during the day.'

'I've heard,' chips in one of the sisters, 'that it's safer to have a house on the beachfront because the German bombers are more likely to attack the centre of a town.'

There was a silence. Elizabeth had heard that too. They were in the centre of town.

'Can we help you clear the table before we go?' asked Mr Smith quickly.

Very few of her PGs over the years had offered to do that.

'That's very kind but we'll manage. Have a good day.'

Whenever things were hard at home – even before the war – Elizabeth had thrown herself into doing something. Not just washing and cleaning but swimming too, first thing before anyone was up. That wonderful cold shock of the water, and then the gradual warming through, set her up for the day. Looking after Robert, of course, even when he was a teenager. Was Henry right that she'd spoiled him? Thank heavens she had Adeline as a confidante.

So when she'd cleared away breakfast and made beds, beaten the rugs and ran the carpet sweeper around, Elizabeth found her feet walking round to her friend's house.

Adeline lived at the top of Cliff Road in Periwinkle Cottage, so-called because of the abundance of that plant's blue flowers in the borders. It was a pretty redbrick house, its back facing the sea. There had been cliff falls during recent years and a few owners found their homes were getting closer to the edge.

Some said that the tunnel didn't help. This had been built in the nineteenth century, when there had been plans for a steam engine to take stone from the eastern cliffs. However, when the steam train arrived, it didn't fit in the tunnel and so it was used to take visitors up and down the front.

It had become a favourite spot for courting couples, including her and Henry all those years ago. How young she had been! Sixteen. Just a year younger than Robert. Then her mother had died. 'I'll look after you,' Henry had said.

Only now did she realize that gratitude shouldn't be the reason for marriage.

Adeline had chosen better. She and George complemented each other with his steady, if slightly dull, approach and her chirpiness.

Maybe, thought Elizabeth, as she went down the path to Periwinkle Cottage, Adeline would be at the hall sorting out any remaining children in need of homes. Perhaps she should have gone there first.

Elizabeth banged the big black lion knocker. A dog barked on the other side. That must mean her friend was in, otherwise he'd be locked in the kitchen.

No answer. She knocked again.

The dog barked once more. Was everything all right? Maybe she ought to go round the back.

The windows were wide, with square glass panes. The view from the inside was spectacular, reaching right across to Lyme Bay.

It was also easy to see in.

Elizabeth froze.

There was Adeline. Embracing a man. A man who wasn't her husband.

15

Horrified, Elizabeth ducked behind a bush. Then she heard the front door shutting. What should she do now? Had the man left? Had Adeline gone too?

Crouching in the borders, Elizabeth waited until there was quiet. Then, carefully, she stood up.

'You saw us then,' said a voice.

Elizabeth jumped.

Adeline exhaled smoke from the cigarette in her hand. Where had she got hold of one? War meant that tobacco imports were in short supply. There was also a rebellious look in her eyes: one that Elizabeth knew all too well from their youth.

'Come inside and I'll explain,' she said.

Stunned into silence, Elizabeth followed her.

Adeline clicked the door shut and then bolted it. No one ever did that during the day. Not even with the threat of an invasion.

'In here,' she said.

They went into her kitchen and sat down at the farmhouse table next to the dresser with the familiar blue-and-white china that Elizabeth had eaten and drunk from for so many years. The silver fluted whistle that her friend used to summon her dog when walking on the beach or on Salcombe Hill hung from one of the cup hooks.

'It's not what you think,' she said.

'Really?' asked Elizabeth. 'You were hugging a man. Who was he?'

Her friend's eyes faced hers without blinking. 'It was a gesture of solidarity, actually.'

'Adeline,' said Elizabeth slowly, 'we've never had secrets from each other before. If something is going on, surely you can tell me?'

Adeline sighed. 'I can tell you, yes. They already gave me permission.'

'Who's they? And what do you mean, "permission"? To do what?'

'That man was giving me this.'

She put her hand in her apron pocket and brought out a small gun.

Elizabeth gasped. 'What in the world are you doing with that?'

'I've joined the secret army, Elizabeth. And we need you too. Tall Chimneys is a perfect cover – and so are you.'

'What secret army?'

She was really beginning to feel scared now. The war had already caused people to have nervous breakdowns. Mrs Reynolds in Cheese Lane had collapsed when Mr Chamberlain had announced the outbreak of war on the wireless. She hadn't been able to go out of the house since then. Rumour had it that a young mother from one of the inland villages near Dartmoor had smothered her children to death before gassing herself, convinced that the Germans had already invaded and were about to do far worse.

Was Adeline losing her mind too? She had so much on her shoulders organizing the evacuees' accommodation.

She must also be worried sick about George, who was somewhere in Italy with his battalion.

'I've not gone mad,' said her friend, as if reading Elizabeth's mind. Then she stroked the small gun in her hands. 'Don't worry. It's not loaded. But I've been taught how to do that when the time comes.'

'But you're not a soldier!'

'When the Germans invade, we're all going to be under Nazi rule. Don't you understand? They'll rape. Kill. Take our children away.'

Elizabeth felt sick. 'That can't be right.'

'I assure you it is. And that's why Gus is doing something about it.'

'Is that the man who was here? I've never seen him before.'

'The government has sent him down to organize a secret army in Sidmouth. There are others being formed right at this minute in other towns along the coast. Churchill has given confidential orders for a select number of local men and women to be trained up to fight back if an invasion takes place. We've been divided into cells of four or five and we practise out in the woods. When the Germans invade – because they will, you know – we'll follow them, taking note of what they're doing, and then we report back.'

'To whom?'

Adeline shrugged. 'Some central government body.'

'What's it called?'

'I don't know. We're not being told everything in case we're captured and blab. The point is that we're defending our home town and everyone in it. We'll organize guerrilla attacks. Kill if necessary.'

Adeline's face was animated. Excited. Elizabeth felt a great wave of misgiving.

'But that's not right,' she began. 'We need to leave this sort of thing to the army.'

'Not right?' Her friend's usually smooth forehead was now creased with frown lines. 'How can it be not right if they are shooting my husband or your son in cold blood?'

Elizabeth winced.

'So are you going to join us or not?'

'I'm not a killer.'

'None of us are, Elizabeth. But if someone tried to shoot Robert, wouldn't you rather he shot first?'

Yes. Of course she would.

'It's our duty to protect others – and ourselves too,' continued Adeline.

'But I don't know how to fire a gun. I'm not sure if I could.'

'You can do puzzles, can't you?'

She and Robert had spent hours doing jigsaws and making up number games. She also loved crosswords. 'What's that got to do with it?'

'They need a wireless operator. Someone who can tap into the messages that the Germans will send each other when they invade. I told them about you and they want you to join us. They'll train you up.'

'Why me?'

'Because you're smart and respected. And because you run a boarding house, you'd be expected to have visitors. Like I said, it's a good cover.'

Elizabeth stood up. 'It all feels so unreal.' A huge lump rose into her throat. 'It doesn't seem that long ago since we were having picnics on the beach, playing tennis or having dinner parties without any of this.'

Adeline gave her a hug. 'I know. It's horrible. All of it. But I can't stand by and let this happen. There's talk of unmarried women and widows being called up too. We've got to do *something*.'

'I'll think about it,' Elizabeth said uncertainly.

'Well, don't take too long.' Adeline took a step back. 'Or the Jerries will have landed. We have to be ready, Elizabeth. I'd rather die than end up under German rule. Wouldn't you?'

16

Elizabeth walked back over Alma Bridge and along the seafront, her mind spinning.

A secret army? It sounded like a spy novel. But Adeline apparently thought it was real enough. Yet surely the army and navy and RAF would be enough to defend them?

Even so, part of her couldn't help feeling slightly envious of Adeline having the guts to join in.

By the time she'd reached the market square, Elizabeth had made up her mind. Of course, she couldn't join this so-called secret army. How could she possibly kill someone? They were mad, all of them. What would Henry say if he found out?

The seagulls were calling overhead. 'Robert, Robert!' they seemed to cry.

That was different. Robert had joined the proper army. Not some hastily put-together Robin Hood band. How did Adeline know that Churchill had organized it? What if this Gus was spinning her a yarn? There were other ways of helping the war effort that didn't break the law, such as taking in those little girls and their teacher.

Walking past the line of people queuing up outside the butcher's with their ration books, she saw the postman rushing towards her. He was late today. 'Mrs Montague,' he called out.

When they'd been children, he had been Bob and she'd

been Elizabeth (never Liz, because her mother hadn't approved of that). He'd always been a jolly chap until the war, when letters could bring bad news. It was every family's dread.

'This one is for you,' he said. 'You're later on in my round but you might like it now.'

A London postmark?

She couldn't think of anyone they knew who was still there. 'Thank you,' she said, opening it on the street. It was written on a scrap of paper with muddy marks on it.

Dear Mother and Father,

I am writing this in haste as one of the lads has to be shipped home so he's taking letters with him. I'm safe and well. Don't worry. I'll be all right.

Yours,

Robert

So formal! There was no mention of where he'd been sent. Perhaps he wasn't allowed to say. But the most important thing was that their son was alive and well.

'Everything OK?' asked Bob.

'Yes, thank you.'

Elizabeth found herself virtually skipping along the pavement towards the building yard, where she found her husband having a tea break.

'Told you the lad would be fine,' was all he said when she gave him the letter.

Yet even his sullen response couldn't dull her happiness and relief.

When she got home, she was met by three sombre

faces in the front sitting room that was reserved for the guests. 'How was school?' she asked.

Little Maisie with her bright blue eyes burst into tears and rushed out and up the stairs, followed by Shirley.

'I'm afraid it didn't go very well,' said Mr Smith.

'Why?'

Please don't say the locals had been unkind to them, she thought. The town appeared to be divided between those who felt it their duty to take in outsiders and those who thought they should 'look after our own first'.

'It's not what they are used to,' said Mr Smith. 'Maisie and Shirley have been very brave but they're homesick. Especially Maisie. She misses her parents and brothers and sisters. I thought school might help but, if anything, all the strange new faces made it worse. They also found the maths difficult. It's more advanced here than at home.'

'Poor little things,' murmured Elizabeth. 'They seemed so happy this morning at breakfast.'

'Children can put on bright faces like adults,' he pointed out.

Her Robert hadn't. He'd worn his heart on his sleeve. It had been one of the many things that Henry had criticized her for. 'You've made that boy into a namby-pamby,' he'd said. 'He needs toughening up.'

'Supposing I make some sandwiches and we have a picnic tea at Weston Beach?' she suggested. 'It's not far from here but there will be fewer people around.'

'What about land mines and tank traps?'

'I go there myself. I know the safe spots.'

'But they won't have costumes and I don't know if they can swim.'

'Then they can paddle, wearing their vests and pants. There's nothing like the sea for lifting the spirits.'

She was right. At first, Maisie and Shirley dragged their feet as they passed the allotments, where she showed them her patch. Then they began to climb Salcombe Hill. 'My legs are aching,' complained Shirley.

'Mine aren't,' chirped Maisie.

But as they dropped down again, past the church and over the fields to where the view opened up, they gasped.

'It's so beautiful!'

'Mr Smith, did you visit the sea much before the war?' she asked as they made their way down the rough wooden steps to the beach.

'No,' he said. 'We didn't.'

We.

Elizabeth waited but he didn't volunteer any more information. Running a boarding house required the skill of making guests feel at home – which often involved talking about their personal lives – and sometimes meant giving them privacy. But treading this tightrope with evacuees who weren't on holiday and would rather be at home was a different matter. It was why she hadn't mentioned her good news about Robert.

'Last one in's a cissy!' called out Maisie.

So much for the girls being scared. Within seconds they were jumping and skipping over the waves as they washed ashore. 'Are you going in too?' she asked Mr Smith.

'Not for me,' he said. 'What about you?'

Only then did Elizabeth realize the potential awkwardness of the situation. Of course, she had her bathing costume on underneath her clothes, as she usually did whenever she went down to the sea, but was it right to expose so much of her body to a stranger?

Why hadn't she considered this before they left the house?

Yet she was longing to feel the water, especially after Adeline's bombshell this morning. Sometimes the sea was the only place she could really be herself. It made her body feel light and, with it, all her fears about the war and revulsion towards Henry just washed away.

'I'll go in further round the bay,' she said.

He nodded, seeming to understand. 'I'll watch the girls.' As he spoke, there were howls of laughter. 'You're right. This is just what they needed.'

It was what *she* needed too. How lovely it was to wade in, to feel that shock of cold and then brace herself, throwing her body and soul into the water.

Her mind grew clearer. She would tell Adeline firmly that she couldn't possibly join her secret army. Maybe the Germans wouldn't invade. Nothing was certain. If the war had taught her anything, it was that.

And then she heard the planes. Thundering towards them.

The Night of the Murder

8.05 p.m.

My mother finally comes downstairs. She kisses my cheek. I want to move away. Yet I want to hug her too.

'Where's Alex?'

I explain.

'That's a shame.'

She means it. Mum's relieved I've found someone at last. She thinks it might make me forget my 'silly story' about what happened in my last summer at Tall Chimneys.

'You're shivering, Nancy,' says Martin.

That's because it's cold inside this horrible stone farmhouse.

'Maybe it's pre-wedding nerves,' says Duncan, winking.

'Not at all,' I retort. 'In fact, I can't wait to get married and be part of a normal family.'

My mother stands up. She looks as though she's going to say something and then goes into the kitchen.

'Can't you try and behave just for once?' says my stepfather.

'It's you who should behave,' I hiss back. 'Though it's a bit late for that, isn't it?'

'What do you mean?' asks Martin, frowning.

'Nothing,' says Duncan quickly.

Nancy

17

I have to get out of here.

So I begin to pack frantically, throwing things into one of the cases I'd brought down. Not too many things. I don't want to draw attention to myself. Just enough to see me through until I can find somewhere else to live. Far from Martin (despite the fact that he's under lock and key). Far from the police.

But what about Claire? She'll be worried sick. I'll have to find a way of telling her I'm all right. I'll miss the baby's arrival too. And I'll miss Alex . . .

'It has to be done, Nancy,' I tell myself sternly. If they knew the truth, they wouldn't want me in their lives anyway.

I drag the case down to the hall. Sheba is standing there, gazing at me mournfully. 'I'm sorry,' I say, kneeling to look into her soulful brown eyes. 'I wish I could take you, but it would be too complicated. Jasmine will find you another home.'

Home. As I say the word, my heart actually hurts. I gaze around the hall with its beautiful staircase rising above me. If only things had been different.

KNOCK! It's the door.

I stumble to my feet. Sheba barks. But it's not a growl.

'Vera,' I say, opening the door slowly.

She looks at the case by my side.

'Going somewhere, are you?'

I nod, not trusting myself to speak.

'I suppose it's because of these.'

She hands over a bundle of newspapers. 'Bought them for you to save you having to go out for them yourself. Knew you'd have to see them eventually. This way, you can prepare yourself at home. Let's go into your kitchen and I'll make you a cup of tea while you take a gander.'

I allow myself to be steered onto a chair. As I feared, the headlines are merciless.

'Farmhouse murderer proclaims undying love for slaughter daughter. What does she really know?'

'The killer and the heiress: were they in it together?'

There's more, but I can't go any further.

'Is it true about the letter?' asks Vera, leaning against the Aga, her eyes firmly fixed on mine.

'Part of it,' I whisper.

Her eyes go steely.

'Martin says he loves me.' Then I pause, trying to choose my words carefully. 'But I don't love him back. And I certainly wasn't part of any plan to kill my mother or her husband.'

'Then you've nothing to worry about,' she says briskly.

I'm tempted to tell her more. But I can't.

'Running away isn't going to help,' she adds. 'It's not as though this stepbrother of yours can hurt you if he's locked up. As for the press, they'll go away eventually. Besides, this house needs you.'

That steely look is still there. 'I remember my mother saying she wanted to run away when the bombs began to fall back in 1941,' continues Vera. 'My father told her to pull herself together and stand up to the enemy if necessary. So she did. We all did. It's called a stiff upper lip – something people don't seem to approve of nowadays. But it's the only way.'

Little does she know that I'm an expert when it comes to hiding how I feel. After all, I've been practising since I was fifteen.

Vera's voice cuts into my thoughts. 'I'm next door for support. And Jasmine is just over the road. She's a good sort, although I thought she was one of those hippies when she first moved in. There are lots of people around here who will be on your side. Folk don't like having their peace invaded by journalists. Besides, it's not like you're a complete grockle. Your mother owned this house, and her mother before her. You're part of a local family, whether you like it or not. So stay here and take whatever comes.'

Wow! I wouldn't want to get on the wrong side of Vera.

'Now, here's your tea. I'll leave you to unpack.'

She's right. No one can make it all go away. No one can stop Martin from hurting me. But there's something about this place that makes me feel I could be strong enough to face what's coming. Maybe I'm meant to be here.

Judith rings with an update. 'You're lucky. The police aren't investigating,' she tells me. 'The ramblings of a convicted criminal don't, apparently, constitute hard evidence.'

I can't believe it.

'Meanwhile,' she continues, 'the newspaper has denied theft and says the letter was sent to them anonymously. My advice is to do nothing. They will find something else to chase tomorrow. But Nancy, I have to double-check. Is there anything else I should know?'

'No,' I lie.

After she rings off, I can't stop shaking. Even when I sit down on one of the kitchen chairs, my right knee begins juddering as if it doesn't belong to me.

Just as it had when I'd leaned over my mother's body, desperately calling out her name.

Sheba, sensing my distress, jumps up and gives me a slobbery kiss.

My mobile rings. *Claire.*

'I saw the paper. Are you all right?'

'Not really.'

'No one will believe him, Nancy. The man's a psychopath.'

'He rang me from prison yesterday,' I blurt out. 'He seemed angry because I haven't visited.'

She sounds aghast. 'What? Did you tell the lawyer?'

'No.'

'Why not?'

'Because he rang me on my mobile. I've no idea how he got the number. I changed it before the trial, but people will think I gave it to him, and that makes me look implicated.'

'Rubbish. Anyone who knows you would never think that.'

But no one really does know me, I almost say.

'Right.' My friend's voice indicates she's going into organized mode. Claire always knows what to do. Or thinks she does.

'If he calls again, tell the lawyer,' she instructs me.

'It's harassment. He's not right in the head. And he's dangerous.'

Not all of this is true, I want to say. But I can't.

'And only pick up numbers that you recognize,' she continues. 'It's weird that he knows your new number.'

'I know,' I whisper.

'He always was devious. What you need is someone with you. Honestly, Nancy. I simply can't understand why you didn't tell Alex everything. He'd have understood. You didn't have to break things off with him. He still wants you back, you know. Just give him a chance. He's a good man.'

'I can't,' I murmur.

'You could have been married by now,' continues Claire. 'You'd be happy like Richard and me. Ouch!'

'What?' I ask, alarmed.

'Nothing. Probably Braxton Hicks.'

'What's that?'

'Some kind of false-alarm thing you sometimes get before the baby arrives. It's meant to prepare your body.'

Of course, I'm excited for her. But when Claire announced she was pregnant, it had created a line between us. I can't share her emotions or understand the difference between second and third trimester: pregnancy terms that Claire now uses casually in a way that suggests I should know myself.

Sometimes I wonder if this is why my friend is so keen for me to hang on to Alex. She wants me to enter her world so we can carry on through life together, in parallel, like we used to do.

'I'd better go,' says Claire, breaking into my thoughts.

'I've got an antenatal appointment. But call me anytime. All right? And please. Don't cut Alex out. It's only going to hurt him more.'

Hurt him? I'm not hurting him. I'm giving him the chance to lead a normal life; one he wouldn't have with me. My head is ringing. I need some air.

I start clearing the kitchen table and come across the letter from the museum. Maybe this is what I need. Helping out might present me to Sidmouth as a decent citizen who wants to do her best. And what else can I do? Wait to get arrested or for the press to come back? I can't bear it.

I pull on my shoes.

I take Cliff Road because I'm less likely to run into anyone over the recently modernized Alma Bridge (the one I remember had virtually fallen to bits, according to Vera). Besides, it's a short walk from there to the museum.

The curator ('Please call me Jeremy') is, at a guess, older than me by about ten years or so. He's wearing a brown corduroy jacket and beige chinos that seem smart compared with my casual trainers and pedal-pusher trousers. After welcoming me warmly with a firm handshake, he launches straight in with some background about the building that was donated to the town by a Miss Constance Radford in 1925. 'Back then, it was known as Hope Cottage.' He is clearly passionate about history. I like him instantly.

'That's fascinating,' he says, looking at the picture I'd taken on my phone of the writing at the back of the wardrobe.

'I was just wondering if one of them might be the missing person,' I ask. As I speak, I find myself desperately hoping this wasn't the case. Their words are so full of life!

'Maisie and Shirley,' he muses. 'There's no telling, really, is there? They might have been paying guests – Tall Chimneys was a boarding house in those days, as I expect you know – but the tone sounds as though the writers were children or teenagers, don't you think? I'll do some research. Can you forward me the picture? Here's my email address.'

'Sure.'

'Thanks. How are you doing, by the way? I gather you're new to the town.'

'Not exactly,' I say. 'My mother owned the house, and my grandmother before that. I'm just staying there temporarily.'

'Well, Sidmouth is certainly a beautiful place to be in,' he says. He speaks in a friendly way as if he hasn't heard any gossip about me. 'Have you time to look round the museum?'

It would be rude to say no and, besides, it might distract me from all the unanswered questions that are zooming round my head. Martin had told me to keep quiet, but he is so unpredictable. What if he's told his cellmate the truth? What would happen then? Would the police find out? How did these things work? And then that phone call, asking me to visit. Clearly that is out of the question. There's no way I can have Martin back in my life.

'I'd love to,' I say, forcing myself to concentrate on the present. 'My father brought me here as a child, but that was long ago.'

'It hasn't changed a great deal, to be honest, although we do have some hands-on activities for children,' says Jeremy. 'Do you have any?'

I shake my head. Why do people always ask that?

'We have three. Just left home, they have. My wife is finding it quite hard. I occupy myself with the past, as you can see. This is one of my favourite exhibits.'

I look at a picture of fishermen from far-gone days, their faces lined by hard work and the wind. But there's a certain peace in those challenging eyes too.

'This is a mammoth tooth. It was found on the beach.'

The one my father had shown me! I blink back the tears, yet at the same time, the memory gives me a warm feeling of comfort.

'And this is some lace from one of the lace businesses. The area was quite famous for that.'

His words are calming as he shows me round. It's almost, but not quite, enough to make me forget.

When I get home, there's a note on the mat. My chest pounds with fear and the words start swimming in front of me. After a moment I can make out a couple. It's all right. It's nothing to do with Martin.

Hiya. Wondered if you fancied popping round for some pizza tonight. Bring a couple of beers if you want. Come about 8? Jasmine.

Beers? I hadn't drunk since the night it happened. I haven't been to anyone's house for dinner either. It's not the kind of thing you fancy doing after your mother is murdered.

But for once, I feel like I wouldn't mind some company. Something else to take my mind off Martin's call.

It might be rather nice to change into a floaty dress and put on some make-up. Almost like the old days when I'd go out for an evening with Alex or a girly drink with Claire, or people from the office.

Then Sheba starts barking furiously. A car pulls up. I can hear its tyres on the gravel. My stomach lurches. It will be the police. They're taking Martin's letter seriously after all.

This is it.

I draw a deep breath. I have to face the music at some time. In a way it's a relief.

I open the door.

'Hello, Nancy,' says Alex.

18

'I told you not to come,' I say.

'Would you believe me if I said I was just passing?'

I take in his lanky frame, his denim jacket that might appear too young on some men in their mid-thirties. Yet somehow it suits his boyish looks.

'No,' I say in answer to his question. 'I wouldn't.'

My head is still reeling with the realization that it's not the police after all.

He shrugs. 'Quite right. The truth is that I couldn't *not* come down to see you. Remember, I grew up near here.'

I vaguely recall him saying he came from the South West. But if he thinks he's going to win me round with flippant small-talk, he's mistaken.

'I said I needed time alone,' I remind him.

'I know. And I'm not going to bother you. I was just worried after those headlines.'

'I suppose Claire gave you the address,' I say.

'I'm not going to deny it. But I can turn right around and go home if you want. All you have to do is say the word. I simply wanted to see that you were OK.'

I hesitate. The truth is that, now he's here, I want him to stay. Of course, that's impossible after what I've done.

A door over the road slams. It's the people next door to Jasmine. I've no idea who they are but it strikes me that maybe it's better for us to be having this conversation inside.

'You'd better come in,' I say. 'Only for a short time.'

'Thanks,' he says, looking around the spacious hall and up through the circular staircase that rises to the second floor. 'Wow! What an amazing place. Some holiday home!'

'Yes,' I say. 'It is.'

I could tell him so much more. Like why I haven't been down here for years. Why parts of it still give me the shivers, including the cellar that I can't – won't – go into. A flash of Martin, those long summer holidays and the smell of apples comes into my head again. I try to blank out all three.

Tears fill my eyes. He notices.

'You've been through so much, Nancy,' he says. 'Don't pretend it's all right, because I know it's not.'

He envelops me in his arms. He doesn't try to kiss me. He just holds me. Gently we rock back and forth.

This is what I love about Alex. He's a good man, kind and genuine.

I break away. 'Do you want to look round the house?'

'Definitely.'

Alex is a culture buff. One of the things that drew me to him was that his favourite gallery – like mine – is the Royal Academy. Leighton House is another of our haunts, with its mosaic walls and heart-faced models. Well, it was.

'It's pretty big,' he says as he follows me up to the top floor.

'It used to be a bed and breakfast – or as they called it then, a boarding house – before my mother inherited it.'

'You could reopen it,' he suggests. 'It would give you something to do.'

Neither of us mentions that I probably won't be able to go back to my job. Or that I don't need the money. Five million will last me a lifetime and beyond. Unless, of course, I go to prison. I wonder what would happen to the money then. Does it even matter? My mother is dead. It still doesn't feel real.

'Sure,' I say. 'They'd all flock here to see the farmhouse slaughter daughter.'

'OK. Bad idea. Still, it's really lovely.'

He flings open a door enthusiastically. It's my mother's old room. The one I hadn't been able to face when I'd cleaned the house before. The dust catches in our throats. The eiderdown is the original. Maroon paisley.

'Shut it,' I say quickly.

He gives me an odd look but pulls the door to.

'Come and see something up here,' I say, hoping to distract him from all the stories I can't tell him.

We go up to the next floor and into the cosy twin-bedded room I've moved into.

'It feels very calm here,' he says, looking around.

'It's why I chose it. As a child, my room was downstairs near my mother and stepfather but . . . I prefer this one.'

Sheba jumps onto the nearer bed. She has been shadowing Alex meekly since he stepped through the door.

'This is what I wanted to show you,' I say, opening the wardrobe and pointing out the writing.

Maisie was here. SO WAS SHIRLEY! 8 October 1941

'Wow!' he says. 'Do you know who they were?'

'No. I forwarded a picture to the curator at the museum

who is doing some research into local houses.' I pause, wondering whether to tell Alex about the missing person Jeremy mentioned but decide not to. I have to put my old love into my past. Not confide in him.

'I do know,' I continue, 'that my grandmother Adeline inherited the house from Elizabeth, her best friend. But according to Mum, Adeline was always reluctant to talk about her.'

Alex is looking thoughtful. 'My grandad got sent to Kent at the age of twelve to live with a blacksmith and his wife while London was being bombed. He loved it and was always talking about it right to the end.'

I'm intrigued. Alex never normally spoke about his family. Whenever I pushed him, he just said they had 'drifted apart'.

Now he is squatting down in front of the old fireplace, running his hands appreciatively over the scrollwork. 'Could be an original. You ought to do some research into this place, Nancy. There's an argument that you owe it to your home to find out its history.'

But the history of Tall Chimneys is best left in the past, in my opinion. At least, certain aspects of it.

'I've got enough on my mind, right now,' I say rather brusquely. It's getting darker. I look at my watch. Alex notices.

'Would you like me to leave?'

When he'd first arrived, that's exactly what I'd wanted. Yet the look on his face – a mixture of disappointment and caring – makes me think again.

'A girl over the road has asked me round for pizza tonight. I could ring and ask if you could come too.'

'You don't have to.'

But I can tell from his voice he wants me to.

There's no reply. No voicemail either.

'I'm sure she won't mind,' I say. 'She doesn't seem like that kind of person.'

'That would be great.'

Neither of us mentions what will happen afterwards. Yet despite my earlier thoughts, I now find myself hoping that he will stay. Besides, we don't have to sleep together. There are plenty of spare rooms.

I give Sheba her supper and then go up to change. I decide that a floaty dress might be over the top and put on a fresh pair of jeans and a crisp white top from Zara. At the last moment I add some stud earrings; the pearl ones that my mother wore during the day.

My father had given them to her. She wouldn't have wanted me to put them away in a drawer somewhere. Besides, they go with my grandmother's necklace.

'You look lovely,' says Alex. 'I didn't bring anything to change into, I'm afraid.'

'You don't need to,' I say. We're crossing the road now and I'm knocking on the door. 'Jasmine's very informal.'

An apprehensive look crosses his face just as the door opens.

Jasmine beams at me and then looks at the man next to me. Her eyes go hard.

'Hope you don't mind,' I say, 'but I've brought a friend.'

She continues to stare at him. 'Hello, Alex,' she says coldly.

19

Here's the thing about coincidences. They sound contrived when you hear about them. But that's exactly what defines them. They are impossibly true.

'How do you know each other?' I say, looking from one to the other.

'We were at secondary school together,' says Alex stiffly. 'A few miles from here.'

A red blotch appears on his neck. It does that when he's nervous. When we met, I found it endearing. Now, it's worrying.

'I was a friend of Jasmine's brother.'

'Some friend,' mutters Jasmine under her breath.

I'm not sure what to say. 'I did try to ring to see if I could bring Alex,' I say. 'He's . . .'

I stop, not wanting to say 'my former fiancé'.

Alex steps in, as if sensing my hesitation. 'Nancy and I knew each other in London. I'm afraid I turned up unexpectedly, but I can go if you'd like me to.'

What's going on here? Clearly there's bad blood between these two.

'You're here, so you might as well come in,' says Jasmine.

It's a mistake. We have an awkward hour or so eating pizza and making stilted conversation. I say 'we' but Jasmine ignores Alex. Instead she asks if I've had any more 'trouble' with visitors, glancing pointedly in Alex's direction. 'Only kidding.'

But she's not and she knows it. We all do.

We leave as soon as possible after that. 'So,' I say to Alex when we're home, 'what's the history between you?'

He looks embarrassed. 'I was a bit of a rebel at school. So was Jasmine's brother. We both got into trouble with the teachers but his parents blamed me.'

'That's it?'

'Yes.'

But I'm not convinced. If I didn't know Alex better, I'd think he was keeping something back.

'There *is* something else, actually.'

I knew it.

'When I went upstairs to the loo, I walked past Jasmine's bedroom.'

'And?'

He makes an embarrassed laugh. 'I took a quick peek.'

'Alex!'

'I know. But I just had this suspicion about her. And I was right. On her dressing table was a letter. From Martin.'

'What?'

He takes my hands. 'Nancy, it was the same letter that the newspaper published. Word for word. It had clearly been torn up, but someone had pieced it together with tape.'

I go cold. 'What are you saying? I put it in my dustbin. One of the journalists must have found it.'

'But what if it was Jasmine and she sold it to them?'

'She wouldn't. She's my friend.'

'You don't even know her. Neither do I any more. We've got no idea what she's capable of.'

It's true. Hadn't Jasmine mentioned she was short of money?

Then again, none of us knows what someone is capable of.

Including ourselves.

20

When I wake in the morning, Alex is getting dressed. We didn't do anything, but still, I let him sleep in my bed. Hold me. It was so comforting.

He comes back to my side and takes my hand. I pull it away. I shouldn't have let him get close. Besides, he wouldn't want to be here if he knew what I had done.

'Please leave now. I should never have let you in. It's made everything worse.'

Hurt is written all over his face. 'I'm always here for you, Nancy. But I can go if that's what you want.'

I nod silently.

And then he leaves. My empty palm burns with loneliness.

Sheba jumps up onto the window seat in the front sitting room, gazing mournfully at Alex's car edging out of the drive. 'You didn't even know him,' I tell her.

Maybe I didn't either. I keep feeling that about everyone right now. Jasmine. Alex. Martin. Even myself.

I need a distraction. What would my mother do? Cook. That's what. I get down the old recipe book that she sometimes used when we came here. There's an inscription in the front: *To Adeline from Elizabeth with love. 1938.*

I flick through the recipes. None of them appeal, but then again, this book came out just before the Second World War started. Stinging-nettle soup. Ox-tail soup.

Besides, there doesn't seem much point in cooking right now. I feel sick rather than hungry.

'Right,' I say. 'Enough of this.'

I march across the road and knock on Jasmine's door. She's in mismatched pyjamas, her face blotchy from sleep. I come straight out with it.

'Alex found the letter Martin sent me in your bedroom,' I say.

'What letter?'

'Come on, Jasmine. The letter that the paper printed.'

Jasmine's eyes harden. 'What was Alex doing in my bedroom?'

'He was on his way back from the loo and, yes, he shouldn't have gone in. But he saw the letter. How much did the newspaper pay you?'

She looks as though I've slapped her in the face. Either she's a good actress or I've made the wrong call.

'How dare you? How could you think that of me?'

'Well, how do you explain it, then?'

Jasmine looks me straight in the eye. 'I didn't want to tell you this but now I have to. Alex was a troublemaker at school. He was always being told off by the teachers and leading my brother – his so-called "best friend" – astray.'

There are tears in her eyes. 'Then he did something evil.'

I stiffen. 'What?'

'They'd already got a reputation at school for drinking and bunking off lessons. Alex was the ringleader. My brother was a model student until he fell under Alex's spell. But then . . .'

She stops.

'Go on,' I say.

'Then, when they were only fifteen, Alex encouraged Paul to help him steal a car. He said it would be fun and that he could drive because his dad had been giving him lessons in a field. So my brother went along with it. But they hit a man and then they ran away.'

'That's awful,' I gasp. 'Was the person hurt?'

'Not permanently, thank God. But Alex said it was my brother who was driving. There were no witnesses so it was his word against Paul's. The judge, for whatever reason, chose to believe him. My brother was sent to a juvenile centre and did three years. It ruined his life. He hasn't been able to get a decent job since he came out.'

This can't be true, surely. But Jasmine's face is so clear and honest that there is no doubt.

'You said last night that you met Alex two years ago.'

'Well, eighteen months actually.'

'Let me guess. Online.'

'My friend got me to do it. I wasn't sure but she was keen to find me someone and . . .'

'Bet he seemed charming.'

I nod.

'Intelligent. Interested in you?'

'Yes,' I say quietly. 'We got engaged within six months.'

She rolls her eyes. 'Did he know your mother and step-father had money?'

Another nod. 'But I broke it off after they died.'

She laughs. 'Let me guess again. He wants you to take him back. So he's making you feel you need him by scaring you into thinking you're with people you can't trust. Like me.'

'Alex isn't like that.'

She leans forward, as if trying to make a point. 'But you don't know him like I do, Nancy. If you don't believe me, check my house. Take it to bits if you want to. You won't find any letter.'

I hesitate.

'Alex will have made the whole thing up,' she says firmly. 'If not, why didn't he just pocket the letter and bring it back to you as proof? Or at least take a photo on his phone.'

I hadn't thought to ask him that.

Suddenly, I feel as if I am back in court giving evidence. What is true and what isn't? Doubt is swirling round my mind just as it did then.

'You see,' she says quietly. 'Men like Alex have an answer for everything. If I were you, Nancy, I'd be careful. Very careful.'

21

I walk down to the sea, my head spinning. Alex had been vague about his past when I'd met him. 'How lovely to grow up by the sea,' He'd agreed when he said he was from a coastal town in Devon, just like me.

But he'd brushed that away with some remark about wanting to get up to 'the bright lights' of London. Had he been running away from his past, just as I was running away from mine?

And if Jasmine was right, what did that say about Alex? He'd run someone over. He could have killed that poor man. And he'd sent an innocent boy to prison, with a record that would blemish his future. So much for me thinking he was genuine.

My mind goes back to the open patio door. Had my ex been hanging around here all the time? What if it was Alex who had taken the letter?

I call the one person I know I can trust.

Claire picks up immediately. 'Are you OK? Did you see Alex? Have you made it up?'

'You know I told you I'd put Martin's letter in the bin when I received it?'

'Yes?' She sounds puzzled. 'Why?'

'Did you tell Alex?'

'I might have done. I can't remember. We've all been

worried about that maniac stepbrother of yours, so it's quite possible. Why?'

I almost tell her but I know she'll think I'm mad, suspecting Alex. 'It doesn't matter. Please don't tell him I asked.'

'Why? What's going on?'

'My lawyer wanted me to find out as much as I could in case the police take it further,' I say. It's not exactly a lie but it's the best I can do.

My phone pings with an email. It's my boss.

I read it resignedly. Part of me had wondered if this might happen. He is 'letting me go'. My presence might 'cause a distraction' after recent 'publicity'.

My eyes prick with tears. It's not like I need the money any more. But I love my job. I am good at it. I know he's right to say it's not fair on my colleagues, but this feels like another sign that my life is being destroyed. I reply, pretending that 'I understand', and then walk on towards the beach. I need to sit on the stones, to watch the waves come in and go out. They give me a sense of rhythm when everything else is falling down around me.

'Nancy!' says a voice.

I look up. It's Jeremy from the museum. He has a dog with him too. Does everyone round here have one?

'Getting some air, are you?'

'Actually, I've just been made redundant,' I say.

I have no idea why I'm telling this to someone I barely know.

His brow wrinkles. 'I'm sorry about that. How very strange.'

'Why?' I ask.

'Because I was about to advertise for someone to help me with a book we're writing on Sidmouth in the Second World War.'

'I'm not an author. I write advertising slogans.'

His voice gathers excitement. 'In a way, that could be very useful. You could draw people in with your skills; get them interested. Forgive me for saying so, but your generation needs reminding about the war just as future generations will need reminding about the virus.'

I've never thought about that before. But he's right.

'The thing is, Nancy, that I believe in serendipity. History is made up of chance happenings that can turn out for the best or not, as the case might be. You live in one of the most historic houses of Sidmouth. You've been through a terrible time, although I haven't liked to allude to it before. Now you've been made redundant. Some might call this a coincidence. History has taught me otherwise. This could be exactly what you need right now. A project! You might even unearth some more information about the person who went missing from your house. Perhaps I've overlooked something in the archives. It's too much for one person to go through.'

There's a lump in my throat. Even though he knows what's happened, this nice man is willing to give me a job. Besides, despite my own situation, I'm intrigued by the missing person. 'May I think about it?' I ask.

'Certainly you may. I won't place this ad until tomorrow afternoon. Does that give you enough time?'

I nod. 'Thanks.'

I walk back home under Jacob's Ladder. Martin and I often used to take this route when my mother encouraged us to 'go out and get some fresh air'. Right here are the little recesses where we sheltered from the rain that day. No one else is around. I stand looking up at the rock where sweethearts over the years have carved their names.

It's got to be here somewhere.

And there it is. *Martin loves Nancy.*

I take a stone from the beach and try to scratch it out. But it remains there. Stubbornly.

Like it or not, we are bound together for ever, as Martin had said in his letter.

But somehow I have to find a way to escape this man.

Whatever it takes.

The Night of the Murder

8.09 p.m.

Martin is frowning as we follow Mum into the kitchen. He leans against the Welsh dresser, doing that agitated thing where his feet are tapping the floor in the way that some people do when they're sitting down.

But he does it standing up. Right foot. Left foot.

His black eyes are suspiciously darting towards his father and then me and then back again.

Twenty years of history is closing in around us. I can feel it. Smell it. Sometimes I forget that Martin didn't know what happened. He'd been sent back to his mother's after that summer and there had been no more family holidays since. In fact, it's the first time this toxic family of ours has been together since it happened.

'What did you mean when you said it was a bit late for Dad to behave?' he asks.

'What are you talking about?' says Mum sharply.

'Your daughter thinks I shouldn't drink so much,' says Duncan quickly.

I've had enough of his lies.

'I'm going to leave now,' I say.

'Please don't,' says Mum. She turns round from the worktop where she's preparing the fish. 'It's my birthday.'

'Don't you think I know that?' I say tightly.

But something in her voice reminds me of my old mum. The one who would have believed me. So I stay.

Elizabeth

22

1941

Was it a fighter plane? Elizabeth stared up in horror as the first one roared above them, racing across the sky. Then another and another.

The Germans? She could feel her heart pounding as if it had moved itself to her throat.

Then she saw the RAF roundels in the distinctive blue, white and red colours on the side.

Elizabeth's heart continued to thump, even though her head told her it was all right. These planes were their boys flying out to defend their island!

Turning swiftly, she struck back to the shore. The girls were already out, wrapped up in the towels she'd brought down for them.

'Are they going to kill us?' asked Maisie, her voice shaking.

'No. They're English planes,' said Elizabeth.

'They're going over the sea to keep us safe,' said Mr Smith gently.

'But what if they don't?' cried Shirley. 'Supposing they get shot down?'

They won't, Elizabeth wanted to say. But how could she be sure? There was only so much you could protect children from. Elizabeth didn't believe in lies. Yet she didn't want to frighten them either.

'Let's go home,' she said brightly. 'I've got some lovely ox-tail stew for dinner.'

It was all the butcher had left this week. No doubt Mrs Norris would raise her eyebrows ('Ox-tail again?') but it couldn't be helped.

'I want me mam,' said Maisie. 'I miss her.'

Elizabeth's heart ached.

'I'm sure she misses you too,' she said, reaching out for the little girl's hand as they climbed back up the hill. 'But she knows you're safe here.'

Maisie frowned. 'She'll need me to help with my brothers and sisters. There are five of us.'

Why hadn't all of them been evacuated to safety?

The teacher seemed to hear her unspoken question. 'Maisie's family are waiting to find somewhere that can take them all. But because her school was bombed, they thought it was best that Maisie, as the eldest, received some kind of education.'

'I don't miss my brother,' said Shirley matter-of-factly. 'It's much nicer here. We get better food and our Billy can't put the stick to me.'

What stories lay behind these children's faces and souls? How was this going to affect them in years to come if – no, *when* – the world was normal again?

Supper was a quiet affair. Even the Patmore sisters refrained from treating everyone to their usual discourse regarding the daily crossword and their current knitting project. Henry came in late without an apology, ate without speaking and then left for drill with the Home Guard.

Afterwards Mrs Norris came up to her. 'May we have a word in private, Mrs Montague?'

'Of course.' Bracing herself for a complaint about the food, Elizabeth led her into their own sitting room.

Mrs Norris puffed herself up with an air of self-importance. 'I'm afraid I have something rather worrying to report. Last night I went for a walk along the beach, to the beginning of Alma Bridge. As always, I had my father's binoculars with me to look out for enemy ships. And that's when I spotted Mr Smith.'

She paused excitedly for a quick breath.

'He had a torch, Mrs Montague. He was flashing it. As if he was making signals.'

'Signals?' Elizabeth repeated.

'Exactly.'

If this wasn't so serious, she might almost have laughed. Then again, there were posters all over town, urging residents to be on their guard against undercover operators. But this was the children's teacher they were talking about.

'You don't honestly think that Mr Smith is a spy?'

Mrs Norris's tone was clipped. 'Without wishing to state the obvious, Mrs Montague, right now, with the state that the world is in, we have to be cautious.'

'I see. Well, thank you.'

'Are you going to tell the police?'

'I will talk to my husband about it.'

Of course, she wouldn't. Henry would use it as an excuse to get rid of him and maybe the little girls too. Mrs Norris was just being a busybody. The war had made plenty of those. The woman had also been extremely cutting to Mr Smith this morning after he'd glanced at her crossword puzzle and given the answer to one of her clues without her asking. Perhaps this was her revenge.

Honestly! thought Elizabeth. She couldn't cope with petty squabbles when there was a war on.

Two more weeks went by, during which she could tell Maisie continued to miss her family. The dear little thing had tears in her eyes at breakfast the other day and slept with a photograph of her mother clasped in her hand. Then Elizabeth bumped into someone from church who had also taken in two evacuees and had invited their parents down so they could see where they were and 'put their minds at rest'. But would Henry agree?

'It sounds like a good idea, don't you think?' she said when they were alone that night. Elizabeth was already in bed. Henry was still undressing. He always did so in the dark. She was grateful for that. It was hard enough talking to him in broad daylight.

'Well, they're not staying here,' he said shortly. 'We're running a business, not providing free bed and board to every Tom, Dick and Harry.'

How could he be so callous?

'Let's just hope that the French don't have the same attitude to our son if he's out there, looking for someone to hide him,' she said.

There was no answer, although she could feel him climbing into the opposite side and pulling the eiderdown in his direction.

'Fine,' she said after a few seconds of silence. 'I'll ask Adeline to put them up.'

*

'A couple of nights?' said her friend when she went up to Periwinkle Cottage the following day. 'Certainly. We have to do what we can. Speaking of which, have you had any more thoughts about . . .'

She didn't need to say the words.

'Yes,' said Elizabeth. 'And the answer's still no.'

She had enough to be getting on with in real life instead of playing silly games in some 'secret army'. Besides, the talk in the fish market this morning was all about the war being over soon. 'Hitler's taken on more than he can chew,' one of the retired colonels in the queue had said. Everyone else had nodded in agreement. It made Elizabeth feel a lot better. She could already picture Robert walking in through the front door. Opening his arms to her. Holding her. *See, Mum! I said I'd be all right!*

Elizabeth shook herself. She mustn't just think of her own situation. There were thousands of other mothers out there, hoping for the safe return of their boys.

Meanwhile, she needed to concentrate on her daily chores. There were beds to make. Meals to be cooked. Washing to be wrung through the mangle in the backyard. The girls had only come with one change of clothes. So, once she'd cleared most of her tasks, she took Maisie and Shirley to Fields to buy them a spare set with coupons and some of her own money.

How she had yearned for a daughter when Robert was small! He'd have loved a sister too. Maisie and Shirley's presence brought an energy to the house. But most important for Elizabeth, they gave her a purpose during this uncertain time.

When she got back, Mrs B was still in the kitchen, even

though she had usually left by now to sort out her own house and family.

'Something came when you were out,' she said quietly, her eyes not meeting Elizabeth's.

Silently she handed over a telegram.

The words swam before her.

Missing on war service. Presumed dead . . . No information should be given to the press.

'No,' whimpered Elizabeth in a voice that wasn't hers. 'No.'

23

This couldn't be true. Her Robert was still alive. He had to be. She could see her boy tucking into his favourite meal – roast beef on Sunday – made by Mrs B, who was now putting her arm around her and leading her to a chair. 'This is delicious,' he'd be saying. 'I don't know how you do it.'

She could picture him as a small boy, desperately trying to master his sums while Henry stood over him, stumbling over the answers until he got it right. Robert as a teenager, saving up his pocket money to buy her a bottle of Blue Grass, her favourite perfume.

'What's happened?'

Henry's voice cut through her thoughts.

'This is your fault.' Elizabeth hissed. 'Look what you have done.'

Her husband's eyes fell on the telegram she was thrusting in his face.

'Let me read it,' he said. There was a tremor in his voice that she had heard only once before, when she told him they had a son.

'It's not certain, Lizzie,' he said, looking up from the paper. He hadn't called her that for years. It just stirred her anger further.

Tears were rolling down her face now. 'If you hadn't encouraged him to go, he'd be here now. You might as well have shot him yourself.'

His face tightened. But he didn't deny it.

Elizabeth was vaguely aware of someone else entering the kitchen. 'Good afternoon, Mr and Mrs Montague. Have you had a good day?'

It was Mr Smith, with the two girls.

'GET OUT,' roared Henry. 'Give us some bloody privacy, will you?'

The children looked up at her in alarm. 'It's all right, dears,' she said to Maisie and Shirley, trying to stifle her sobs. 'I just need some time on my own.'

Then she ran out of the house, unable to see through the tears.

The next thing Elizabeth knew, she was on the beach. The same stretch that she and Robert used to come to. Somehow she'd made it past the defences without being harmed or stopped. The waves were choppy; grey and brooding. There was a sharp edge to the wind.

Come on in, Mum!

She could almost hear his voice.

Now gone for ever.

There was a howl. Like the unseen animal that she and Robert had once heard when walking on Dartmoor.

But it was coming from her own mouth.

'My boy,' she wept. 'My boy.'

When she returned an hour later – she really couldn't neglect the children or the PGs any longer – the house was quiet. Maybe Mr Smith had taken the girls out. Hopefully Henry had made himself scarce. She went into the kitchen.

Mrs B was there, wiping dishes. On seeing Elizabeth,

she took her hand. They'd never, in all the years they'd known each other, had any physical contact before today. 'You need a lie-down,' she says. 'You've had a shock.'

'No,' said Elizabeth. Then, despite everything, she remembered her manners. 'Thank you, Mrs B, but no.'

'Beryl,' said Mrs B, touching her on the arm. 'Please call me Beryl.'

Such familiarity made her sob even more.

'I've got to *do* something,' she choked.

'We could register with the Red Cross,' said a voice behind her.

It was Henry. She almost hadn't recognized the subdued tone.

'If he's a prisoner of war,' he added, 'they might know about it.'

A tiny ray of hope began to creep in.

'That's right,' added Mrs B eagerly. 'My Reg's sister in London knows someone who received a telegram like this. Turned out her lad got sent to one of those camps in Germany. Better there than dead.'

Elizabeth winced.

'I'll go into town and find out how to do it,' said Henry.

She rounded on him. 'Well, why are you still here then? Just do it.'

'I wanted to wait until you came back,' he said. 'I was worried. What will you do?'

For a moment, she saw the old Henry, concern and even love in his eyes. The one she had fallen for, all those years ago.

'I'm going to carry on knitting the hat I'm making him,' she said.

'But he might never wear –'

'Stop right there, Henry. You've got your job to do, so get on with it. I've got mine. I've also got two small evacuee girls in our care. I have responsibility for them. Where are they?'

She was feeling scarily calm now. Rather as if she was acting a part in a film.

'They're in the garden with Mr Smith,' said Beryl.

'Then I'll go and get them. They'll want to have their tea. We can't afford to waste any food.'

'Mrs Montague,' called out Maisie when she went out to find them in the apple orchard. The dear little thing ran into her arms. 'Have they found your son?'

Someone must have told her.

'Not yet,' she managed to reply. 'But they will soon.'

They had to.

24

'I won't believe he's dead,' Elizabeth told herself in her private moments.

The more she said this, the more she convinced herself. Yet she could tell from the sympathetic faces around her that no one else felt the same.

Even Henry continued to be kind to her, which was strangely unnerving.

In public, she went on as usual. Her list of jobs was endless. Helping Mrs B (she couldn't switch to Beryl after all this time) to look after their guests. Keeping an eye on the little girls. Mr Smith was very good with them, but there was nothing like a motherly touch. Working alongside Adeline to find more billets for the children who were arriving daily. Digging the allotment and planting more cabbages for the spring. Listening to the hourly bulletins on the wireless. She also managed to get accommodation for a group of pregnant women in one of the large local houses that had been requisitioned by the government.

But top of Elizabeth's list was to sit the children down at the dining-room table every Sunday after lunch with her Basildon Bond notepaper so they could write their regular weekly letters home. The agony in her heart made her even more aware of how much their parents must miss them. Of course, it wouldn't have been right to read what the girls had written.

The shock of Robert's 'temporary disappearance' as she called it ('missing' seemed too final) had almost made her forget Adeline's kind offer of beds until her friend reminded her again.

So Elizabeth wrote to Maisie and Shirley's mothers, suggesting a trip to Sidmouth. She wouldn't tell the girls, she decided, in case the train fare was too expensive or the women couldn't leave their other children.

But letters from them both arrived in the same post shortly afterwards.

I wood be delited to take you up on your kind offer, read the one from Maisie's mother. *My hart aches to see my girl.*

The spelling might not be correct but the love shone out.

The one from Shirley's mother, written in uneven capital letters, simply said *YES*.

The children's excitement was worth putting up with Henry's grumpiness for, when she suggested that they all eat together during their stay. 'We're already giving their offspring bed and board,' he complained. 'Now you say we've got to feed two extra mouths for two days without any payment.'

'Let's just hope that Robert is being fed, wherever he is,' she said quietly.

Henry said nothing.

Meanwhile, there was no news from the Red Cross. That didn't mean anything, she told herself. There were so many young men out there. Older men too. It would take time to find Robert. She had to be patient and have faith. The alternative was too terrible to contemplate.

*

Maisie and Shirley were leaping up and down with excitement as they made their way to the station the following week.

'Not so near the edge of the platform,' she kept warning the girls.

'But I want to see the train as soon as it comes round the corner,' said Maisie.

'Here it is!' yelled Shirley.

Elizabeth began to feel apprehensive. Maisie and Shirley's mothers must be desperate to see their children. They must also be in need of reassurance that their precious daughters were safe in her hands. It was up to her to give them that comfort. What a responsibility!

'There's me mam!' yelled Maisie, breaking away from her and flying up to a jolly-looking round woman with rosy cheeks and a jaunty little hat. That must be Mrs Evans.

Elizabeth felt a terrible surge of envy. She wanted to hold Robert like that. To feel his face against hers.

'Shirley?' said a sharp voice. 'Is that you?' It came from a tall, gaunt woman.

'Mum.'

Despite the child's previous excitement, Elizabeth could see an odd expression crossing Shirley's face. It almost looked like trepidation.

'Well, I must say. I hardly recognized you. Aren't you the posh one? Just look at them clothes you're wearing.'

Shirley went red. 'Mrs Montague bought me a new coat.'

'Did she now?'

Elizabeth put her hand out to the woman, who now had a sour expression on her face. Her hair was jet black like her daughter's but it was tightly permed and the effect was quite severe. They'd all had to learn to do their own since war started and some results were better than others.

'How nice to meet you,' said Elizabeth.

Shirley's mother gave her a cold stare. 'I hope you're not spoiling my girl. The rest of us have had to make do.'

So have we, Elizabeth wanted to say. She'd bought the girls' coats out of her own money because it was so cold and there weren't any that fitted them in the bag of donations from the locals.

'Mrs Montague?'

Maisie's mother was coming towards her with Maisie still clinging to her. 'Thank you so much for looking after my little girl. I can't thank you enough.'

'Please, call me Elizabeth.'

'Ta. I'm Julie. We're in your debt, ma'am. We really are.'

'I don't know about that.' Mrs Penny's lips pursed. 'From what I heard on the train, it's just as dangerous down here as it is in London. If I'd known that the Jerries might land here any minute, I'd have kept our Shirley with us at home.'

'You're staying at a friend's house,' said Elizabeth nervously as they began walking back. 'It's just round the corner from us.'

'We're not good enough for you, then?'

Oh dear! This was getting worse. 'We have paying guests so we don't have any extra room, I'm afraid.'

'I see.' Her lips pursed again. 'I'll go straight there then and have a rest. I'm dead beat from that journey.'

'Don't you want to come for a walk with us, Mum?' asked Shirley. 'We always do that on Saturdays. Mrs Montague is teaching us to keep a nature diary.'

'Is she now?'

'And you can see the sea!' piped up Maisie. 'We can't go on the beach – well, not all of it – because of the mines and –'

'Mines?' Shirley's mother began to tremble. 'What if the bleeding Germans invade when we're here? Just get me to this friend of yours so I can have a lie-down.'

Later that afternoon, they all went to collect her. 'Everything all right?' whispered Elizabeth to Adeline.

Her friend raised her eyebrows in answer.

If it had been my daughter, Elizabeth thought, *I'd have spent every minute with her instead of having a rest.*

'Blooming heck,' said Shirley's mother as they walked into Tall Chimneys. 'Where I come from, this place would put up the whole street. Wait until I tell the girls on the line about this.'

Both women worked nights in a munitions factory. Elizabeth didn't like to ask who was in charge of the other children while they did that.

'What's that?' shrieked Mrs Penny.

'It's the bell for dinner, Mum,' said Shirley.

'A bleeding bell to tell you when grub's up? Are you having me on?'

'It's like a dream,' said Maisie's mother. 'Aren't you girls lucky to end up in a place like this, and with such a nice lady? I have to say I was really worried. You hear all kinds of stories about evacuee kids having to work like navvies.'

'The only hard labour they do is their school work,' said Elizabeth brightly. 'Isn't that right, Mr Smith?'

The teacher was coming down the stairs at that very minute.

'They do indeed,' he said.

Shirley's mother glared at him. 'What kind of place have you brought my girl to? You're meant to be responsible for them.'

'I'm sorry, Mrs Penny. I'm not sure what you mean.'

'We was told they'd go somewhere safe. Not to some town where the Jerries could land any minute.'

'We've been very lucky to have been billeted here, Mrs Penny,' said Mr Smith firmly. 'In fact, Mrs Montague offered to take us on even though she also runs a boarding house.'

'Well, I hope the guests are the right sort.'

They were going into the dining room now. The PGs were already there. Had Mrs Norris or the sisters heard them? Elizabeth could only hope not.

'What are those things?' demanded Mrs Penny, pointing to the trolley. 'They look like helmets.'

'They're silver clocks, Mum. I mean *cloches*. They go on each one of our plates to keep the food hot.'

Shirley was blushing as Mrs B was putting them onto the table.

'What hoity-toity nonsense.'

Elizabeth could see the horrified looks on the faces of her PGs. Even so, her heart went out to Mrs Penny. It must be awful for her to be in a strange place and watch someone else looking after her child.

'We put them on our heads sometimes when we have practice air raids,' piped up Maisie.

'That's a good idea,' said her mother.

'Yes. And then we sit under the table wearing them,' added Shirley.

Mrs Penny let out a little scream. 'How's that going to save you from the Jerries?'

'You'd be surprised,' said Maisie's mum. 'You hear of all kinds of things helping people when the bombs fall.'

Shirley's mother got up. 'That's it. I've had enough.'

She burst into tears. The poor thing was scared witless. Instinctively, Elizabeth got up to comfort her, but the woman pushed her away.

'Get off me,' she scowled. 'I don't want no pity from the likes of you. You have no idea what it's like to be away from your kid and wonder if some bomb is going to smash you all to smithereens any time.'

'Actually,' said Henry, who had just arrived, 'we do. Our only son has been reported as missing, presumed dead.'

A tense hush fell in the room. It stayed that way for the rest of the meal.

'Tomorrow will be better,' Elizabeth told herself after seeing the mothers back to Periwinkle Cottage and then finally climbing into her own bed. It was always difficult when you arrived somewhere new, even in normal times. Mrs Penny would come round.

But when she went down to breakfast the next morning (having overslept, rather embarrassingly) only Maisie was there.

'Where's Shirley?' she asked.

The child started sobbing. 'Her mum's been round. She's taken her back to London.'

25

Tall Chimneys felt so quiet without Shirley and her constant chatter. Maisie was, understandably, very subdued. Elizabeth felt as though she had failed by not meeting Mrs Penny's expectations.

'I miss her,' she said to Elizabeth when they went for their usual nature walk the following Saturday. 'And I miss my mam too.'

She should never have asked the mothers down. How selfish of her to meddle like this, partly as a way of forgetting her own problems.

'Do you miss your son?' asked Maisie quietly.

The unexpected question made Elizabeth's eyes blur. To hide her grief, she knelt down and picked a little red wildflower growing by the verge. 'Yes, I do.'

'I'm sorry,' said the child simply.

'Thank you.' For two pins, Elizabeth would have thrown herself on the earth and wept. But she had to hold herself together for Maisie's sake. 'Do you remember what this is called?'

She'd been teaching the girls the names of the local flora.

'Pink campion?'

'Nearly! Red campion. Here you are. You can press it in your nature book.'

'Can I pick another? I'll put it in Shirley's book too. She

left it behind but I'll finish it for her for when we meet up again.'

'What a lovely idea! Now, how about this?'

'I know! I know!' Maisie's face was shining with excitement. 'This was Shirley's favourite 'cos it's SO pretty. It's Queen Anne's lace, but sometimes it's called cow parsley.'

'Clever you!'

Thank goodness! thought Elizabeth, grateful that she'd managed to distract the child – and herself too – for a few minutes.

Days passed. There was still no news of her boy. Meanwhile, there had been even more servicemen arriving in town, many of them Canadians. Everyone was talking about what they'd do if enemy ships or submarines were spotted in the Channel. It all felt so unreal. To think that nearly three years ago, they'd all been living normal lives without fear of being wiped out at any minute. Still, if the Americans joined – there was a lot of talk about that too – it would 'help to put the boot in', as Henry put it.

His attitude towards her had become colder again; perhaps because she could barely talk to him. She couldn't stop thinking about Robert, starving in some camp. Or worse.

Elizabeth would have liked to discuss her fears with Adeline, but her friend hadn't been at home the last few times she'd knocked on her door. And when she'd gone to the Manor Hall to sort out donations for evacuees, Adeline hadn't been on duty.

'May I help you with that?' asked Mr Smith one afternoon when he saw her set off from Tall Chimneys with a shovel and fork.

'Thank you, but I'm fine.'

Elizabeth rather liked her time on the allotment. It gave her space to think and be herself.

'Please allow me. We used to have quite a big garden. I'd like to see what you're growing.'

There was that 'we' again.

'What was your life like before the war?' she found herself asking.

He paused for so long that she wished she'd stayed quiet.

'I was married with a son,' he said. 'But then . . . I lost them.'

How awful!

'I'm so sorry.'

'Thank you. I'll tell you more one day.'

'You don't have to,' she said awkwardly. Her heart went out to him.

He looked at her in a way that made her blush. 'I want to,' he said. They were at the allotment now. 'Shall I start with these weeds?'

Two hours later, they walked back to Tall Chimneys together, Elizabeth feeling calmer than she had for some time. 'Thank you so much for your hard work,' she said as they got to the driveway.

'It's a pleasure,' he replied.

At that moment, Henry came out of the house. His look went from her to the teacher and back again.

'Where have you been?' he said coldly.

'At the allotment. Mr Smith was giving me a hand.'

'So I see.' His eyes took in the mud on their clothes. 'I've got some news.'

Elizabeth gasped. 'Robert?'

'No. One of the schoolteachers has been round. It's the girl, the one who left. Their house took a direct hit. The whole family's dead. Every single one of them.'

26

'I've told the other one,' said Henry. 'I think she was a bit upset.'

'Where is she now?' whispered Elizabeth. The poor child. What must she be feeling?

'She went to her room,' said Henry awkwardly. 'I thought I'd let her be.'

Elizabeth flew upstairs. 'Maisie! Maisie!'

There she was, sitting on Shirley's bed. There was no sound. Not even a tear. Maisie looked as if she was in a trance. It must be the shock. Elizabeth held her, trying to find some words of comfort but none would come. Then the child began to shiver. She could even hear the little girl's teeth chattering.

'Let me make you some hot Bovril,' she said. 'It will help.'

But Maisie shook her head. Elizabeth began to feel frightened. What should she do?

There was a knock on the door. 'May I come in?'

It was Mr Smith, carrying a glass. 'I know this is terrible for you, Maisie. It is for all of us, although especially for you as her best friend. But I'm sure that if Shirley was here, she would want you to have some water. It will help you. Then after that, maybe a little lie-down.'

What kind words. He must be a very good teacher.

To Elizabeth's relief, Maisie took a few sips.

Mr Smith left so silently that she didn't even notice him exit the room.

'Please . . . don't go,' the child whispered to Elizabeth.

'Of course not, if you don't want me to.'

Pulling up a chair, she sat by the side of the bed, holding Maisie's small cold hand. After a while, the child's eyes closed and her breathing grew steadier. Elizabeth stood up quietly. As she did so, she noticed the door of the wardrobe was open. There at the back in round loopy writing was written '*Maisie was here. SO WAS SHIRLEY! 8 October 1941.*'

Elizabeth had to blink back the tears.

Maisie was still asleep when Elizabeth finally went to bed. But she was unable to do the same. Thoughts about Shirley and her family kept going round and round.

They would have heard the air-raid warning, surely. Why hadn't they left the house for the public shelter? Or hadn't there been time to do so? What terrors must have passed through their heads as the bombs began to fall and the house shake? Was Mrs Penny the type of mother who would have comforted her children or would she have been in hysterics?

It was all too terrible to think about.

Then an awful screaming pierced the air.

'What the hell is that?' said Henry sleepily from the far side of the bed.

Without bothering to answer, Elizabeth leaped out of bed and ran up the stairs. Mrs Norris was hovering outside Maisie's room with small spiky brown rollers in her hair. 'I wasn't sure whether to go in or not,' she said nervously. It wasn't like her to be so indecisive.

'It's all right, Maisie,' said Elizabeth soothingly as she opened the door.

The little girl was sitting up straight and staring as if a demon was in front of her, still screaming.

Tentatively, Elizabeth held the child to her, stroking her back as she used to stroke Robert's when he'd been ill as a small boy with those continuous winter coughs. 'You're having a night terror,' she said as calmly as possible. 'It will pass. Think of something nice, like Queen Anne's lace.'

Gradually Maisie's screams became shuddering sobs. Still Elizabeth held her, stroking and talking quietly about the things she knew that the child loved: the sea, collecting eggs from the farm coop, helping Mrs B make bread.

Slowly her breathing evened out and she sank back on the pillow, her eyes closing.

Elizabeth sat for a while, waiting until she was sure Maisie was asleep, and then crept out. Everyone apart from Henry and the sisters was in the kitchen.

'How is she?' asked Mr Smith.

'Quiet now,' she said, trying not to look at his silk Paisley dressing gown, which was rather more expensive-looking than one might have expected for a teacher.

'Poor little lamb,' murmured Mrs B.

'Thank you, everyone, for your concern,' said Elizabeth. 'I think the best thing we can do is go back to bed. I'll keep an ear out for her. It will take time for it to sink in.'

She was right. As the days, passed, the pattern continued. Maisie barely spoke a word. At mealtimes, she rarely ate more than a few mouthfuls, and even those had to be coaxed down her. At night, she woke regularly, screaming Shirley's name.

Elizabeth's doctor prescribed something to calm her down, but it simply made her sleepy. When she woke, she would start crying and screaming all over again.

One day a letter arrived, the envelope addressed to Maisie in a childish hand. Probably from one of her brothers or sisters, Elizabeth assumed. This should cheer her up.

As Maisie opened it at the breakfast table, her eyes widened.

'It's from Shirley!' she said.

Everyone fell silent. Elizabeth froze.

'She's not dead at all! Look!'

She waved the letter in the air. 'Shirley says she likes being back in London with her family, even though she misses us. There haven't been any raids for ages. They reckon Mr Hitler's gone back to Germany. Isn't that wonderful?'

Her face was wreathed in smiles.

'Goodness,' said Elizabeth. 'May I have a look?'

As she feared, the letter was stamped the day before the bombing. How cruelly ironic.

'But . . .' began Mrs B.

Elizabeth flashed her a warning look. Mrs Norris seemed to take her cue too, as did the teacher. Somehow, this didn't seem the time to smash the child's hopes.

'There must have been a mistake,' trilled Maisie. 'Someone else must have died instead of her.' Her face fell. 'I know that's awful. But the thing is that my Shirley is all right! Can I write to her please? Now?'

'Of course you can,' said Elizabeth, 'as soon as you've finished the rest of your breakfast. Then maybe you should go to school.'

'Good idea,' said Mr Smith. 'It's English this morning and you know how you love reading.'

No one else at the table said anything. Had she done the right thing by allowing her to write back without explaining the letter had been written before Shirley's death? (She'd already asked Mr Smith to explain the situation to the head at school.)

Perhaps she should ask the doctor for advice.

'It's a difficult time,' he said slowly. 'But in my view, we could be causing terrible harm by forcing her to see the truth.'

'But what will happen when she does find out?' asked Elizabeth.

'Let's face that one when we come to it, shall we?'

The good thing was that Maisie's night terrors ended. She began to eat again. 'I wonder why Shirley hasn't written me another letter,' she would say occasionally.

'I expect she's busy, dear,' Mrs Norris would say. 'Now tell me what you learned in school today . . .'

Excusing herself, Elizabeth quietly slipped away. Today was Robert's birthday – something that Henry had either forgotten or decided not to mention. She needed to walk along the seafront. Imagine that he was next to her, holding her arm.

'Look, Mother,' she could hear him saying, 'it's a perfect day for a swim.'

When she got home, Henry was waiting. She knew instantly from his expression that he had news. 'Robert's commanding officer rang,' he said. 'Our boy was taken prisoner . . .'

Yes. *Yes!*

'But he tried to escape and . . . and he was . . .'

Henry burst into tears.

'He was what?' Elizabeth said, grabbing his lapels.

'He was shot dead.' Henry was now sobbing like a baby.

'Dead?' she whispered, releasing him. 'No. No. He can't be. I'd have known.' She thumped her chest. 'I'd have felt it here when it happened.'

Then she sank to her knees, howling. Yet at the same time, she was aware of a strange calm. The worst had happened. Nothing could ever be as bad as this again.

Henry was shaking. 'I'm so sorry, Elizabeth. You were right. This is all my fault.'

'Yes,' she said, stumbling to her feet. Cold fury had taken over now. 'It *is* your fault. And I will never, ever forgive you.'

Slamming the door behind her, she almost ran up Cliff Road. This time, Adeline answered the door.

'The secret army,' gasped Elizabeth, breathlessly. 'How do I sign up?'

The Night of the Murder

8.15 p.m.

Duncan has had too much to drink.

'When's dinner ready?' he asks rudely.

'I'm afraid I'm running a bit late,' says Mum.

'Then I'll just have to have a snack, won't I?'

He takes an apple from the fruit bowl on the kitchen table and bites into it. 'Delicious,' he says, looking straight at me.

He's trying to goad me. But he's not going to win.

'Why don't you open my birthday present, Mum?' I say.

Nancy

27

I've been back at Tall Chimneys for nearly two weeks now. At times it feels as though I've never left. So many memories are returning, mainly about my dad. How he taught me to swim just opposite the Riviera Hotel. How we'd walk over the hills to Branscombe and swim in the clear water there. How we'd look for crabs in rock pools. Read stories together. Make up our own as well.

But there are other memories, too, which scare me. Like this heart that Martin carved on the cliff all those years ago. I can't seem to stop searching it out whenever I walk past.

I stare at it now, running my finger along it, feeling the warmth of the stone in the sun. Feeling the pain.

It feels like yesterday when Martin scored it into the rock, using the Swiss Army knife he carried everywhere. I was fourteen. He was sixteen. It was the summer before 'it' happened. We'd come down to Sidmouth for the annual holiday, as we'd done every year after our parents had got married. We were company for each other, they said.

Claire was even more desperate to have a boyfriend that summer. Lots of the other girls in our class had one. 'If we don't do the same, people will think there's something wrong with us,' she'd say. It was true. Bullying was rife. You could be made fun of or shunned simply because of the size of your nose, let alone the lack of a boyfriend.

I could even sense a jealousy on Claire's part when I said Martin was coming again. That seemed odd, given that she'd called him 'creepy' last year. Or maybe it was because she was miffed that she hadn't been invited to come with us. Mum had thought we should have 'family' time.

'Why don't you two take yourselves off for a walk?' my mother suggested when my stepbrother arrived from France. So we did – but his hand kept bumping into mine. 'Sorry,' he said.

Martin had grown a wispy blond moustache since I'd seen him the previous Christmas and he was taller. But he still had that habit of staring intently at me when I spoke, as if he was hanging on to every word. It unnerved me. So too did that childish smile and those piercing black eyes.

One afternoon, when we were reading on the lawn, I was putting on sun cream. 'Let me,' he said, seeing me struggling to reach my back. I didn't like the touch of his hand on my skin but I didn't want to be rude. He was just helping. Wasn't he?

In the evenings, Mum would suggest charades or some other game in her efforts to make us into this 'family' she wanted us to be. But I didn't like being near Duncan. He made my skin crawl and he was always shouting at Martin. 'Nancy and I are going to listen to some music in my room,' Martin said. He hadn't asked me but I was glad to escape the adults. We sat side by side on the carpet listening to Black Sabbath, which I didn't like very much but felt I ought to because he did, and he was older. He listened to me when I said how much I missed Dad. 'I hate the way Duncan bosses Mum around,' I confessed.

'I get that,' he said. His face darkened. 'He can be a real

tosser. It must be shit having a dead dad. At least my mother is alive.'

One day, when we were walking along Jacob's Ladder, he startled me with a question. 'Do you have a boyfriend?'

'No,' I said, embarrassed.

Just as I spoke, it began to rain. He took my arm and steered me into one of the cave-like inlets to keep dry.

'I'll be your boyfriend if you like,' he said. Then he whipped out a knife from his pocket so fast that, for a scary minute, I thought he was going to hurt me. But he proceeded to score a heart shape on the wall of stone with our names next to it.

I'd laughed awkwardly.

'Why are you laughing?' he said tightly.

'Because . . . because I didn't know you felt that way,' I said.

'Our parents are married,' he replied, putting the knife away. 'We have to love each other.'

So he meant it in a brotherly way. That was a relief. 'Sure,' I said, trying to be cool.

'You know,' he said one evening when we were sitting in his room listening to Leonard Cohen (I liked this more than some of Martin's other music), 'we ought to make up our own secret code.'

'Why?' I asked.

'I've been reading about Bletchley Park and how people decoded the German messages during the war.'

'But why do *we* need a code?' I asked.

'We could use it to moan about your mother and my father in our letters when we write to each other after I go back.'

Martin was at yet another boarding school. From the conversations I had overheard between my mother and stepfather, it appeared that his mother couldn't cope very well having him at home. He wasn't an 'easy' child. No one told me why and I didn't like to ask. But I felt sorry for him, passed from his mother to his father and then from one boarding school to another.

Martin and I had never written to each other before but he spoke as if it had all been arranged. It seemed unfriendly to say I wouldn't. And it would be good to have someone to share family stuff with. Claire's family were so normal that she couldn't be expected to understand.

'OK,' I said.

He got up and grabbed a notebook. 'I've made a start. See? You use a mixture of ordinary words and then substitute numbers for certain letters. We can throw in a bit of French and Latin too. You do them both at school, don't you?'

His first letter arrived two days after he went back to school, and I decoded it. It was like a game! I showed it to Claire. 'It's a love letter,' she said.

'No it's not,' I laughed.

'It *is*, Nancy. Don't you see? He says he misses you.'

'That's just because we had fun together on holiday.'

'Honestly! You're so naive.'

Turned out she was right.

Sheba starts to bark, interrupting my thoughts. Someone is knocking at the front door. Please don't let it be any more journalists.

To my relief, it's just Jeremy from the museum. People

seem to call round far more often here than they do in London.

'I'm sorry to bother you but I wondered if you'd had a chance to consider my job offer. It's just that if you're not interested, I need to advertise.'

I hesitate. 'I'm afraid I haven't had much time to think . . .'

'You might like to know,' he says, 'that I found something out about your Maisie and Shirley.'

I feel my arms prickle with goosebumps.

'We discovered a list of evacuee names and they were on it.'

'That's amazing,' I say.

But Jeremy is looking solemn. 'I also came across some records from the church school from around that time. It seems that Shirley was killed in a bombing raid.'

I gasp. 'In Sidmouth?'

Jeremy shook his head. 'In London. Maybe she went back to visit her family.'

My eyes sting with tears. I might not have known her, but what a terrible thing to happen. 'What about Maisie?'

'There's no mention of her apart from her name on the evacuee list.'

I suddenly have a compelling need to find out more. Perhaps it's because Tall Chimneys has become my safety net. What was the story behind this girl who lived in my house? Did she have anything to do with the missing person? Was it her?

'The job,' I say. 'I'll take it.'

I might as well. I need to do something or I'll go crazy.

I have to fill my brain with something other than the horrors that keep elbowing their way into my head.

Otherwise, I might lose my mind. Just like I did, for a while, after the murder.

28

Jeremy is right. The records are in a mess. No wonder he wanted me to start straight away. There's too much here for one person to look through and oversee the museum at the same time. How on earth am I going to find out something about a missing person when I don't even have a definite name?

Still, at least I can make myself useful by trying to catalogue some of this. I sit in the little office at the back, wading through wartime instructions on what to do in the event of a bombing raid and the importance of keeping gas masks close to hand. There are several warnings on how residents should conduct themselves during the war. There are also some posters with slogans such as *Careless Talk Costs Lives* and warnings about German spies masquerading as 'the ordinary man or woman on the street'. There's even a scary leaflet on what to do if there's an invasion.

Seeing it written down like this makes the war feel horribly real and not just a date in a history book. People must have been terrified.

There are photographs, too, of Sidmouth between 1939 and 1945. The streets are recognizable and the people don't look that different. It could almost – but not quite – be today. I shiver. How can we have come on so far in years but still be fighting?

I open a box file and take out another bundle of papers. Something falls out and hits the floor with a metallic sound. I pick it up. It's a pin; the type you might fix to a lapel.

'Look at this,' I say to Jeremy.

He gives a little start. 'Good heavens. Someone donated that to us a few years ago but it got lost in the archives. Clever you!'

'Does it signify something?' I ask.

'Well,' he says slowly. 'There was talk – still is – of a group of men and women in Sidmouth who were training undercover to feed information through to Churchill in the event of an invasion.'

Vera had alluded to something similar during one of our walks.

'Rumour also has it,' he continues, 'that they were trained in the use of firearms. At the end of the war, there was a big explosion on top of Peak Hill. The word was that they'd blown up their weapons so they couldn't get into trouble.'

'Wow!' This sounds like something out of James Bond. 'What about the pin?'

He touches it in the palm of his hand, almost reverently. 'In 1944, it was given to those who were in the secret army as a token of recognition for their courage. By then, most of their work was over.'

'So they didn't wear it before, while they were under-cover?'

'No. But some of them wore Home Guard uniform with a battalion number on it that identified them to those in the know. They operated in cells. Many of them might have known each other socially but not been aware that they were in the same cell. The butcher might not have known he was fighting alongside the postmistress, for instance. But one way of identifying them was that many carried a Fairbairn-Sykes knife.'

'But how do you know this? Is it written down in one of these accounts?'

Jeremy looks awkward. 'No. I was actually told by a relative of a man who was involved. She didn't want her name mentioned. Or his. But she felt the pin had historical significance, which is why she gave it to me.'

I feel a sense of rising excitement inside me. 'Can't you ask her if she'll be named in the book? It's just the sort of thing that would get the museum publicity.'

Jeremy places a hand on my arm. It's only brief but I feel his anxiety. 'Not so fast, Nancy. The Second World War might seem a long time ago, but this is Sidmouth. Families carry secrets like they do in many small communities. It wouldn't be right to expose them.'

'But why not? They were doing good, weren't they?'

Again there's that flash across his face. 'One would like to think so. But like any group under threat, tensions must have run deep.' He gives a little shake. 'Now let's keep going through these boxes, shall we?'

'What about the pin?' I ask.

'I'll keep that safe,' he says firmly.

Part of me wants to tell this man everything about the night of the farmhouse murder; he seems so trustworthy, so forgiving. But instead, I force myself to stay quiet. It's what I'm good at, after all.

When I get home, everything seems as I left it. Sheba is asleep by the Aga.

I'm about to put on the kettle when my mobile rings. *Alex.* I press Decline.

Then I get out the vacuum cleaner and fiercely clean the carpet in the hall. As I do so, I notice a letter that must have fluttered under a chair. It has a postmark showing it had been sent a few days earlier – as well as an HMP franking print. I don't remember hearing any post being delivered and hadn't been aware of Sheba's usual barking. Maybe we'd been out for a walk.

Shaking, I tear it open, deciphering as I read.

Dear Nancy,

How are you doing? Everything is fine here. The sun is out and I can hear the birds singing through the bars of my cell. My pad mate is in for killing his wife. Once a day, we go out for exercise round the yard.

Meanwhile, I am on the cleaning rota for the wing. Yesterday I found a razor blade on the floor in the shower. It happens. You have to keep your wits about you.

Sorry about the other day. I had to ring off because the guy behind me said he'd 'get me' if I didn't. I needed to hear your voice, Nancy. You've got to visit me. It's awful here. My pad mate is a psycho. He should be in the mental wing but there's no room.

Remember to do everything I told you. Also remember that I'll always love you. You owe me, Nancy. So visit. NOW.

Love Martin

It takes me a while to figure out all these ramblings because my memory of our teenage code is a bit rusty. He hadn't used it in the first letter, but he had clearly wanted to signal something in this one. The 'you owe me' bit. Thank goodness he hadn't written this in plain English.

But what if Martin goes public? Would anyone believe him? It's possible.

Then it comes to me. Maybe I should change tack. Perhaps I ought to visit him after all. If I can see him face to face, I might be able to put an end to it.

I do a Google search. I find the number.

And I ring.

'HMP Knockton,' says a voice.

'I would like to visit one of your prisoners,' I say, my voice trembling. 'Martin Greenfield. As soon as possible, please.'

29

It's taken over a fortnight to organize the paperwork. I've had to fill in various forms and, ridiculously, wait for him to agree that Martin is happy to see me.

He is.

I have been instructed to bring in identifying documents.

And now, here I am, on the 7.53 train from Honiton to Waterloo.

The passing countryside is pretty, with its oxbow lakes and outlying farms, but I can't relax. What is it that Martin wants me to do? Is he ever going to leave me alone?

Then again, I don't deserve peace. I should be in prison. Like him.

To distract myself, I get out my phone and scroll through my pictures. They go back months. Years. There's Mum and me – we're doing a selfie during a day out at Hampton Court. It was taken two years before she died. In the picture we both look as though we're really happy. We were good at hiding our feelings.

There's Alex. This one was taken just before I called off the wedding.

'I can't marry him without telling him what happened,' I remember telling Claire.

'He'd understand,' she assured me. 'Why don't I tell him?'

'No,' I said. Shouted, actually. 'I'm too ashamed.'

Claire held me. 'But it was years ago, Nancy. You were still a child. It wasn't your fault.'

I think of Martin and how he would flick back my hair gently when we were sitting next to each other, listening to music. It seemed rude to ask him not to.

'I know. But it's damaged me, Claire. And I can't make it go away. It wouldn't be fair on Alex.'

'I think he'd help you.'

'No one can,' I sobbed.

Sometimes I wonder if I am imagining what happened. According to the books I've read, people can have false memories. But now, ironically, as I go back through the older pictures on my phone, I find one of Martin just after my graduation. We're having a celebratory pub lunch with our parents. He has his arm around me. I remember that he'd put it there just before someone took the shot for us. Afterwards, I'd stepped quickly away.

I scroll back to more recent pics. One in particular makes me stop, even though I've looked at it enough times. It's the picture of the letter Martin had sent me, which I'd photographed on my phone before throwing it in the bin.

At the time, I just wanted to put it behind me. But some kind of instinct, which I can't explain, makes me go online to find the original newspaper article. It screams out at me along with the picture of Martin's letter with the caption 'Murderer proclaims love for stepsister'. Again, something isn't right, but I don't know what.

So I go to a website where people comment on articles. And there it is. 'The bloke can't even spell,' says someone.

Of course. I'm a copywriter, aren't I? How did I miss this? It changes everything.

The prison is on the other side of London, an hour away from Waterloo plus a forty-minute walk. I decide to get a taxi instead. After all, I can afford it now.

'Been here before, have you?' asks the driver as we approach the prison.

He talks as if I'm here on holiday.

'No,' I say shortly.

We turn right suddenly and go down a drive to what looks like a stately home. I hadn't been expecting this.

'Are we here?' I ask.

'That's the administration block,' says the driver. 'They keep the men locked up on the right.'

He jerks his head towards a high wall with coiled barbed wire on top.

'Ever visited a prison before?' he asks.

'No,' I say quietly.

'Good luck, love,' he says.

I make my way to the entrance, holding my head high. Telling myself that I can do this. That prison is no big deal. I've been in worse situations.

The huge door is firmly shut. There's a notice on one side declaring that anyone who enters with illegal substances could be prosecuted.

I glance at the people in the queue. They're the kind you might see anywhere. At a bus stop. In the supermarket. In the office.

They talk in hushed whispers. One or two nod at each other, suggesting they are regulars.

My mouth is dry. I don't belong here. But I deserve to.

When the huge door is opened, we go in, one at a time.

There's a list of items that we aren't allowed to take in. It includes mobile phones, any other electronic devices, chewing gum, sticky tape and umbrellas.

'They can use gum to duplicate keys,' says a well-dressed woman, noticing my confusion. 'Sticky tape can be used to gag people. And umbrellas have a sharp point. Don't worry. You'll soon get the hang of it.'

I've no intention of 'getting the hang of it'. I am here for one visit only.

'Sit here,' says an officer sharply. She indicates a strange-looking seat. There's a notice that states that the chair contains a 'body camera' and that this might not be suitable for anyone who's pregnant.

'It's to check you're not carrying drugs inside you,' says the officer. Her tone is softer now. Perhaps she realizes I'm new at this.

My fingerprints are then taken on an electronic pad. I have to put my bag in a locker. Finally, I go into a hall that looks like a school gymnasium, except that there are several small tables with men in green tabards sitting at them.

I realize I'm clenching my teeth so hard that my jaw hurts. I look for Martin but can't see him.

Maybe it's because the hall is quite full already. The people who were in front of me in the queue are already sitting. Talking in loud voices. Whispering. Arguing.

There are children too. I'm surprised by this. Some are playing at the back with toys. There's a coffee bar at the side. It's a surreal mixture of normal and abnormal.

That's when I see a hand raised high. 'Nancy! I'm over here!'

'No shouting,' barks an officer.

Martin is sitting at a table, wearing a green tracksuit under his tabard. He is thinner than when I last saw him. He needs to shave. But his childlike smile is the same. I want to be sick.

'You came!' he says, jumping up to give me a hug. He speaks as if we're a caring brother and sister – which I suppose, in some people's eyes, we were. The press would have it that we still are. 'About time.'

'No touching,' roars an officer.

I sit down. He smells of sweat. Martin had always been fastidiously clean to the point of fussiness. He would stay in the bath for hours and use up all the hot water. My mother was forever complaining.

Then his face stops being friendly and his eyes narrow. 'Why didn't you visit earlier? How could you just leave me here in this hell-hole? Do you know what it's like to be the only one in my wing who hasn't had any visitors?'

'I've come here for one reason,' I say, looking down at the floor. I don't want to see his face. It will take me back there.

'To tell me you love me?' he asks.

I have to look up now. 'You know that's not true, Martin. Stop messing around.'

He makes a sarcastic 'sorry' clown-like face. 'I'm not. You were the one who kissed me, remember?'

'That's not true,' I say sharply, glancing at the people either side of us to check if they had heard him. Thankfully they seem engrossed in their own conversations.

'I know you wanted me to, though,' he says.

A memory comes back to me as he speaks. We'd been sitting side by side on the carpet during one of our Leonard Cohen nights in Tall Chimneys. To my surprise, he had suddenly leaned towards me and put his mouth on mine.

'I just want to be friends,' I'd said, pulling away.

'Sure,' he'd replied. But after that he kept giving me secret smiles that made me feel even more uncomfortable. I tried sitting away from him during family meals. But he always found a way of sidling up next to me. It was a huge relief when he finally went back to his mother for the rest of the holidays.

I'd been so shocked by the kiss that I made the mistake of telling Claire. 'So you got there first,' she said coolly.

'Did *you* fancy him?' I'd asked.

'Course not, silly. I meant that you've kissed a boy before I have.'

'It's not a competition,' I said, surprised.

'Of course it's not,' she said, laughing as if I'd just said something very stupid.

It was after that when she ignored me for a bit and hung out with other girls. Later, when she got a boyfriend of her own, she started being friendly again. Neither of us spoke about this estrangement, but it was always there in my mind. She'd really hurt me.

I'm also aware that there were occasions when I treated him like the big brother I'd always wanted, phoning him that time when I thought I was being followed down the street. I hadn't known who else to call and I was scared. But looking back, I can see that I might have sent out the wrong message.

'There's nothing between us,' I say now. 'There never has been.'

His face darkens. 'That's not true. Besides, aren't you forgetting the night our parents died?'

Bile rises into my mouth.

'Actually, I'd like to talk about something else first,' I say. 'Two things, actually. How did you get my new phone number?'

He looks pleased with himself. 'That's the one good thing about this place. There's always someone who knows someone who can do something for you. At a price, of course. Tracking down phone numbers is much easier than I thought. So don't bother changing yours again, 'cos I'll find it.'

I'm trying hard not to show the fear inside me. That fear that there really is no escape from this lunatic step-brother of mine.

'What's the second thing?' he asks, sitting forward on his seat as if he's a bright pupil keen to get the next answer right.

'That first letter you wrote to me,' I say. 'The one that said you'd always love me. The one that wasn't in code.'

He grins. 'Thought you'd like it. I didn't expect you to hand it to the newspapers, mind you.'

There he goes again. Turning everything round.

'Why would I do that, Martin?'

He shrugs. 'I don't know. Why would anyone do anything?'

I'm not letting him do this to me any more. Confusing me so I say things I don't want to or mean to.

'The thing is, Martin, that you wrote two letters, didn't

you? One for me and one for the press. You thought they were the same, but you made a mistake.'

His brows knit together the way they used to as a child when his father told him off for some minor demeanour, like not sitting still at the table.

'What are you talking about?'

'I took a picture of the letter you sent me before I tore it up. I compared it with the picture of the letter in the papers. The handwriting was the same. But there was a spelling error in one. Remember that line, "We are bound together for life because of what happened in the farmhouse"?'

He nods.

'Well "life" is spelt "live" in the newspaper article. But in the letter you sent me it's spelt the right way. "Life". They don't match, Martin. You must have made a copy and sent it to the press.'

A flash of fear crosses his face. Then it goes and he shakes his head. 'Why would I do that, Nance?'

He knows I hate it when he calls me that.

'Because you wanted to create public suspicion about what happened. I don't see why.' I drop my voice. 'You told me to stay quiet.'

I can see anger now in his face. 'But I expected you to write and visit.'

'So you *did* do it.'

'All right, it was me. I wanted everyone to know that I'll never give up on you. Don't you see, Nancy? We can make a life together when I get out.'

If this wasn't so mad, I would laugh. 'That's not going to happen. Besides, you're never going to get out after what you did.'

His face turns dark again. His eyes narrow. I see his father in them. I can smell apples in the cellar. Bile rises in my throat and my stomach turns itself inside out.

'Yes I am,' he hisses. 'Because I've got a new lawyer. She's going to see if I can appeal against my conviction. I've had enough of your behaviour. Do you know how humiliating it is to queue up for post on the wing and be the only one who never gets a letter? You've let me down. Remember, I could tell them everything.'

It's true. He could. I need to get out of this place.

'Please don't go,' he says as I stand up. 'You're my only link with the outside. I might not have long. Someone's going to kill me in here one day. I just know it. Last week, a kid on my wing threw boiling water and sugar at an older man in the queue because he wouldn't hand over his tea rations. Now the poor bloke is in intensive care. They say no one will recognize hm. Not even his own mother.'

I'm shocked. 'Can't the officers do anything about it?'

Martin laughs scornfully. 'Some of them encourage it, especially if it means a troublemaker is going to get moved on as a result.'

He grabs my wrists, squeezes both of them tight, just as he did on the night it happened, and drops them before one of the guards notices. 'You have to help me, Nancy. You need to back me up. Not just to save my skin. But to save your skin too.'

His voice softens again. 'You've got such a beautiful face, Nancy. I wouldn't want anyone to spoil it.'

30

'Appeal?' snorts Judith when I ring her as soon as I get back. 'Martin hasn't got a leg to stand on. There's no fresh evidence. Prisoners often talk about appealing after they've been sentenced. They can't take the thought of a long stretch. He's harassing you. We can file a complaint to the prison about that.'

'No,' I say quickly. 'I don't want to antagonize him.'

'Then my advice is to ignore him and not visit again,' she says. Her brisk tone suggests that is the end of it.

But I can't get Martin's threats out of my head.

Then there's the matter of the two letters. Martin's now admitted he sent a second letter (the one with the misspelling) to the press. But what really happened to the one I put in the bin?

Is it possible that Alex lied about it being in Jasmine's room because he feared Jasmine would tell me about his past? It would give support to his argument that she wasn't to be trusted.

Do I believe my new friend? There was no doubting the passion and hurt in Jasmine's eyes when she'd told me how Alex had ruined her brother's life.

We all make mistakes. Don't I know that myself? Alex had been very vague about his childhood when we'd first met. And even when we got serious, he kept making excuses for not introducing me to his family.

When I'd pressed him for more details, he'd become brusque and then withdrawn. 'I don't want to talk about it.' He didn't even want them on the wedding-guest list.

Part of me accepted that because, after all, hadn't I kept things hidden from him about my earlier teenage life?

But running someone over and not stopping, and then claiming someone else was driving, is unforgivable. Perhaps I've had a lucky escape. You can't commit to someone if they're not honest about their past, can you?

Then again, who am I to talk? It's not as if I've been honest with Alex about *my* past.

Minutes after I speak to Judith, the phone goes again.

'Yes?' I say tersely. I've stopped answering with my name.

'Nancy? This is Jeremy. Sorry to bother you but I've just come across something rather interesting in a cutting from the *Sidmouth Herald* in 1941.'

I'm about to say that this isn't a good time to talk but he carries on.

'It says – and I quote – "There is still no news of the two people missing after the recent bomb raid. Names will not be released until they are found, out of respect to their next of kin."'

Despite being so stressed over Martin, I feel disappointment in Jeremy's finding. 'So we don't know if it's linked with the earlier story you found about someone going missing from Tall Chimneys?'

'Unfortunately not. As far as I can see from later editions, the newspaper doesn't mention these two people again. In fact, it's almost as if it was hushed up. Then again, it was wartime. It wasn't that long after Exeter was bombed. People didn't say much in public in case the Germans got hold of a rumour or snippet of news and used it in some way. The whole town was terrified about being invaded.'

Hadn't Vera said something similar?

I think of the eagle statue in commemoration of the Allied Forces. And I think of the writing on the wall in my bedroom.

'Have you found out any more about Maisie?' I ask.

Privately, I have a picture of her and poor Shirley in my head. Two rosy-cheeked friends, rather like Claire and me the first time she had joined me here for the holidays, though in old-fashioned clothes. Gingham dresses. Clean white socks and patent shoes. Poor Maisie. She must have been devastated at losing her friend. Just as I would be if I lost Claire.

'Afraid not. Presumably she went back to London after the war. Most of them did. But it would have been a big upheaval for them. When you read real-life accounts, many of the evacuees didn't settle. They'd got used to being away from home. Some stayed on and married locals.'

'Are any of them still alive?' I ask.

'The last one died a few months ago, sadly.'

So I've missed them. Missed the chance to ask any of them about Tall Chimneys and this person who disappeared. Still, I've got enough to worry about right now.

Like being arrested.

My mind is whirling after Jeremy's call. Is history repeating itself? Had there been a murder here? Just like there had been at the farmhouse?

What if there are some people who make death happen

around them? What if it's following my family? My mind goes to the cellar, and I can feel the panic rising. My chest is tight. I can't breathe properly.

There's only one person alive now who knows what happened that summer when I was fifteen. Only one person I can trust. So I ring her.

'Someone went missing from your house during the war,' repeats Claire when I tell her. 'And they never found the body?'

I shiver, even though it's not that cold. 'I knew this a few weeks ago actually . . .'

'Why didn't you tell me?'

'Because I wanted to brush it under the carpet, perhaps,' I admit. 'I've had enough of death.' My voice rises to an almost hysterical level. 'Maybe it's my fault, Claire.' Then I voice my earlier fear. 'Perhaps I bring death to every place I've been in.'

Her voice is reassuring in the same way my mother's used to be when I was a child and crying about my father. 'Take a deep breath, Nancy. That's right. Now, let's try to be logical about this. You don't know for certain that either of these missing people actually died.'

'I'm also talking about the other thing.'

Her voice changes. 'I told you before, Nancy. You've got to forget it or you'll never have a proper relationship with anyone. If you'd only told Alex about –'

'Stop!' I say. 'I can't talk about that.'

But instead of being sympathetic, Claire sounds angry. 'All right, we won't. But how do you know Jasmine is telling the truth about Alex and her brother? You've barely met her. She's clearly bitter about him going to prison, so

I suspect she's trying to shift the blame away from him. I know who *I'd* believe. Alex is a good guy, Nancy. He's much better suited to you than you realize.'

'Why are you so sure? I haven't known him that long. I don't know that much about him. I've never even met his family. In fact, I was crazy to agree to getting married. It was only because he seemed kind and I was . . .'

I stop, tears filling my eyes, before continuing.

'. . . I was lonely,' I sob.

'I know.' Claire's voice is softer now. 'But I think you should see him and listen to what he has to say.'

'I'll think about it,' I promise. Then, partly to get her off the subject, I tell her about my visit to Martin and the letters. It works.

'You can't afford to ignore threats like that. Ring the police.'

'There's no point. What are they going to do? Put a twenty-four-hour watch on me? They don't have resources for that kind of thing.'

'Are you sure you're all right there on your own, Nancy?'

'Quite sure,' I say firmly. And I am. I feel a bit calmer after speaking to her.

'Good,' she says. 'Because if it was me . . . Ow!'

'Are you all right?'

'Probably Braxton Hicks again.'

I still can't believe at times that my friend is going to be a mother.

Don't leave it too late for me to be a grandmother, my mother used to say. At the time I was annoyed. It was none of her business. Now it makes me desperately sad.

'You'd better go,' I say.

'Yes,' she says. 'I've got a check-up with the clinic. See you soon. And don't worry. This will all pass in time.'

But it won't, will it? I know she means to be helpful. But nothing can bring back Mum.

And nothing can take away my guilt.

31

The knock comes at my door just after 7 a.m. Sheba races there but she's not barking in the way she does for strangers. It's an excited bark.

Jasmine is there.

'Thought we could go for a swim,' she says, handing me a wetsuit. 'Take this. It's a spare.'

I hesitate, thinking of what Claire had said. Supposing Jasmine was lying about Alex and her brother?

'I'm not sure. It's pretty cold.'

'Come on,' she says. 'You'll love it. It'll blow your mind.'

I think of my father and how he had loved swimming in the sea before breakfast.

'You're crazy,' my mother would laugh when he came back in his trunks.

'Nothing like it,' he'd say, giving her a hug.

'Don't get me wet!' she'd squeal.

Then he'd reach out an arm to me and we'd all cuddle each other.

Maybe swimming with Jasmine will be better than sitting at home and worrying what Martin is going to do next.

'It's FREEZING!' I scream when we get in.

'Brilliant, isn't it?' grins Jasmine. 'I love the shot of adrenalin. Don't you? Better than sex if you ask me. Keep swimming and you'll get warm. The water becomes sealed inside the suit. You'll see.'

She's right. Before long, we're swimming side by side in the water. 'So,' she says, 'what were you up to in London?'

'How did you know where I'd gone?'

'Vera told me.'

Of course. I'd asked my neighbour to have Sheba while I'd gone.

'I was visiting someone,' I say vaguely.

'Was it Alex?'

'No.' Then I blurt it out. 'I went to visit my stepbrother in prison.'

'Why?' She stops swimming. We're not far out. Our feet can just touch the bottom.

I take a deep breath. 'I owe you an apology. I realized Martin must have sent a copy of the letter to the papers. I'd taken a picture of the one I tore up, you see. But the letter printed in the paper had a word that was spelt differently.'

'OK.'

Jasmine is giving me an odd look.

'So Alex must've been lying. I'm sorry I thought you'd sold it to a journalist.'

Her eyes are focused straight on me. Unwavering. 'I'd never do anything like that. It's not me.'

She sounds so honest. But how can I be absolutely certain? What if there's some other reason for all this?

My own eyes are beginning to water, and not just from the sea. 'The thing is that it's really important for me to be able to trust people.'

'It's important for all of us, isn't it?'

'Yes but . . . well, my dad died from leukaemia when I was young and then my mother married Martin's dad, who was horrible, and then she . . . well, she didn't stand up for me when she should have done, and now Alex . . .'

Tears are pouring down my face and I'm shivering.

'I think we'd better get out,' says Jasmine. 'Let's go and have a nice hot drink.'

'Don't you have work?'

'The kennels let me go.' Jasmine is looking upset. 'The virus knocked us for six and it's never really picked up. I've tried to get some extra work in town but there's not much going.'

'I'm sorry.'

'It's OK.' Jasmine is linking her arm through mine as we make our way out of the water. 'Something good will turn up. And it will for you too. You'll see.'

We buy a takeaway chocolate at the Fort Café on the way home. 'My treat,' I insist.

I can almost pretend that we are just two friends having a drink together without a care in the world.

When I get home – the house is beginning to feel like that – I check my mobile to find a missed call from an unknown number.

I check to see if the sender left a message.

There's nothing.

Then it rings again.

'You're there,' says Martin. There's loud shouting in the background and the sound of doors banging. 'Thank God for that. This is my last chance to use the phone before I have to go back to my cell.'

'What do you want?' I say. 'We said everything we needed to on my visit.'

'But I miss you, Nancy.' His voice is beseeching, like a

child's. 'I need you. I can't live without you. Ever since your visit, I can't stop thinking about you. I want to smell your hair. Run my hands through it. Hold you against me. We have to be together again. You've got to get me out of this place. Please.'

'We don't have to be together again, Martin, because we were never together in the first place.'

Anger is rising up now in my chest. 'I've had enough of these games. My lawyer says your appeal will never work. You're in prison for life. I don't love you. And I'm never going to see you again. I'm sorry, but you have to accept the truth. None of this would have happened if it hadn't been for you. And the sooner you accept this, the better.'

Then I slam down the phone.

32

Despite my words, I am shaking with fear. I try to reassure myself. Prison is a secure place. He can't get out. Then I remind myself of Judith's words. No grounds for appeal.

I try to think of something that will calm me down. I know: I'll get down the recipe book and start making a cheese quiche. It was one of my mother's favourite recipes. How often had I watched her make pastry by hand? 'The trick is to get all the lumps out of the flour,' she would tell me.

I pick some spinach I had spotted in the overgrown vegetable patch. I parboil it and line the case before adding garlic, grated extra-strong Cheddar cheese and sliced vine tomatoes. Then I put it in the Aga. The simple domestic routine helps.

Until the phone rings again.

Alex.

He rushes in before I can speak. 'Claire's told me about Martin harassing you. I don't like the sound of it.'

'It's not your business any more,' I say curtly. 'Especially after what you did. It turns out I don't know you as well as I'd thought.'

'If you're referring to the car accident, Claire told me that, too. Jasmine's lying. Her brother *was* driving.'

'Why should I believe you?'

'So you believe someone you've hardly met rather than the man you were going to marry?'

He sounds hurt. 'We have to meet. Please, Nancy. We could go somewhere neutral. How about Stonehenge the day after tomorrow? It's halfway between us and I have a job near there.'

'I don't know . . .'

'I beg you. Give me a chance to explain myself.'

And against my better instincts, I agree.

When I pull up at Stonehenge, Alex is already waiting in the car park.

Despite myself, my heart gives a flip.

'You came,' he says. He doesn't move to hug me. Maybe he knows I'd step aside if he did.

'Did you think I wouldn't?'

'I wasn't sure. Shall we walk?'

Sheba is straining on the lead. I can't let her off here. There are tourists, and the main road is not far away. Besides, she has become my security blanket.

'We need to talk about how to keep you safe.' His mouth is set. His jaw clenched.

'You're not engaged to me any more,' I point out. 'It's not your responsibility, Alex. What I really want to know is why you lied about seeing Martin's letter in Jasmine's room? Did you want to make her look bad because she knows about your past?'

His mouth sets again. 'First of all, I didn't lie. It was there. I saw it. It was pieced together with sticky tape as if it had been torn up and put back together.'

Alex speaks so firmly that I almost believe him. Then his voice gets quieter. 'But you're right. I do have a past that I am ashamed of. Jasmine doesn't know the half of it.'

'Tell me,' I say grimly.

We're standing in front of one of the huge stones. What stories have they heard in their time? Worse than the one I suspect I'm going to hear now? Sheba sits by my feet, as if waiting too.

'I was a bit of a troublemaker at school,' says Alex slowly. 'Nothing awful at first. I'd answer back in class and once I was caught with a bottle of wine at break time. It was my birthday and I was just showing off in front of my mates. We all thought we were pretty cool, and Paul – Jasmine's brother – was desperate to be part of the crowd. I felt sorry for him. So I asked him to come along to this party I was going to.'

His brow creases. 'I should never have done that. Or it might not have happened.'

'What might not have happened?' I ask nervously.

Alex sighs. 'When I left the party, Paul tagged along too. There was a car outside the house – a really smart sports car – and the keys were still in it. Paul talked me into taking it for a drive. We were both having driving lessons but neither of us had passed the test. I know. You're right to look like that. It was crazy. But I'd had a few drinks – we both had – and it seemed like a good idea.'

He lets out a groan. I steel myself. 'We weren't going that fast but it was icy on the roads and we kept sliding around. Then . . .'

His face crumples. 'Then someone stepped out in front of us from nowhere. There was this awful thud. We got out and saw this body lying in the road and we freaked out. We both ran off. Me to my place and Paul to his. Then, that night, the police knocked on the door and hauled me down to the station. Paul told them that I was driving.'

'I know,' I say. 'Jasmine told me.'

'But she's wrong.' His voice rises and someone nearby looks at us. 'It was Paul at the wheel. He told his family and the police that it was me because he was scared. Luckily, forensics showed otherwise, but he always claimed they'd made a mistake and that I was the real culprit.'

He puts his head in his hands. 'In a way, I was.'

'Why? You said you weren't driving.'

'I wasn't. But, like I said, I'd had some drinks and I taunted him for not driving faster. So he did. If I hadn't done that, he might not have had the accident.'

I gulp, trying to take this in. 'And the man you knocked over – was he all right?'

'Yes, apart from a fractured leg. But he must have been traumatized.'

'Yes,' I say. 'He would have been.'

'I left Devon to try to make a fresh start. Besides, my family didn't want anything to do with me. They said I'd brought shame on them, whether I'd been driving or not. I started my own life in London and have never broken the law since then. I've not seen Paul, or his family – including Jasmine. But I've always been aware that one day, someone would tap on my shoulder and bring it all back.'

I know the feeling. Alex and I share more than he knows. More than I want to admit.

'Then I met you, Nancy,' he continues, 'and I realized from the minute we spoke that you were the one. But I also guessed you wouldn't want me if you knew the old Alex.'

'Does Claire know any of this?'

'No.'

'If she did, she might not be so keen for us to get back together,' I say.

'Haven't you ever done anything wrong, Nancy?'

I stiffen. 'Why do you say that?'

'I'm just saying that we all make mistakes. Yes – I was reckless, dangerous even, in my teens. But please don't hold it against me now.'

I'm so close to making my own confession that I daren't say anything.

Alex's voice thickens. 'I can't bear the idea of not having you in my life any more.'

'I can't be with you, Alex. Things are too different now.'

I'll miss him too. But I have to protect him as well as myself.

'You might not feel that way for ever,' he says.

'I think I will. I'm sorry, Alex.'

He gives a quick nod as if trying to absorb this.

'OK. But we can still keep in touch, can't we? Meet up every now and then? Phone calls? I need to know you're all right, Nancy.'

'I will be,' I say.

Then we part.

I cry all the way home. How I yearn for Alex to put his arms around me.

But if he knew the real Nancy, he would run a mile.

When I pull up outside the house, Vera is there.

'A courier left something with me for you,' she says.

'Thank you.'

Her eyes search mine. 'How are you doing?'

'Getting there,' I lie.

Her eyes are now focused on the small box that she hands over. 'Something for the house, is it?'

If she expects me to open the package in front of her, she's wrong. I wait until she's gone and I've shut the door behind her. It takes ages to open all the protective cardboard layers. When I do, I feel sick.

It's a packet of sugar. And a note.

33

PUT THE KETTLE ON. I'M ON MY WAY.

The note is one of those gift messages that you can get with online deliveries.

Could this mean what I think it does?

Martin's words from my visit come back to me. *'You've got such a beautiful face, Nancy. I wouldn't want anyone to spoil it.'*

My whole body starts shaking. I want to be sick.

Should I tell the police? But if I do, and they interview Martin, he might be angry enough to tell them what really happened.

Yet can I risk *not* telling them?

A memory comes back into my head from when Martin was about sixteen.

'He scares me,' I heard Mum telling Duncan. 'I don't want him in the house.'

'But he's my son.'

'Look what he did to his own mother!'

'What?' I asked, coming into the room after overhearing the conversation.

'Nothing,' they both said. If only Mum hadn't been trying to protect Duncan, as always. If only she had told me that my stepbrother could be violent.

Later, during the court case, it came out that Martin had frequently punched his mother, leaving her with bruises.

She'd refused to report this to the police because she didn't want him to be charged and get a record.

It's why I am so scared of him now. If Martin could attack others, he could do the same to me.

I rush round the house, closing the windows and locking the doors. Then Sheba makes a whining noise. She's nosing at the side door. I freeze. 'Who's there?' I call out.

'It's me, Jasmine.'

Speak of the devil. If it hadn't been for the shock of Martin's package, I would have gone straight to her place to confront her with Alex's side of the story.

I open the door.

Jasmine doesn't look her usual self. Her mascara is streaked. Her hair is a mess.

'I'm so sorry, Nancy,' she blurts out. 'I have to tell you the truth. Alex didn't lie. He *did* see Martin's letter in my bedroom – the one that you ripped up. I taped it back together I'd seen you from my window, putting it in the bin. One of those journalists who came round said he'd make it worth my while if I kept an eye out for anything that you did. I know it sounds awful but I've been struggling to make the rent. So I sneaked over and took the bits. I was going to sell it to the papers but then you were so nice to me and my conscience got the better of me so I didn't. When it appeared in the paper anyway, I thought someone else must have got hold of a copy. I panicked when you asked me about it. I wish I'd just told you the truth then. I'm really sorry.'

'Why are you confessing all this now?' I ask coldly.

'Because it's been preying on my mind for so long that

I thought I'd go mad if I didn't come clean. Besides, you're my friend and –'

I cut in. 'We're not friends any more,' I say icily. 'I should have believed Alex in the first place instead of trusting someone I hardly know.'

'Nancy, I am so –'

'Just leave!' I shout.

I sink to the kitchen floor, in front of the Aga, wrapping my arms around my knees and rocking back and forth like a child. I can't trust anyone.

A whole day passes. Nothing happens.

Maybe I'd overreacted. Martin had only wanted to scare me.

I go into the museum to help catalogue more archives. 'You seem a bit quiet,' says Jeremy.

'Just tired,' I tell him.

'Why don't you go home early,' he says kindly. 'Besides, there's going to be a storm tonight. We'll all be battening down the hatches. Rather cosy, don't you think?'

It might be if there was someone else with me. I think of Alex for a minute and then tell myself that there's no way it could work. Not now.

I'm nervous when I let myself into Tall Chimneys. But there's no need to be. It all seems fine. No more deliveries. No open doors. No notes.

Sheba nudges me. She needs her evening walk. Just as I get her lead on, my mobile rings.

UNKNOWN CALLER

'Nancy?'

I recognize the DI's voice immediately.

'Yes?'

'I need you to listen carefully.' His voice is taut. 'Stay inside. Lock the doors. We'll be with you as soon as we can.'

'What's happened?' I ask, even though I already know the answer.

'Martin has escaped from prison. We think he's on his way to you.'

I drop the phone, my hands clumsy with fear.

Sheba is growling now. A low, throaty growl. She's standing up on her paws against the kitchen counter, snarling.

I haven't drawn the blind yet. The light from Vera's house is on and I can see outside.

A wind must have whipped up. The apple tree's branches – the ones that Vera had advised me to prune when I first arrived – are rattling against the window.

Sheba is getting frantic.

Then I leap back in fright.

Martin's face looms up before me through the glass.

The Night of the Murder

8.16 p.m.

My birthday present to Mum is a photograph album. I have care-fully stuck in photos of me and Mum and Dad from the days when it was just the three of us.

It's a gift that, I admit, was designed to annoy Duncan.

But I didn't know it was going to backfire on me.

'I remember that one,' he slurs, pointing to a picture taken not long before Dad died. 'It was when I started to comfort your mother. She found it so hard to cope, poor dear. You needed a loving pair of arms around you. Isn't that right, Violet?'

My mouth goes dry. 'Tell me he's lying, Mum.'

Her moment's hesitation is enough. Anger and disbelief bubble up inside me.

I turn to Martin. 'Do you want to know why I told your father it was too late to behave?'

And then it all comes tumbling out of my mouth.

Elizabeth

34

Christmas 1941 onwards

The man appeared out of nowhere.

Elizabeth was walking slowly back home from town with the weekly ration of margarine and sugar, thinking of Robert, as she always did these days, when a tall man stepped out in front of her.

She jumped, shaken.

'I'm so sorry,' he said. Then he appeared to do a double-take. 'Mrs Montague?'

'Yes,' she said. Then she realized the man was Jim from the garage.

'I'm glad to see you, actually,' he said. 'I was wondering if we could have a word about your car.'

'The car?' Ordinary words didn't feel ordinary any more. She sometimes found that she had to keep repeating them before they made sense. 'But we don't use it because of petrol rationing,' she said. 'It's in the garage.'

'Exactly what I want to talk to you about,' he said. 'A mutual friend suggested I gave you some advice about it.' Then he gave her a quick wink.

That's when it began to dawn on her. Hadn't Adeline told her that someone would approach her in the next few days to 'vet' her? But could Jim really be part of the secret army?

'The second bridge in the Byes in five minutes,' he said quietly. Then, in a louder voice, he added, 'I'll call your husband then about the car, shall I?'

'That would be best,' she managed to say.

Five minutes? She'd have to rush. It was dark, but she could hear the sound of the water as the River Sid gushed its way past.

'Has Adeline told you what we do?' he asked as they huddled by the bridge. He used her friend's first name quite naturally.

'Only that you are preparing in case of invasion.'

'That's right. We need to be able to report back on the enemy's activities to headquarters if they come and, if necessary, fight.'

He said this in such a matter-of-fact way that Elizabeth wondered if she'd heard him right. Could this really be the man who mended their car during peacetime?

'Can you use a knife or a gun?'

'I've never used a knife, but I shoot rabbits sometimes,' she said, without mentioning that she didn't like it. It was something she had to do in order to help feed the PGs. 'But that's with a shotgun.'

'A pistol isn't that different. But would you be prepared to use a gun on a person?'

She thought of Robert being shot as he tried to escape. Dear God, please may he have died instantly. And she thought of little Shirley blasted to smithereens in the Blitz.

'If necessary, yes.'

Her answer seemed to satisfy him.

'To begin with, we'd have you on messenger duty. You'd

have to carry messages during our practices from one point to another.'

Was that all? Adeline had talked about her being a wireless operator. She wanted to be doing something useful.

'It's actually very important,' he said, as if reading her thoughts. 'It might be the only way we can communicate if the Germans reach us.'

'Where will I find these messages?' Her voice, she realized, still didn't sound like hers. It hadn't since the telegram.

'They'll be hidden in dead-letter boxes.'

'What are they?'

'Hiding places in farm gates, hollow trees and the like. Sometimes they're hidden in split tennis balls. Don't worry. You'll be given instructions soon enough.'

Then his tone turned heavy.

'Prove your salt and we'll put you on other duties. But if you're no good, you're out. We can't afford any weaknesses. And if you collaborate with the enemy when they invade, you will be shot yourself.'

'Of course I wouldn't,' she said indignantly.

'You'll also need to sign the Official Secrets Act.'

'Really?'

'This is serious work. It goes without saying that you cannot tell your family or anyone else.'

But *Adeline* had told her!

'If there is an invasion, you will be expected to leave your home immediately and rendezvous with the rest of the cell. And if you are captured, you will have to take the cyanide pill we will provide you with. We'll also give you training in unarmed combat.'

Elizabeth's mind was racing. This felt like a spy thriller.

He must have seen her expression. 'Are you up to this?' he asked.

She thought of Robert, killed by German bullets. 'Yes.'

'Good. We need folk like you who seem ordinary on the outside. We'll be in touch.'

'But when do I start training?'

'You'll be contacted. Remember. Patience is one of the greatest skills we need in our kind of work. That and ingenuity.'

Then he was gone.

Christmas was coming. Elizabeth tried, for Maisie's sake, to make it as cheery as possible. Together they made a little tree out of twigs, as suggested by one of the government leaflets. There was a shortage of spruce trees because of the war effort.

The Canadian and American soldiers held a party in town for the children. Some of the older residents complained about Sidmouth becoming 'foreign', but the Allies added a distinct flavour to the area. They really were so jolly and kind.

One evening, Henry actually came home with a turkey, though God knows how he'd got it. He was trying, at least.

But whenever she started to talk about Robert, he either went quiet or cut her down with some brusque remark like 'It's no good talking about things we can't do anything about.'

Sometimes he'd say this in front of the guests and more

than once she caught a comforting glance from Mr Smith, or even Mrs Norris.

Meanwhile, the secret army wasn't what she'd thought. Every now and then Elizabeth would receive a message. On it would be directions on how to find another note that might be in a farm gate or a milk churn or down by the sea under a rock. Once it was in a hole in the ground in the woods with a plank on top. That had taken some finding.

In that note would be instructions on where to leave the next one. But what was the point? It felt like a children's game.

On one occasion, she bumped into the Patmore sisters on a walk up on the hills. Elizabeth had been about to leave a message in a farm gate and panicked. 'Swallow it if you meet someone you know,' Jim had instructed her, 'even if it's someone you think you can trust. Don't worry. You won't choke. It's made of edible paper.'

Desperately she turned her head, hoping the sisters wouldn't see, and stuffed the note (luckily it was small) into her mouth. Ugh! She began coughing with the effort of getting it down.

'Are you all right?' called out the older one.

'Yes, thank you,' she managed to gasp. They insisted on giving her a swig from the whisky flask they carried for 'emergencies', which made her feel even guiltier.

'I don't understand what good I'm doing,' she complained to Adeline later. 'It's not as though it was for real – just a dummy run.'

Adeline was unusually serious. 'It's still important. When

the Germans invade, we'll have practised enough to pass on vital messages.'

When the Germans invade. Not *if*. In a way, Elizabeth was excited. It was her only means of avenging Robert's death. So what if she died in the process? It wasn't as if her own life was important now.

'Any news from George?' she asked.

'Yes. He's in North Africa.'

Adeline spoke in a tone that suggested she didn't want to say any more, so Elizabeth left it at that. Meanwhile, she'd started unarmed combat training with Jim in the woods. This was usually in the evening – she had to pretend to Henry she was 'going for a walk'. 'Not bad,' said Jim after she'd thrown him to the ground for the first time.

Spring arrived with white buds and sorrow that Robert wasn't here to see it. Elizabeth could tell from the chat in town that she wasn't the only one who felt a mounting sense of anxiety and fear coupled with frustration and uncertainty. When would this war end? It had gone on for so long. They'd said it would be over in a year. And now look. Here they were in 1942 and still no prospect of peace.

Then came the German raids on Exeter. Every night, again and again they heard them roaring overhead on their way to the city.

'God knows how many people have died,' said Adeline. 'Some say it's hundreds.' Her eyes watered. 'Children have perished too.'

It was tragic. So many lives. Elizabeth stopped complaining about the uselessness of delivering fake messages and threw herself into it with more enthusiasm.

'You're doing well,' said Jim approvingly. 'Before long you'll be given other jobs.'

'What?' she asked eagerly.

'You'll find out when the time comes. Meanwhile, I reckon you're ready for this.'

He took out a gun and handed it to her. 'Let's have a bit of practice in the woods, shall we? I'm going to be very clear on this. If you come across any German invaders, you are to shoot them. Can you do that?'

Before the war, Elizabeth would have been appalled at the thought of hurting anyone. But now it was different. Shoot the men who had taken her Robert? Of course she could.

Meanwhile, Singapore had surrendered to Japan and, in March, the RAF had launched a blistering attack on a German city called Lübeck. 'Good on them,' Henry had said. Yet despite her hatred of the Germans, Elizabeth found herself wondering about the foreign families who had been torn apart. Families who, maybe, had been caught up in a war they'd never wanted to happen.

Was she being disloyal to have thoughts like this? It was all so confusing.

Maisie stopped asking questions about Shirley and talked instead about nature trips and shell hunting and what they were doing at school. She also ceased writing to her friend. 'If she's moved house she won't be getting them any more, will she?' But she did carry on writing to her own mother every Sunday.

Then, one evening, when Elizabeth was walking Adeline's dog through the woods, she caught a glimpse of

Henry. His back was to her. He was standing very close to a tall blonde woman, their hands entwined.

Just as she was about to call out, they slipped away through the trees.

Stunned, she returned the dog and walked home. When he came back half an hour later, her husband was as cool as a cucumber.

'Where have you been?'

'Home Guard,' he said shortly.

'Dinner is ready,' she said, trying to keep her voice steady.

'I'll wash my hands.'

The strange thing was that she didn't care. Before the war, she might have had it out with him. Asked him to leave perhaps, even though divorce was a word that had never smeared her family.

Yet everything was different now. When the war was ended, maybe that would be the time for decisions.

'What do they tell *you* to do?' she asked Adeline when she went round to borrow an extra baking dish for some blackberries she had gathered. 'Are you still delivering messages?'

'I can't say,' she replied. Then she crossed one leg over the other, as though wanting Elizabeth to notice.

Elizabeth glanced at her nylons. 'Are those new?'

There wasn't one ladder on them. Elizabeth couldn't remember the last time she'd been able to buy new stockings.

'In fact, they were a present,' said Adeline.

Elisabeth gasped. 'From one of the Americans?'

'A Canadian, actually.'

She'd heard about the lavish gifts that the Americans and Canadians gave. Chocolates. Stockings. Cigarettes. The younger girls were all too happy to take the gifts. But many of the older women were concerned.

'If you accept a gift you might be expected to give something back in return,' one had said in the baker's the other day. Elizabeth couldn't help thinking she had a point.

'Where did you meet him?' she asked Adeline now.

'He came round to the hall with some chocolate bars for the children and we got chatting. Don't look like that, Elizabeth. There's nothing in it.'

'I hope not.'

'And there's no need to sound so prissy either. This is war, Elizabeth. Nothing is what it was.'

'Exactly. And what about George?'

Adeline laughed. 'I'm not having an affair, if that's what you're getting at. It's just a bit of fun, that's all.'

But fun could be dangerous. Elizabeth thought back to the man she'd seen Adeline hugging. Had she been telling the truth about him being part of the secret army? Her friend had changed since the war started.

Then again, didn't something in her tremble when she looked at Mr Smith at the dinner table or when he brought Maisie back from school, talking to the child kindly as if he was her father rather than a teacher. Henry had never been like that with Robert. He'd always been bossy and hard, expecting him to do more than his best.

'Have you heard about the mystery guest at one of the hotels on the front?' asked Adeline, interrupting her thoughts.

'No.'

Her friend lit a cigarette. 'Apparently there was some-one with a foreign accent staying there before the Exeter raids. Then afterwards he disappeared.'

Elizabeth felt a tremor running through her.

'Where did he come from?'

Adeline breathed out a blue ring of smoke. 'That's just it. No one knows. The registration papers he filled in had a false address.'

'That's awful. Don't you see? It's even more reason why you can't take gifts from strangers.'

'My Canadian friend isn't a stranger,' Adeline scoffed. 'He's on our side.'

'So he *is* a friend, is he?'

'Elizabeth.' Adeline reached out for her hand. 'I love you dearly. But, please, keep out of things you don't know anything about. Concentrate on your own marriage.'

She froze. 'What do you mean?'

'I wasn't going to tell you this but . . . well . . . there are rumours Henry's been seen with another woman . . . Polly Bright from the bakery.'

So that's who it was. 'I know,' said Elizabeth quietly.

Adeline stared. 'Why didn't you tell me?'

'Because I've chosen to ignore it.'

'Why?'

Elizabeth shrugged. 'Maybe I'm a coward.'

'I thought you were made of sterner stuff than that.'

'Well, maybe I'm not. Maybe I've more important things on my mind, like my son's death.'

Adeline touched her lightly on the shoulder. 'I'm sorry.'

Elizabeth turned away. She and Adeline rarely had disagreements but lately it seemed they had nothing in common. They parted on cool terms.

To cap it all, when she got home, water was dripping steadily through the ceiling into the kitchen.

'Looks like it's coming from Mr Smith's room,' said Mrs B. 'I went to find Mr Montague but he wasn't around.'

'Is Mr Smith out?' asked Elizabeth.

'Yes. He's at the school.'

'Of course. I'll go and see what's going on, then.'

She felt rather anxious about entering without asking him. Still, she needed to find out what was going on or goodness knows what damage there might be.

So that was the problem! A pipe was leaking; the one that fed his washbasin.

She'd bind a towel round it to make do, and then go to see the plumber. But as she went to leave the room, Elizabeth's gaze fell on the desk. There were papers on top. Piles of school work and, underneath, something poking out. A piece of paper with the word 'Ausweispapiere' on it. Below was a picture of Mr Smith with a signature beneath. Stefan Schmidt.

Elizabeth froze. These looked like identity papers.

Suddenly it all made sense.

Mrs Norris's sighting of the man on the beach with a torch, which she had foolishly disregarded.

'Stephen Smith' making himself indispensable at the boarding house.

'Stephen Smith' worming his way into her affections.

A foreigner staying at one of the local hotels, liaising, perhaps, with others.

The truth was staring her in the face.
Stefan Schmidt was a spy.
She had to tell the police!
But as she moved towards the door, it swung open.

35

Mr Smith – or rather Herr Schmidt – looked at her face and then at the document in her hand.

He seemed startled

'I can explain . . .' he began.

But then there was a high wailing sound. The air-raid siren.

'Quick, everyone,' shouted Mrs B from downstairs. 'The Germans are coming!'

'Help!' she started to scream, but he caught her by the sleeve.

'Please don't say anything. I can explain.'

Shaking him off, Elizabeth tore down the stairs to find Maisie in the kitchen before he killed them all. The siren was screaming in her ears. 'We've got to go to the shelter,' she said, gathering the child up in her arms. With any luck she could shut the door behind them all, leaving him on the outside.

But to her horror, he was behind her, helping to shepherd in Mrs B. Elizabeth began to shake. Only she knew what danger they were in.

The man even had the gall to position himself next to her. 'I'm not going to hurt anyone,' he said quietly. He sounded sincere, but how did she know he was telling the truth? Perhaps it was just as well that her earlier cry for help had been smothered by the wail of the siren. If she exposed him now, Herr Schmidt might pull out a gun. He was bound to have one on him. Spies did, didn't they? She edged away from him.

'I'm scared,' whimpered Maisie as they huddled together in the home-made shelter that Henry had put up at the bottom of the garden. He'd spent days digging the pit and then banking it up with bricks and wire and goodness knows what else.

At the time, it had felt ludicrous. Unnecessary. After all, he could have bought an Anderson shelter, but Henry insisted on doing it himself. Now it looked like the only thing that might – dear God – possibly save them from the bombers overhead. From the sound of the planes, there were more than there'd ever been before.

'It's all right,' whispered Elizabeth, trying to sound brave. 'Let's play noughts and crosses on the walls, shall we?'

The Patmore sisters were holding each other as if they were children. Even Mrs Norris, usually stoical, was panting so loudly that Elizabeth could feel her breath on her neck.

'The planes have passed over now,' said the man whom she'd thought of as Mr Smith until an hour or so ago.

'How do you know?' growled Henry.

'Listen.'

He was right. It was quiet. Maybe he had inside knowledge.

'Don't move, anyone,' ordered Henry. 'It could be a trick. Those bloody Jerries might be sending over another lot.'

Maisie began to weep again. *I have to do something to distract her*, thought Elizabeth.

Instinctively, she began to hum a tune that Robert had loved. It was a rhyme that she had made up when he'd been scared about starting school. The words, once so familiar, but cloudy with lack of use, came back to her. 'We're strong and wise and brave as knights. Our courage will shine in the darkest of nights.'

'Do shut up, Elizabeth,' growled Henry.

How dare he dismiss her like that in front of everyone? Besides, the enemy in their midst was probably going to kill them all anyway. She carried on, louder this time. Slowly the PGs took it up. Then Maisie. Even the spy had the audacity to do the same. Only Henry remained silent, his lips pursed in the flickering torchlight.

By the time they had finished several rounds, it was still silent.

'It looks like Mr Smith is right,' she said, pronouncing his name with a leaden sarcasm that she hoped he would pick up on. 'The noise has stopped.'

They all climbed out one by one. Now was her chance to denounce the man. But he was standing behind her. Whispering in a low voice. 'I've told you, Elizabeth. I'm not going to hurt anyone. Please believe me.'

'I'm not stupid,' she hissed.

The sky was a flickering red. 'I wonder if something's burning in the sea,' said Henry.

'You'll be able to see from my room,' said Maisie.

They all found themselves running up, including Mr Smith. Would he kill them there? wondered Elizabeth.

Maisie stood on a chair but the rest could glimpse it standing up. An orange ball sat on the water in the distance. It looked as though the waves were on fire. Above it was a plane doing a loop, almost as though it was triumphant.

'That's one of ours,' said Henry. 'You can tell from the shape.' His voice was excited. 'Our boys have got one of the bastards!'

'Is the German pilot dead?' asked Maisie, quivering.

'He bloody deserves to be. They got our son, didn't they?'

Elizabeth's eyes swam with tears.

'I'm sorry,' said the teacher quietly.

'What's it got to do with you?' demanded Henry.

This was it. This was where she should expose him. But before she could say anything, he spoke.

'Mrs Montague,' he said. 'Could I help you make hot drinks for everyone?'

His eyes were pleading with her.

'All right,' she said. If she didn't, he might hurt the others. Maybe she could find a way to get him first. 'Mrs B, can you take everyone downstairs into the sitting room, please?'

Henry left, muttering something about checking on the houses down the road as part of his Home Guard duties. He was probably going to see his fancy woman. But right now she didn't care.

The teacher followed her into the kitchen. As soon as they were inside, she grabbed the bread knife and held it in front of her. 'You've got two minutes to explain yourself.'

'I'm not a spy,' he said firmly, holding up his hands and backing away. 'You've got to believe me.'

'Then why is your name Schmidt?'

'Because my father was German.'

She thought for a moment. 'Was he a Jew?'

Rumours were circulating that Jewish men, women and even children were being stripped of their homes and possessions and herded into camps like cattle for no reason other than their religion.

'No – but he had several friends who were and he didn't like the way things were going in Germany. So he sent me and my wife over here in 1935 to some cousins on my mother's side. We decided it would be safer if we changed our surnames to avoid any confrontation. What you saw were my original identity documents. Perhaps foolishly, I kept them in case I needed them.'

He sounded so plausible. But liars did, didn't they? 'Where is your father now?' she asked.

He looked at her steadily. 'He was shot because he spoke out about the treatment of the Jews. Not all Germans are bad. There are a lot of families who are too scared to disobey. They know that their loved ones will be murdered if they do.'

'And your mother?'

'She died of natural causes when I was a child.'

'How do I know you are telling the truth?'

'You don't. But if you are still suspicious, you have a right to be. Because there is something else I must tell you.'

Her hands began to sweat on the handle of the bread knife she was still holding. If necessary, she could overpower him, thanks to Jim's training. 'Go on.'

'I trained in England to become a teacher because teaching is a reserved occupation, so I wouldn't be called up to fight. You see, I'm a conscientious objector. I don't want to kill anyone, whatever their nationality.' He shuddered. 'I just couldn't live with that guilt.'

In one way, Elizabeth could understand that. In another, it was a cop-out. Look at Robert risking his life.

'I'm afraid I misled you earlier when I said my wife and child were lost. In a way, that's true. My wife left me when I became a "conchie" as she called it, taking our son with her.'

Then he put his hand in his pocket and withdrew a photograph of a boy with a shiny smile and tidy haircut. He placed it in her hand.

'Alastair is five now,' he said. Tears were glistening in his eyes. 'He was born in England after we arrived. My wife didn't leave a forwarding address. I can only hope they are still alive. This photograph is all I have. I dropped it on the beach and only realized later on. I can't tell you what a panic I got into. I had to go out in the middle of the night to find it.'

Perhaps that explained Mrs Norris seeing him with a torch? But it didn't take away the fact that he had lied to her all this time. Or that he had refused to fight.

Elizabeth took a step away from him. Every bone in her body burned with fury. 'I want you out of this house, Mr Smith – or rather, Herr Schmidt. Now.'

'Of course,' he said. 'What will you tell your husband?'

'Exactly what you have told me.'

'Then I might be sent to an internment camp.' His eyes pleaded with her. 'I didn't have to tell you, Eliz— Mrs Montague. I wanted to.'

'Why?'

'I think you know the answer to that question.'

'What are you saying?'

'Only that I've felt ever since I met you that we . . . well, we understand each other.'

How dare he be so impertinent! 'I have no idea what you're talking about. I'll give you time to find a new billet and then you're out.'

'Thank you,' he said.

Now was the time to call the police. Elizabeth waited until she could hear his footsteps go up the stairs. Then she crept out into the hall and picked up the phone.

'So I said to the air-raid warden . . .'

Bother! Mrs Brown from down the road was on the phone. That was the problem with having a party line. She'd just have to wait until her neighbour finished. But when she tried again, Mrs Brown was still talking. She could interrupt politely and say she needed to make an urgent phone call but then Mrs Brown would be curious (she was that kind of woman). Still, a spy was a spy. Or wasn't it?

Elizabeth thought about the picture. The boy's smile . . . Somewhere out there was a child who needed to be reunited with his father. What if Stephen Smith – or rather Stefan – was telling the truth? Supposing that boy in the photograph had been her own son? How would she feel then?

Slowly, very slowly, she put down the receiver.

36

Every morning when Elizabeth woke up, it came flooding back. Had she made a terrible mistake? Was the teacher telling the truth? Or was she hiding a spy under her roof? What would the authorities say if they knew? Elizabeth couldn't even bring herself to think about Henry's reaction.

But Stephen Smith, as she still had to think of him in order to maintain this charade, went out of his way to be a model guest. 'I promise you,' he would assure her at every opportunity when there was no one around, 'you have nothing to fear from me. Thank you for giving me this chance.'

'Have you found anywhere else to live?' she demanded.

'I am afraid not. Everywhere is full. Now, what can I do to help? I noticed the back kitchen door has a loose bolt. I can sort that for you, if you like.'

'My husband is perfectly capable,' she replied stiffly.

'Then I will help Maisie with her homework.'

Meanwhile, when the phone rang or the postman knocked, Elizabeth leaped in case there was news of Robert. But there never was. Of course there wasn't. He'd been shot, hadn't he? Yet sometimes it helped to pretend to herself that he was still out there somewhere.

'You're very twitchy today,' said Adeline a week or so later.

They were sorting out clothing donations for the evacuees in the Manor Hall. The other volunteers had left. It was just the two of them: the first time for a while since their argument.

'Am I?' she said, trying to sound normal. Wouldn't anyone be twitchy if they'd discovered a German in their house? Maybe she should tell her friend. But what if Mr Smith was genuine? Her gut instinct told her that he was.

'I'm sorry I was tetchy last time,' added Adeline.

'That's all right,' said Elizabeth stiffly.

'The thing is, I haven't been totally honest with you.'

Elizabeth looked up from a jumper that had clearly seen better days. It was surely time to pull it apart and reuse the wool.

'What about?'

'About me.' Her face was glowing. 'You see, I'm in love.'

Elizabeth's heart sank. 'With the Canadian who gave you stockings?'

She nodded, flushing. 'Brian loves me. I can't tell you how wonderful it is to be truly loved.'

'But what about George?'

'He wasn't right for me any more than Henry is for you. You know that.'

'But you always said it would be different when you had children.'

Adeline was younger than her. There was still time. Or there would be, if her husband came back.

'That's just it.' Adeline stroked her stomach.

'You're not!' Elizabeth gasped.

Her friend glowed. 'It's early days but I'm being sick

and there's this strange taste in my mouth, just like when you were pregnant with Robert.'

'But Adeline, what are you going to do? Everyone here will know that George can't be the father.'

'I reckon I can keep it hidden for a bit. Then I'm going away. I have a cousin in Wiltshire. She's quite liberal-minded. She'll understand. We'll tell her neighbours it's my husband's. They won't be any the wiser. Then after the war, Brian and I will make a new life in Canada.'

'You've got it all worked out,' whispered Elizabeth.

'You've got to, haven't you, as far as you can with this bloody war? I thought you'd be pleased for me. You know how much I've always wanted a baby.'

'Of course I'm pleased for you. But it's so . . . so untidy.'

'Life is untidy right now. Please don't disapprove, Elizabeth. I need some love. The war has taught me that. I don't want to waste one more day.'

'Of course.' Elizabeth thought about some of the unfriendly – even hostile – comments about the overseas airmen 'taking our women' that she'd heard around town. There might be some who would think nothing of punishing both Adeline and her Canadian in some horrible way.

'You won't tell anyone, will you?'

Elizabeth sighed. 'Of course not.' How could she judge, when she was harbouring a man who was, at the least, a conscientious objector and might, at the worst, be a spy?

Elizabeth glanced at her wrist before remembering that she'd taken her watch in to be melted down for metal to help the war effort. 'I've got to go back now to sort out tea for everyone.'

'Thank you for understanding,' said Adeline. 'Are things still difficult with Henry?'

She nodded. 'It won't change.'

'It can if you want it to, Elizabeth.' She took her arm. 'It's not as if you have to consider Robert any more, is it?'

Elizabeth flinched before giving Adeline a kiss on the cheek. 'Be careful.'

'You too.' Adeline laughed gaily. 'You're going to be the godmother, by the way! If you want to be, of course.'

'I'd be honoured,' she said solemnly. Who was she to puncture Adeline's vision of the future? If she wanted to dream of a new life with her Canadian, then that was surely her right.

If nothing else, the war was teaching them all to live for the moment.

Because the next day might not come.

On her way home, a woman brushed against her, pressing a piece of paper into her hand.

By the time she turned, the woman was out of sight round a corner.

Swiftly she glanced at it. The instructions told her to drop it off at Western Mouth. It would take a while to get there, and she'd miss tea. Mrs B would hold the fort, but Henry wouldn't be pleased.

Too bad.

Making her way alone across the top of the cliffs, Elizabeth passed the Frog Stone: a boulder so called because it had two bulges like a frog's head and stomach. When Robert had been little, he had loved jumping on and off it.

Was that a seagull? Sometimes their cries sounded very much like a person's.

Heavens. It *was* a person!

'Hier, hier!'

Halfway down the cliff face was something red. Dear God! It was a parachute.

'Who's there?' she said, trying to sound braver than she felt.

'Bitte,' said a voice. Elizabeth didn't know many German words but she was pretty sure that meant 'Please'.

Then she saw his blue-grey jacket and black leather boots. Jim had taught her that was the Luftwaffe uniform. He'd also warned that spies could speak good English. Then again, a spy was surely more likely to be dressed in civvies.

'Help me,' he pleaded.

Swiftly she pulled out the gun that Jim had given her.

His face stared up, pleading. 'No,' he begged, in a German accent. He looked younger than her own son. 'Please. Do not shoot.' Tears rolled down his face.

'How old are you?' she called out, her voice wobbling. Any minute now and he might shoot *her*.

'Eighteen.'

Only a year older than Robert. But not too young to kill her. Her skin went clammy with terror.

He was holding his hand up to her. The other was clinging to a bush.

'How did you get here?' she demanded.

'I was in a plane when it was attacked. I was the navigator. The pilot told me to bail out. He said it was my only chance.'

'You've been bombing Exeter,' she shouted, furious. 'Do you know how many innocent people you killed?'

He was crying again now. 'We are at war. We had no choice.'

'Everyone has a choice.'

'Please. Help me. For my mother's sake, help me. She is a widow. I am all she has left.'

Elizabeth's feet rooted themselves to the ground.

If Robert were still alive and on German soil, wouldn't she have wanted someone to help him?

What was it that Mr Smith had said?

'Not all Germans are bad. There are a lot of families who are too scared to disobey. They know that their loved ones will be murdered if they do.'

Of course, she should tell the authorities in town about the boy's existence and then he'd be put in a camp. But the secret army's instructions had been quite clear. Jim's words came back to her: *'If you come across German invaders, you are to shoot them.'*

If she disobeyed, there might be reprisals against her own family. Her own life would not be worth living. She would be shot if discovered (another of Jim's warnings). Hadn't there been a story in the paper about a German sympathizer in the north of the country who had been strangled in the dark when she was walking down the street? Wasn't it bad enough that she already had a German under her roof?

There was the sound of falling rocks. Elizabeth's heart skipped a beat. He had slid a few feet further down the cliff. Below, the sea reared up, roaring with fury.

It was no good. She couldn't help it. 'Can you make your way to the left?' she called out. 'There's a ledge there.'

His voice was terrified. 'But I might fall.'

Why risk her own life for the enemy? But thoughts of Robert were urging her on. *He's a kid. Wouldn't you want someone to help me if I was in his position?*

'Can you throw your parachute towards me?'

'I am too scared to let go.'

'What is your name?'

'Karl.'

'Listen to me, Karl. This is your only chance. I don't know if it will work, but it's worth trying. Do you understand me?'

'You will not shoot me?' he said.

'No.'

There was a rumble. More earth was falling.

'Karl,' she said, her mouth dry. 'Do what I say.'

He heaved at his parachute, trying to throw part of the silk towards her. Step by step, she inched down the sloping cliff edge towards it.

'Be careful,' he called out.

There appeared to be genuine concern in his voice.

Once or twice she nearly fell but each time managed to right herself.

Finally, she grabbed a handful of the silk and began pulling him towards her. His eyes were wide with terror.

'You are nearly safe,' she repeated.

His hand stretched out for hers. He was so heavy that for a moment she thought she was going to fall. Then she pulled him back and they collapsed into the bracken. He was panting, his eyes wide with terror.

'Are you going to shoot me?' he whispered.

'No, I promised you,' she said. 'But there are others here who might.'

'Who's there?' boomed a voice.

She froze. 'Lie there,' she said. 'Don't move.'

Making her way out of the clearing, she found Jim standing by the path.

'What are you doing?' he asked sharply.

'Delivering a message,' she said, remembering the note in her pocket which she should have swallowed when she'd seen the young boy.

'Better be quick, then, hadn't you?'

'Yes, but . . .'

'But what?'

'I've lost my watch,' she lied. 'I'd like to find it first.'

'If this was an invasion, would you spend time looking for your precious watch?' he snapped.

'No.' She hesitated. 'But it's not an invasion and it was my last birthday present from my son before he was shot.'

Something gave in his eyes. 'Very well. I'll let you off this time. But there won't be any other chances.'

'Thank you.'

She slipped back through the woods. Karl was huddled into a ball, his arms around his knees. He was rocking back and forth like a child in spasm.

'Listen,' she said. 'I can't help you. I've got to . . . go somewhere. You'll have to walk down into town and hand yourself in.'

'But what if the people you spoke of find me first?'

'It's not my responsibility,' she said. 'I got you off that cliff, didn't I?'

His eyes watered. They were a pale blue, she noticed. Just like Robert's.

'Please, I beg you, kind lady. Do not leave me.'

Even if he got into town, questions would be asked. She'd been seen by Jim. They were bound to put two and two together.

Maybe it would be better if she hid him somewhere overnight. Then he could hand himself in and say he had bailed out over another part of town.

But where could she put him? When Jim had asked if she had the courage to shoot a German, she'd insisted she did. But this boy was so young.

'I'll be back as fast as I can,' she said. 'Hide in these bushes.'

Never had Elizabeth run so fast. Dashing into the kitchen – thankfully, Mrs B had gone home – she grabbed some bread and cheese and a flask of water.

Running back out of the house, she almost collided with Mr Smith.

He glanced at her dress, which was, she now realized, ripped and covered with mud stains. 'Are you all right?'

'Perfectly, thank you,' she said.

'You have twigs in your hair,' he said quietly.

'It's none of your business,' she said.

'I only mentioned it because your husband is home now. I believe he is in the study.'

She froze.

'Elizabeth, are you in trouble?' he said quietly.

'Yes,' she heard herself whispering. 'Yes. I think I am.'

37

She had no choice. At least it felt that way right now. 'Tell me where this lad is and I will go for him,' said Mr Smith. 'If anyone is going to get into trouble, it should be me.'

Elizabeth's heart was thudding against her ribcage. 'But where can we hide him?'

The word 'we' had slipped out without her realizing.

'The allotment,' he said. 'You have a hut.'

Elizabeth was about to ask how he knew but then remembered that he had helped her dig over the vegetable bed.

'Yes,' she said. 'But there might be others around.'

'Not at this time of day. It's too dark. He will have to stay quiet, of course, once he is there. I'll explain that.'

'His English is good –' she began, but then stopped. 'I presume you speak fluent German,' she said quietly.

He nodded. 'Our parents brought us up to be bilingual. My father was an English-language professor.'

'Us?' she asked.

'Me and my sister.' He spoke as if he was choking.

'Where is she now?'

His eyes were wet.

'In Berlin. She was meant to have come with me but she would not leave her fiancé.'

'So your sister is at the mercy of our bombers? You

must hate us. Is that why you want to help this German boy?'

He made to take hold of her hands but then stepped back. 'I've told you before, Elizabeth.'

He was using her first name, as he had done once before. Was this another ploy to make her trust him? So why didn't she stop him?

'I don't believe in war,' he continued. 'No one ever wins. I will help anyone in need, regardless of their race or their creed.'

'But –'

'Elizabeth?'

It was Henry, yelling from the floor above. 'Where have you been?'

'Just out for a walk with Adeline,' she said.

'You know that we are discouraged from going out after dark.'

'Quickly,' hissed Mr Smith. 'Where is he?'

Swiftly she gave him directions, hoping they were clear enough.

'Don't worry. I'll find him.' He reached across. For a moment, she thought he was going to touch her. Her breath quickened. Then he took something from her hair. 'Check the mirror,' he said, handing her a twig. 'There are more.'

Then he was gone.

Elizabeth lay awake all night, waiting for a sound to indicate that he was back.

Nothing.

What if he was caught, and the boy too? Supposing

Mr Smith really was a spy? Was that why he had insisted on going – to help one of his own? Was it even possible that he had directed the plane to 'crash' here so the young man could join in an uprising? She'd been mad to trust either of them. And yet what if both were telling the truth?

Eventually, around 3 a.m., her anxiety became so great that she tiptoed out of bed, leaving Henry to snore loudly.

Mr Smith's door was shut. Had it been closed when he left? She couldn't remember and she didn't dare open it – supposing one of the sisters heard her?

Then she heard a voice.

'Aunty Elizabeth?'

Maisie's door was slightly open. The child was afraid of the dark and had always slept that way, even when Shirley had been there. She looked in. 'Yes, dear?'

'I went down to the kitchen to get some water and saw Mr Smith coming home. Why did he get back so late?'

So he *was* back.

'I don't know,' she said. 'But I do know that we mustn't say anything about it to anyone.'

'Why?'

Elizabeth felt her palms sweating. 'You just have to trust me.'

'Is it one of those adult secrets?'

Elizabeth swallowed. 'Yes.'

'I can't sleep.'

'Would you like me to sit next to you on the bed until you drop off?'

'Yes please.'

It wasn't until the dawn chorus started that she realized

she must have nodded off briefly. Getting off the bed quietly, so as not to disturb Maisie who was fast asleep, she headed for the bathroom. It would give her a good excuse for being up at 5 a.m.

When she came out, she could see that Mr Smith's bedroom door was now ajar. Trembling, she slowly peeped round. The room was empty.

Then she heard a noise in the kitchen. It was too early for Mrs B. Tiptoeing down, pausing at each creak of the stairs, she found the teacher cutting a slice of bread from the loaf that Mrs B had bought from the bakery the day before.

For a moment he looked terrified, before realizing it was her.

'I hope you don't mind,' he whispered. 'I know rations are tight but we have to feed the poor boy.'

She could barely talk for fear. 'So you found him?'

'Yes. I took him to your allotment shed. I suggested he stayed there for a couple of days and then walked into town to hand himself in. I've made him swear he won't mention your involvement. Instead, he will say that he landed in Lyme and then slept rough on the cliffs.'

That should be long enough after being spotted by Jim for the two events not to be connected. Or would it? It was a chance she'd have to take. There's no way they could feed him for longer.

'He's very grateful.'

Elizabeth thought of her son and all the people who had perished in the air raid on Exeter and everywhere else. One of the local farmers was still missing, presumed dead in a ditch somewhere.

'You're not in league with him, are you?'

'Of course I'm not. You must believe me.'

He seemed so genuine, and yet . . .

'What have we done?' she said, bursting into tears.

'Shhh. It's all right.'

How it happened, she didn't know. But somehow Mr Smith's arms were around her. Holding her. Cloaking her body with a warmth she hadn't felt for years.

Then he stepped back. His face was flushed. 'I'm sorry,' he said. 'Forgive me. I'll go now.'

Elizabeth was left standing in the kitchen.

'You bloody little fool,' she told herself. 'What have you done now?'

38

'I'm sure we had more bread than this,' said Mrs B when she arrived two hours later to help Elizabeth with breakfast for the PGs.

'I'm afraid I got hungry in the night,' said Elizabeth quickly. 'I couldn't sleep so I had my slice early.'

'None of us are sleeping much at the moment, are we?' said Mrs B. They were laying the table together. 'I keep thinking the Jerries are going to come over again. My Reg is more of a bundle of nerves than ever.'

Poor man.

At breakfast, Elizabeth sat and watched everyone eat, her stomach grumbling. Yet at the same time, she wasn't hungry. How could she be, knowing what she had done? If someone had told her last week that she'd be hiding a German – two if you counted Mr Smith – she'd never have believed them.

What if the boy made a noise? Supposing he opened the door to get some light?

She would go to prison or perhaps be hanged by the authorities. That's if the secret army didn't get to her first. Traitor. That's what she'd be branded as. And quite right too. How could she possibly be helping the enemy? The same people whose U-boat had caused all those poor innocent children to drown by sinking the *City of Benares* evacuee ship on its way to America. Except that this Karl was just a kid himself. A boy whose widowed mother was waiting for him. Unless he'd made all that up.

Maybe the shock of Robert's death had disturbed her mind, making her act irrationally.

'You seem a bit on edge,' said Adeline, as they folded yet more donated clothes together two days later.

'Well, I'm worried about you,' said Elizabeth. It was part of the truth. 'When you start to show, what will happen?'

Adeline was unable to hide the excitement in her voice. 'Brian's got it all sorted out. He's asked for a transfer to an RAF camp near Oxford. He'll take me with him and I'll find lodgings nearby. We'll say we're man and wife.'

'And when George comes home?'

She shrugged. 'I'll get a divorce. Reckon I won't be the only one. The war has made lots of us have another think about who we want to spend the rest of our lives with.'

Maybe Henry might want a divorce himself when the war was over to marry that Polly woman, wondered Elizabeth. The thought didn't trouble her as much as she would have expected.

That evening, after supper, Mr Smith offered to give her a hand washing up. It was Mrs B's night off. Everyone else had left the table, including Henry, who had announced he was 'going out'.

'We've got a problem,' Mr Smith said. 'Karl is sick.'

'What?'

'I went over just before dinner to give him one of my blankets. I hope you don't mind. He's got a fever. I didn't want to worry you before but I'm concerned it's gone to his chest. The hut's very damp.'

Robert had been prone to bronchitis. She had sat up with him, night after night, helping him to cough up the thick green phlegm.

'What should we do?' she asked.

'I think we need to bring our plan forward. He'll have to leave the hut tomorrow and hand himself in. At least then he might get some medical help.'

'I've got some syrup that I used to give my son.' She caught her breath. 'I wanted him to pack it in his haversack but he told me not to fuss.'

He touched her arm briefly. Electricity coupled with shame shot through her.

'I'll take it up,' he said.

As he spoke there was a knock on the front door. It was one of the other teachers, wanting to speak to him.

'I'm sorry,' he said, coming back. 'There's a problem with one of the children in my group.' His eyes were wet. 'His family in London has been . . .'

He stopped.

'Bombed?' Elizabeth whispered.

He nodded.

'He's asking for me.'

'You must go,' she said.

'I'll see to Karl when I get back,' he said.

The heavy wooden clock in the hall ticked on. Elizabeth paced around the kitchen trying to decide what to do. It was far beyond curfew now. Maybe he'd been pressed into staying the night.

Maisie was in bed. Henry was out. The guests were in their rooms. It wouldn't take her long.

Swiftly she took down the cough syrup from the bath-room cupboard, as well as some aspirin. She'd use her bike. It would be quicker than walking. Obviously she couldn't switch on her lights in the blackout but she knew the way. She'd just have to take care not to hit anyone. Every now and then, the moon came out from behind a cloud to give light.

Through the Byes, past the river, which was swirling after the rain, and over the first bridge. Through the little gate into the allotments and past the beautifully kept patches with their cabbages and parsnips, towards hers.

She could hear the coughing from outside the hut. Sup-posing someone else had heard it too?

The boy was huddled in a corner with a blanket around him. There was that 'illness' smell that she remembered from Robert being poorly as a child. 'Who's there?' he whimpered, putting up his hands in surrender. 'Please don't hurt me.'

'It's all right,' she said. 'It's me, Elizabeth. I've brought you this.'

Gently she gave him a teaspoon of the syrup. His coughing was so bad that he brought most of it back up again. Mr Smith was right. He was definitely running a temperature. She could feel the heat radiating off him.

'Mutter, Mutter,' he whispered. This was another word that Elizabeth recognized. He wanted his mother.

'Karl,' she said, gently. 'I need to get you to the doctor. We can't wait for you to hand yourself in tomorrow because you're too ill. I can help you to his house but I can't go in with you. Otherwise they might suspect me.

You must not tell them that I hid you here. Do you understand?'

He nodded. 'I say I sleep on the cliffs. Stephen tells me that.'

'Exactly. We need to go now. Can you lean on me?'

Even though he was thin, he was tall, and his body almost crushed her as they made their way outside the hut.

'I feel too ill to walk,' he moaned.

How was she going to do this? She should have waited until Mr Smith was back after all.

'You have to,' she said desperately. 'Think of your mother. She will be waiting for you.'

'You are such a kind lady.' He was weeping now. 'How can I thank you?'

The moon came out again, just as she was about to reply.

'What in Christ's name do you think you're doing?' boomed a voice.

Frozen, Elizabeth stopped. 'Henry?' she whispered.

'I knew something was up when you kept sneaking off. It's why I followed you tonight. But this . . .'

Henry wasn't usually lost for speech.

'This,' he repeated, staring at the boy's uniform,' is unforgivable. How could you possibly be helping a Nazi?'

'He isn't a Nazi,' said Elizabeth, trembling. 'He's a young boy who was told he had to fight. He's only a year older than Robert. And he's ill. He needs a doctor.'

'Doctor?'

Henry was spitting and blustering now in the way he did when he was irate, but this was worse than she had ever seen him before. 'He should be shot. And so should you. What would our son think if he knew his mother was trying to help the very people who had killed him?'

'At least he isn't here to see you carrying on with that Polly woman from the bakery,' she snapped back.

'And what about you? Hanging around with that teacher – I've seen the way you look at him over the table,' he snarled. 'You meet him, don't you, when you go out on your walks on the hill.'

'No,' she said.

'Then what do you do?'

It was on the tip of her tongue to tell him the truth. But nothing mattered now. Not after Robert.

Then Karl let out a groan and fell to the ground.

'Leave him,' thundered Henry.

'Can't you see? He's really ill.'

'Good. Let's finish him off then, shall we?'

Elizabeth stared with horror at the gun that Henry had pulled out of his pocket. In that instant, she realized she'd left her own pistol in the house. 'No,' she screamed. 'Don't do it!'

'The Germans killed our son, Elizabeth. An eye for an eye. What are you? A traitor?'

'Of course I'm not,' she shouted back. 'But another death won't make it right.'

Karl was whimpering. 'Please. Do not kill me.'

'Stop blubbering, you coward. Die like a man.'

Her husband was aiming the gun. He meant it, Elizabeth realized. He was going to kill the boy.

'Don't you see,' she screamed, 'that this is just like Robert. He probably begged for his life. And he was only there because you egged him on. You're no better than a murderer.'

'STOP IT! STOP!' he roared.

Suddenly, he turned the gun towards her. Just as the moon retreated behind the clouds again.

Looking back, Elizabeth found it hard to remember exactly what happened and how. Perhaps it's because Jim's training suddenly kicked in. All she could recall was flying towards him and hearing a shot that rang out into the darkness, causing birds to scatter from the trees and bushes.

Then an awful silence.

Looking around, she realized – to her horror – two terrible things.

Firstly, that there was a body on the ground.

And secondly, that she was holding her husband's gun.

The Night of the Murder

8.17 p.m.

'You touched my girl,' says Martin when I'd finished speaking. His face is thunderous as he faces his father. His bushy eyebrows are knitted with rage.

I want to tell him again that I'm not his girl. Yet part of me feels grateful. I want Duncan to suffer.

Birthdays can be terrible things. Like anniversaries, they can bring out the worst in everyone by reminding you of the past.

Then he picks up a knife from the rack.

Nancy

39

There's a terrible noise. A crash. An explosion of glass.

I jump to one side as shards come flying into the kitchen. Martin's face looms against the broken window. He puts his arm through, trying to grab the latch.

'Shit, that hurt. Open up, Nancy. Or I'll have to carry on breaking my way in.'

I begin to shake uncontrollably with sheer terror. 'Come round through the back door,' I manage to blurt out. 'I'll open it.'

As he stumbles inside, Martin's face is pale, but he is grinning manically, as if on a high. There's a big gap in the front of his mouth where he's lost a tooth. 'God, it's good to see you again, Nancy.' He holds out his arms, despite the blood that is dripping onto the kitchen slate floor.

Sheba barks furiously. Martin cringes. 'Get that dog away from me or it will be sorry,' he yells. He'd never liked dogs, even as a teenager. Apparently one had bitten him as a child.

'Give me a minute,' I say, trying to sound in control.

Scared that Sheba might be hurt, I attempt to calm her down and put her in the sitting room for safety, along with a bowl of water. I need to pander to Martin. Anything, so as not to upset him. This man is unpredictable. Dangerous. He'd assaulted his own mother, after all.

'Let me bandage that arm,' I say. Maybe if I'm kind to him I can find a way out of this.

He sinks on to a kitchen chair and holds out his arm like a child. There's a first-aid kit in the cupboard left over from Mum's day. I can't help but touch his skin as I wind the bandage round. It makes me recoil with disgust. The cuts aren't as bad as I thought, but I have to extract some pieces of glass with tweezers. 'Hold still,' I say.

Martin's wearing the same green tracksuit he'd had on when I'd visited him in prison. 'I could do with a cup of tea,' he says.

Our conversation seems bizarrely normal. He grins at me. 'No sugar in this one. Just boiling water.'

'You don't frighten me, you know,' I lie.

He puts his head to one side. 'Come on, Nancy, that parcel was just a joke.'

'No it wasn't,' I say. 'You wanted to scare me.'

'Would I really want to do that to my girl?' Then he reaches out his good arm and strokes my hand. It's so unexpected that it takes me a second to jump back.

'You like that, don't you, Nancy? You were the first woman I kissed. It creates a bond, don't you think?'

If I deny this, it might aggravate him even more. But if I agree in order to keep him happy, that might make it worse. How do I get him to go?

'Say something, Nance,' he says. He tilts my chin and holds it up so I am forced to look at his face.

'We have a bond because our parents married each other,' I say. 'But that's as far as it goes.'

His eyes glitter. 'If it wasn't for me, you'd be on trial for murder.'

'Please don't say that,' I whisper. As I speak, the screams come back to me. *Mummy! Mummy!*

'It's all right,' he says soothingly, cupping his hand under my chin. 'I'm here now. After I sent you that little present, I started thinking. I realized that Alex must have got to you again and persuaded you to leave me. So I decided to come down here and rescue you.'

'Rescue me?' I say.

'Rescue both of us. We each need each other.'

It's no good. I can't carry on with this front any more. 'I don't need you to rescue me,' I say.

His eyes are hard. Unflinching. 'Do you know what I've just risked for you?' he says. 'If they catch me, they'll send me to an even tougher prison. I might even end up in Solitary. Come on, Nancy. I know you want me too. Why else would you have visited me?'

'To tell you to leave me alone.'

'Then why did you send me your new mobile phone number when I went down?'

'What? That's rubbish. You said someone in the prison traced it for you.'

'I lied so you wouldn't get into trouble. It was you.'

'No it wasn't,' I say firmly.

Martin used to do this to me when we were younger. He'd tell me I had done something when I hadn't. It made me doubt myself. Just as it is doing now. But there's an added layer this time to his coercive control. He's a prisoner on the run.

'Nancy,' he says, 'don't try to correct me. We both know I'm right.'

He isn't. But I'm too scared to get into an argument over this.

Sheba is barking loudly from the sitting room.

'I need to check she's all right,' I plead.

'Not now, Nancy. We've got to get going.'

'Where?' I tremble.

'France.' He speaks as if I should know this. 'Don't bother taking any stuff. We can get it when we're there.'

'But . . .'

He carries on talking over me as he always used to. So rude, my mother used to say. 'There's a ferry from Plymouth. I've checked out the times. We can buy tickets when we arrive.'

'How did you escape?' It occurs to me I should have asked this before, but the glass and the shock had taken away my reasoning.

Martin grins again. 'I got my cellmate to help me knock out a tooth. I knew they'd then have to take me to the dentist, which meant a trip to the outside. I made sure I did it when a certain guard was on duty – she fancied me.'

He smiles smugly. 'When we got to the dentist, she let me go to the toilet without my handcuffs and I made a dash for it out of the window. Then I hot-wired a car – you learn all kinds of things in prison – and got down here as fast as I could.'

I can hardly take this in.

And yet I can. All too easily. Martin is clever like that. And dangerous.

'Come on,' he says now, tugging my sleeve.

'I'm not going anywhere,' I say, backing away.

Sheba is growling from behind the sitting-room door.

'If you don't,' Martin says slowly. 'I'll have to make you.'

His voice is low. Menacing. It's as if he has changed the hot tap to cold in seconds.

'Nancy, I can't risk leaving you here so you can tell the police where I'm going.'

He has me backed up against the kitchen cupboard with the loose panel below it. I step forward and pretend to put my arms round his neck. 'Maybe you're right, Martin,' I murmur. 'Why don't we stay here, just for a little while.'

He appears to relax a bit, smiling. Good.

'Let me just pick this piece of glass off the floor,' I say.

Then I bend down and whip out the knife I'd hidden the day after I got here.

'Oh no you don't.' He almost sounds amused, but his iron grip on my wrist suggests something else. We grapple for a few seconds, but I am no match for his strength and I drop the knife on the floor. My arm is agony and red marks are welling up.

'Nancy,' he says in a voice that chills my bones. 'You disappoint me. You can't do things like that. What would your mother say?'

'Stop it,' I say. 'Don't talk about her.'

'Your mother, your mother,' he taunts. 'If she'd listened to you, none of this would have happened. Isn't that what you told her?'

'You disgust me as much as your father did,' I hiss.

Instantly, he has me pushed up against the wall, the knife at my throat. His voice is hard. Brittle. 'I'm glad that man is dead. He deserves it. So did your mother. Don't you see, Nancy? They damaged us. It's why we need to go through the rest of life together. We're soulmates.'

'Please, Martin, don't.'

'You should be a bit nicer, then, Nancy.' He teases the

blade against the side of my throat. 'I love you, Nancy, but I won't go back to prison.'

'OK,' I gasp. 'I'll come with you. Just put that knife down.'

He nods as if satisfied. 'Actually, we won't drive to Plymouth. They might be looking out for us. We'll take a boat.' He grins again. 'It will be an adventure.'

'Are you crazy?'

As soon as I say this, I know I've made a mistake.

'Nancy,' he says softly. 'Don't ever, ever call me crazy. Got it?'

'Yes,' I squeak, terrified he'll use the knife this time.

'And leave that mobile of yours behind,' he adds.

Reluctantly I place it on the kitchen table.

Then he pulls me by the arm, out of the door and into the night.

40

The wind is so fierce that I can barely walk. But I have no choice because Martin is dragging me along firmly by the arm.

We stumble over fallen branches on the pavement. He takes the quieter route down a side road, past the bowling green and the church. Past the museum and Kennaway House. Please God let us run into someone.

'Faster,' Martin keeps saying.

'I'm going as fast as I can,' I yell out.

I've decided to pretend I'm doing what he wants. But somehow I have to find a way of escaping. We're getting nearer to the front. As we do so, the wind is increasing. Massive waves are fiercely slapping over the promenade like waterfalls. No one is here as far as I can tell. Martin heads for the far end, towards Jacob's Ladder. 'I want to leave from our place,' he says, pointing up to the rocks where he'd carved our names all those years ago.

He's crazy. Stark raving crazy. Fear makes me unable to think properly. I want to be sick.

'HELP!' I call out.

'SHUT UP!'

Martin's eyes are glaring at me like a devil's in the moonlight. 'If you make a fuss, Nancy, I'll kill you here and now.' He's still holding the knife.

There are some boats moored on this part of the beach.

One of them has a motor, and the key is inside. People are trusting here. It's tied with a knot to a lobster pot. Martin swiftly cuts it with the knife.

'Help me pull it out,' he commands.

I stare with horror at the waves. Some are as high as a house. It's freezing. 'We'll die out there,' I shout over the wind.

'No we won't,' he yells back. 'It's safer than the road, where someone will spot us.'

'Not in this weather!' I scream.

'We have no choice! I'll die if I have to go back to prison. Come on, Nancy. It's this or I kill us both.' He looks mad enough for me to believe him.

I push one end of the boat out down the shingle with Martin taking the lead.

'Nancy!'

A voice calls out into the air.

I turn round. It's Vera in her old raincoat, flashing a torch.

'What's she doing here?' growls Martin.

Her voice rings out across the beach as she walks towards us. 'I heard Sheba barking and came round to see if you were all right. Then I saw you heading down here. You can't possibly take a boat out into weather like this. You'll drown.'

As Vera speaks, she sees Martin. Too late. He smashes the torch out of her hands.

'What are you doing? Stop it. Or I will call the police.'

There's a scream. Mine or Vera's. I don't know.

All I can see is Vera falling to the ground and Martin's knife glinting in the moonlight.

'What have you done?' I yell.

'I had to,' he yells back. 'Now get in.'

He shoves me into the boat. A wave tosses us up and out. I look back at the body on the beach.

'Help!' I scream out again. '*Help!*'

'Too late,' he says, as the wind whips my voice away. 'They can't hear us. We're on our own now. Us against the world.'

41

Please God, don't let Vera be dead. And please don't let me drown.

I'm not a particularly religious person. But I find myself recalling a line from a prayer that my father and I had come across in an old church near here: *Preserve us from the dangers of the sea.*

'The sea is a beautiful place, Nancy,' Dad had said to me. 'But don't be fooled. It can turn against you. That's why I'm teaching you to swim.'

Right now, I am scared in a way that's beyond terror. Each wave tosses us into the air. Each wave feels like the last chance I have to draw breath. There's no way we'll survive if we get thrown into the water.

We're going past the cliffs now and heading towards Branscombe.

'You don't honestly think we're going to make it to Plymouth, do you?' I scream. 'Besides, we're going the wrong way.'

'All right,' he shouts irritably. 'I'm just trying to get this thing away from the rocks.' He's struggling with the engine but it's no match for the waves.

Then there's a noise from above. A rumbling. A huge splash a few feet ahead of us. Then another, even closer this time. It must be rocks falling down from the cliff. Hadn't Vera talked about the danger of landslides?

'Look out!' yells Martin. I can't help ducking instinctively, even though common sense tells me this won't help. A big-gish rock lands on the boat. It tips us sideways.

'Move to the other side,' he roars.

I do as he says while he heaves the rock over the side, and the boat rights itself again.

But now we're being dragged out to sea.

'I don't want to drown,' I whimper.

I put my fingers inside my jacket pocket to keep warm. They close around something hard. My grandmother's whistle! The one I've been using to call Sheba back on walks.

I blow on it as hard as I can. The sound is carried away by the wind.

Martin laughs. 'No one can hear you, Nancy,' he yells.

'You're right,' I say.

Then I lean forward and blow it again straight into his right ear.

'Bitch,' he snarls. 'Don't do that ever again.' He smacks my hand away and the whistle falls into the boat.

'I'm sorry,' I say, scared.

'It's OK, Nance. I know you're frightened. But you've got me here to look after you.'

We flounder on for I don't know how long. Ten min-utes, maybe. Fifteen? Each time a wave tosses us up in the air, I think it's the end. We don't seem to be making any headway. The pull of the current is too fierce.

Then he swears.

'What is it?' I yell, trying to be heard over the wind and water.

As I speak, I see a light coming towards us from the esplanade. It's a boat.

'It must be from the lifeboat station,' I call out. 'They can see we're in trouble.'

'No, no.' Martin's voice is disbelieving.

There's a sea plane overhead too. Looking for us. Please may it find us in time.

We're both soaked to the skin now. My fingers won't move. My heart is beating so fast that I don't have the energy to argue back.

'Watch out,' yells Martin.

The highest wave I have ever seen is coming towards us. I can't breathe. The fear in my throat is so thick that I feel I'm being choked. Martin grabs my hand. 'I've got you, Nancy, my love. It's all right. Don't be scared.'

I feel myself being dragged. He's going to take me with him. 'We'll die together,' he screams.

'No!'

Clutching the side of the boat as an anchor, I use a strength I didn't know I had. Water smashes against my face as we somehow ride the wave. God knows how but we are still upright. Exhausted, we fall back into the bottom of the boat, clutching each other with blind terror. If he still has the knife, I can't see it.

Another wave is coming. This one seems even higher. The sight makes my stomach freefall with panic. I look towards Martin's eyes. I can't see them in the dark. But I can feel them. Boring into me. 'I love you, Nancy,' he calls out. 'Remember that.'

Then the wave hits us. The force is stronger than I could have imagined. I am knocked to one side. My ears sing with the pressure of the water. I can't see anything, but somehow I'm still in the boat. My hair is plastered to my face. I brush it away from my eyes, searching desperately in the dark.

'Martin?' I scream.

There's no answer.

I feel around in the darkness. But there is nothing there. I go to the other side of the boat. Still nothing. I pause, my heart pounding, preparing myself for the moment when he will surely rear up like a sea monster, his eyes glittering in triumph.

But he doesn't.

I search around the bottom of the boat. He's not there. But my hands close around something else. The silver whistle that Martin had knocked out of my hands earlier.

I blow on it. 'Help!' I call out. Where did the lifeboat go? Then I blow again.

Nothing happens for a while. I've no idea how long. The waves seem to have subsided slightly, as if recognizing Martin is no longer there.

I blow the whistle once more in desperation.

And then I hear it.

'ARE YOU ALL RIGHT?'

It sounds like a loudspeaker.

'Yes,' I gasp.

The lifeboat pulls up alongside me. Its searchlight blinds my eyes. It also lights up the sea around. I search the surface for a body.

Nothing.

Someone climbs over, picks me up and carries me back. 'Where's the person who was with you?'

'He went over the side,' I weep.

'Shine the light,' orders someone else on the lifeboat.

We all stare.

Nothing.

I burst into floods of tears. Not just for Vera, who might be dead. Not just for my mother. Not for Martin. But with relief.

Please let it be over now.

It has to be.

42

'Are you all right, love?'

'Put this round her. She's shaking.'

'Hang on to me. That's right. You're safe now.'

'What happened?'

I'm aware of these questions and well-meaning gestures as my rescuers help me ashore. It feels like their words are coming from miles away.

Then I remember.

'Vera,' I gasp. 'Is she all right?'

'The woman on the beach?' says someone. 'She was taken away by ambulance.'

'She tried to help me,' I weep. Please. Don't let me be responsible for another death.

There's another ambulance there. Someone from the lifeboat station must have called it. They want to take me to hospital to be checked out, but I tell them that I am all right. 'I need to go home to see to my dog,' I whimper.

'I'll look after them both,' says a voice I recognize as Jasmine's. 'I saw the sea plane hovering. I'm a registered first-aider so I came down to see if I could do anything.'

My first thought is that I don't want her anywhere near me after her betrayal. But I'm in no state to argue.

'Let's go home,' says Jasmine.

I allow her to take me back to Tall Chimneys. She runs a bath. When I come down, she is in the kitchen stirring a pan of tomato soup. 'I found a tin,' she says, handing me a mug. 'I know it's your favourite.'

Gratefully, I sip it.

'It rang while you were in the bath,' she says, pointing to my mobile that I'd left behind in the kitchen when Martin had dragged me off. 'I answered it. Hope you don't mind. It was Alex. I told him what happened.'

'What did he say?'

'He was really worried. Says he's on his way. Don't worry. I won't cause any trouble.'

But the only thing that matters now is Vera.

Jasmine is still here when Alex arrives at Tall Chimneys.

'I didn't want to leave Nancy alone until you came,' I hear her say as she opens the door.

'Thanks,' he says.

'I did it for her, not you.'

'Is she all right?'

'Go into the kitchen,' says Jasmine briskly. 'I'll give you some space.'

Sheba is sitting by my side. If it wasn't for her size, I think she'd be on my lap.

'Nancy,' Alex says. And then he wraps me up in his arms. I smell his sweat. His panic. His love. 'Thank God you're all right. I don't know how I would have lived without you.'

But I'd ended it with him. Did he still really care?

'We're waiting to hear if Vera is all right,' I sob. 'I seem to bring trouble wherever I go.'

'You can't think like that,' he says, stroking my back. I'd forgotten how good that felt.

And then my mobile rings.

I grab it. 'Thank you,' I say quietly after listening for a couple of minutes.

Jasmine walks back into the room and both she and Alex look at me expectantly. 'That was Vera's niece,' I say. 'She thought we'd like to know that . . .'

I pause, struggling to accept the news.

'. . . that the knife missed any vital organs. She'll be in hospital for a good while but it's not life-threatening.'

'Thank God,' say Jasmine and Alex at the same time.

I still can't believe it. I had been certain that she had died, like so many others I had loved. The relief is overwhelming.

I sleep fitfully that night. Alex is holding me and wakes me up when I have my nightmare. It's always the same. Duncan grabbing me. My mother screaming as the knife goes in. And now there's another. Martin and me in the sea. '*We'll die together.*'

'It's all right,' soothes Alex.

But it's not.

How can it be, after what I've done?

There's only one way out, I realize. To do the thing I have been trying so hard not to do. To set myself free with the truth.

After all, Alex has laid his past bare to me. That couldn't have been easy.

Now I must do the same – even if I go to jail.

43

I decide to tell Alex in the morning. I need one more night with his arms around me. It's so comforting. I might have denied it to myself, yet the truth is that I've missed him terribly.

But I must have overslept with the exhaustion of everything that had happened because the next thing I know, the clock on the bedside table says 9.15 and someone is saying my name.

'Nancy?'

I wake up bolt-upright, terrified it might be Martin or Duncan. Then I realize it can't be. It's Alex.

'Sorry to wake you, love,' he says tenderly. 'But something's happened.'

A body has been washed up on the shore, further along the coastline towards Exmouth. It's wearing a green prison tracksuit. They want me to identify it.

'Are you OK about doing it?' asks Alex when he's finished explaining.

I get out of bed and wander over to the window. The sun is streaming through, in stark contrast to the terrible weather of the storm yesterday. I can see the sea over the rooftops of my neighbours' houses. Glinting. Sparkling. Cleansing. Lighting up the hidden secrets in my mind.

'I don't want to see him,' I reply. 'But I have to.'

'Someone else could do it. One of the prison officers, perhaps.'

I come back and sit on the bed. 'I have to do it myself. I owe him that.'

'You don't owe that monster anything,' says Alex.

But I do.

Of course, I've seen a dead body before. But this is different. There is no blood. No glazed eyes open. No horror written over the face. No screams.

It's just Martin. In the morgue. A pale, bloated Martin who bears little resemblance to the man I knew.

The first boy who kissed me.

The 'brother' who stood up to his father for me.

The man who nearly killed me.

'Yes,' I say turning away. 'That's him.'

Alex is waiting for me. He puts his arm around me. I move away. Despite everything, I don't feel right touching anyone straight after saying goodbye to my stepbrother's bloated body.

We drive back to Tall Chimneys in silence. I don't want to talk. If I do, I will either have to lie or tell Alex what really happened. And I don't want to do either.

When we open the door, Sheba bounds up to me. I kneel down, burying my face in her fur. I almost feel like telling her instead. In the short time I've looked after her, I've learned how understanding she is.

I'm quiet for the rest of the day, weighing up this terrible decision about whether to tell Alex. Last night it had seemed so clear. But seeing Martin had changed it. Duncan had hurt us both in different ways. Martin had also hurt me. Didn't I deserve to be free after all that?

But I can't get the farmhouse out of my head. '*Mummy! Mummy!*'

Alex makes cheese on toast, but I can't swallow a mouthful.

'Do you mind if I go to bed early?' I ask Alex.

'Good idea,' he says, getting up at the same time as if coming with me.

'Alone,' I say.

Something flickers in his eyes. Hurt? Doubt?

'Of course,' he says. 'I'll sleep in one of the other rooms. Just wake me if you need anything.'

I toss and turn, counting the pros and cons on my fingers. But it's no good. I'm not the kind of person who can hide things easily. The last year and a bit since my mother died has been agony. There is only one thing to do.

In the early hours of the morning, I tiptoe downstairs to the room where Alex is sleeping.

He looks so calm. So peaceful. What I have to say now is going to wreck his life for ever.

'Alex,' I whisper.

He wakes, startled. 'Nancy? Are you all right?'

I kneel by the side of his bed, taking his hand in mine. 'I've got something to tell you. You won't like it. In fact, it's terrible.'

'What?' he says. Alex is usually someone who takes ages to wake up. But right now, he's fully alert.

As soon as he speaks, I wish I'd stayed silent. But it's too late now. I've said something that can't be taken back.

'Remember the first time we went to bed?' I say slowly.

'Yes,' he says.

'I couldn't . . . I was too frightened to . . .'

'I know,' he says.

'You were so patient.'

'I loved you,' he said. 'And I felt you needed time.'

'But I didn't tell you why,' I said.

'You're shivering, Nancy. Come into bed and tell me.'

'I can't,' I say. 'You won't want me to when I have.'

He looks uncertain. 'You're scaring me, Nancy. It can't be as bad as all that.'

But it is.

I take a deep breath.

'I'd never liked Duncan. There was something creepy about him. I remember thinking that, even when he was just a friend of Dad's. Then he married Mum, and he treated me as though I was a nuisance, always telling me to go and play or "amuse" myself.'

I take a deep breath to try and still my heart, which is thumping madly. It doesn't work.

'When I was twelve, Claire started to come on holiday with us down here. Mum bought us a pair of matching pink bikinis. I remember Duncan giving me a look when I put mine on. I didn't know how to describe it then but now I can see it was . . . well, almost lascivious.'

Alex makes a sound of disgust.

'After that, he started to take notice of my appearance much more than usual. He'd compliment me on what I was wearing and do seemingly "fatherly" things like tuck a stray strand of hair behind my ear when I was going to school. Mum would say he was just being a good dad whenever I said anything to her about it.'

I swallow hard, forcing myself to continue. It's too late to turn back now.

'Then, the summer after I turned fifteen, we drove down here for our usual break. Claire came too. One day, Duncan asked me to go into the cellar with him to help bring up the garden apples we'd been storing there. Claire was hanging out washing. It was Mum's birthday. We were going out to dinner later to celebrate. But when we were inside the cellar, he . . . he locked the door behind us.

'"Why are you doing that?" I asked.

'"In case it slams shut and locks us in," he said. "I had a bit of trouble with it the other day. Now let's sort out the apples."

'Some were rotten – they had a horrid smell to them that still turns my stomach when I think of it. Others were ready to eat. He bit one in front of me. Juice dribbled down his mouth. "Delicious," he said. "Try one."'

I hear Alex groan as if he knows what's coming.

'Duncan's hand closed over mine as I picked one up. He made up some excuse about helping me choose the best ones. I stood up because I felt uncomfortable. He stood up at the same time. He tucked that stray hair of mine behind my ear like he'd done before but this time he was standing very close to me. He . . . he said I had very beautiful eyes and that I was an extremely attractive young woman. Then he reached out and grabbed me by the waist. I was so shocked that I stood stock still. Maybe he took that as permission because then . . . then he stroked my breast. I was still dressed, of course, but . . .'

I begin to cry. Alex takes my hand. 'The lecherous bastard.'

I want to stop there. But Alex needs to know everything if he's going to understand what really happened on the night of the murder.

'I stepped back, and asked him what he was doing. He pretended to look shocked and said it was one of my silly made-up stories. Said I should help him tidy up the apples that I'd knocked when I stepped away from him. He made me feel foolish, as though I'd dreamed up the whole thing. But I knew I hadn't.'

'What did you do next?' asks Alex tightly.

'I ran out of the cellar. Duncan had left the key in the door. All I wanted to do was find Mum. She was in the kitchen. Claire had finished hanging out the washing and gone down to the beach. I was in tears. I told Mum everything but she wouldn't believe me. She said I must have mistaken that . . . that touching.'

'*Duncan is trying his best to be a good father to you, Nancy. Maybe he was giving you a cuddle. It's what fathers do. I don't want to hear any more about it. You've ruined my birthday.*'

'That's awful,' breathed Alex.

'I was so ashamed that I didn't even tell Claire. Duncan behaved perfectly normally when we went out to dinner later, involving me in the conversation with little remarks like, "What do you think, Nancy, love?"

'Inside, I felt sick. I knew what I'd seen and felt. What he'd done was no accident. But most of all, I felt angry with Mum, who was being very quiet. She should have believed me.'

'Why do you think she didn't?' asks Alex.

'I've asked myself this so many times. Maybe she was scared of losing Duncan – she'd hated being alone after Dad died.'

Alex makes an angry sound.

'I distanced myself emotionally from Mum after that. I was hurt and angry. Over the years, that anger grew and grew. Duncan would continue to give me lustful looks. I could tell. And Mum just didn't seem to notice. I took care to stay well away from him and refused to go back to Tall Chimneys again. Mum was very upset but I dug in my heels and said I'd stay with Claire instead. I couldn't wait to get away to university. I wasn't able to tell anyone until I was in my mid-twenties, when I finally told Claire. She was shocked.'

'So am I.' He holds me tight. 'Does anyone else know?'

I shake my head.

'You've had to carry this all by yourself?'

I nod. 'After university, I saw as little of Mum as possible and often ignored her calls. When we met occasionally, I refused to see Duncan. It put me off having long-term relationships because the idea of . . . of intimacy always brought me back to the cellar. Claire frequently encouraged me to "give it a go", but I couldn't. That's why she put me on that dating app, which is how I found you . . .'

He kisses my hand. 'I'm so glad you did.'

He won't be glad in a moment.

'I didn't want to go to Mum's birthday party,' I continue, 'because of the memories that the date always brings back and because I knew Duncan would be there. But I thought it would be all right if you were with me.'

I think back to his call, telling me that his flight from

Paris had been delayed. I'd so nearly not gone then. But I'd told myself that our impending marriage was giving me a clean start and that maybe I ought to try to restore my relationship with Mum.

His face darkens. 'I ought to have been there for you. Martin could have killed you too.'

This is where I have to tell him. Yet it's like holding a pistol to my own head.

I could stay quiet. Carry on, hiding the lie that will continue to eat me up like a snake, until it swallows me whole. Or I could tell the truth and destroy this man's love. But deep down I know I have no choice.

'It was me who killed Mum, Alex,' I hear myself blurt out. 'I'm a murderer.'

His face changes. He stares at me, horror in his face. 'You couldn't have done, Nancy. Please tell me that's not true.'

'But it is,' I cry.

The Night of the Murder

8.20 p.m.

Duncan's blood is everywhere. It's even in the grouting between the floor's flagstones.

Martin's face is demonic with fury.

There's no knowing what he's going to do next.

I grab the handle, trying to wrestle it from him. Mum is looking at me in terrified disbelief.

'Save me, Nancy,' say her eyes. 'Save me.'

Elizabeth

44

Elizabeth stared at the pool of blood, spooling wider and wider in the moonlight. Pressing her hands against her mouth, she willed herself not to scream. This couldn't have happened.

She couldn't have shot her husband. Not Henry. The father of her son. The man she'd promised to love until death do us part. She dimly remembered running towards him and pushing him away (something, she thought shamefully, which might not have been possible were it not for his bad leg). But she didn't recall grabbing the gun from him.

Yet she must have.

It was a reflex reaction, she reasoned. Her husband had been pointing the gun at her. She'd acted in self-protection, helped by the training which Jim had given her. Or had she wanted to kill him?

Initially she stood rigid, her body motionless. Then those suppressed screams rose up like waves of sickness. She couldn't stop them.

'Elizabeth,' said a voice. Someone was holding her arms. 'Stop, or someone will hear.'

In the fog of shock, she couldn't understand why Mr Smith had suddenly arrived. Then she remembered.

He must have come back to the house and seen that she and Henry were both missing. Had he guessed she would be here?

'I thought he was going to kill me,' she said, shaking. Telling herself it was true.

'It's OK. I believe you.'

He was shaking too. Then he looked up to the sky. 'Listen,' he said.

'What?'

'German planes,' he frowned. 'We have to go.'

An air raid? Elizabeth couldn't think straight, let alone move.

'Go home. Quickly!' He was shouting over the noise as the bombers got nearer and nearer.

'What about . . . him?'

Elizabeth couldn't even say the name 'Henry'. That body couldn't be him. Not that *thing* on the ground. How could a living, breathing person end up like that? How could she be responsible?

'Leave him to me. I'll sort this out. Now run.'

'Oh my God. Where's Karl?' She'd forgotten all about him.

'I don't know. But you can't worry about him now.'

'What if he wasn't really ill? What if he's signalling to the enemy?'

'There's nothing we can do. You have to get back. If anyone asks, just say you were looking for Henry but you couldn't find him. Now *go!*'

Elizabeth ran as fast as she could back through the Byes, narrowly avoiding her neighbour, Jim's sister, out with her dog. War was so hard for animals. They still had to do their business, even during raids. Had they seen her? Please no. Racing up the road, she headed for Tall Chimneys. In the past, its height had always given her a feeling of safety. But not now. Not after what she had just done.

BANG!

Elizabeth jumped at the sound of a bomb going off in the distance. It sounded close. She tried to shut the front door quietly behind her and then realized she wasn't alone.

Maisie was standing at the bottom of the stairs, eyes wide. So too were the paying guests huddled around her. The roar of the planes was overhead now. One after the other.

There was no time to get to the shelter. 'Under the dining-room table,' she said, grabbing Maisie and taking her with her.

One of the Patmore sisters began to whimper.

'Come on, ladies,' said Mrs Norris sternly. 'Where's your wartime spirit?'

'I'm frightened,' said the little girl. 'Are we going to die?'

'No, we're not.'

Elizabeth held Maisie to her under the table, stroking her hair as she might a daughter's. She used to do this to Robert when he was young, especially when he wasn't well. 'It will be all right,' she crooned.

'Listen,' she said after a while. The air was silent. 'They've gone.'

Indeed, there was the sound of the all-clear. Sweating with fear and relief, they crawled out.

'Is everyone all right?' asked Elizabeth, taking in the

sisters with their curlers in and Mrs Norris, standing as upright as any soldier.

'Yes, thank you,' retorted the latter. 'What about you?'

'We're all right, aren't we, Maisie?'

'But where's Mr Montague?' asked one of the sisters.

'I don't know,' said Elizabeth, her voice shaking.

'And what about Mr Smith?'

'He went to help someone.' At least that was true.

'Well, I hope they're both safe.'

She distracted them all with cups of hot cocoa, using the last of her precious supply. Then she went to bed, waiting. Trembling. At one stage she thought she heard someone coming in. It must be Mr Smith. Should she get up? But if she did, someone might see her talking with him. Better to wait until morning.

How could she think and rationalize so coldly? Didn't she care that her husband was dead?

But to her shame, all she could think about was Mr Smith. What if he was seen? What would he say? And if he had been spotted, would he tell them what she'd done?

45

In the morning, Elizabeth woke early. Going downstairs, she found Mr Smith in the kitchen, washing his clothes in the sink. She was just in time to see a streak of red go down the plughole. Vomit rose up into her mouth.

'It's all right,' he said gently, holding her hair back as she retched over the basin. 'Now take a sip of water.'

'What did you do with my husband?' she whispered.

'It's best that you don't know.'

'Did you find Karl?'

'No.'

'But what do I tell the police? The guests know Henry wasn't here last night.'

'Wait until lunchtime. Ask around to see if anyone has seen Henry, as you would if – you know . . . Then report him as missing.'

They looked at each other, each thinking the same thought, or so Elizabeth felt. Terrible as the enemy's raid on Exeter had been, it might be an excuse for Henry's disappearance. Other people – poor souls – might have gone missing too. Bodies weren't always found after a bombing. And if they were, they were frequently unrecognizable.

Elizabeth was sick again. What kind of a person was she, she wondered, to think this way?

Within a couple of hours, reports were coming in thick

and fast of the damage to the Exeter area. Frequently Elizabeth found herself weeping with shock and guilt.

Mrs Norris patted her back, reassuring her that Henry would be found soon. Eventually, unable to eat lunch, she summoned up the courage to go to the police station.

'Where do you think your husband went when he left the house last night?' asked the officer.

Elizabeth could feel from the heat of her face that she was blushing furiously. 'I don't know, but I am aware that he had . . . had a friend.'

She hadn't known she was going to say this until it came out of her mouth.

The policeman went silent. He nodded. 'I'll have a word at the bakery.'

She flushed even more. Had everyone else in the town known apart from her?

Later in the day there was a knock. A tall blonde woman stood there, her eyes red from crying. It was Polly Bright.

'What do you want?' demanded Elizabeth, trembling on the inside.

The woman was pale. Not exactly repentant, but not brash either. 'I need you to know that your husband wasn't with me last night. It isn't what you're thinking.'

Elizabeth could hear her own heart thudding. This woman might be telling the truth, but she had been sleeping with her husband. She couldn't deny that. 'Isn't it? What *do* I think then?'

Polly shrugged. 'I can't say.'

This time, a distinct look of guilt passed over her face. Elizabeth recognized it all too well. It was how she felt inside.

'Well, I'll tell you then. You and my *husband* have not been very discreet. You've been seen together. Several times, in fact, in the woods at the top of Salcombe Hill. Do you think I'm a fool?'

'I'm sorry,' the woman burst out. 'Really I am. We didn't mean to hurt you. It's the war. It changes everything. Please, let me explain –'

Elizabeth slammed the door in the woman's face. Afterwards, she stood with her back to it, letting the tears flow out. She might not have loved Henry any more. In fact, she had hated him. But they had shared a history. A past. A child. It created a bond that you could never forget, no matter how much you wanted to.

Later, she forced herself to go round town and ask if anyone had seen Henry, as Mr Smith had advised. No one had. Their concern made her feel like a fraud.

What would they do if they knew the truth?

She passed the postmistress leaving her shift. 'Have you heard the news?'

Oh my God. Had Henry's body been found?

'What?' Elizabeth said nervously.

The postmistress clearly couldn't wait to tell her. 'A German pilot bailed out during the raid. Hid in the woods overnight. Limped into the police station this morning and gave himself up, claiming to be ill. In one of the camps now, he is. Deserves to swing, if you ask me.'

46

Elizabeth waited for the police to arrest her.

Surely Karl would tell them about the woman who had helped him and then shot her husband in cold blood? It might enable him to make some kind of deal.

But nothing happened. No one knocked on her door to take her away. Instead, a steady stream of callers came to express their sympathies that Henry was missing. The body of a man from Lyme Regis, who had been walking on the cliffs when a bomb fell, had been washed up on a nearby beach. The general unspoken assumption on these callers' faces was that the same fate must have befallen Henry.

'I've been keeping an eye out for a body in the river,' said one of his former army cronies from the Conservative Club bluntly. 'No sign of him. But I'll keep looking.'

The men at the yard had organized a search party, combing the woods and the land right down to the sea. 'I'm so sorry, Mrs Montague,' said one of them after a few days. 'We've found nothing.'

'Thank you for looking,' Elizabeth said shakily. But she couldn't help wondering about Karl as well. Was he getting the right medical treatment? What if he'd died too? Was she a traitor to worry about him? Or was she transferring her grief over Robert to concern for another woman's son?

The following week Mr Smith and Maisie went back to London. Maisie's mum and family had been given accommodation and they had decided they'd be better off all together. Several other evacuees were going home too now that the intensive bombing on London was easing up. Besides, after the Exeter raid, there was a feeling that the South West might be just as dangerous.

'I will miss you, Mrs Montague,' wept Maisie at the station. 'But I do want to be with Mum and Dad and my brothers and sisters.'

'Of course you do,' she said, hugging the child tight, partly to hide her own tears. 'Remember that Tall Chimneys will always be your second home if you want to come back – and after the war too.'

Then she shook hands with Mr Smith. Part of her wanted to beg him to stay. But another part was relieved. He was the only connection to her terrible crime – apart from Karl – and his presence was a constant reminder.

'Thank you so much for your kind hospitality, Mrs Montague,' he said formally.

'It's been good to know you, Mr Smith,' she said. Then she whispered 'Have you heard if he's all right?'

Instinctively, she knew there was no need to say Karl's name.

He shook his head.

Elizabeth watched as he walked away.

'Wait,' she heard herself call out.

Then she reached into her handbag. Quite what had made her put it in there before leaving the house, she didn't know. It had been in one of her drawers ever since she had returned from that futile trip to London. Until this moment, she hadn't been certain. But now she was.

'Take this, please,' she said, running after him. It was the navy-blue scarf she'd knitted for Robert. 'It will keep you warm.'

His eyes widened. 'Isn't this . . .?'

'Just take it, Stephen,' she said urgently.

Then she turned and walked away.

It was only then that she realized she'd called him by his first name.

Tall Chimneys was oddly quiet, especially after Mrs Norris went home. 'My great-niece in Northumbria has had a baby and could do with another pair of hands. It's such a job to get help nowadays. You've been so kind to us. As a token of my gratitude, I'd like you to have these.'

She pressed her binoculars into Elizabeth's hand. 'They might come in useful.'

'But they belonged to your father.'

'I am sure he would want you to have them,' said Mrs Norris briskly.

The Patmore sisters went back to their home shortly afterwards amidst effusive thanks.

'We do hope you get some news on poor Mr Montague,' one of them said.

'It must be so hard not to know what happened,' said the other.

Elizabeth swallowed the giant ball of guilt in her throat. 'Yes,' she said. 'It is.'

But she couldn't help thinking that the women were going because Henry was no longer there. It had made them feel safe, having a man in the house. The mystery of his disappearance unsettled them. It unsettled her too. At times, she thought he was calling out to her in that commanding manner of his. '*Elizabeth? Those PGs have eaten all the jam again.*'

It was almost as if the house was haunted by his absence.

Nightmares about shooting him dogged her, and every night she would wake, screaming.

She might not have been arrested for his death, Elizabeth thought as she tried to calm herself in the small hours of the morning, but it was as though someone had given her a jail sentence nevertheless. A silent sentence that she couldn't tell anyone about.

There was something else that occupied her greatly. People were beginning to whisper about Adeline, who was getting larger by the day, try as she did to conceal her pregnancy with loose clothing.

One day her friend arrived on the doorstep, shaking. 'Someone put a stone through my window this morning and then I found a note under my door, calling me a tart. I'm going to leave the day after tomorrow to stay with my cousin in Salisbury.'

No! Adeline couldn't go! How would she manage here on her own? Elizabeth knew that was selfish, but she couldn't help herself.

If only she could drive there to see her! But you weren't meant to drive unless you had special permission or good cause, like an emergency.

'I'll miss you,' said Elizabeth, unable to hide the catch in her voice.

'I'll miss you too, but I can't stay here any longer. Brian says that as soon as the war is over, he'll take me back to Canada and we'll pretend we're married until I can get a divorce. No one will know.'

Trust Adeline to have it all sorted.

Then her voice changed. 'I'm so sorry about Henry. Maybe he'll turn up alive and well. You do hear about these things.'

Time and time again, Elizabeth had wanted to tell her friend what had happened. But what if Adeline then informed her cell handler? Elizabeth might be shot.

Two days later, when she was in town and about to walk home, she saw the church flag flying at half-mast.

Her heart caught in her chest. Had they found Henry, wherever he was? No. They'd have told her first. Wouldn't they?

'Haven't you heard?' said one of the women from Fields who was passing by. 'A Canadian plane from the base was shot down last night. The pilot was killed.'

'Do you know his name?' Elizabeth asked, a sinking feeling in her stomach.

'Brian somebody.'

Elizabeth ran as fast as she could to Adeline's house. 'I've just heard,' she panted, flinging her arms around her.

Her friend was pale and strained. Her face exhausted from crying. There was a battered case by her feet.

'Surely you're not still going?'

'I have to. I can't stay here. They'll ostracize me for being an unmarried mother. When George gets back,

God knows what he'll do.' Her voice rose in panic. 'I have no one to look after me.'

Suddenly Elizabeth felt a new life and courage rising up inside her. She grasped Adeline's hands. 'Yes you do. You have me. Come and live at Tall Chimneys. We'll brazen it out. I'll help you. We'll bring up your baby together.'

A brief look of hope fluttered across Adeline's face. Then it fell. 'But what will happen when George comes home?'

'We'll face that when he does.'

She had nothing left to lose. And if the town shunned her for supporting her friend, well, so be it. The three of them would somehow manage alone.

47

'Hold my hand, Violet,' said Elizabeth encouragingly as they walked over the beach towards the water. 'One step at a time. That's right. Clever girl! Doesn't it feel lovely?'

Many children were scared when they went into the sea for the first time. But not Violet. Then again, Elizabeth and Adeline had taken her into the water, each holding a chubby little hand, almost from the beginning of her young life. Not down at the seafront, of course – that was still strewn with barbed wire and other deterrents like logs and railway sleepers to stop the tanks getting through the beaches – but in the little spot to the side of Weston Beach which was usually quiet, even in peacetime.

Violet was such a striking little girl! She had dark glossy curls – Adeline said they were just like her father's – and a determined manner that made it clear, almost from the first, that she was in charge and that she would do exactly what she wanted in life.

Long may it last, thought Elizabeth. Any child born outside wedlock would need confidence and strength to counter the disapproval she would surely receive from society.

As for Henry, she tried to block him from her mind. It was the only way she could cope with the guilt. Yet there were times when she wished she'd pushed Mr Smith into telling her where he had put her husband's body. Indeed, the need to know grew so strong last year that she had written to his school, asking him to get in touch. The reply came back within a fortnight. Mr Smith had left. His whereabouts were 'unknown'.

'Where's Mummy?' demanded Violet, breaking into her thoughts.

'I'm here, darling.'

Adeline emerged from behind a rock, where she'd been changing into her costume. Violet – both women had agreed she couldn't be called anything else with eyes like those – held out an arm and the three of them walked in. Today the sea was flat. So calm that it didn't seem real. Last week it had been furious, waves pounding against the rocks.

But then the world was like that now.

People said that Hitler was on the run. Yet it wasn't over yet. There was talk of the 'last push into Europe'. But how and when it would happen was anyone's guess.

'I can't see anyone else, can you?' asked Adeline, glancing around.

'No – and it doesn't matter if there is,' replied Elizabeth firmly.

Adeline didn't look convinced. It wasn't any wonder, really. Most of the folk in town had given her the cold shoulder, refusing to even acknowledge the baby in Robert's old pram, which Elizabeth had brought down from the attic.

'Of course you must use it,' she had said when Adeline had given her a questioning look. 'Robert would have wanted it.' Sometimes it helped to say her son's name out loud. It forced her to acknowledge that he was gone for ever. And also that he had once lived.

Maisie wrote to her every few months, telling her about all the things she was doing at school and how she loved being back with her mum and dad. '*But I doo mis you,*' she wrote.

'Look, Violet, there's a seagull!' said Adeline, pointing.

'Bird,' trilled Violet.

'That's right. Clever girl!'

Adeline was correct. Violet was bright. Elizabeth could only hope that her friend's child would be the same. Women who had babies out of wedlock were outcasts, and their children were tarred with the same brush. With any luck, opinions might soften after the war. After all, Adeline wasn't the only one. Mrs B's niece in London had fallen in love with an airman who had neglected to tell her he was married. Now she was on her own with his baby and Mrs B's sister. 'A real tragedy, it is,' Mrs B had declared.

But how could anyone call a baby a tragedy? Just look at Violet. So full of life. So content.

'She has her father's happy-go-lucky attitude,' Adeline said, as if reading her mind.

Elizabeth squeezed her friend's hand in comfort. 'I'm sorry.'

Adeline had wept for months after news of Brian's death. And Elizabeth could tell she still wasn't over it.

'Don't be. She gives me comfort.'

Adeline had written to Brian's family after Violet was born. His parents had sent a short, stiffly worded letter back saying that they were glad their son had had some happiness before he died. They enclosed some money.

There had been nothing to suggest they wanted to see their granddaughter.

'And what about George?' asked Elizabeth gently.

Writing a letter to her husband, who was now fighting in France, had been one of the hardest things Adeline had ever done. Elizabeth knew because she'd helped her phrase the wording. But they couldn't put it off any longer, as she'd said. Someone was bound to let someone else in his platoon know that Adeline was pregnant with another man's child.

'He plans to divorce me as soon as he's back.'

But what if he didn't return? A shameful part of Elizabeth couldn't help thinking it would help her friend's situation. Divorce was so shameful. No! What was she thinking? George deserved to live. Just as Henry had deserved to.

'You'll feel better when it's all sorted out,' said Elizabeth, knowing as she spoke that this wasn't necessarily true.

'Will I? What will happen when Violet goes to school? Supposing the other kids make fun of her?'

'People's attitudes will change,' replied Elizabeth with a forcefulness she didn't really feel inside. 'You'll see.'

'And what about you?' said Adeline.

'I'm fine,' said Elizabeth quickly. She didn't deserve anyone's pity. 'Now, let's have a bit of a splash about, shall we, Violet?'

Swimming had become even more of an escape for her after Henry's death. The shock was the only thing that could clear her mind for a few moments. But the following day when she got up and looked out of the window, the sea seemed black! Then she realized why. There were hundreds and hundreds of ships in convoys going out across the water towards France.

Mrs B came rushing in through the door, early for work. 'Have you heard?' she asked excitedly. 'Have you seen the boats? Word has it that the Allied Forces are going to invade Normandy! By sea, air and gawd knows what!' She jumped up and down. 'We've won the bleeding war!'

48

She wasn't quite right.

It took almost a year before the end of the war looked certain. The BBC broadcast a report from Richard Dimbleby as he entered Belsen with the troops in April 1945. There had been terrible stories about gas chambers before but not everyone had believed them. They were too horrific. But it was all true.

How could anyone be so evil?

On the 30th, Hitler committed suicide.

For Elizabeth, nothing felt real. Even when VE Day arrived a few days later and there was singing and dancing in the streets in Sidmouth and throughout the country, Elizabeth felt numb. After everything they'd been through, it seemed impossible they could just make merry as though nothing had happened.

They'd been at war for so long that the abnormal now felt normal.

It was hard to accept that you could walk down the street without fear of being bombed, or that men were now beginning to pull up the barbed wire on the beaches.

Or that Henry and Robert were gone for ever.

Meanwhile, little Violet was chatting away, an early talker, and proving very agile on her feet. The three women – including Mrs B – had their hands full making sure she was always in sight. They survived on Henry's pension and by taking in paying guests again. The sisters and Mrs Norris sent letters to say that they were holidaying elsewhere – 'as a change', said the Patmores. Maybe they wanted to forget about the war as much as Elizabeth did.

Thank goodness for Violet, Elizabeth often thought. She brought a welcome energy to their lives. Yet at the same time, her very existence added a level of fear every day.

'I'm terrified about what George will do when he comes home,' said Adeline.

'Don't be. You and Violet are safe here with me.' Inside, though, she wasn't so sure.

George hadn't been a violent man, but he'd written vitriolic letters to Adeline when she'd told him about the child and made it clear that he was going to drag her name through the mud when he returned.

He must have had time to reflect, however, because a few months later, Adeline received another letter from him. He declared that he couldn't come back to a town where she had caused him so much shame. He was going to make his life elsewhere.

'It's a relief, to be honest,' Adeline said as they sat in the garden. 'Maybe I should do the same. I could pass myself off as a war widow in a new place. Then Violet would be accepted.'

'No,' said Elizabeth quickly. 'Please don't. I would miss you both terribly.'

'We'd miss you too.' Adeline glanced across at Violet, who was sitting in Elizabeth's lap. 'She adores you.'

'And I adore her. It's so lovely to feel a little one in my arms again.' She steadied her gaze on a beautiful apricot rose outside the sitting room. 'If it hadn't been for the war, Robert might be a father by now.'

Adeline reached out and touched her arm. 'I'm so sorry.'

For a moment, Elizabeth's eyes blurred. 'Thank you.' Then she stood up. 'Right. Let's have our own celebration. I've made some butterfly cakes with eggs from the farm.'

'Eggs?' trilled Violet. 'Real ones?'

They laughed. 'Yes. Real ones.'

'You know,' said Adeline, 'before the war, we had real flour in cakes. Not the kind we have now.'

'Like flowers in the garden?' asked Violet.

Her speech was amazingly advanced for a three-year-old.

'I mean a different kind of flour. In fact . . .'

Adeline stopped at the sound of the gate. Looked up. Her face blanched.

Elizabeth, who had been cuddling Violet, looked up too.

No. It couldn't be. He was dead. She'd seen his body with her own eyes.

But now here he was. Coming in through the back gate and over the lawn. Standing in front of her. His eyes cold. His face set.

'Henry?' she whispered. 'You're alive?'

The Night of the Murder

8.25 p.m.

'Listen carefully,' says Martin. 'This is what we have to do.'

In my shock, his words come to me as though from under water.

'Got it?'

I nod. And I ring 999, just as he'd told me to.

'What happened?' demand the police when I let them in through the front door of the farmhouse.

I try to talk but the words are jumbled up in my throat.

'Who did this?'

My mouth is glued shut, paralysed with fear and shock and disbelief. I can feel sweat running down my back. Urine trickling down between my legs. This couldn't have happened. It couldn't.

'Nancy,' says a policewoman. She must have got my name from the emergency call. 'You have to tell us.'

Nancy

49

'You are a murderer?' repeats Alex. He gets out of bed and looks at me as if I am a stranger. In that instant, I know I have changed our lives for ever. There is no going back. There is no new start.

'Let me explain,' I sob.

He makes a strange sound, indicating that you can't simply 'explain' something like that. Maybe he's right. But I can try. My mind goes back to the night of my mother's birthday. To Martin meeting me outside the farmhouse, as if pretending we are a couple.

Me telling Duncan to behave. Martin overhearing our conversation and following us into the kitchen, pushing me to explain. My birthday present to Mum – an album of photographs showing just me, Mum and Dad to purposefully piss off Duncan. Duncan's revelation that Mum had been carrying on with him while Dad was alive. Me blurting it all out, word for word:

'Your father is no better than a paedophile, Martin. He came on to me in the cellar at Tall Chimneys when I was fifteen. Didn't you, Duncan? You actually touched my breast. Goodness knows what else you might have done if I hadn't got away.'

As I try to describe it all to Alex, it's as though I am there now. Seeing it in the present.

'You touched my girl,' says Martin. His face is rigid with

fury. His bushy eyebrows are knitted with rage. And then, as if he can barely believe it, he says, 'You touched her, Dad?'

Duncan looks nervous. 'Steady on, son. She's lying.'

'Please, Nancy,' begs my mother. 'Stop.'

Anger is boiling up inside me now. 'It's Duncan you should have told to stop. You chose to side with him so you didn't upset your bully of a husband. If you'd stood up to him, none of this would have happened. Do you know how much damage the two of you have done to me?'

'Oh, come on,' snarled Duncan. 'You're making a mountain out of a molehill here. It's not as though we ever had sex.'

My mother went very quiet. 'So you did touch her?'

'If I did, Violet,' he slurred, 'you've only yourself to blame. You should have showed me more affection instead of constantly talking about your bloody first husband, even though – let's face it – you cheated on him. Besides, you'd let yourself go. Can you blame me for looking elsewhere?'

'You fucker.' Martin's voice was cold. Chilling. 'You touched my girl, Dad. You're going to pay for this.'

The knife rack is on the side. I've always thought it was a dangerous thing to have in the house. An armoury of lethal weapons, hiding under the guise of domesticity.

But isn't that exactly what a family is like?

At least, it is with mine. Sharp tongues, bedded next to each other, simmering with resentment.

'It's all your fault!' someone screams.

I realize the someone is me.

Duncan flinches.

Words are pouring out of my mouth like a battle cry.

326

Words I have been hiding for years, which are now flying through the air like bullets.

Everything happens so fast that it's hard to remember the exact order of events. But this is what I do recall. My mother dropping the fish knife. Martin picking it up. Examining it briefly and then tossing it to one side to choose a sharper one from the rack instead. The blade glinting in the ceiling spotlights. My stepfather thudding to the floor with a terrifying cry as Martin plunges the blade into his chest before pulling it out again. The knife falling. Me reaching for it so that no one else can be hurt.

Duncan is bleeding on the floor. My mother is crying, shaking him. 'Don't die! I don't want to be alone.'

'How can you say that, Mum? He admitted touching me.'

Martin's chilling voice. 'You should have believed my girl, Violet.'

Then he snatches the knife off me. I fight him for it, scared he's going to kill Mum too. But my hands slip on the bloodied handle. I steer it in one direction. Martin pulls it in another. We're both screaming and shouting at each other. The knife is back in my hands now. He pushes me towards Mum. And then suddenly – shockingly – a fountain of blood spurts out of my mother's throat. She collapses on the ground, screaming in agony, and then goes silent. Her eyes are open, fixed on those spotlights.

My stepfather lies next to her. Motionless.

An eerie silence settles.

'No,' I whisper.

We had each killed our parent.

Together, we stare in horror at the two bodies.

'Listen,' says Martin tightly. 'This is what we have to do.'

50

'Is that the full story?' asks the DI when I've finished. We're in the police station at Honiton. Alex had driven me there, at my request, after my confession. Neither of us spoke to the other. He doesn't want me now, I realize. And I don't blame him.

'Yes,' I sob. 'That is everything.'

'So, to get this straight, it wasn't your stepbrother who stabbed your mother. It was you, but you didn't mean to.'

I try to sound clear. 'I didn't even know I'd done it until the knife went in.'

'Your fingerprints weren't on the weapon,' she says.

'It's because Martin wiped them off,' I say. 'He said he wanted to protect me and that he'd go down anyway for stabbing his father so he might as well confess to two murders. I was in shock. So I agreed. Later, when the police questioned me, I was too terrified to take it back. I told myself that what Martin had said was true. He was going to go down anyway. So why not let him take the blame for both murders? But the guilt burned away at me, minute by minute, hour by hour. My mother kept coming back with that glazed expression in her eyes to haunt me in my nightmares. To make it worse, Martin was continually reminding me from prison of my "debt" to him. He used it to try and get me to agree to go away with him when he escaped. I tried to escape but he pulled me out of the house to the coast.'

'I see.'

I'm not sure that I do. Accident or not, I had killed my mother.

'What happens next?' I ask.

'I need to submit a report for the Crown Prosecution. They will decide if there is enough evidence for us to charge you.'

Her voice suggests that there should be.

'I loved my mother,' I sob.

'A killer told me that . . . ,' says the DI. She doesn't finish her sentence. She doesn't have to.

It's quite clear.

I am as responsible for my mother's death as Martin was for his father's.

What am I meant to do now, while I wait for the police to arrest me? I almost feel like catching a ferry as Martin had suggested and running away. But I've been told I can't leave the country. And besides, it's time to face the truth.

Vera comes round to see me, her arm in a sling.

'Thank you for trying to save me,' I say.

'I only did what any decent person would have done,' she replies. 'Do you know the worst thing one can do in life?'

There are so many, I want to say.

'Not stand up to evil. My uncle Jim was in the secret army, you know, during the war. He used to own the garage in Bridge Street. It provided a good front. He trained your grandmother Adeline and her best friend Elizabeth. My mother told me after it was all over, instructing me not to tell a soul. But I think it's important for you to know that brave blood runs in your family.'

Vera's uncle had trained my grandmother? 'Is it true that they were given a pin as recognition of their work?' I ask.

'Yes,' she says. 'In fact, I gave Uncle Jim's pin to the museum along with some other papers. I asked Jeremy not to disclose the name of the owner. Not everyone agreed with what he did. People can be odd about these things, even all these years later.'

So that explains the pin I'd found in the archives. Had Jeremy really 'mislaid' it or had he deliberately buried it?

'You don't have to worry about me telling anyone,' I say slowly. 'I may not be around for much longer.'

Then I explain why. I don't want any secrets from this woman, even though I barely know her. I feel I owe her the truth. I tell her everything that happened from that last summer in Tall Chimneys to the night at the farmhouse.

'It's why I broke off my engagement to Alex,' I add. 'We were going to be married. But then Mum died and I couldn't go through with it without admitting that her death was my fault. I was also too ashamed to tell him what Duncan had done to me as a teenager. Sometimes I wondered if it had been my fault for leading him on in some way.'

Vera wraps her good arm around me. 'You poor child,' she says. 'Are you going to tell Alex all this now?'

'I have done.'

'How did he take it?'

'He was very understanding about Duncan – but then

I told him about . . . about what I did to Mum. He said he needed time to think.'

'I see. Where is he now?'

'I don't know,' I gulp. 'I haven't heard from him since he left.'

'Look, dear.' Vera had never called me 'dear' before. 'I'm no expert in love. But may I make a small suggestion?'

51

There's an inquest into Martin's death. The verdict is 'Death by drowning'. I leave the coroner's court in a daze. None of this feels real.

'Disgraceful,' I hear someone mutter. 'The pair of them put others' lives at risk by going out in such terrible weather.'

'I heard he forced her to go with him,' says someone else.

I walk on quickly, pretending I haven't heard.

I wish I could talk to Alex, but he hasn't rung. And, despite Vera's suggestion that I write him an 'old-fashioned letter about what happened because written words might sink in better', I am too ashamed to make contact with him.

Shortly afterwards comes a phone call that casts a ray of hope into the darkness. It's Richard, Claire's husband. 'We've got our baby girl!'

How wonderful! I wait for a pang of jealousy but it doesn't come. Besides, I wasn't responsible enough to be a mother after what I had done.

'The thing is that Claire's a bit down in the dumps,' continues Richard.

'Why?'

'Well, she had to have an emergency caesarean, and they think she's got the baby blues. But also, honestly, I think she's worried about you. And . . .' He hesitates. 'And she says she needs to see you to tell you something.'

'What?'

'I don't know. But it would be great if you could get here as soon as possible. I'm concerned about her, Nancy.'

So I catch the train up to London, leaving Sheba with Jasmine. We've had several talks about Alex and her brother but have agreed to leave it there. If I'd had a real brother, I might have stuck up for him too.

Claire is lying in bed, looking very pale. The baby – they haven't named her yet – is in a cot by the side.

'I'll leave you alone,' says Richard.

Claire reaches out a hand to me. 'I need to tell you something,' she says. 'I've been wanting to do so for years, but having this little one has made me realize I can't keep it back any more. I'd kill anyone who hurt her.'

'Go on,' I say nervously. I've got a bad feeling about this.

'Remember when you told me that Martin had kissed you?'

I nod.

'I was jealous.'

'Why? You said he was creepy.'

'He was. But I wanted to be the first one who got kissed.' Claire shakes her head as if she's cross with herself. 'Sounds silly, I know, but you know what it was like. Teenage girls can be awful to each other – so competitive.'

I remember all too well. 'Was that why you shut me out?' I ask.

She nods. 'Yes. I'm sorry. But there you were, getting all this attention from a boy, and I wasn't.'

Then she hesitates. 'There's something else, and I'm so

sorry, Nancy. During that holiday at Tall Chimneys just after our fifteenth birthdays . . .'

She hesitates. 'I never told you this, but I saw him . . .'

'Martin?'

'No. Duncan.' Her voice is shaky. 'I was in the garden hanging out washing for your mum and heard voices from the cellar. I peered through the half-window and saw Duncan touching you where . . . where he shouldn't. Then I saw you arguing.'

The image is so clear in my head that I want to be sick.

'After you ran out, I must have made a noise because he saw me through the window and came out to find me,' continues Claire. 'No one else was around. I didn't know where you'd gone. He said that if I told anyone, he'd deny it. I still remember his exact words: "No one will believe a young girl. Your parents will be ashamed of you, and you won't have any friends ever again."'

'That sounds like him,' I say through gritted teeth.

'It's worse, Nancy. The following day, your mother approached me privately, saying that you'd told her that Duncan had touched you "inappropriately", as she put it. She asked me if it was true. And I . . . I said I didn't think it could be because you would have told me.'

'I can't believe you did that,' I say, my ears ringing with shock.

'I'm so sorry, Nancy. I was so scared of him. I didn't know what to do. And you seemed OK. So in the end I convinced myself I'd got it wrong.'

The full implications of my friend's betrayal are beginning to sink in.

'It was only when we were grown-up and you told me

about Duncan that I realized what a huge mistake I had made. And then I couldn't find a way to say something. I should have been brave enough to be honest. Can you ever forgive me?'

'I don't know,' I say slowly.

'I appreciate it's a big ask.'

Suddenly I feel anger flashing through me. 'A big ask? It's a lot more than that. If my mother had believed me, she might have left Duncan and still been alive today. Yes – you're right about the psychological damage. I refused to go out on a date for years because I couldn't bear the idea of anyone touching me, until I met Alex. But the worst thing was not being believed by my own mother.'

Claire puts her head in her hands. 'I should have told you, but I knew you'd probably never forgive me. I thought maybe if I found you someone kind it would be a way for you to heal.'

I recall how insistent she'd been about getting me to sign up for a dating site and then selecting the 'right' person.

'You helped me find a boyfriend because you felt guilty?'

'I suppose so, yes. But it worked out, didn't it? Alex is a good man.'

I think back to what he'd told me about his past. He might not have been driving that car but he *had* encouraged Paul. Someone could have died. 'He hasn't always been,' I say.

'Have any of us?' Claire's voice is beseeching. 'Which one of us can honestly say we haven't done anything wrong?'

She's right. I was going to keep this to myself but I can't.

'Claire,' I say, trembling. 'The night Mum died, I . . . I did something awful. Or I think I might have done.'

My best friend is staring at me in an odd way. 'I don't understand.'

'It wasn't Martin who killed her,' I whisper.

'What?'

I want to stop but I've gone too far. 'We fought over the knife after he'd stabbed Duncan. I was scared he was going to kill Mum but I was furious with her too, partly because she hadn't believed me about Duncan but also because I discovered they'd been having a relationship when my poor dad was dying . . .'

I burst into tears. 'Martin pushed me towards her and . . . and the knife went into her throat. But the fact is that I was so angry that I'm not sure if I meant to put that blade in or not. So I've been to the police and given a statement.'

Claire is staring at me as if she can't believe what I've just said. Nor can I.

'If you had told Mum the truth at the time,' I repeat, as if trying to justify my actions, 'none of this might have happened.'

'You're right.' She looks down at the bed covers. 'I should have done. But if you're saying what I think you are – that you might have killed your own mother – you can't put all the blame on me.'

That's true too.

Then the baby stirs. She's so tiny. Like a little doll with that rosebud mouth.

'Would you like to pick her up?' asks Claire. Her voice is strained as if she wants to change the subject.

'Not now,' I say, getting up. 'I think I need to leave.'

'What does Alex say?' she asks, her voice wavering.

'He hasn't rung me since I told him what I've just told you.'

The baby's cries are getting louder. They remind me once again of how different Claire's life is from mine. I make my way out of her house. She must have phoned Alex after I'd gone because my mobile rings within the hour.

Alex and I meet up in 'our' wine bar near his house. I feel an overwhelming wave of regret as I look around, remembering how many happy hours we'd sat here, planning our future.

I tell him about Claire's confession.

'She was wrong to lie to your mother,' he says when I finish. 'But she was young, and I can see why she did it. We all make mistakes.'

'This wasn't just a mistake,' I snap. 'It changed everything. If she had told the truth then I wouldn't have . . .'

'I know. I'm sorry. I'm here for you, Nancy. I really am. Look, I won't lie. I was shocked when you told me about your mother. Just as you were shocked when I told you about the car accident.'

'My crime is worse,' I blurt out.

'How can we honestly grade a crime? I know the courts do it, but there's so much more to it than that, isn't there? The man we hit could easily have died. The thing is, Nancy, that I've been having a very good think. I'm still here if you want me.'

'All I want right now,' I say, 'is to go home.'

'Your flat is still being watched by the press. They got interested again after Martin drowned.'

I wince. 'Not that place,' I say. 'My real home. Tall Chimneys. If I leave now, I can get the last train from Waterloo.'

He stands up. 'Let me drive you.'

My heart lifts a little to see the house as we come into Sidmouth. The towering chimneys make me feel safe and secure. Perhaps it's their height, which elevates it above the others in the road. *We will protect you*, they seem to say, like sentinels on guard.

This really is home now, I realize. Despite everything that happened in the cellar all those years ago.

But when I open the door, there's an official letter on the mat.

I have to stand trial. For the murder of my mother.

52

I look through the glass screen in front of me at the barristers in their gowns and wigs. The gallery is packed with some familiar faces (Alex, Vera, Jasmine) and many whom I don't know. Some are holding notebooks. Of course. The press. I look at the judge, a youngish-looking woman with a prefect-like expression. And I look at the jury.

'They are the ones who will decide your future,' Judith had told me. 'There's no knowing which way they will go.'

One woman is staring at me hard, as if trying to work out if I am guilty just from my face. A young man seems as though he would rather be somewhere else. Judith has found a defence barrister who has several years of experience in murder cases. She has asked me so many questions in preparation for today that I am drained. But I have answered each one as truthfully as I can. I have had enough of lies.

Judith and the barrister have also explained the 'order of proceedings', as they call it. But I am so exhausted that I cannot follow it. The barrister had pleaded for me to be granted bail but the judge had refused.

So I've spent the last three months in a remand prison. I'm lucky it wasn't longer, but it was enough. My cellmate was a woman who had hit her husband on the head with a spade after discovering he'd had an affair. When I told her about my mother, she said she would have done the same. It didn't reassure me, especially when I saw her make coffee for another woman in the communal kitchen and slip a used tampon into it. 'She deserves it,' she whispered, seeing I had spotted her. 'That one's a right bitch.'

But it was the isolation that I found worse. The intense need for fresh air. We only had an hour a day outside in the yard for exercise. My cellmate said it was more than she got at her last prison.

At night, I would close my eyes and think of Tall Chimneys. Then nightmares of my mother would take over. Her glassy eyes. Blood spurting from her throat. Duncan touching me in the cellar.

The women had wished me good luck when I'd left this morning. Some cheered me on as I left the dining room to get into the prison car that would take me to court. 'If you did it, Nancy, I wouldn't blame you,' yells one.

I listen to the voices now in court. Some of them make sense. Some of them don't. I am here. But I am not here. I want my mother. I don't want my mother. I want Alex here. Yet I don't want him here. What is he thinking? I don't want Claire – if she'd told my mother the truth, this might never have happened. But then I see her rushing into the public gallery, late. I turn my head away. Maybe I'm going out of my mind. Perhaps she's not there at all. Maybe I'm not, either.

There's a stirring. The guard turns to me. 'You're on,' she says brusquely. I walk in a daze to the stand. I take my oath.

Then the prosecution launches into me. 'Nancy. Can you tell the court exactly what happened that night?'

So I do. I tell them about Duncan touching me. I tell

340

them about Claire not telling my mother. I tell them about my mother not believing me. I tell them of the resulting coolness between us. I tell them about the birthday party that I hadn't wanted to go to but went to because my then fiancé had persuaded me. I tell them about Martin's obsession with me. I tell them how my mother heard Duncan admitting that he'd touched me. And I tell them about Martin picking up the knife and stabbing Duncan.

'I took it off him again, hanging on to it, scared he might hurt someone else. He tried to get it back and in the tussle, pushed me towards her. And . . . the knife went into Mum.'

Tears are flooding down my face. The young juror who had seemed disinterested earlier on is staring at me in horror.

'It was an accident,' I cry out.

'Are you sure?' asks the barrister. 'You'd been angry with your mother for many years. You'd just found out that she had an affair with your stepfather when she was still married to your father. Perhaps, subconsciously, you wanted to kill her.'

'I've thought of this,' I say. As I speak, I see my own barrister from the bench look horrified. This isn't something I have shared with her. 'Sometimes I wonder that too. But I'd like to think that wasn't true. I just wanted to get the knife off Martin before he did anything else. I loved my mother. I think of her every day. I miss her.'

I look at the jury, whose faces are glued to mine. 'Every child needs a mother. Even if they are adults.'

A woman nods. The young man wipes his eyes.

'And I want mine back. But for the rest of my life I will

have to live with the knowledge that it was my action that killed Mum. I will never, ever, forgive myself.'

I am led back to my place behind the glass screen.

More people take the stand. My own barrister asks me questions. I can only tell her what I told the prosecution. Then the jury goes out.

'What happens now?' I say as the guard leads me out of the courtroom and into a cell below.

'You've got to wait for the verdict,' she says.

'What do you think they'll decide?' I ask.

She looks at me. 'I'm not meant to say.'

'You've seen enough trials,' I beg.

'OK.' Her eyes harden. 'If you want my honest opinion, it doesn't look great to me.'

53

'The guard shouldn't have said that,' says my barrister while we are waiting for the verdict. 'I could put in a complaint.'

'Don't,' I say. 'They might take it out on me when I go to prison.'

'If, Nancy. Not when.'

But I'm not so sure.

'The police don't have much evidence,' adds my barrister.

'They have the knife,' I point out. 'And my recorded 999 call.'

'But none of these show that you did it.'

'I told them I did,' I remind her.

She sighs. 'Yes, but, as I've said before, there are mitigating circumstances.'

'The press won't think so.'

'It doesn't matter what they think.'

'Doesn't it?' I reply, thinking how they'd hounded me after Martin's trial. 'You think I was too honest, don't you?' I can't help adding.

'I didn't know you were going to admit that you might, deep down, have intended to put that knife in.'

We sit in silence for a bit.

'How long has it been?' I ask. I'm too nervous to look at the clock on the wall.

'Fifty-three minutes,' says my barrister.

'How long could it take?'

'Remember what I said before? A jury can make up its mind within minutes. Or it could take days. But we should discuss some practicalities. If you *do* get sent down –'

'So you think I will be.'

'That's not what I said. If you do get sent down, you can order things like deodorant and toothpaste items from what's known as the canteen. This isn't just where you eat. It's also the name for a sort of mobile shop with items delivered by staff on a trolley.'

'I know,' I say. 'It was the same in the remand prison.'

'Of course.' She says this as though she's forgotten I've already been behind bars for three months. It must be hard for her to keep track of all her clients. 'You'll be allowed visitors after a certain time required for paperwork . . .'

I have a flashback to the time I'd visited Martin. Would Alex visit me? Or Claire?

'And then there's the –'

She stops at the knock on the door. It's the guard.

'They're ready,' she says.

I can barely walk back to my seat behind the glass screen. When we are told to rise for the judge, my legs nearly give way beneath me.

'Has the jury reached its verdict?'

The foreman nods.

'Do you find Nancy Greenfield guilty or not guilty of murder?'

Elizabeth

54

1945 onwards

When Elizabeth came to, Adeline was leaning over her, mopping her face with a cold flannel, a strange expression on her face.

'Did I pass out?' Elizabeth gasped. 'I thought I saw Henry.'

'No,' said her friend gently. 'It's not Henry. It's . . .'

She stopped.

Elizabeth eased herself to a semi-sitting position on the lawn. She saw khaki trousers, covered with what looked like dried mud. A belt. A jacket. A man.

Grabbing the deckchair beside her, she staggered to her feet.

'Where's Father?' said the man.

'Robert?' she whispered.

No longer did he look like the young man who had gone to war. His face was lined and worn. His auburn hair (so like Henry's) had been cropped and there were bare patches as though someone had shaved him for nits. He had a beard too; long and straggly. War had ravaged her son.

'We thought you were dead,' she said faintly. 'They told us you had been shot after you escaped the prisoner-of-war camp.'

'I was,' he said, pulling up his right trouser leg to reveal a hideous mass of scarring. So that explained the limp. 'But the German soldiers who were running after us, firing, ran off when one of our planes flew over. I played dead for a while, in case they were still around. The other poor sods who were with me were well and truly dead.'

Hadn't Elizabeth hoped and dreamed for years that a miracle like this would happen? Yet now it didn't feel the way she'd always imagined. Her boy seemed so cold. So unloving. So unlike himself.

'How did you survive?' asked Adeline.

'For some days – God knows how many – I lived on what I could find in the forest. Then a farmer found me. I thought he was going to hand me in, but he took me back to his home and he and his wife hid me in the attic.'

Rather like I hid Karl, thought Elizabeth.

'How long were you there for?'

'Until a few weeks ago. Then they told me war had ended.'

'That must have been over three years then?'

'I stopped counting.' His voice was clipped. Curt. 'Where is Father? I've already asked you twice.'

Elizabeth faltered. She saw Adeline shooting her a worried glance. There had been times when Elizabeth would have loved to have told her the truth. But she hadn't dared. And it wouldn't be fair on her.

'Come on, woman. Tell me,' demanded Robert.

Woman? How could this be her son? Was he an imposter?

'I'm sorry,' she said. 'He went missing during one of the bombing raids. We think he must have had an accident . . .'

'Missing?' His brows knitted together. 'Someone must have found him. It's not like this place is a battlefield.'

'Actually, you're wrong,' said Adeline. 'It *was* at times. Hundreds of men, women and children died in Exeter. People died in Sidmouth too. Three were blown up after stepping onto mines laid as part of the coastal defences – two were evacuees.' She shivered. 'Your mother's had a really difficult time and –'

'Why don't you go back to your own house?' he said.

'Robert! That's rude. Adeline lives here now with little Violet.'

'What?' he scowled. 'Did George cop it, then?'

Elizabeth winced.

'We keep each other company,' she said, ignoring his question. 'And I like having Violet . . .'

'Hello.' Violet, on hearing her name, gave him a big smile.

'Get away. I don't want some kid here.'

But Robert had always got on so well with Adeline. He'd loved children, and he'd been as frightened of Henry's temper as she had. It was her, his mother, whom he'd been close to. Yet now his father was the only person he seemed to want.

What would he do if he knew what she had done?

'Robert,' she said gently, touching his arm. 'It's been a shock for you, coming back and finding everything changed. Why don't you lie down for a bit?'

He pushed her away roughly. 'A shock? Of course it's been a bloody shock, Mother. If you'd seen the things I had, you'd never . . .'

Then he shook his head. There were flea bites on his

scalp, Elizabeth noticed. 'It doesn't matter. I'm going to my room.'

'What about a bath first?' she suggested.

'I SAID I WANTED TO GO TO MY ROOM, DIDN'T I?' he thundered, just as Henry used to.

But he couldn't go up there! It was the room where Maisie and Shirley had been and now it was Violet's, with the pretty eiderdown on the bed and her toys and the row of children's books. Elizabeth had given away Robert's things, unable to face the memories, although she'd kept his W. B. Yeats poetry book that he'd studied for his exams. She'd often cried over the poem 'An Irish Airman Foresees His Death'.

What would he think?

Too late. Despite that limp, he could move at quite a pace. As she ran up the stairs behind him, she saw him going in.

'What have you done? Didn't you want me to come home?' He was staring at her with a steeliness that terrified her.

Tears streamed down her face. 'Of course I did. But we were told you were dead.'

'But I wasn't.'

'I didn't know that, Robert.'

He was opening his wardrobe now. Throwing out Violet's dresses onto the floor. 'Who the fuck are Maisie and Shirley?'

He'd seen the writing inside.

'Two little girls who stayed here during the war. They were evacuees.'

He gave an ironic laugh. 'You couldn't wait to get rid of me, could you?'

This was hell. Pure hell. 'Robert, you know I didn't want you to go to war.'

'But you soon forgot me, didn't you?' He waved towards the dolls on the bed.

She put her hand on his arm again but once more he shook it off. 'It wasn't like that,' she pleaded. 'We all had to do our bit. I had to use your bedroom for children who were being bombed in London.' Her eyes misted with tears. 'Tragically, one of them . . .'

She stopped. What was the point? He wasn't listening. Instead, he was advancing towards her, shaking his fist. 'You wanted me dead, didn't you?'

Elizabeth was really scared now. She moved back towards the door. 'No, Robert. That's not true. What's wrong with you?'

Instantly she knew she shouldn't have said that.

'What's wrong with me?' he roared. 'I'll give you what's wrong with me.'

His hands were on her neck. Tightening and tightening around her throat until she couldn't breathe.

Maybe this was how it was meant to end. Punishment for having murdered Henry.

And then there was a terrible screeching sound in her ears and the world went black.

55

It was quite common, said the doctor. Robert was suffering from an illness of the mind from being shot, the stress of hiding in an attic for so long, and the terrible things he had seen and been made to do during the war. Killing was not in her boy's nature. Or at least it hadn't been before he had left.

It hadn't been in hers, either.

But the truth was that, if it hadn't been for Adeline who had heard the commotion, she might not still be alive. Even so, it had taken both her friend and Mrs B to prise Robert off her unconscious body.

'A convalescent home is what he needs,' the doctor said. 'There are some very good ones around.'

How could she let her boy go when he had only just come back? But it wasn't Robert who had returned. It was a different man. Another Henry.

Other people's children had sustained physical injuries that elicited sympathy, but 'trouble in the head', as it was referred to, was something that no one seemed to know how to deal with. Least of all her. Reluctantly, she agreed, and Robert was sent to a sanatorium near Plymouth.

'Maybe it's for the best,' said Adeline. 'Are you sure you don't want Violet and me to leave when he gets better?'

'Quite sure,' said Elizabeth. But inside she was beginning to wonder. Of course, she couldn't turn out her friend with little Violet. But Robert hadn't wanted them there. Supposing he felt the same after his convalescence?

'It must have been a shock for him, finding out about Henry.'

Elizabeth froze.

'If Henry had been wounded in the raid, it's possible he might have lost his mind, like Robert,' Adeline continued. 'Indeed, Henry could return too, one day.'

'Maybe.'

'You don't sound very enthusiastic.' Adeline was looking at her in a strange way. 'I've often wondered. He was an impossible man. One could argue it was quite convenient he went missing in a raid –'

'Adeline!' Elizabeth cut in. 'How could you? Yes. Henry was difficult. But I would never have wished him harm.'

That much was true.

'I'm sorry,' said Adeline, flushing. 'Come on, Violet. Let's go and play, shall we?'

When Robert returned, nearly a year later, he wasn't angry any more. Rather, he hardly said a word. Elizabeth's once bright, confident son now spent his days either in his room or limping through the house, like a creature finding himself in a new world. Perhaps it was the drugs that, the doctors said, were 'crucial' to his recovery. She had to administer them to him every day. He was incapable of counting the tablets himself.

'Such a shame,' said Mrs B. 'I had an uncle who was like that after the Great War.'

'Did he get better?' asked Elizabeth.

Mrs B was silent, but her expression was answer enough.

There was no question of Robert being able to hold down a job. Instead, he helped Mrs B in the kitchen, peeling potatoes and washing up – there was a steady influx of paying guests now that people were able to go on holiday again.

But often Elizabeth would hear the sound of smashed crockery and Mrs B's soothing 'There, there. It was just an accident.'

Elizabeth's heart wanted to break. Her clever boy had gone for ever. Still, at least he was only occasionally violent; usually when he'd refused to take his tablets.

Maybe it was because they felt sorry for her, but people in the town were beginning to be kinder to the residents of Tall Chimneys now. Much to their relief, little Violet started school without any signs of being bullied and Adeline no longer attracted disapproving looks wherever she went.

'I've got a job at the library,' she said excitedly one day. 'I didn't think they'd give it to me because . . . well, you know. But they have.'

'They're lucky to have you,' said Elizabeth.

Meanwhile, the country's recovery from war was slow but steady. Rationing was still in place, but more food products were coming through, like fresh meat, though they were still unable to buy things like bananas.

'I can tell you,' said Mrs B, 'I shouldn't care if I never saw Spam again in my life!'

Even Robert smiled at that.

Two weeks later, an uncleared mine was triggered by a man out walking further along the coast. He lost an arm but was lucky not to have died. Another reminder that the past was still lingering.

Yet at the same time, there was such beauty around them. The sea. The chestnut trees in the Byes that were laden with conkers.

'Let's go for a walk,' Elizabeth suggested to Robert, but when a conker fell from a tree, Robert threw himself to the ground, his arms over his head. 'They're coming,' he cried.

'No,' she said, getting down herself on the ground and cradling him. 'It's all right.'

It took her ages to get him back home. Then she had to call the doctor who prescribed something to calm him down.

A year later, on a bright almost-hot September day, Elizabeth was walking up the driveway with the shopping for the night's supper.

'May I help you with that?' asked a voice behind her.

She turned.

A well-dressed man in a trilby and brown checked summer suit with shiny brogues was standing there. His gaze was steady, even though his eyes betrayed apprehension. He had a scarf around his neck. Navy blue.

'Mr Smith?' she asked, trying to keep her voice steady.

'Mrs Montague.'

His was not a question.

'I hope you don't mind me turning up like this. I have taken a room nearby. I wondered if you would let me buy you dinner tonight.'

56

They went to a restaurant on the front. It was a pleasant, white-stuccoed building facing the sea. Elizabeth kept finding herself touching her pearls nervously. Since Henry, she'd had nightmares about them strangling her as a punishment for what she'd done.

'This is nice,' he said, looking around.

'One of the staff is an Italian who was a prisoner of war here,' she said. 'He chose to stay.'

Mr Smith raised his eyebrows.

'A lot has changed,' she said.

'The whole world has changed,' he said. 'Does it feel odd to you that we can sit here like this?'

'Yes. It does. I still keep expecting the sirens to go or planes overhead.'

He nodded. 'That as well.'

What exactly did he mean? Was he referring to what they had done? Her skin became clammy with fear.

She had so many questions. So much to say. But she was scared of starting.

'I tried to contact you after you left,' she said, feeling her palms sweat as she spoke. 'I rang your school in London but someone said you had moved on.'

His eyes widened, as if surprised she had done this. 'I felt I needed a new start,' he said. 'So I went to Scotland.'

'Did you like it?'

'Yes. It was beautiful. I found a job on a farm and kept myself to myself. It also gave me time to think.'

His fingers were playing with the clip that secured the tablecloth to the table. 'After the war ended, I left and came back to London to try and find my wife and son.'

Her heart began to pound against her ribcage. 'And did you?'

He smiled. A lovely warm smile that met his eyes. 'I did. It turned out that she'd sent a letter to my old digs.'

Placing a hand inside his pocket, he drew out a photograph of a smiling boy standing next to him and a woman.

How wonderful. Yet at the same time the news was like a punch to her stomach. 'You look so happy.'

He nodded. 'I can't tell you what a relief it was to see them alive and well.'

A picture of Henry, bloodied on the ground, came into her head.

'Of course it was.'

To steady herself, Elizabeth looked through the window at a seagull that was eyeing her from the low wall outside. It had a steely gaze. 'You fool,' it seemed to say. 'What else had you expected?'

'Everything is reasonably amicable,' he went on.

Elizabeth was so busy trying to adopt a calm demeanour that she almost missed his words.

'Amicable?'

'Yes.' His eyes held hers. 'We're divorced now. My wife wanted it and, to be honest, so did I. The good thing is that my son and I see a lot of each other. He doesn't seem to hold our break-up or my political feelings against me.'

His voice fell. 'I'm sorry about Robert. Though, obviously, I am glad he returned.'

'How did you know?' she asked sharply.

'I ran into one of the teachers from the school who told me. There are so many poor men and women who suffered in the war.'

'Thank you.' She swallowed the lump in her throat. 'He saw some terrible things.' Her voice wobbled. 'He was painfully thin when he came back. Before he was taken in, he was so hungry that he actually ate raw beef cut from a dead cow he found in a field. He can't eat meat now. There are times when he seems happy enough, in his own simple way. But on the odd occasion, if I am late with his medication or something triggers a memory, my boy is a different person. Sometimes . . . sometimes he scares me.'

Elizabeth shuddered, thinking how Robert had crawled under the kitchen table the other night, quivering from head to toe. This time it was because she had clattered a pan when putting it away. Noise always upset him.

His eyes sharpened. 'Does he hurt you? Is that why you're wearing a high-necked, long-sleeved jumper even though it's warm?'

'Yes,' she said shortly. 'But it doesn't happen as much as it used to.'

She told others that her occasional bruises were from walking into a door or falling in the garden. Yet Mr Smith didn't deserve that. That was the thing about him. She had always felt she could be totally herself when they were talking. It was a relief to find it was still the same now.

'Are you with anyone?' he asked.

The question took her by surprise. Perhaps he realized this because he quickly followed it up with another. 'Someone who can look after you?'

'Adeline lives with me. She had a child by her Canadian pilot. Poor man was shot down before the birth.'

He bowed his head in silent acknowledgement of the tragedy. 'They must be a great comfort for you.'

'They are.' A burst of joy came into her voice. 'Violet is such a character. She's very strong-willed although she can also seem vulnerable. Quite an actress too! Somehow she manages to get her own way without us even realizing it until it's too late. She brings a certain energy to the house. A sense of life . . .'

Then she stopped.

Life. How could she talk about life? Especially with this man sitting opposite her. He'd been an accomplice to murder. That's what the law might say.

'You're wearing the scarf I knitted for Robert,' she said, feeling stupid.

'I always do, even when it's not cold.' He looked at her unwavering. 'It means a great deal to me.'

He untied it and handed it to her. 'Would you like it back for your son?'

She shook her head. 'I have to make sure he doesn't wear anything that is . . . well, dangerous,' she said. 'He might try to strangle himself or others with it. Besides, it belongs to you now.'

But she couldn't stop looking at the scarf, remembering how she'd knitted her grief of Robert's leaving into it. 'It's lasted a long time.'

'Some things do,' he replied. 'Like feelings.'

Did he really mean that? But even if he did, she didn't deserve it.

She glanced around. The restaurant wasn't very full and those tables that were occupied had couples who were too busy talking to each other to overhear them.

Elizabeth leaned forward again, whispering. 'Do you ever wonder about what we did?'

He looked around too, his eyes nervously darting from face to face. 'I'm not sure if this is the place.'

'I need to know.'

She had to make him tell her before he disappeared for ever. Wasn't that why she had rung the London school? Not just because she had feelings for him. But because of the other thing. The terrible, terrible other thing.

'For my own peace of mind, Stephen.' All pretence of formality was gone. 'Where did you put Henry?'

Nancy

57

One year later

'They'll be here soon, won't they?' says Vera who's just popped round. She's steadier on her feet now, although it's taken a while for her to recover. The consultant said she was 'very lucky', especially in view of her age.

I feel so guilty. She wouldn't have been hurt if she hadn't been concerned enough to find me that night. But even without that, I've also learned to really care for this plucky woman who has become so much more of a friend than simply a neighbour – especially after the trial.

'Farmhouse murder heiress moves jury to tears,' said one newspaper after the verdict.

'Leave Nancy alone now,' said another, as though the writer was on first-name terms with me. 'Hasn't she suffered enough?'

'Innocent,' said a third, in huge bold lettering.

The truth is, as my barrister told me, that the prosecution didn't have enough evidence to prove that I had intended to kill Mum. 'But it was the jury who saved you. That bit about every adult needing their mother was the clincher. So, ironically, was your confession that you sometimes wondered if you'd meant to kill your mother.'

Really?

'That part might have sent you down,' she added. 'Then

again, it might also have saved you. The jury seemed to respect your honesty. There are probably a few who wouldn't mind killing members of their own families – or at least have thought of it. Frankly, I'm amazed you weren't charged with manslaughter instead. That would have made it much easier to gain a conviction.'

But I wasn't. And now, here I am. A free woman.

'Sure you've got everything you need?' adds Vera, bringing me back to the present.

'Yes thanks,' I say.

'Make sure you bring them up to the kennels,' adds Jasmine who's here for support as well.

I am excited, but also nervous. We're expecting visitors.

It was my old boss's idea. He'd rung me after the not-guilty verdict to offer me my job back, and was quite surprised when I'd told him I was staying put in Devon.

'How about this then?' he said. 'We've taken on a new client; a charity that provides holidays for disadvantaged children. We need a freelancer to write a regular newsletter that will encourage people to open up their home to them for a week or so.'

It so happened that I'd been twiddling my thumbs. The book on Sidmouth at war has been written and is about to be published by the museum. It means a lot to the locals, of whom I count myself as one.

'I think I could do that,' I said. I'd been digging the allotment that my mother had rented from the council, which I had now been allowed to take over. I'd never seen myself as a gardener before but it gives me peace to work where her hands had toiled. There's also a joy in growing things when there has been so much devastation in the world.

That night, I sat down and began brainstorming the newsletter idea. Yet the words wouldn't come. Something was troubling me and I wasn't sure what. At one point, I got up and went into my bedroom. As if someone was guiding my hand, I opened the wardrobe doors and looked once more at the writing there.

What did these two little evacuees, taken in by my grandmother's best friend Elizabeth, think about being uprooted from London to a smallish seaside town? Did they feel nervous? Did they love it here? And did they have any idea what lay in store?

I went downstairs, sat at the table and watched my fingers fly across the keyboard.

THE STORY OF TALL CHIMNEYS AND THE PEOPLE WHO LIVED HERE

I typed for an hour, but eventually I had to stop. Writing about my house's history was a nice idea, but I didn't know enough about it.

The next day I rang my London boss. It's sometimes easier to talk than email.

'Sorry,' I said. 'I can't write about this charity's work. At least, not without experiencing it myself. I'd like to offer some kids a week here.'

'Are you sure?'

I could picture his face. I'd been to his place once to collect some papers. It was a glass-enclosed penthouse suite. The kind that was definitely not child-friendly.

Tall Chimneys isn't like that. It loves children. I can feel it in its bricks and mortar. Sense it in my bones as I run my hands down the mahogany bannister rail. Absorb it as I sit at the foot of the Aga, Sheba's nose nuzzling mine. (That's right. I've formally 'adopted' her from the re-homing centre.)

'Quite sure,' I said. 'Can you put me in touch with the charity?'

I spent the next few weeks organizing the spare bedrooms and getting ready for our visitors. I bought some children's books from the two bookshops we have in town, and then I found an old volume of W. B. Yeats poems in a bookcase downstairs. It had the name 'Robert' inscribed in the front and a school stamp. It might be considered too adult for children nowadays, so I decided to take it to bed myself and read it.

And now they're here!

There's the sound of tyres on the gravel drive at the front. Sheba starts barking. I get down and put my face next to hers. 'You've got to be nice to them,' I whisper. 'None of that "I'm pretending to be fierce when I'm actually scared inside" nonsense.'

We both know what that's like.

'That dog understands every word you say,' says Jasmine. 'Big softie. I knew you were made for each other the minute I saw you together.'

Just what Claire had said about me and Alex.

But I don't want to think about her now. My priority is to make sure these children have the break they deserve. I also want to restore some good energy into this house that has seen so much pain.

'Wow!' says a little girl, running through the door in trainers and a dress that looks too small for her. 'Are we really staying here? It's ginormous!'

'Can we go to the sea now?' demands a little boy running after her.

She puts her arm around him protectively. 'This is my brother. He wants to go looking for pirates.'

'Then we'll have to see what we can find after lunch,' I say.

'Ajani! Gilly! You're not meant to go in without me! Where are your manners?'

A harassed-looking woman comes rushing in.

'I'm sorry,' she says. 'I couldn't stop them. They're so excited to be here.'

'And I'm excited to have you,' I say. 'Welcome to Tall Chimneys.'

It's the evening when Beliska, who is the woman in charge of the group, brings up the elephant in the room. The children are asleep upstairs, zonked out after a day of running up and down the beach, digging sandcastles and wanting to know if those 'high-rise cliffs are going to fall down on us'.

We are sitting in the back of the house in my favourite sitting room overlooking the garden. She's had a glass of wine. I've had my usual elderflower that I make myself from the flowers in the allotment.

'You've been through a pretty tough time yourself, haven't you?' asks Beliska.

I wondered when this would arise. After all, this time last year, my face was all over the papers.

'Yes,' I say. 'I have.'

But to my surprise, she doesn't come out with any of the things I was expecting.

'Bad things can happen in life,' says Beliska quietly. 'Gilly and Ajani were in the house when the police broke down the door to arrest their mum for possession. She was with her dealer at the time, who then smashed a glass into her face 'cos he thought she'd set him up. The dealer got five years. Mum got a scarred face and eighteen months.'

I shivered. 'Poor kids.'

'Their nan is their legal carer now. Best thing for them, if you ask me.'

Then she looks at the high chair in the corner. 'Looks like you cater for all ages.'

'That's for my friend's toddler,' I say. 'They're coming down to stay next week.'

I feel nervous as I speak. Here I am, trying to help strangers whose lives have fallen apart because of family crises. Yet I haven't been able to fully forgive my own best friend for not telling Mum the truth about Duncan.

'That's nice.' She looks at me. 'You're a good woman, Nancy.'

'I'm not sure about that,' I say, blushing. 'But I do feel that this house needs to be full of people.'

She nods. 'It's got a good vibe about it and yet . . .'

She pauses.

'. . . Yet there's something that's not quite right.'

My skin breaks out in goosebumps.

'I know this sounds weird,' Beliska continues, 'but I often have a bit of a sixth sense about places. And I've got a strange feeling about this house. Did something happen here?'

My mouth is dry. 'No,' I say. 'Not that I know of, anyway.'

She shakes herself. 'I don't know. Maybe it's just to do with your stepbrother dragging you out of here. Sorry. I read the story in the papers like everyone else at the time.'

A cold chill passes through me as I think of the person who'd gone missing from Tall Chimneys during the war. We never did find out who it was and, to be honest, it had slipped my mind during the trial and the aftermath.

But what if this missing person had been buried right here?

In my home.

In Tall Chimneys.

58

'Why didn't you tell Beliska about the missing person?' asks Alex when I recount the conversation.

He's come down with Claire and Richard. And, of course, little Charlie (short for Charlene). It was Alex's idea. I've seen Claire a few times since the birth but our relationship isn't the same as it was. I can't help it.

'I don't know,' I say. 'I just felt spooked.'

Then I glance at Richard. 'You're an architect. What do you think?'

He shrugs. 'I believe that every house has a life. Emotions might well get absorbed into bricks and mortar. They leave good and bad behind them. But that's only my personal opinion.'

'Well, let's just concentrate on the good, shall we?' says Claire, stroking Charlie's cheek as the baby slumbers in the Moses basket next to her. She shoots me a 'Please let's be friends' look, but I pretend not to notice.

Beliska's question about whether something had happened here unnerves me more than I care to admit. Every now and then I wake in the night and swear I can hear creaks that weren't there before. Once or twice, I fancy I hear whispering.

And on one occasion, a scream.

I wake to find it has come from my own mouth during one of my regular nightmares about my mother. 'Please,

Mum,' I whisper. 'If I did kill you, I didn't mean to. Not really. Give me some peace.'

Strangely, the nightmares seem to ease off a bit after that.

Then, one morning, just after Alex goes back to London for a couple of days, there's a knock on the door.

I'm not expecting anyone. Sheba cocks an ear but doesn't get up. That's unusual.

The woman on my doorstep must, I guess, be in her late eighties if not older. Her face is wrinkled and her back is bent. But when she lifts her face to meet mine, it's her eyes that really strike me. They are a brilliant blue.

Next to her is a younger woman. I can tell instantly from their likeness that they are mother and daughter.

'Miss Greenfield?'

I nod.

'I'm so sorry to trouble you but we were driving by and my mother was absolutely desperate to see the house again.'

'Again?' I say.

'Yes,' says the old lady. Her eyes positively sparkle. 'My name is Maisie. My surname used to be Evans. I lived here during the war.'

59

'This is where Shirley and I slept,' Maisie says, her voice sounding like a child's at Christmas. 'I'd never shared a room with just one person before. It was like living in a palace!'

Her eyes go all watery as she stares around the twin-bedded room. She insisted on coming straight up here, despite my offer of a cup of tea first.

'I loved Shirley like a sister. Still can't believe she's gone. If her mother hadn't taken her back, she might have lived, you know. But her mum didn't like it here 'cos she thought it was too posh. The lady who owned Tall Chimneys — her name was Mrs Montague — employed a lady called Mrs B who would ring a bell for dinner. And we had these silver tops to cover the dishes and keep the food warm. Cloches, they were called, though Shirley used to call them "clocks".'

She speaks in a rush, as if there might not be enough minutes left to get it all out.

'My mum and Shirley's mum came down to visit us. Mrs Montague said we were to think of this as our second home, but Shirley's mum didn't like that. She said it was too fancy for them and that her daughter might get ideas above her station. I think she was jealous of Mrs Montague in case Shirley got too fond of her. Anyway, she took her home and then the bombs got them.'

There's a sob in her voice. 'The whole family was wiped out.'

'I'm so sorry,' I whisper. Of course, I know from Jeremy that one of the little evacuees had died during the war. But hearing it from Maisie's mouth makes it so much more real.

'The strange thing was that I got a letter from Shirley. It arrived after she'd died, so I thought she was still alive, you see. Mrs Montague didn't tell me any different and nor did the others. Reckon they must have been trying to protect me. But it was an awful shock when I finally went back to London and found my friend had been killed after all.'

A tear rolls down her wrinkled cheek.

'I'm so sorry,' I gulp.

Maisie takes the tissue her daughter hands her and gives me a quick smile. 'I'm all right, love, thank you. I don't blame Mrs Montague for hiding the truth. She was doing her best. It weren't all bad times. We had a lot of fun swimming and walking. And once, when we were in a bombing raid, she taught me this song.'

The old lady begins to sing.

'"We're strong and wise and brave as knights. Our courage will shine in the darkest of nights." Always remembered it, I did. I taught my kids it too.'

'That she did,' says her daughter, putting her arm around her mother.

I can't help feeling a familiar flash of jealousy. They seem so close. Mum and I should have been like that. Then she continues.

'I went back to London after the Blitz died down. I wrote

373

the odd letter but then stopped. I should have carried on. I was a teenager by then, and somehow other things seemed more important. I feel bad about that now. Mrs Montague was so good to us.'

'I'm sure she'd understand,' I say. Of course, I don't know that for certain, but a weird feeling obliges me to speak for my grandmother's best friend.

'We first saw Mrs Montague on the train from London to here, you know,' continues Maisie. 'We was being evacuated and she had gone up there to try and find her son to say one last goodbye before he went to war. Then we ended up being billeted with her. Our teacher was with us. Nice man by the name of Mr Smith. I never heard what happened to him either. But I do know that Mrs Montague's son Robert was killed in the war. Terrible business. I was there when she got the telegram. Can't believe I'm still here, to be honest.'

Maisie's daughter holds her arm again. 'My mum's a survivor.'

'That's partly thanks to your dad,' she says. She turns to me. 'I met Ronnie in the factory where I worked when I went back to London. Couldn't wait to start a family, we couldn't. Nothing like it for healing old wounds.'

Her bright blue eyes fasten on me like a little bird's. 'Are you married, Nancy?'

'*Mum!*'

'You don't mind me asking you that, do you?'

Part of me *does* mind, but I have a feeling that Maisie isn't one to take no for an answer, much like Vera.

'No, I'm not married.'

'Shame.'

'*Mum!*'

'I mean it. A nice girl like you – I can see that in your face – needs lots of kids.' She looks around the kitchen where we are standing. 'You've certainly got the space for it here.'

'Nice' girl? Doesn't she know about me? Or is she pretending not to? Is it possible that she's been sent here to find out more on behalf of one of the papers? But something tells me that Maisie is genuine. She is who she says she is.

'I remember.' She chuckles. 'Mrs B – the lady I mentioned before who used to help Mrs Montague – used to give us a right old telling-off when she caught me and Shirley sliding down the bannisters! "You'll kill yourselves, you will," she'd say. But of course we didn't.'

Then her face falls. I sense she is thinking of her friend.

'Can you tell me,' I ask, 'about the other people who lived here?'

'Well, there was our teacher, Mr Smith, like I said. He was a lovely man. Taught me to play chess during one of the air raids. Kept me calm.'

'Mum still plays,' says her daughter. 'She's in a local league.'

Those eyes twinkle. 'I'm not bad, if I say it myself! I remember the PGs too. That's the paying guests. They came down here to escape the bombs. There were two single sisters – the Patmores, I think they were called – who'd come on holiday and stayed because they were too scared to go home, and a widow too. Her name was Mrs Norris. She acted all strict but her bark was worse than her bite. She'd lend us her radio so we could listen to *Children's*

Hour in our bedroom. They were very good to us. And then there was Mr Montague, the husband. He was in the Home Guard like a lot of them. But I didn't take to him.'

My skin begins to prickle. Please don't say he was another Duncan.

'Why not?'

Maisie is looking around wonderingly. I've put up some more of Dad's paintings as well as landscape pictures by a local artist called Cathy and a beautiful seascape montage from another artist, Julia, whom I've got to know and is now a good friend. I've also met some others round here too, including Anne Lois Marples, who does a lot of charity work.

'Mr Montague didn't want any evacuees. Said that our ration books weren't enough to cover our keep and the government had a cheek to expect hard-working people like him to take us in.'

'That's awful,' I say.

'I often heard him telling Mrs Montague that she should have turned us down, but she stuck up for us. And he was horrible to her when their son died, didn't like her talking about him. Even as a child I remember this tension whenever he was in the room. Then the Germans did all those terrible raids on Exeter. They dropped a few bombs on their way back. One of them got him.'

I shiver. Suddenly the sun emerges from behind a cloud and the room instantly brightens.

'Oh,' she breathes. 'I'd forgotten the light. It's so different from London.'

I take it for granted now, but she's right. It streams through the window, bathing us all in a shaft of dancing golden dust. 'You can just about see the sea,' she says. 'Shirley and I had to stand on a chair to do that.'

She looks as if she's going to do that now, but her daughter takes her arm again.

'And there's the wardrobe,' she says in a hushed voice. She opens the doors without so much as a 'by your leave'. But I don't mind. It's further proof that Maisie is real. Not an imposter.

There are no clothes inside. I've been keeping it empty for guests.

'It's still here! Look at this,' she cries to her daughter, who stares in wonder at the writing inside.

Tears are streaming down her face. 'It was Shirley's idea. She wanted to do it. I said we'd get told off and that it wasn't fair to mess up Mrs Montague's home but she went right ahead, putting my name first as if I was the naughty one! "We need to make our mark," she said. Well, she did that, didn't she?'

Then she sits down on the bed and weeps, her shoulders shaking.

I don't know what to do apart from put a hand briefly on her shoulder.

'It's all right,' says her daughter. 'She needs to let it out. The grief has been inside her for too long. She really loved Shirley. There's nothing like a best friend.'

I think of Claire and how close we had been.

'Please let me make you a cup of tea now,' I say.

So we go down to the kitchen and I put the big old copper kettle on the Aga.

'Shirley and I used to love sitting on the floor, our backs against it when it was cold,' sniffs Maisie. 'I can see your dog does the same. Mrs Montague's friend Adeline had a dog.'

'She was my grandmother, you know,' I say. 'Adeline was, I mean.' Maisie has been talking so fast until now that there hasn't been a chance to explain this.

'Is that right? Well, we used to take her dog for walks sometimes. I wanted one, but it was difficult during the war. Pets went missing during bomb raids. God bless Mrs Montague, that's all I can say. Or we could have been killed right here. She used to take us down to the garden shelter during the raids.'

'I found it,' I say. 'There were noughts and crosses on the walls.'

'That was us!' beamed Maisie. 'Our teacher wrote something too that made us all feel better. I can remember it still because it's helped me through difficult times: *There is nothing to fear in life but fear itself.*'

I would do well to remember that, I tell myself as I place her tea in front of her with the two sugars she'd requested.

'I know you said you didn't write to her, but do you know what happened to Mrs Montague?' I ask.

'No idea.'

I hesitate. 'It's just that my mother told me that Elizabeth gave Tall Chimneys to my grandmother.'

Maisie whistles. It makes her seem almost girlish. 'Did she now?'

'I always thought that was a pretty generous gift. But Mum said that my grandmother didn't like talking about it, perhaps because she still missed her best friend. Who knows?'

She shrugs. 'I suppose we can't know everything about the past, can we?'

'Can you tell me anything else about Adeline?' I ask. 'She died of cancer before I was born and my mother never spoke about her much.'

Maisie seems to hesitate. 'Well, she was a very beautiful lady. She let my mam stay at her house when she visited from London to check we were all right. It must have been terrible to let your kids go to a stranger's during the war.'

I nod.

'People aren't always what you think they are,' she adds.

'I've read about some evacuees having a bad time with their host families,' I say.

Maisie's bright eyes look away. 'I didn't mean that . . .'

Her voice tails off.

'What *did* you mean?' I ask. I have a feeling that Maisie is holding something back.

'Well, one day when . . .'

She stops.

'When what?' I ask. 'Please, Maisie. I've so little family that I want to know as much as I can about Elizabeth and Adeline.'

She blushes. 'It's not really for me to say, but they must be all dead now, so I suppose it doesn't make much difference. Well, one day Shirley and I saw Adeline kissing someone in the woods. We thought it was ever so naughty because her husband was away, fighting.'

'My grandmother was having an affair?' I can't help feeling rather shocked. 'Do you know any more?'

'Sorry, Nancy.' Maisie gets to her feet. 'We've got to go

now.' She speaks as if I have detained her. 'My daughter's taking me to some fancy hotel in the Cotswolds on the way back. It's been wonderful to see Tall Chimneys again and' – she catches her breath here – 'to see Shirley's writing on the wall. Thanks ever so much for having us.'

Then she swiftly brushes my cheek with hers. Her face is soft.

On her way out of the kitchen, her eye falls on the dresser with its various knick-knacks from my mother's time here. 'Oh,' she says, her eyes brightening. 'There's that dear little wooden toast rack with the heart. Shirley and I loved that!'

That means it must have been Elizabeth's! How amazing that it's survived. Once more, I get that lovely warm feeling. Tall Chimneys really is home now.

'Oh dear,' Maisie says as her daughter unlocks the car (a rather smart BMW) and plumps up a cushion on the front seat. 'I think I might need the loo again. It's my age, you know. Nancy won't mind taking me back, will you, love?'

I sense she wants to tell me something privately. And I'm right.

'I haven't mentioned this to anyone else,' she says, as soon as we get into the house, 'because, well, it seems a bit silly. But it's something that keeps coming back into my mind over the years.'

Why do I feel I have been waiting for this ever since she arrived?

'The night Mr Montague went missing . . . well, I couldn't sleep.'

'Wait,' I say. 'He went missing? You said he was killed in a bombing raid.'

'Yes. Well, he must have been or he'd have come back that night. I remember someone saying that he'd probably been hit and his body lost in the sea or the Byes or over a cliff. It happened to a few other people along the coast, apparently.'

'Did his body ever turn up?' I ask tightly.

'Not when I was here.'

I catch my breath. Could this be the missing person that Jeremy had talked about? The one who had disappeared from Tall Chimneys?

'There's more.' She grabs my hand as if to get my full attention, although she already has it. 'That night, after the raid, I couldn't sleep as I just said. I was thirsty. So I came downstairs to get some water from the kitchen and saw our teacher Mr Smith coming in. His clothes were dripping with water. I thought that was strange because it wasn't raining.'

My mouth goes dry. 'Did he see you?'

'Yes.' She goes silent.

'What did he do?'

'He put his finger to his lips to show I should stay silent. Then I scooted back upstairs. Shortly after that I went back to London because the Blitz had ended. But it haunted me, that finger on his lips. Why had he wanted me to stay quiet?'

She's gripping my hand now. Her grasp is surprisingly strong. Her eyes are wide and troubled. 'All my life I've worried that I should have told someone about this before. Then again, it might mean nothing, mightn't it?'

She wants me to agree with her. How can I not? The poor woman needs peace of mind.

'Of course it might mean nothing,' I reassure her. 'But sometimes it's good to share these things.'

She gives me a quick hug. 'Thank you. I can't tell you how lovely it is to see this place again. I'm glad you're here, Nancy. You suit it. Now I really must use your downstairs loo, if you don't mind. You see? It wasn't just an excuse!'

After they've gone, I go round to Vera's. It occurs to me that she and Maisie must be around the same age. Maybe Vera remembers her.

That's strange. The door is partly open. Something seems to be blocking it on the other side.

I squeeze through the gap and then gasp in horror.

There's a crumpled heap on the floor.

60

'Vera!' I rush to kneel down next to her.

Memories of Martin attacking her come flying back. I check to see if she's breathing. Thank God, she is. She seems to be conscious. 'Did someone hurt you?'

'No,' she groans. 'I tripped on the stairs and couldn't get to the phone.' She lets out another groan. 'My hip hurts.'

I get her to hospital and after the operation – the bones are shattered so badly that she needs an entirely new hip – I insist that she comes back to Tall Chimneys so I can look after her.

Resting in one of the guest beds now, Vera eases herself onto her elbows. 'It's lovely here,' she says, looking out of the window at the palm trees that are shedding long thin leaves after last night's storm. 'You know, I get a good view of your place from my house.' She chuckles. 'So did my mother. She was quite nosy. Always looking out onto the road and taking note of who went where.'

I lean forward. 'Did she ever mention someone called Maisie Evans?'

Vera put her head to one side as if thinking. 'Not that I can recall.'

A surge of disappointment shoots through me. 'I actually found you after your fall because I'd come round to tell you I'd had a visitor. It was a woman called Maisie who said she had lived here during the war as an evacuee.'

'Wasn't she one of the names on the wall you asked me about?'

'Yes.'

'Still doesn't ring any bells, but it was a long time ago and there were lots of people going in and out then, what with the paying guests.'

Maybe I can jog her memory. 'Maisie said her teacher had come down with them and that one night, he came in, dripping with water even though it hadn't been raining. It was a few hours after an air raid.'

Vera's black eyes dart quickly out of the window and back again.

'You know something, don't you?' I say.

She sighs. 'During my mother's final months, she used to ramble a lot. I couldn't understand much but there was one thing that stood out.'

My heart quickens. 'What?'

'She kept saying, "The allotment. I saw Elizabeth coming back from the allotment that night." Well, she would have done, wouldn't she? They both had a plot. But I did wonder what she meant by "that night". Night seems a strange time to be gardening, and "that" makes it sound significant in some way.'

'It does,' I agree.

'But there is one other thing. I do remember that when Mrs Montague was preparing to leave for Canada after the war, she spent a great deal of time in the cellar, packing up boxes. She asked me to help tape up them but said I wasn't to look inside. In fact, she paid me some pocket money to do so. I was thrilled to bits! She wrote NOT TO BE OPENED DURING MY LIFETIME on top of one.

384

When I asked why, she said it was a secret and I wasn't to tell anyone. But I suppose it doesn't matter now.'

'In the cellar?' I say. A cold, clammy feeling comes over me.

'If I were you,' says Vera, 'I'd take a look down there.'

She sees the repulsion on my face.

'I know. It's where that wicked man . . .'

She stops. Perhaps she senses I can't bear to hear the words. Her bony hand reaches out and clasps mine. 'But maybe, Nancy, it's time for you to face your demons.'

61

As I go down the hard cellar steps, I am shaking so much that I almost fall.

There's still that smell of apples but instead of that sweet, ripe odour, it is rotten. I trace its source to a crate of shrivelled, mouldering fruit.

Damp drips down the walls.

Every bone in my body is telling me to get out of here. But my head is telling me something different.

'Fuck you, Duncan,' I say out loud.

This is not a word I am in the habit of using but it feels good at this moment.

'Fuck you,' I repeat. 'I'm glad you're dead. You deserve it.'

There are stacks of boxes here. They are all unsealed. I begin opening them in case the tape has come off with the damp over the years. My heart jumps. Inside are some of my father's early paintings. I could sell them, but I'm not going to. They're one of my last remaining links with Dad. I can see him now, sitting at his easel. Not knowing that fame would finally come to him too late.

Most are little watercolour sketches, mainly of Sidmouth. Dad had loved this place. I recall how my mother always used to say that he had taken to it as if it was he who had been born here rather than her. I immediately decide to hold on to these ones, however much they might fetch on the market.

There's a box with old china and some newspapers dating back to the war. I leaf through one. It's the edition that Jeremy had found in the museum.

I read it out loud to myself.

"'There is still no news of the two people missing after the recent bombing raid. Names will not be released until they are found, out of respect to their next of kin.'"

Next to it, in the margin, there is some writing in ink with beautifully formed letters: 'John Tebbit from Home Farm. And H.'

Who was H? It must have been someone familiar for the writer to have used just an initial.

There's only one crate left. It's near where Duncan had pressed himself against me.

I walk towards it, my legs wobbling. The crate is nailed at the top, unlike the others. My heart quickens as I read the faded lettering on top. NOT TO BE OPENED DURING MY LIFETIME: E. MONTAGUE. I remember seeing a palette knife in one of dad's art boxes and I use it to prise off the lid.

There are old children's books inside. This one was published in 1926. The illustrations take up a whole page and there is a thin paper cover over each one inside as if to protect it. I hold one to my cheek impulsively. I can almost imagine a young boy reading it. I say 'boy' because it has a daredevil adventure cover, typical of that era.

I go deeper into the crate. There is a soldier's uniform. It's torn and dirty. It almost looks as if it has been returned from war unwashed.

There are loose photographs too.

One – of a beautiful young woman – looks just like

my mother but it is dated 1939, before my mother was born. She's standing close to a handsome young man in uniform.

I turn it over. *Adeline and George*, says the pretty, sloping writing.

But who was George? Mum had always told me that my grandfather was called Brian. He was killed in action when my grandmother was pregnant with my mother. I know she didn't have any brothers. Could this George have been the man that Maisie had seen my grandmother with in the woods? Still, who am I to judge? If nothing else, the events of the last few years have taught me that relationships aren't what they might seem.

There's another photograph too. It's of two little girls sitting on a farm gate with big smiles on their faces. Their hair is neatly plaited in matching styles with ribbons at the ends, and they are both wearing gingham dresses with ankle socks. Just like the ones in my imagination.

Maisie and Shirley, says the same writing. Poor, poor Shirley, killed in the London raids when she could have stayed safe here. I must get a copy made and send it to Maisie. Or would that upset her too much?

A young man is now staring up at me. He is in uniform too; a uniform very similar to the one I found at the top of the crate. *Robert, 1941*, it says on the back. Who was he?

And then there's a picture of two women, their arms around each other's waists and happiness simply glowing out of them. It's dated 1932. *Adeline and Elizabeth*. The writing is different.

Elizabeth! My grandmother's best friend. The one who had left her the house. But why? Did she no longer need

388

it? Where did she go? She is also wearing a pearl necklace that looks very much like mine. Maybe that's just coincidence. But I hope it isn't.

And then, right at the bottom, are several old folders. I take one out.

Inside is a huge sheet of paper with a red seal. It's already been broken.

I've found the deeds to Tall Chimneys. And there's something next to it, wrapped in a blanket.

Oh my God. It's a small pistol.

62

I call the police. They come to take the gun away. 'And you found it in this old crate?' asks the officer.

'Yes,' I say. 'It had newspapers going back to the Second World War, so I think it dates from then.'

His face looks suspicious. Do they know who I am? The farmhouse slaughter daughter? Are they going to believe me?

'Is it loaded?' I ask.

'We'll let the experts tell us that,' he replies with a 'you tell me' expression.

After they leave, I go up to Vera, who had tried to come downstairs when she saw the police car and is clearly agitated. 'A gun,' she says. 'Well I never.'

I've a feeling she's about to say more but she doesn't. Then I show her the deeds.

'Open them up then,' she demands imperiously.

Inside the other folders are several flimsy paper documents, each beautifully folded, some with seals that are broken. The writing is exquisite, perfectly formed in black ink. The dates go back to the early part of the nineteenth century. You can smell the history. I feel almost like an intruder. So many people have lived in my house over the centuries. People with amazing names like Ebenezer Browse. A Doctor Grey. A woman described as a 'spinster'.

Together we leaf through. I can't help wondering how

clean they are. The last few years have made us more aware of touching things, let alone old documents that had lived through the Spanish flu, smallpox and goodness knows what else.

'Look at this,' crows Vera triumphantly.

It's dated 1947 and shows that one Elizabeth Montague had gifted Tall Chimneys to Adeline Palmer. My grandmother, whom I had never known.

A shiver passes down my spine.

Inside the document is a sealed envelope. On it is written *To Adeline's Descendants*. I hesitate. I've been looking for the story behind my house for so long, partly as a distraction from the awful things I've both done and endured. But now it could be right here, in my hand, and I'm scared. Haven't I got enough to deal with?

'Open it,' commands Vera.

I read the letter aloud.

I hope you are still living here. Tall Chimneys is a beautiful place. But it deserves to have the truth told. The following is an account of my war years, and the reason I had to leave the place I loved.

In 1942 my friend Adeline invited me to join a group called the secret army. I wanted to do my bit because I'd been officially informed that my son Robert had been shot dead by the Germans.

Robert! The boy in the photograph.

We were each trained to use a gun.

A gun! The one I'd found in the box?

Vera doesn't look surprised. 'I'd heard rumours about

that,' she says. 'Highly illegal, of course, although some said it was sanctioned by the authorities.'

One night I came across a terrified young German airman who was stranded on the cliff edge on Salcombe Hill after bailing out. Karl reminded me of my son, so I hid him in our allotment shed. If I'd been discovered, I would have been shot by the other members of the secret army or arrested by the police. Yet I couldn't help it. I was just one mother trying to help another.

But my husband Henry found out. He followed me and was about to shoot us. I shot him in self-defence.

Stephen Smith – the teacher who was billeted with us along with Maisie, one of our evacuees – said he would get rid of the body. I think he felt sorry for me. He had seen how Henry had bullied me. At the time, he wouldn't tell me where he'd put my husband. But Stephen assured me that it wasn't in the house.

A huge wave of relief washes over me when I read this. So he hadn't been killed here, in Tall Chimneys. But I also feel fear along with a strong sense of déjà vu. Henry had been a bully from the sound of it. Just like Duncan. Both had received justice, two generations apart.

Some might call it a crime. Others might feel both men deserved it.

I read on.

At the end of the war, my son Robert came home. I cannot describe my shock and joy. Shock because he was not the same. Joy because my son was alive when I'd been led to believe he was dead.

I stop reading for a moment. Wasn't that the son that Maisie had referred to? The one she thought had been killed?

I am writing this because Stephen and I are to be married. We are going to Canada with Robert to make a new life. I am therefore gifting Tall Chimneys to my best friend Adeline with instructions that she is to pass it down to my goddaughter Violet and her descendants. I am also giving her my pearl necklace that was Henry's wedding present to me. I'd kept it because, despite everything, I'd loved him once. Now, however, I want no reminders of my old life.

Wow! So my necklace IS the same set of pearls that my grandmother had passed to Mum. I touch it again. It gives me that warm sense of security I'd had before my mother's death. The letter continues.

Violet, if you are reading this, I want you to know that you were a much-wanted baby. Adeline was going to go to Canada with Brian, the Canadian pilot who was your real father. Your mother might well have told you this by now but if not, I'm sorry if it comes as a shock. They were deeply in love, and you were conceived while her husband George was away fighting. We argued about that – I'm afraid I thought Adeline should honour her marriage vows. But then I realized that she was entitled to some happiness. Tragically, Brian perished when his plane was shot down in action. This was before you were born, so you and your mother came to live with me.

I gasp out loud. So I'd got it all wrong. George in the photograph had been my grandmother's husband. My grandfather Brian, whom my mother had told me about, had been her Canadian lover. My mother had been illegitimate! The result of a love affair. That must have been a big deal in those days.

After the war, Adeline tracked down Brian's mother and told her about her granddaughter. She and Brian had already agreed that if they had a girl, they would call her Violet after Brian's mother and have Nancy (from Adeline's mother) as the middle name. But the Canadian parents didn't reply to any of her letters apart from the first, when they'd sent money without expressing a wish to see Violet. It broke my friend's heart.

How awful!

'Your grandmother had a hard time of it, according to my mother,' says Vera looking at my face. 'People shunned her. It was why her friend Elizabeth took her in. Your mother carried the stigma of illegitimacy all through her childhood. Couldn't wait to leave home and move to the bright lights of London. I was surprised when she kept this place after Adeline died. But memories had faded then, and your dad loved the house.'

'So you knew all this and didn't tell me?' I say.

She shrugs. 'Round here, you have to earn someone's trust. But you've more than done that.'

I continue reading. There is more.

Two years after the war ended, I received a letter from a Frau Blome in Hamburg. She was the mother of the young German I helped to hide. I have enclosed it here.

There is a brief letter in an envelope with a German stamp. It reads simply: *From one Mutter to another. Thank you for saving my son's life.*

'Is that all?' I say. 'What happened to him?'

Vera shrugged. 'There were lots of questions after the war that no one could answer. But his mother's words make it sound like he survived.'

Elizabeth's letter is not quite finished.

I hope that whoever reads this will find peace in Tall Chimneys. Look after my home. It will always look after you. Look after the allotment too.

I brush the tears from my eyes. This fills in so many gaps. Of all people, I can understand too well why Elizabeth didn't want anyone to open this letter during her lifetime. But why write it down at all?

'She could have taken the secret with her to her grave,' I say out loud.

'Maybe it wouldn't have rested easily on her conscience,' says Vera.

I understand that.

'Want my advice?' she continues.

I have a feeling I don't have a choice.

'Block up the cellar. It will help you mentally. Get someone to fill it with bricks so no one ever goes in it again. Then enjoy the rest of the house. You were wrong just now when you said it hadn't given you peace. It has. I can see it in your eyes. In your face. In the good things you have done since moving in. It was meant that you should come back.'

'Do you think so?' I ask hopefully.

'I know so. Just as you do in your heart.'

But there's something else.

'Did you think it was a bit odd that Elizabeth especially singled out the allotment in her letter?' I say. 'It's not as though it's part of the house. It belongs to the council. And you say your mother kept rambling about Mrs Montague and the allotment too.'

'I've been thinking the same myself,' says Vera. 'Maybe you should do some digging.'

Elizabeth

63

'We need to take a walk,' Stephen said firmly.

One or two people were looking at them now. How much had they heard?

Leaving a generous tip, Stephen led her out of the restaurant with a touch on the small of her back that was barely noticeable to anyone else. Yet she felt scorched.

In unspoken agreement they crossed the road, just as the Toastrack drove past, and stood facing the sea.

'I've missed it,' he said, watching the waves pound against the rocks. 'Do you still swim?'

'Yes. It's the only thing that keeps me sane. That and little Violet.'

He bent his head in acknowledgement, an action he had performed frequently in the last few hours. It made her feel understood.

'Shall we walk along the beach?' he suggested.

But there were too many people there. Some might gossip and put two and two together. *There's Mrs Montague with the schoolteacher who boarded with her during the war. Her husband went missing, you know . . .*

'How about up Salcombe Hill?' she said.

For a while, they walked in silence. It was steep enough for speech to be an effort, a useful excuse. Once, after reaching the woods, she stumbled and he put out his hand to steady her, but she moved away. 'I can manage, thank you,' she said.

'I'm sorry.'

They'd got to the fields now, overlooking the cliff. As they approached the Frog Stone – not far from where she'd discovered Karl the airman – Elizabeth found herself asking again.

'Where did you put Henry? I have to know, Stephen. Or I can't move on.'

This time, he told her.

She stood in shock, trying to take it in.

'I had to,' he said. 'I couldn't drag him far. He was too heavy and someone could have come any minute.'

That felt cowardly. Or was she being unfair?

'It wasn't me I was worried about,' he added, as if sensing her thoughts. 'It was you, Elizabeth. But if I had been discovered, I was going to say that I had shot him so you didn't get into trouble.'

She could believe that.

'So no one suspected anything, then?' he went on.

'No.'

'What about the gun? I meant to ask you at the time.'

'I hid it in the cellar,' whispered Elizabeth, sinking down on the grass. 'I was too scared to throw it away in case someone saw me.'

'Did you know he had a knife in his pocket too?'

'No,' she gasped. 'I wonder why he didn't use that on me?'

'Maybe the pistol was closer to hand.' He touched her arm. 'Thank God you weren't hurt.'

The earth below swayed up and down. 'Sorry. I feel a bit dizzy.'

'Here. Have some of this.' He took a flask from his inside pocket and held it against her lips.

Then, unable to stop herself, she retched.

He held her until she stopped.

'I feel so guilty,' she whispered, taking the handkerchief he offered.

'Henry was a bully, Elizabeth. We all saw that. And that night – he was going to kill you.'

'But I shot him instead, didn't I? If I'd been found out, I'd have gone to prison or been hanged. Instead, I've been living a lie. Everywhere I go in town, every compassionate face I see, reminds me of the wicked thing I did. And Robert – he will never see his father again.'

'I know. I feel for you.' His arm was still around her even though she had stopped being sick. 'In fact, I've thought about you every day since I left, Elizabeth.'

How could the use of her first name make her heart jump like this?

'Then why didn't you leave a forwarding address?' she retorted.

'I didn't think you'd want anything to do with me. I knew you'd feel guilty and I thought that my presence might make it worse.'

'So why did you come here and look me up?'

'It was something that Monika said.'

'Monika?'

'My ex-wife. When she asked me for a divorce she said it was because the war had taught her that you couldn't waste time any more. You had to move on if things weren't right and you had to make decisions that might have seemed hasty before the war. You had to be bold.'

'I can see that,' she said.

They had started to walk on now. The warmth of his hand on her shoulder remained, even though their arms now swung side by side.

'What about Robert?' he asked. 'What is his future going to be like here?'

She sighed. 'I suppose he'll just carry on working at Tall Chimneys until I die. After that, I don't know. I'm not sure he'd cope with running it on his own. My son is never going to be accepted by society ever again. The world used men like him as cannon fodder. Now, because his nerves are shredded to bits, they treat him like an idiot. Yes, some people are kind to him. But they don't want to employ him or let him near their daughters.'

'Poor lad.' Stephen sounded angry but not in an aggressive, Henry way. 'It's so unfair.'

'And I don't see it changing,' she added. 'None of us are going to be what we were before. Adeline is no longer regarded as a respectable married woman. Although more people accept her now, there are still those who won't walk on the same side of the street as her because little Violet is . . . because she doesn't have a father.'

They'd reached the stile that led onto the flat part where the sundial stood. Any further towards the edge of the cliff and you could fall.

'None of us are going to be what we were before,' he said. 'And I don't want us to be. The end of the war has brought us a clean slate, Elizabeth. We can put up with situations we don't like, or we can be brave and change them. It's why I've decided to emigrate.'

'Emigrate?'

She hadn't expected this.

His face shone, yet it was nervous at the same time.

'It's why I wanted to come here one last time, Elizabeth.'

If he went, no one would ever know the truth about Henry. If he stayed, there was always the chance it might slip out somehow. So why did she feel so upset? So taken aback. So empty at the prospect of losing him again just as he'd come back? All these were feelings that she hadn't allowed herself to consider before, let alone express out loud. But now the prospect of his departure physically hurt.

'The thing is, Elizabeth, that I meant it when I said I've thought of you every day. We share something. Not just that night in the allotment . . .'

She flinched.

'That night in the allotment,' he repeated as if to reinforce the gravity, 'because at the time it felt like the only thing to do. But I have also thought of you every day for so many other reasons that I can't even put a name to.'

It was true. She felt the same. But she couldn't say so. It would mean forgiving herself. And that she couldn't do.

His hands were reaching out to her now. A lifebelt on the edge of a cliff.

'Come with me, Elizabeth. You *and* Robert. It will be a new start. Please.'

Go with him?

Go with a man whom she scarcely knew and yet at the same time whose thoughts she felt as though she understood – as he did hers? Go with a man who had lied during the war about his background until she'd caught him out? A man whom she now trusted implicitly? Was she mad?

'Yes,' she heard herself say. 'Yes!'

64

Of course, she needed to tell Adeline about her decision before anyone else. So she headed down to the beach where her friend was with Violet, making sandcastles.

Elizabeth sat down next to them on the warm pebbles. 'I've got something to tell you,' she said.

'You're going away with Stephen,' replied Adeline.

'How did you know?'

'Because I'm your best friend and because you've always been right for each other. Where are you going?'

'Canada,' said Elizabeth.

There was a short silence. 'Where I was going with Brian,' said Adeline quietly.

'I'm sorry.'

'Don't be. But I'll miss you.'

Elizabeth squeezed her hand. 'I'll write.'

'I'll send you my new address when I find a place for Violet and me.'

'There's no need for you to move,' said Elizabeth quickly. 'I should have said that at the beginning. I'm going to give you Tall Chimneys.'

Adeline's eyes widened. 'Give me Tall Chimneys? Why?'

'Because, as you've just said, you're my best friend. Stephen and I are taking Robert with us. I want you and Violet to have a safe base for the rest of your lives.'

'But what if Henry comes back? I hate to say this,

Elizabeth, but he might have used the air raid as an excuse to go off and make a new life. He wouldn't be the first. There was a story about a man who did exactly that in the papers only the other day.'

'He's not going to come back,' said Elizabeth quietly. 'I shot him.'

The words came out of her mouth as if they had a will of their own.

Adeline looked at her with horror. 'You what?'

'You can't tell anyone,' said Elizabeth, shaking.

'Darling, I promise I won't. On Violet's life.'

Slowly, Elizabeth told her what had happened, only stopping when she reached her conversation with Stephen.

'I'm not going to tell you where his body is because I don't want you to carry that load. But I can promise you he's not in Tall Chimneys.'

Adeline hugged her. 'I know I shouldn't say this but I'm glad you got him first. Otherwise he'd have killed you, from what you've said. You're a brave woman, Elizabeth.'

'I don't feel like it.' Elizabeth wiped her eyes. 'But I know I can't stay here any more. It might be better for Robert to have a new life. And I do love Stephen.'

As if realizing the enormity of the conversation, Violet toddled up and sat on her lap. Elizabeth rested her face against the child's. 'Have a wonderful life here, the two of you.'

'We will,' said Adeline, hugging her again, 'although I can't bear the thought of not seeing you.'

'You could visit.'

'I get seasick,' said Adeline. 'And . . . well, to be honest,

I don't want to go to the country where Brian and I were going to make our fresh start. It would hurt too much. And don't say sorry again. I'm glad for you. Besides, we can write.'

'Of course we'll write,' cried Elizabeth, hugging her tightly. 'I can't wait to get long lovely letters about Violet growing up and the sea and Tall Chimneys. I know you will love it as I do.'

'I'll miss you so much,' sobbed Adeline. 'But thank you. Thank you.'

Nancy

65

They'll be here soon! The first visit from the children's charity went so well that I offered to make them monthly, and I live for them now. I've also been impressed enough by the organization to make a substantial donation. Mum's money has finally been put to good use.

My young visitors give me a purpose. Many come from troubled backgrounds. If I can help just one of them to experience a little happiness and safety, then I'll feel my life has been worth it.

There's one little girl – Summer – whom I bonded with almost from the moment she arrived. She's sassy. Smart. Quite rude, and cocky in a way that makes her seem older than her eleven years. But underneath I knew she was hurting. I recognized it.

Of course, one mustn't have favourites, but it's hard not to.

Sometimes Beliska and I take them swimming, and I noticed Summer's calm attitude immediately. She didn't shriek or scream with terror like the others at the coldness of the sea or the crashing waves. She set her face and plunged straight in.

'When did you learn to swim?' I asked one day as we were walking back.

'When my mum's dealer threw me into the Thames,' she answered matter-of-factly.

I didn't quite know what to say. 'Did anyone stop to help?'

Summer looked at me as though I was mad. 'It was night, wasn't it? 'Sides, people don't want to get involved. When I got out, I ran to the cop shop and told them.'

I didn't want to ask more. I'd already asked too many questions. But when Beliska and I were alone later – we were quite good friends by now – I told her about the conversation, wondering if it had been the child's imagination.

'All true, I'm afraid. Her mum was a drug addict and she owed the guy money.'

'Didn't a social worker step in?'

'Let's just say that the family weren't on their radar. Summer's with foster parents now. They're good people.'

At least she was safe and secure, then.

Meanwhile, I've given up on the allotment clue, if that's what it was in Elizabeth's letter. I've gone back through the archives in the museum and can't find anything referring to an incident there. I've also been down several times to the plot itself. I haven't found anything unusual, although I have managed to grow a few runner beans. My patch looks like an untidy teenager's bedroom next to the others, which are pristine with earth so fine that it looks like sieved flour.

But one day when I reach the allotment gate, I find it's got a notice on it. DO NOT ENTER.

'They've discovered an old well that has sprung a leak,' says one of my plot neighbours. 'It's why there's been all that trouble with some of the plots getting waterlogged. They thought it was pipes at first.'

I think back to the watery ground when I'd first arrived

and the remark about pipes that one of the locals had made to me.

There's a digger here too. Then a police car turns up.

Quite a crowd of onlookers has gathered. 'Keep back, everyone,' says someone in an orange jacket.

'What's going on?' I ask her.

She seems excited. 'Looks like they've found a skeleton at the bottom.'

66

Should I tell anyone about the letter in the cellar? Or my suspicions about the skeleton's identity? But what good would it do? I feel protective of Elizabeth. I don't want her name sullied, even though she must be long dead by now.

I think of what Vera had said about her own mother talking about Mrs Montague. And I think of Elizabeth's instruction about 'looking after the allotment' in that letter. Was that a clue? Had she been trying to tell us something?

So I keep quiet. I don't even tell Alex when he calls from London for our evening chat. That night when I go to bed, the house seems more peaceful than ever. But I can't work out why.

The next morning, Jeremy from the museum rings. He's excited, I can tell, and when he asks me to come into the museum, I cycle round immediately.

I expect him to talk about the skeleton but instead he places a hardback journal in front of me, filled with perfectly formed copperplate handwriting.

'It was dropped through the letterbox this morning. Unfortunately, the writer hasn't put his or her name. I think I know why. Take a look at this.'

The journal contains the unknown author's observation of the town at war. (*We said prayers in church today for the*

Browns, who have lost a second son in action.) But there are also brief references to *reconnaissances* and *rifle practice in the woods* as well as a *huge bonfire at the top of Peak Hill, where we destroyed all our weapons when peace was declared.*

Yet it's the final page that stands out: *I miss Henry terribly. I know she had something to do with it. I feel it in my heart. He couldn't just have gone missing like that. If only I could prove it.*

Who was 'she'? A shiver goes through me as I think of the gun I found in the cellar. A gun that clearly hadn't been handed in. But I say nothing.

'I suppose we'll never know who Henry is,' says Jeremy.

I say nothing. I'd never told Jeremy about this part of the letter. I feel Elizabeth would want me to keep it quiet.

'I suspect, continues Jeremy, that the journal was donated by a descendant who didn't want to be identified because of the weapons reference.'

'What's this at the end?' I ask.

It's very faint but it looks like initials: *P.B.*

'Well done,' says Jeremy patting me on the back and then stepping away as if he'd thought better of it. 'I didn't see that. Must get my eyes checked again. Mmmm . . . *P.B.* Peter someone, perhaps? On a different subject, did you hear about the skeleton in the well?'

'Yes,' I say.

'It will be interesting to see how old it is, don't you think?'

'Do you believe there's a connection with the diary arriving today?' I ask, unable to stop myself.

'Possibly. Or it could just be a coincidence.' Jeremy gives a wry smile. 'History is full of those.'

Much as I'd like to, I say nothing to Jeremy about Elizabeth's letter. I feel an empathy with this woman, even

413

though we've never met. Maybe it's because she bailed out my grandmother and mother by giving them a home when they needed it.

Meanwhile, the mystery skeleton gets into the local paper and onto BBC's *Spotlight* as well as ITV's *West Country News*.

One of the announcers adds that a knife was also found at the bottom of the well. I go into a cold sweat, thinking of my mother.

Immediately, I ring Jeremy. 'I was about to call you about that,' he said. 'I gather it's a Fairbairn-Sykes.'

'The type you told me about before? That signifies someone was in the secret army?'

'Yes.'

I can almost hear him nodding gravely

Another shiver goes through me.

'So the skeleton . . . he might have been part of it?'

'Maybe. But it would be hard to prove.'

After a few weeks of speculation in the press, without any obvious leads, everything goes quiet. Good.

Not long after that, Beliska rings. She gets straight to the point.

'Summer's foster parents can't look after her any more. Their daughter is sick and they need to be with her to help with the grandchildren in Scotland, so they're moving. They say they've got too much to cope with to continue fostering.'

'So what will happen to her?'

Beliska makes a despairing sound. 'Back into the

system. That's what I wanted to talk to you about. Have you ever considered being a foster parent yourself?'

'No, and even if I did, they might not take me on with my background.'

'You don't have a criminal record.'

'Some people think I should have gone to prison.'

It's true. I still get letters about it from total strangers.

'I'm sorry. Look, I thought you might say this. But the fact is that Summer is so much happier when she's at Tall Chimneys. What do you say, Nancy? Will you give it some thought, at least?'

67

How could I say no after everything I've been through? Don't I know how important it is to have a stable family life? This is my chance to make a difference.

And somehow, almost as if it is meant, applications are made and interviews are given and some months later, after various training courses, I am approved. This makes it sound much simpler than it was. Perhaps the truth is that I keep expecting someone to tap me on the shoulder and say 'You? Suitable as a foster parent? You have no right to look after a child.'

Yet it happens. Summer comes to live with me. I am on trial, of course. Or so it feels. And that's exactly as it should be. People come to check up on me and make sure that I am doing a good job and that Summer is happy.

'I love it here!' she tells them every time, with a shiny face and bright eyes, waving her arms in enthusiasm – arms that have filled out since she's been here. She's no longer that skinny, spiky little thing that first arrived at Tall Chimneys.

She gives the house, and me, a new lease of life. Sheba adores her too and they follow each other like shadows.

I've put her in my old bedroom with the writing at the back of the wardrobe. 'Who are Maisie and Shirley?' she asks.

'Two little girls who lived here during the war,' I say.

'Which war?'

'The Second World War,' I say.

She frowns, creating a wave of wrinkles in a forehead that should be unblemished at that age. 'What was that?'

What do they teach them at school nowadays? Then again, I didn't learn much about that period either.

'Back in 1939,' I tell her, 'the Germans invaded Poland. Then they began to invade other countries too and tried to do the same to us.'

'What does invade mean?'

'Take over. Occupy. Steal.'

Her little snub nose wrinkles in disbelief. 'But that's wrong.'

'Yes. It is. But at the time, we were scared they might succeed. Many people in Sidmouth were frightened they might come in boats across the sea and kill us.'

'Did they?'

'No. Luckily there were some very brave people who were ready to fight back.'

I'm aware this is a simplistic way of putting it, yet it's a start.

'But what about Maisie and Shirley? What happened to them?'

I swallow the lump in my throat. 'Shirley died,' I say.

'How?'

'She went back to London and a bomb fell on her house.'

'Shit! Did you know her?'

I almost pull up Summer for her language but decide this isn't the right time. I'm also amused that she thinks I might be that old.

'No, I wasn't born then. But I do know Maisie, her friend. She's an old lady now. She came to visit me the other year.'

Then Sheba bounds up and Summer loses interest in the story about two little girls who lived here so long ago. 'Can we take her out for a walk, please?'

It's a welcome relief. Summer's energy is exactly what Tall Chimneys needs.

She also loves cooking with Vera and comes back bearing home-made cookies. 'That one's a real poppet, isn't she?' says my neighbour.

'Yes,' I say. 'She is.'

'Have you ever thought of having a baby yourself? You're not too old, you know.'

Vera's accident hadn't done anything to stop her straight-talking habits.

'It's not for me,' I say shortly.

'Sorry. Didn't mean to interfere. Wasn't for me either, as it turns out, although that's another story.'

Her lips purse. Clearly it's not something she intends to share. And why should she?

Life with a child, I'm discovering, is a mixture of challenges! Apart from trying to reassure her that she's safe now, I have a struggle to get Summer to do her homework instead of swimming in the sea, which she's taken to like a duck to water.

'I hate equations,' she says. 'I won't need them when I grow up. Not if I'm going to run a paddleboard school.'

I've booked my foster daughter (how wonderful it is to say that!) in for some lessons with a local instructor and they are really paying off.

'That's it!' I call out, standing next to her, shoulders deep.

The water is flat today even though it's late September. Some tourists who've waited until the summer hordes have dispersed back to towns and schools and ordinary lives are standing on the esplanade, watching us.

So is someone else.

'You're doing great,' he calls out.

Summer flicks her wet hair out of her eyes. 'Come on, Alex!' she calls back. 'Why don't you have a go?'

'Not for me, thanks. Sheba and I are happy to watch.'

Alex has come down to Sidmouth for 'a few months'. Neither of us has actually said the words 'let's see how it goes' but it feels like it's understood. He still has his place in London and goes back every now and then.

'More of us are doing it,' says Jasmine, who has a live-out 'bloke' now. 'We don't need to prove anything to the world with wedding rings or stuff like that.'

Sometimes the four of us go out for a pizza at the Marine or a takeaway beer from the Bedford (fizzy lemonade for Summer), which we'll drink overlooking the sea in the evening. The sunsets look like burnished gold. If that sounds like a cliché, it's because it really does feel as though we are living in one of those fairy tales where everything is perfect.

As long as I can focus on the present, that is.

It's good to see there's no tension between Alex and Jasmine any more. People change, I tell myself. They might have made wrong decisions in the past. But they can become better people. None of us are perfect.

If only I could apply the same judgement to myself.

68

Remembrance Day

It's a bright, crisp November morning.

I am standing in the churchyard with a crowd of faces, many of whom I've got to know. I'm no longer the 'farmhouse slaughter daughter', as the newspapers had called me. I'm just one of the locals. Summer is next to me. She is wearing a poppy that she has knitted with the help of Vera. She made one for me too.

Nearby is a monument erected in honour of the American and Canadian forces who were stationed here during the war. I wonder for the hundredth time what Sidmouth was like when they were here. I hope there was some laughter amidst all the fear and loss.

My heart is aching with gratitude to all those brave men and women who died during both world wars – both civilians and those in the forces – whose courage and fortitude meant that future generations could walk freely down the streets, open and draw their curtains when they wanted, swim in the sea and live a life free from fear.

Their names are being read out.

'John Tebbit, farmer.'

I give a little start. Tebbit? Wasn't that the name that was written in the margin of the newspaper in the cellar?

Then there's another who catches my attention, perhaps because she died the week before VE Day.

Polly Bright. My breath catches in my throat.

P.B.?

Could that be the author of the diary handed in to the museum? The one who mourned the missing Henry and accused a woman of having 'something to do with it'?

'That's my great-gran!' says a small child near me.

'That's right, love,' says the woman holding her hand.

My breath catches in my throat.

Had Polly Bright really had a child? Was it possible that it had been Henry's? And – once more – should I tell the police of my suspicions about the skeleton in the well?

Or am I letting my imagination run away with me?

Stop, says a voice inside my head. *Let sleeping dogs lie.*

'What do you reckon?' asks Maisie, her eyes shining. We are standing on the promenade. It's a choppy day but a bright one. The waves are glinting merrily in the autumn sun. It's a week after the Remembrance Day service.

Maisie is leaning on a stick, with her daughter hovering protectively next to her. But her eyes are sparkling and I get a glimpse for a minute – or so I feel – of the nine-year-old girl who had arrived in Sidmouth during the war.

'I think she'd have loved it,' I say. 'So would my grandmother.'

I'm not sure why I'm saying this. After all, I never knew either. But if it was me, I would have loved it, and Alex says he thinks I take after Adeline. 'From what you've told me,' he says, 'she was a gutsy woman who stood up to life in the face of adversity. Just like you, Nancy. It's one reason I love you so much.'

I look at the writing on the bench.

Maisie was here. SO WAS SHIRLEY! 8 October 1941

'She would have loved it and all,' says Maisie. Her eyes are glistening.

'It's all right, Mum,' says her daughter, softly.

'I know it is, love.'

She stands for a minute. A figure unbowed by the past. Looking out across the sea as far as the eye can see. 'Cracking view, don't you think?' she says.

Then she takes her daughter's arm and links her other through mine. I take Summer's right hand. Together, the four of us walk back home.

But I can't help thinking about the words on the bench.

How can I expect to be forgiven if I can't forgive others? The truth is that I miss my best friend. Just as Elizabeth and Adeline must have missed each other after the war. And what if I lost Claire as Maisie lost Shirley? Yes, my mother might have supported me against Duncan if Claire had told her what she'd seen, but my friend had stood up staunchly for me in other ways over the years. And she'd also 'found' me Alex.

So after Maisie and her daughter leave, I pick up the phone.

'Hi,' I say. 'It's me. I was thinking about coming up to London for a few days. Shall we meet somewhere?'

I can hear the tears in Claire's voice.

'That would be lovely,' she says. 'I've missed you, Nancy.'

Epilogue

Of course, I'd lied.

Not about everything. Just one 'little' fact. My mind goes back to the night I'd nearly drowned. The night of Martin's death. *Another wave is coming. This one seems even higher. The sight makes my stomach freefall with panic. I look towards Martin's eyes. I can't see them in the dark. But I can feel them. Boring into me. 'I love you, Nancy,' he calls out. 'Remember that.'*

Then the wave hits us. The force is stronger than I could have imagined. I am knocked to one side. My ears sing with the pressure of the water. I can't see anything, but somehow I'm still in the boat. My hair is plastered to my face. I brush it away from my eyes, searching desperately in the dark.

'Martin?' I scream.

There's no answer.

That's what I told the police. That's what I'd pretended to myself.

The real truth is this.

'Martin?' I scream.

'Nancy.' It was Martin.

He's in the water, holding on to the side of the boat with one hand and holding out the other.

'Grab me,' he shouts.

So I do. I grasp his hand. I look into his eyes. I think of the young boy bullied by his father. Of the teenager who became obsessed by me. Of the man who stabbed his father. His declaration that we

423

would die together. I know that I will never be free of this man. He will love me one minute. And he could murder me the next.

I can't take that chance.

I need to be safe.

So I let go of his hand.

He looks at me for a few seconds. Am I imagining it or is there forgiveness in his eyes? And then he disappears under the water.

The truth is that I deliberately chose to abandon him to an almost-certain death.

Yet part of me wanted to save Martin at the same time.

I honestly don't know which one is the real me.

Sometimes, that's just the way you have to live, isn't it? Not knowing.

It's my very own silent sentence.

Evacuee's account of WWII,
My War by the Sea, by Maisie Evans
(as told to Nancy Greenfield), tops the best-seller list.

Author's Note

When I moved to Devon some thirteen years ago, I was amazed to discover that there had been a secret army during the Second World War. The idea of civilians forming a guerrilla movement in the event of invasion seemed almost too fantastical to be true. We had the armed forces to protect us, didn't we?

Then I discovered that East Devon was not the only place to have secret armies. Churchill was, in fact, behind this scheme of training local men and women to protect their home territories using their local knowledge. The correct names for these groups were the Auxiliary Units and the Special Duties Branch, although together they were popularly known as Churchill's Secret Army. More recently, information has come to light that has identified another highly secret civilian resistance organization called Section VII. This particular group of brave civilians would act only once Britain had been defeated militarily and was occupied. This book represents a fictional combination of all of them. Most of those who took part went to their graves without telling a soul.

While I have tried to be as faithful to the truth as possible in my novel, I have taken certain liberties. For example, as far as I can find out, there wasn't a secret army unit based in Sidmouth, although men and women from the town might have belonged to local cells in surrounding towns and villages.

I should also mention that, although I have used real places and geographical features, I have occasionally tweaked them slightly. None of the names or characters are real.

But I have not changed Sidmouth's heart. It beats today as warmly and embracingly as it seems to have done during the Second World War and, I would guess, throughout the ages.

Acknowledgements

I am extremely grateful to the following stars at Penguin:

Harriet Bourton and Katy Loftus for their editorial talent and for taking my characters to heart; Lydia Fried for her cheerful emails and coordination of audio readers et al.; social media queens Ellie Hudson and Georgia Taylor; Natalie Wall for her efficiency in production planning; Amelia Evans, Monique Corless, Penny Liechti, Ann Katrin Ziser, Annamika Singh and everyone else in PRH Rights; Sam Fanaken, Ruth Johnstone, Kyla Dean, Eleanor Rhodes Davies, Linda Viberg and the wider sales team who all work so collegiately on selling my books; publicity magicians Rebecca Gray and Jane Gentle.

Also huge thanks to my fantastic agent Kate Hordern; my wonderful film/TV agent Italia Gandolfo; Trevor Horwood, my copy-editor (we work well together as a team!); and proofreaders Sarah Barlow and Mandy Greenfield. (The fact that Mandy and my lead characters share a surname is one of life's strange coincidences that I discovered only *post facto*.)

In case you're wondering how authors choose names for their characters, I sometimes ask friends and family if they will donate theirs. Trevor kindly provided the surname 'Browse' because a schoolbook (dated 1810) had been found under the floorboards in his house in Devon for a boy called George Browse. The name Anne Lois

Marples was chosen by Karen Jarvis who was the successful bidder for a character name in aid of Young Lives vs Cancer. By the way, I made up that slogan for vitamin tablets. I did search the internet to see if it already existed but couldn't find anything. Just saying . . .

Although I have set *Coming to Find You* in a real place, all characters both past and present are fictitious. Any similarity to real names or events is entirely coincidental. Certain liberties or 'tweaks' have been made with regard to geographical locations. I have worked hard to ensure that historical facts are accurate. Please forgive any mistakes.

Everyone needs a champion. Hats off to Dead Good and Page Turners, among others, for being so supportive.

Where would a writer be without bloggers, reviewers, booksellers and readers? Thank you. Thank you. Thank you. (Many of you have become good friends.) In case you don't know, authors usually receive sales figures on a Tuesday afternoon/early evening. That's when you'll find me nursing a cup of peppermint tea and keeping my fingers crossed.

And what about authors who are asked to review other people's books when they're busy writing their own? Not everyone has the time. Many thanks to those who said 'yes'.

As part of my research, I spoke to a group of courageous men and women who had been evacuated to Sidmouth during the Second World War, as well as local families whose parents and grandparents had passed down memories. Special thanks must go to Ivy Jones, Sheelagh Michelmore, Julia Creeke, Carey Cave, Tom Griffiths and the Royal York Hotel (a boarding house during the Second World War).

I would like to draw attention to those families of criminals who, through no fault of their own, live a 'silent sentence'. As I discovered when I worked as a writer in residence of a high-security male prison, there are many law-abiding folk out there, struggling to come to terms with the atrocities their loved ones have committed. There are also numerous families whose loved ones were the victims.

A writer tries to get it right, so I am much obliged to Nigel Hyman from Sidmouth Museum (Sid Vale Association) for sharing his knowledge and taking the time to read an early draft of the manuscript. Nigel is also the co-author, along with Christine Hardy, of *Sidmouth: The War Years 1939–1945*. Please read it and do visit the museum.

I am indebted to author Andrew Chatterton, whom I came across just as we were at the copy-editing stage. His book *Britain's Secret Defences* (Casemate Publishers) is riveting. He was kind enough to give me extra information as well as reading the edited version.

Whenever I need to source books for research, I go to my friend the military historian Jonathan Walker. He came up trumps again. He also took time to read the proof copy. Thank you!

I'm running out of substitutes for the words 'thank you', so I'm just going to repeat myself:

Thanks to my husband for giving me space to write; my amazing children and grandchildren; my father and his war stories, like the time he was blown off the loo by the blast of a bomb while reading *Jane Eyre* (he wasn't hurt); my sister, brother-in-law, niece and cousins; and my wonderful circle of friends.

We All Have Our Secrets

YOU KNOW SHE'S LYING . . . BUT SO ARE YOU.

Two women are staying in Willowmead House.

One of them is running.
One of them is hiding.
Both of them are lying.

Emily made one bad decision and now her career could be over. Her family home on the Cornish coast is the only place where she feels safe. But when she arrives, there's a stranger living with her father.

Emily doesn't trust the beautiful young woman, convinced that she's telling one lie after another. Soon, Emily becomes obsessed with finding out the truth . . .

But should some secrets stay buried forever?

Praise for Jane Corry

'Clever, gripping, nuanced'
Phoebe Morgan

'An unputdownable read'
Emma Curtis

'The twists just keep on coming'
Celia Walden

The Lies We Tell

**YOU DID WHAT ANY MOTHER WOULD DO . . .
AND NOW SOMEONE ELSE'S SON IS DEAD.**

Sarah always thought of herself and her husband, Tom,
as good people. But that was before their son Freddy
came home saying he'd done something terrible.
Begging them not to tell the police.

Soon Sarah and Tom must find out just how far they are
willing to push themselves, and their marriage, to protect
their only child . . .

As the lies build up and Sarah is presented with the
perfect opportunity to get Freddy off the hook, she is
faced with a terrifying decision . . .

Save her son . . . or save herself?

Praise for Jane Corry

'Everything I love in a book'
Lisa Jewell

'Jane Corry's best yet'
B. A. Paris

'Brims with suspense'
Louise Candlish

I Made a Mistake

IT STARTED WITH A KISS . . . AND ENDED WITH MURDER.

In Poppy Page's mind, there are two types of women in this world: those who are faithful to their husbands and those who are not. Until now, Poppy has never questioned which she was.

But when handsome, charming Matthew Gordon walks back into her life after almost two decades, that changes. Poppy makes a single mistake – and that mistake will be far more dangerous than she could imagine.

Someone is going to pay for it with their life . . .

Praise for Jane Corry

'Gritty, real, interesting and clever'
Gillian McAllister

'Clever, compulsive and twisty'
Claire Douglas

'Absolutely brilliant'
Angela Marsons

I Looked Away

**YOU MADE A MISTAKE.
BUT THEY'RE SAYING IT'S MURDER.**

Every Monday, 49-year-old Ellie looks after her grandson
Josh. She loves him more than anyone else in the world.
The only thing that can mar her happiness is her husband's
affair. But he swears it's over now and Ellie has decided
to be thankful for what she's got.

Then one day, while she's looking after Josh, her husband
gets a call from *that woman*. And – just for a moment – Ellie
takes her eyes off her grandson. What happens next will
change her life forever.

Because Ellie is hiding something in her past.

**And what looks like an accident could start to
look like murder . . .**

Praise for Jane Corry

'Sensitive and thought-provoking'
Adele Parks

'Thrilling, emotional and pacy'
Claire Douglas

'Dark, sinister, compelling'
Nicci French

my husband's wife

FIRST COMES LOVE . . . THEN COMES MARRIAGE . . . THEN COMES MURDER.

When lawyer Lily marries Ed, she's determined to make a fresh start. To leave the secrets of the past behind.

But when she takes on her first criminal case, she starts to find herself strangely drawn to her client. A man who's accused of murder. A man she will soon be willing to risk everything for.

But is he really innocent?

And who is she to judge?

Praise for Jane Corry

'Jane Corry is the new queen of the psychological thriller'
Kate Furnivall

'Chilling and suspenseful'
Elizabeth Haynes

'Twisty, feverish and utterly gripping'
Eva Dolan

the
dead
ex

HE CHEATED . . . HE LIED . . . HE DIED.

Vicki's husband David once promised to love her in sickness and in health. But after a brutal attack left her suffering with epilepsy, he ran away with his mistress.

So when Vicki gets a call one day to say that he's missing, her first thought is 'good riddance'. But then the police find evidence suggesting that David is dead. And they think Vicki had something to do with it.

What really happened on the night of David's disappearance?

And how can Vicki prove her innocence, when she's not even sure of it herself?

Praise for Jane Corry

'Compulsive, edgy and fabulous twists!'
B. A. Paris

'Few writers can match Jane Corry'
Cara Hunter

'Totally hooked me'
Peter James

blood sisters

THREE LITTLE GIRLS. ONE GOOD. ONE BAD. ONE DEAD.

Kitty lives in a care home. She can't speak properly and she has no memory of the accident that put her here.

At least that's the story she's sticking to.

Art teacher Alison looks fine on the surface. But the surface is a lie. When a job in a prison comes up she decides to take it – this is her chance to finally make things right.

But someone is watching Kitty and Alison.

Someone who wants revenge for what happened that sunny morning in May.

And only another life will do . . .

Praise for Jane Corry

'A fearsomely good thriller'
Nicci French

'I raced through this'
Teresa Driscoll

'So many brilliant twists'
Claire Douglas